TAILS FLUFFED, FANGS BARED

they prowl their territories, ready to defend against invaders both seen and invisible. They are our conquerors, our comrades, and our closest companions. So settle back in your favorite chair, with your furry friend comfortably curled on your lap, and share the adventures of felines brave and bold. . . .

"Papercut Luck"—Imprisoned by the emperor's soldiers, could a cat talisman made real prove the answer to their prayers?

"In Bastet's Service"—Her beloved cat gone, she is gifted by the goddess with another, a poor creature sorely in need of loving care. But who will prove the true protector when danger invades their home?

"Quest of Souls"—Soul robbers had claimed those the boy held dear. Could he possibly triumph over such powerful foes with only his cat for an ally?

These are just a few of the far more than nine lives portrayed in this delightful romp along the secret ways known only to those incredible felines in—

CATFANTASTIC II

CATFANTASTIC II

EDITED BY

ANDRE NORTON &
MARTIN H. GREENBERG

DAW BOOKS, INC.
DONALD A. WOLLHEIM, PUBLISHER

375 Hudson Street, New York, NY 10014

DAW Book Collectors No. 839.

First Printing, January 1991

1 2 3 4 5 6 7 8 9

DAW

CONTENTS

INTRODUCTION

We have been informed by those patient researchers who really enjoy delving into facts and figures that cats are now the most popular pets in the United States. Several reasons are listed with solemn sincerity: a cat can become an "inside" animal in a small apartment; it does not have to be escorted on "walks" but is more civilized about intimate functions; it is a pleasant lap sitter and comfort; it is less expensive (Ha, have you priced food and cat litter, or vet bills recently?); and so on. So much for official recognition.

However, no matter how sensible one imagines oneself to be, still the cat remains a mystery either intriguing or irritating or both. We cannot help but believe that cats, always choosing to go their own way, do possess a quality for weighing the human with whom she or he chooses to live, and have a masterful way of training the whole household into a system most benefiting the cat.

Is this some form of magic? Of course not. Magic has been placed beyond the boundaries of acceptance. If we suspect that we are chess pieces to be played for fun or profit by our "pets," then we have definitely courted insanity.

Magic and cats, however, have been linked in our minds for generations. Cats have been worshiped and reviled, studied and misunderstood for generations upon generations. They are still masters of themselves—magic or no magic.

BOMBER
AND THE BISMARCK

by Clare Bell

Bomber and Feathers, all met on May 23, 1941 aboard the British aircraft carrier H.M.S. *Ark Royal.* The meeting didn't change Bomber much, for he was a cat. It left a more indelible impression on Lieutenant "Feathers" Geoffrey-Faucett.

H.M.S. *Ark Royal* was part of Force H, a fleet of battleships and destroyers sent out from Gibraltar to protect British convoys in the Atlantic. One of the newer British aircraft carriers, she was equipped with an aircraft control tower to monitor the takeoffs and landings of the antiquated Fairey Swordfish torpedo-biplanes aboard her. If she'd been a carrier of the old "flat-iron" design, her decks all runway and all operations controlled from below, no one would have ever spotted the half-drowned animal struggling in the seas alongside.

Geoffrey-Faucett was sharing a cup of tea and a rare idle minute up in the tower with the air controller while the "airedales" in the deck crew brought his Swordfish biplane up from below decks on the lift. He had straight sandy hair and aristocratic features except for a slightly snub nose. He also had a reputation for sending his torpedoes into the aft end of a target ship, "right up the bastard's tailfeathers," as he often put it. That led to the nickname of "Tailfeathers," which was quickly shortened to "Feathers."

Jack Shepherd, the air controller, put his cup down so hard that spoon and saucer clattered. He pointed through the tower window to the heaving swell just off the starboard quarter and said, "What the devil is that?"

Shepherd took his field glasses, squinted through once, scratched his black curly hair and squinted again. "Eyes must be playing me false. Here, you have a look." He handed the field glasses to the pilot.

Feathers focused the binoculars, scanning the white-caps that splashed along *Ark Royal*'s sides as she kept her station several hundred miles off the Spanish coast. He frowned. Was that dark spot just a bit of flotsam caught in the chop? It moved in a funny way. And did he see the outline of a head and ears and, God bless, even the end of a tail sticking up from the gray-green Atlantic?

"It's a cat. It really is a cat," he said, slinging the field glasses back to Shepherd. "Must have fallen off some passenger transport. Look, see if you can get the helm to hold off on the upwind run."

"What are you up to now, Feathers?" Shepherd glanced down at a Swordfish biplane rising up through the lift hatch. "The airedales will have your plane ready."

"Bugger the old Stringbag," Feathers threw back over his shoulder as he clattered down the iron spiral of steps. "She'll keep. I'm going to fish that cat out. Can't let the thing drown."

He drew his sheepskin jacket collar tight about his neck as he butted his way into the wind sweeping across the flight deck. The *Ark Royal* was giving short hard bounces in the chop, which made it hard for the pilot to keep his footing. Ignoring the waves of the flight deck crew who were prepping his aircraft, Feathers ran to the bow, threw open a locker, grabbed a life ring and hurled it out in the direction where he had last seen the cat. Behind him he heard footsteps, the unmistakable gimpy-leg gait of Patterson, his gunner.

"Who's gone in the drink?" the gunner asked in a voice made raspy from scotch and tobacco. "I didn't hear no man overboard alarm."

"Nobody. It's a cat." Feathers frowned, shading his eyes against the hazy sun. "Can you spot him, Pat?"

"Go on, you're daft, Feathers. The old man will have your nuts for a necktie if you hold up the reconnaissance flight."

Geoffrey-Faucett scanned the seas, feeling a bit fool-ish. All this fuss about an animal, especially during wartime, when human lives were being lost. And had he really seen a cat?

The white ring bobbed up and down in the troughs. The dark spot began to move toward the ring. Its progress was terribly slow, but Feathers felt a sudden surge of unmilitary delight. The animal was still alive, a miracle in the freezing North Atlantic. It fought its way to the ring and Feathers saw it scramble on.

Carefully he drew in the line attached to the ring, fearful that the rough seas might sweep the cat away before he got it aboard. But at last the ring hung from its line over the *Ark Royal*'s bow rail. On the life ring, spreadeagled with its claws driven deep into the white-painted cork, was the castaway.

Feathers reached down with both hands, grabbed the outside of the ring, and brought it aboard. Yellow-gold eyes the color of sovereigns glared at Feathers as he tried to pry the cat's paws from the ring. The brine-drenched animal held on tenaciously, growling deep in its throat.

"Grateful one, he is," said Patterson. "Take your face off if you're not careful."

"You take a swipe at me and I'll chuck you back," said Feathers to the cat. With a clasp knife from his pocket, he cut the line from the life ring, then carried the ring like a platter with the cat sprawled out across the top.

"What are you going to do with him?" Patterson asked, trotting after.

"Give him to old Shepherd in the tower. He won't have anything to do once the squadron takes off. I'll let him coax our friend here off the life ring and nurse him with some tea and biscuits."

The crackle of the *Ark Royal*'s public address system sounded on the flight deck, breaking through the shouts of the airedales and the sound of Swordfish engines warming up.

"Attention, air and deck crews. All scheduled air operations are canceled. Repeat, all scheduled air operations are canceled on orders from the War Office. Stand by for further announcements."

As the system shut off with a sharp crack, airedales and pilots alike stared at each other, dumbfounded.

"Operations canceled?" squeaked Patterson incredulously. "What's happened? The bloody war's over?"

"Might be worse." Matthews, a grubby airedale with carroty hair and freckles came up beside the pilot and gunner. "The Nazis might have invaded. U-boats in the Thames and the swastika flying from the House of Parliament, I shouldn't doubt."

"Don't think so," said Feathers. "More likely this has something to do with that new German battleship we've been hearing about over the wireless."

"The one named after that Prussian. Otto von something-or-other."

"Bismarck," Patterson supplied in his smoky rasp. "Ah, she's no threat. Remember, lads. We've got the *Hood*."

A cluster of men had come up behind Feathers for a look at the cat. They all broke into shouts when they heard the flagship's name. "The *Hood*, the *Hood*, the mighty *Hood*. Three cheers for the *Hood*!"

Fists lifted in the air and voices bellowed out. Feathers, still encumbered with the life ring and its occupant, couldn't lift his hand, but he shouted along with the rest. For twenty years the battleship H.M.S. *Hood* had been the staunch symbol of British sea power. With her 42,000-ton displacement and her fifteen-inch guns, she was the most powerful battleship in the world.

The cheering faded as the *Ark Royal*'s loudspeaker crackled to life again. "This is the Captain speaking. The War Office and the Prime Minister have requested that the following information be announced to all members of the British Armed forces. This morning, at six hundred hours, the H.M.S. *Hood* blew up and sank during an engagement off the coast of Iceland with the enemy battleship *Bismarck* and the heavy cruiser, *Prinz Eugen*. Three survivors were taken aboard H.M.S. *Repulse*. Their names are . . ."

Feathers stood, stunned. The *Hood* gone? Bang, just like that? And three survivors out of how many? The *Hood* had carried a crew of more than fourteen hundred. He felt a burning lump in his throat. Three survivors out of fourteen hundred! And he had been messing about with a bloody cat after the pride of the British Empire had gone down beneath the waves.

The "bloody cat" gave a sharp meow. Feathers meant to answer its imperious glare with an indignant one of his own, but he noticed something about the animal's neck. It was a brown leather collar with a buckle and bronze nameplate. As Feathers turned the collar, letters in a flourished engraved script came into view. They read, "H.M.S. Hood."

At the sight, the pilot felt his face flush, then pale. He stared at the half-drowned shivering cat, then at the collar. The words didn't change, as he half-expected them to.

"It can't be," he muttered.

In principle there was no reason why the animal couldn't have been the *Hood*'s ship's cat. Many British vessels had cats aboard, whether officially or otherwise. The stores of food aboard were too tempting to the rats that infested the most well-run ships. Therefore a cat, or perhaps a pair were an essentail part of a warship's crew.

Feathers was still baffled. According to the announcement, the *Hood* had gone down in the Denmark Strait, between Iceland and Greenland. The *Ark Royal* was, at this moment, only a few hundred miles off the coast of Spain.

How could this cat have gotten here, more than three thousand miles from the *Hood*'s last known position. No. This had to have another explanation. Perhaps the cat had been on another ship, being brought to or from the *Hood*. Maybe it had fallen ill or grown too old and had to be retired. The *Hood*'s crew might have let it keep the collar and nameplate as an honor for years of service.

Feathers admitted his reasoning was pretty flimsy, but it was the only explanation that made sense.

And then he noticed something else about the cat. In the light gray fur on its left haunch, the pilot saw a sooty mark. When Feathers touched it, the cat flinched and stiffened. Even though the fur was soaked, the hairs looked black and brittle. Burned. And in the cat's fur was the lingering smell of cordite.

Suddenly an image came into his mind. A small four-footed figure darting across the tilting deckplates while guns roared and fire licked out from the superstructure of a doomed battleship.

The *Hood* had blown up. A tower of fire amidships. Fire and smoke and scorched fur. And the collar.

"Well, some cook could have thrown a hot kettle at you in the galley," muttered Feathers, looking down at the cat, but suddenly all his contrived explanations fell apart.

As he backed through the hatchway with cat and ring still held out in front of him like a tea tray, Feathers Geoffrey-Faucett could not help wondering if he held a fourth, if unrecognized, survivor from the H.M.S. *Hood*.

Since the orders had been changed and the Swordfish biplanes were again being stowed below decks, Feathers Geoffrey-Faucett decided that he could spare a moment to look after the cat. The animal was shivering after its drenching in the sea, though it clung as stubbornly as ever to the life ring.

As the pilot carried the cat between decks to his cramped cabin, he felt the deck vibrate as a roar shook the carrier, then subsided into a rumble. The *Ark Royal*'s engines were coming up to full throttle; she was no longer at station but bound for some destination. Feathers guessed that they were heading for the North Atlantic, where the battleship *Bismarck* must be lurking.

As he was tilting the cat and life ring against his chest to squeeze them and himself through the narrow cabin hatchway, he heard Jack Shepherd's voice. The air controller stopped, stared, then broke into a grin beneath his neatly clipped mustache.

"So there really was a cat out there. You weren't just ragging me, Feathers."

"Get some rum from your kit, would you, Jack? This little perisher needs it and I could use a nip as well."

Feathers spread a slicker on his bunk, laid cat and ring down, then grabbed a terrycloth and toweled the animal until its fur stood up in spikes. When Shepherd came in with the bottle, Feathers laid a gentle hand over the top

of the cat's head and slipped his fingers into the corner of
its mouth, prying its jaws apart. Shepherd filled the bottle cap with a small dose. Feathers deftly poured it down
the animal's throat, then followed with a second.

"My, you know how to handle it," said Shepherd
admiringly.

"My mum kept moggies and vetted them herself. Always had a soft spot for the creatures. All right," Feathers said to the cat. "Sit up and let's have a look at you."

By now the cat had released its grip on the life ring.
Feathers gently lifted the ring off over the cat's head.
The castaway shook itself, grimaced, and raised its flattened ears. It was a compact little animal with the short
thick fur and the rounded head characteristic of the
sturdy British shorthair. A few more rubs with the towel
and the fur was soft and fluffy, if still a little damp.
The cat opened its gold eyes and stared Feathers full in
the face.

Now that the beast was halfway clean and dry, Feathers could see its markings. All along the back, sides,
chest, and down the front legs on both outside and inside, the animal's fur was a rich leathery brown. The
brown ended in a border just behind the animal's middle
and its flanks, hind legs and tail were gray. Two white
wristlets encircled the forelegs just above the paws. The
paws themselves were black.

"Well, aren't we the natty little gentleman," said
Feathers, leaning over with his hands on his knees. "Look,
Jack. He looks like he's got on a bomber jacket."

The cat arched its back and rubbed against Feathers'
hand, then butted his palm with its nose. Its head and
neck were tan, with a slightly darker color on the ears.
And the ears themselves were a bit odd. They stood up
like normal cat's ears, but the outside edge of each one
curled outward and the tips pointed together like little
horns.

"Poor beggar. The wind's blown his lugs inside out,"
said Shepherd."

Feathers guffawed. "No Jack. That's just the way he
is. Looks a bit jaunty with those ears, doesn't he? Doesn't
need an R.A.F. cap to match the rest of him."

Feathers' fingers touched the collar as he stroked the cat. He remembered the nameplate and its upsetting message. He didn't want anyone else in the crew to see that. Quickly he slipped it round and started to undo the buckle, but the cat raised a paw to stop him. No claws, just a firm press of one black foot and a gaze into the eyes.

Luckily Jack Shepherd was occupied at the other end, doing a quick inspection to be sure they were using the correct gender when referring the animal.

"Definitely a little tom, all right," he announced, proud of his first venture into the veterinary field. "Got all the equipment intact, far as I can see."

Feathers, who had kept his hand on the collar, made a decision. "Jack, what do you make of this?" He showed Shepherd the bronze nameplate and the scorched spot on the cat's side. He saw the air controller flush, then go pale, just as he himself had done.

"H.M.S. *Hood*. Well, of all the queer happenings. . . ." Shepherd sat down beside Feathers on the bunk. The cat walked onto the air controller's lap, stood on his thighs and tilted its head back, watching him expectantly.

"He doesn't want me to take his collar off. Pushes my hand away."

"If the sinking hadn't just been announced, I would have said that the collar was a prank," said Shepherd.

"Jack, no one's been at him since I hauled him over the rail, I swear. The only thing I can think of is that he belongs to the wife or child of someone on the *Hood* and he fell off a transport in rough weather." He looked at the cat. "But it just doesn't seem to fit."

Shepherd agreed. "They don't have room for pets on the transports. Look," he said, switching the subject. "Why don't you nip down to the galley and coax some tinned mackerel out of the cook while I look after Bomber?"

"What? You're already given him a name?"

"Well, we don't know what he was called aboard the *Hood*. There was no name on the tag and his markings do look like a bomber jacket."

Feathers grinned as he walked down the hallway on his errand. Bomber. It wasn't a bad name. And it was certainly appropriate for a cat aboard an aircraft carrier. When he returned to his cabin with the fish on a saucer, he heard Shepherd's voice querulously scolding the cat.

"That's the property of the Royal Navy, you ungrateful animal!"

Feathers stepped through, mackerel in hand. Bomber spotted it and made a dive for the plate as Feathers laid it on the floor. The pilot stared at the air controller, who rolled his eyes at the cat.

"What's the matter?"

"I shouldn't have given him that name," Shepherd said. "I bet he thinks he's got to live up to it. He's perfumed your cabin like a bloody bug bomb."

Feathers took a sniff. The smell was redolent and well remembered from his childhood among his mother's feline household. "He's just staking out his territory. Obviously knows his way about a ship."

"Well, I'll think I'll be getting along," said Shepherd, making a hasty exit. "I'd keep the cabin door shut until he . . . ah, makes himself at home. Cheerio."

While Bomber was still preoccupied with the mackerel, Feathers made one more foray into the galley for an old baking tin and some newspapers. He fled under assault from the cook, who had grown indignant at such raids upon his territory. A ladle clanged against the wall behind Feathers as he made a quick exit, bearing pan and papers. Once he had regained his cabin, he shredded the papers, stuffed them in the pan, took the cat by the scruff and pointed his nose at the makeshift sandbox.

"You'd bloody well better use that, or you'll find yourself right back in the Atlantic," he growled, then pulled the slicker from his bunk and stretched out on top of the blanket. He noticed that Shepherd had, in his haste, forgotten his bottle of rum. He uncapped it, took a pull and lay back for some quiet thoughts.

After scruffling about in the shredded papers for a while, Bomber came over, leapt onto Feathers' chest and settled there, kneading with his paws and exhaling a faint odor of mackerel.

Feathers put one hand behind his head and dabbled in the cat's fur with the fingers of the other. "Where did you come from, eh? Are you really the *Hood*'s ship's cat? If you are, I'll wager you'd like to be in on a scrap with the *Bismarck*."

Bomber's ears twitched back and his tail wagged briefly while his eyes slitted. In them, Feathers thought he saw the unmistakable glint of anger. He sighed, laid his head back, wondering if his imagination was getting the best of him.

The captain called the ship's company out on the flight deck for an announcement that Feathers expected. Force H was being sent north to join in the hunt for the German wolves that had destroyed the *Hood*. The two enemy ships now lay poised to prey on the transatlantic convoys that were the only resource keeping England in the war.

"Though what good we'll do is beyond me," whispered Shepherd, who had come up behind Feathers. "Flying outmoded Swordfish chicken coops with only one torpedo each. If we had some decent carrier-based aircraft. . . ."

"Don't you count out the Stringbags yet," snapped the gunner Patterson, standing nearby. "Remember the ships we sunk at Taranto Harbor? Knocked out half the Italian fleet."

Feathers said nothing. Though he felt a fierce loyalty to his airplane, he knew Shepherd was right. The Fairey Swordfish torpedo biplane, while reliable, maneuverable and easy to fly, was no match for the guns and armor of enemy ships and aircraft. If any of the Swordfish saw service in the coming fight, it would be as a last-ditch attempt after all else had failed. And it would likely end in disaster.

There was nothing they could do about it in any case. Pilots and crew would have to sit out the hours drinking coffee, studying maps, and listening to reports on the wireless while *Ark Royal* and the rest of Force H churned their way north to join the hunt.

Feathers returned to his cabin. When he stepped in, he saw Bomber nosing about the corners of the cabin.

The little cat stopped, turned his gray hindquarters to the wall, and began a meaningful quivering of his tail.

"Oh, hell," growled Feathers, lunging forward to grab the offender, but he was too late. A misty aerosol formed in a cloud behind the cat's tail, Bomber's benediction to the wall. "One stinker on this ocean is enough, but I'm blessed with two. You and the bloody *Bismarck*."

But even as Feathers was drawing back his open hand for a slap at the cat, Bomber spun around, pointing his head at the wall. His fur bristled and rippled as if some unseen hand were stroking it backward. His head ducked, pointing his ears toward the bulkhead.

Undulations swept through Bomber's jacket, up his neck to his ears. The air around the cat grew electric with static. With a crackle, a hot white spark leaped from each eartip to the damp spot on the bulkhead.

Feathers jumped back so fast he nearly fell on his rump. "I've heard of a cathode," he muttered to himself. "But I never thought it would be attached to a cat!"

And then he stared even harder, for Bomber's show wasn't over yet. The spot on the whitewashed cabin wall started to smoke and glow, making Feathers wonder if it would ignite like petrol and burst into flame. But instead the bulkhead started to ripple, just as Bomber's fur had done. Rainbow-colored rings bloomed in the center, spreading outward. And the once-substantial metal bulkhead was somehow becoming hazy, transparent.

Feathers quickly snuck a glance at Shepherd's rum bottle to see how much he had actually consumed before falling asleep. It did not reassure him to see that the level had only dropped by a half-inch. So it wasn't spirits that were causing this. Not alcoholic ones, at any rate.

The wall continued its alarming transformation until it contained a medium-sized hole. Bomber turned to Feathers and crooked the tip to his tail.

The pilot dropped down on his knees and peered through the hole. It did not lead into the next cabin, as he had assumed. It seemed to go somewhere . . . else. Feathers quickly got up and locked his cabin hatch from the inside. He returned to cat and wall, finding both as he had left them. The hole, if anything, was a little larger.

Tentatively, Feathers put his fingertips to the edge of the opening. They tingled strangely. He peered through. The somewhere else definitely resembled the inside of another ship. But not the *Ark Royal*. He was looking at walls and decking that had a different color and texture from the ones on the carrier or any other Royal Navy ship he'd ever been on. They were a heavy blue-gray and the air had the factory smell of newly manufactured metal. The rumble of engines sounded though the opening, but their sound was foreign.

The click of footsteps sounded on the other ship, making Feathers draw back from the gap. They grew louder. Feathers felt himself break into a sweat. Whoever was coming could hardly fail to notice a three-foot hole that hadn't been there a minute before. He waited, expecting the steady click of the footsteps to cease and exclamations of astonishment and dismay to break through from the other side.

The steps did stop. But the expected outcry didn't come. Unable to stand the tension, Feathers knelt and peered through the gap. He saw the hem of a double-breasted navy blue coat with two rows of buttons. The cuff bore a single stripe and a gold star on the sleeve, the insignia of a lieutenant in the German navy. The man had stopped right opposite the hole! But he wasn't doing or saying anything. Perhaps he was simply struck dumb. Feathers waited for all hell to break loose.

The pilot shifted so that he could gaze slightly upward. Yes, a young German naval officer. He could see the Reich eagle on the cap. The man didn't look as if he'd seen anything unusual. He was leaning slightly against the bulkhead on the opposite side of the corridor, finishing a cigarette. He took a last draw, tossed the butt down, and strode off.

Feathers wiped his sweaty hands on his trousers, scarcely able to believe that the officer hadn't seen anything. Apart from the hole itself, the noise coming through from the *Ark Royal* should have drawn the man's attention. Unless. . . .

Unless the gap only worked in one direction, like a

one-way mirror. Perhaps the officer had glanced down and seen only the unbroken expanse of metal.

Bomber came up and butted Feathers impatiently, as if urging him to go through the opening. Feathers took a pen from his pocket and edged it into the gap, half-expecting the pen to be chopped off by the sudden reappearance of the bulkhead. There was something on the other side, on the metal floor. The officer's discarded cigarette end. Feathers snatched it up and whipped his hand back through the hole.

He stood up, staring at his prize. It still smoked between his fingers. It was crushed and dingy, nevertheless, he could still read what remained of the tobacconist's imprint. Three Castles. A German brand, popular with naval officers. He had stuck his hand through the hole and brought back the end of an enemy fag. That clinched it. That ship on the other side. It must be one of those that sank the *Hood*. *Prinz Eugen*. Or *Bismarck* herself.

His brain suddenly came alive with crazy plans. With this entryway to the German ship, men from the *Ark Royal* could slip aboard the *Bismarck* and cause all kinds of havoc. A charge could be planted in her engine room. Her captain and high officers could be picked off. The ship itself could be taken from within! What a triumph for the Royal Navy if the mighty *Bismarck* could be seized and turned against the Axis nations who built her.

But even as dreams piled atop each other in the pilot's head, the hole trembled, shrank and popped shut. Shaking a little, Feathers touched the bulkhead. It was as solid as ever. Bomber gave Feathers a look halfway between resignation and disgust.

Feathers sat back on his bunk. He was tempted to take a large gulp of rum and dismiss the entire thing as a feverish hallucination. Until he looked at the German cigarette butt in his hand. There was no way to explain that.

He scratched his head. Apparently the effect was transitory, perhaps lasting only as long as the concentrated essence that created it. But if that was true, why hadn't Shepherd noticed anything when Bomber first began to display his proclivities? Feathers hadn't remembered any unexplained dimensional apertures in his cabin when he'd returned from the galley with a plate of fish.

Feathers sighed. Even if he could get the cat to perform again, no one in his right mind would believe him or be ready to duck through the interstice before it closed. And how would they get back? Could Bomber reverse the route from the German ship back to the *Ark Royal*?

The pilot flung himself back on his bunk, his arm across his eyes. Anyone in his right mind? Was he even in his right mind or was he going completely round the bend? He felt a heavy warm weight on his chest and saw the cat once more curled up on top of him.

"I don't know what the hell you are, but as a secret weapon, you leave something to be desired," he growled.

Bomber, however, didn't answer.

The carrier *Ark Royal* plowed ahead on a northwest course along with the other craft of Force H who were hoping to intercept the *Bismarck* and *Prinz Eugen*. The men aboard cheered at reports over the wireless that the *Bismarck* appeared to have taken a hit on the bow during the final engagement with the Home Fleet. The radar-equipped heavy cruiser H.M.S. *Sheffield*, which had been shadowing the German battleship, reported that *Bismarck* was leaving a wide swath of oil in her wake. But the excitement slowly died down when further reports indicated that the warship was not losing any speed and appeared essentially undamaged.

And then came the news that *Bismarck* had given her pursuers the slip and vanished into the fogs and rain squalls of the North Atlantic. Now all that the British forces could do was to wait and hope that air reconnaissance would spot her.

Force H kept steaming north, hoping the intercept *Bismarck* if she made a run for ports in Spain or France. But no one knew where the great ship had gone. It was as if she had vanished from the sea.

During the run north, Feathers had more free time than he wanted. He spent it drinking more than he should from Jack Shepherd's rum bottle and pursuing Bomber about the cabin, trying to persuade the cat to repeat his extraordinary performance. But Bomber, perhaps in disgust at having to deal with creatures of such low sagacity and perception, was behaving in a maddeningly normal manner. He even used the baking tin and its nest of paper for its intended purpose without creating the tiniest of interspatial holes.

Feathers braved the cook's wrath to abscond with more tinned mackerel, hoping that something in the fish had contributed to the cat's display. But even though Bomber consumed every morsel with relish, nothing happened.

At last Feathers decided that the whole thing must have been a total fantasy or a dream. He could not bring himself, however, to toss out the German cigarette butt. The pilot resigned himself to the fact that if the *Bismarck* was to be taken, it would be done without any feline assistance, fantastic or otherwise.

May 26 dawned with gray heaving seas underneath the *Ark Royal* and an even grayer mood among her crew. *Bismarck* had been sighted again by a Catalina flying boat off the coast of Ireland, but the ensuing attacks against her were ineffective.

The battleships H.M.S. *Prince of Wales* and *King George V* plus the cruiser *Suffolk* had tangled with her briefly, only to be driven off by the German ship's deadly and accurate shelling. And a flight of Swordfish from *Ark Royal*'s sister carrier, H.M.S. *Victorious*, had loosed nine torpedoes at *Bismarck* with only one hit. It hadn't fazed her in the least. She was still running at 20 knots, well ahead of the pursuing Home Fleet and likely to escape. The only way to slow her down lay in the *Ark Royal* and her aircraft.

The Ark Royal had already sent two Swordfish equipped with long-range tanks to shadow the *Bismarck* and make sure she did not slip from sight again. These relays of shadowers were continually replaced during the day. Then came the announcement that the fifteen Swordfish not engaged in shadowing operations would mount an afernoon torpedo attack on the *Bismarck*.

Feathers ate his lunch, then he and Crockett, his observer, went up to the briefing office with the other aircrews to plan the attack. When he went down to his

cabin to collect some last-minute gear, Bomber tried to
follow him out.

"Look, sport," said Feathers, pushing him firmly back
inside. "You had your chance to put some holes in that
bloody battleship. Now I'm getting mine," With that, he
locked the cat inside the cabin, although he wondered
whether Bomber might use his unusual talents to make
an escape.

He didn't have time to think about Bomber once he
reached the flight deck. At two-thirty, the airedales had
his Swordfish prepped and ready, torpedo slung underneath. Despite the tossing seas and rolling deck, he,
Crockett, and Patterson made it off and buzzed away
with the rest of their squadron, all hungry for a shot at
the *Bismarck*.

About two hours later, a chagrined crew of Swordfish
were circling about *Ark Royal* while the carrier headed
upwind for their fly-on. The whole attack had been a
fiasco from start to finish. Emerging from heavy cloud
cover in an attack formation, the Swordfish had dived at
a lone ship, thinking it was their sought-for target. But it
wasn't. Confused by the weather and over-eager for combat, they mistook the cruiser *Sheffield* for the *Bismarck*.

"God, what a bloody-balls-up," groaned Feathers as
he scrambled out of his cockpit onto the rain-swept deck.
Patterson followed quickly so that the airedales could
hustle the plane onto the lift and below decks before the
next Swordfish made its approach. "They send us out
and what do we do? Nearly sink one of our own ships!"

"I don't know what those other blokes were about,"
said Patterson. "We've used the *Sheffield* for all our
dummy practice runs. As soon as I saw that superstructure, I knew it was the old *Sheff* and I told you to hold the
torpedo. Was right, wasn't I?"

"I imagine the War Office has lost all faith in the
Stringbags and they won't give us a second chance," said
Feathers gloomily.

"Boyo, they don't have a choice. We don't have anything else to throw at the bugger." With that cheerful
observation, Patterson shoved open the tower hatchway
and held it for Feathers. "You'll feel better when you've

got some grub in you. I have an itch that the old man is going to give us a chance to redeem ourselves."

"If the *Sheffield* isn't sunk," said Feathers. He trooped along with the others into the canteen and ate as much as he could hold, though the food might have been sawdust for all he cared. He was slightly cheered when news came that *Sheffield* had managed to maneuver so deftly that none of the torpedoes had hit her. He perked up even more when the captain announced that a second wave of Swordfish would depart the *Ark Royal* at 6:30 P.M. for one more crack at the *Bismarck*.

After the meal, Feathers was tempted to go immediately to the briefing room and then down to the hangar below to check his plane. But he remembered Bomber, still locked in his cabin. He hadn't left the cat any water. Feeling guilty, he made his way down to his quarters and opened the door. Bomber was still there, nosing about the corners of the room. Feathers patted him roughly, then fetched him water in the empty mackerel tin. As he did so, he talked to the cat, telling him what a mess the attack had been.

"If you could just do your trick again and let me get aboard *Bismarck*, I'd have a better chance of wrecking her than I have flying that firecracker-carrying chicken coop."

Bomber drew back his ears and narrowed his eyes. For an instant Feathers hoped that he had understood after all. The pilot was ready to grab his sidearm and dive through the moment that Bomber created a passageway between the *Ark Royal* and the *Bismarck*. But instead, the cat sprang away from Feathers, out the cabin door, and down the hallway.

"Where the devil are you going," Feathers shouted out the door as a gray tail disappeared around a corner. "I don't have time to chase a cat about. Dammit, come back!"

But Bomber was gone.

Perhaps he had decided to tackle the *Bismarck* on his own. Feathers could just imagine Bomber waging his own sort of guerrilla war with the enemy. He could almost hear the harsh Prussian voices scream in bad

World War One movie dialogue about "eine verdammt
geschpritzen-katzen!"

Feathers Geoffrey-Faucett shrugged. Bomber had gone
off on some mission, now Feathers had to attend to his
own. He jammed his cap back on his head and made his
way to the briefing room, where the aircrews were already assembling.

The plan was essentially the same as before, except
this time, presumably, they would attack the right ship.
A subflight of three Swordfish would approach in a steep
dive behind the quarry. As the planes pulled out of the
dive, they would fan out and approach the enemy in line
abreast. At ninety feet, flying a flat course, they would
drop their torpedoes into the sea and sheer away from
the barrage of flak from enemy anti-aircraft guns.

The trick was getting close enough before dropping the
torpedo. The optimum distance was 900 yards, but Feathers doubted that *Bismarck* would let anything get within
that range before blowing it out of the air. He felt his
hands begin to sweat. *Sheffield* had held her fire from
the attacking planes. *Bismarck* would give it all she
had.

They would have to fly low and hope for luck.

Bad weather had dogged the first attempt and threatened to scuttle the second. The rain squalls that gusted
fitfully around the carrier became a full gale. Feathers
pulled his leather flying cap down over his head, pulled
his jacket collar up around his neck and braved the
pelting rain. The sky, already dimmed by twilight, was
darkened almost to blackness by the storm. The deck
crews could only work by floodlights.

As he approached his Swordfish, a sweating crewman
in a grime-streaked slicker was rolling a torpedo on a
dolly toward the plane's undercarriage. Between the rain,
the glaring lights and the seesawing deck, the airedale
was having a struggle to get the torpedo in place. Feathers hastened his steps to help the airedale, fearing that
man, dolly, and torpedo might be swept over the side by
the rush of white water spilling over the carrier's bow and
sluicing down the deck.

Before he could reach the dolly, he saw a little four-footed shape gallop from the shadows toward the torpedo. With a yell, the airedale shouted and flailed, driving the animal off. What the hell was Bomber doing out on the flight deck, Feathers wondered, but he had no time to go after the cat. He overtook both airedale and dolly, adding his strength to the crewman's. Together they wrestled the torpedo back toward the airplane, raised it and secured it in the rack between the Swordfish's wheels.

"Thanks, sir," panted the crewman. "Might have lost 'er over the side if you 'adn't 'elped. Rum thing, that cat running out from nowheres. Gave me a start, it did."

Feathers squinted against the rain and the glaring floodlights but saw no sign of Bomber. He spotted the shapes of Patterson, his gunner, and Crockett, his forward observer. With a few last words to the two about the attack plans, he boosted them into their cockpits, then took one futile look about for Bomber.

Before he knew it, a lithe shape launched itself from somewhere behind the Swordfish's tail, bounded across a stream of seawater, scrambled up his trousers, and tunneled beneath his jacket. Feathers swore in a mixture of delight and annoyance. He was glad the cat hadn't been swept overboard, but what the hell was he going to do with him? There wasn't time. The other Swordfish crews were in their planes and one was starting the tracking run down the deck line. As the biplane skittered and wobbled, Feathers wondered how it would ever make it through the curtain of heavy spray and crashing waves from the ship's bow.

Somehow the carrier's deck lifted at the critical moment, giving the plane an additional boost into the air. Feathers saw it wallow unsteadily, on the edge of a stall, then gathered speed, circling away from the carrier. He prayed that he would be that lucky.

Bomber, tucked away beneath the pilot's jacket, had sunk his claws into Feathers' shirt in a way that suggested it would be difficult and time-consuming to remove him. And even if he did pry the cat loose, the airedales had their hands too full to bother with a cat.

"All right, you're going," said Feathers to the furry

lump underneath his jacket. "I just hope you know what you're letting yourself in for."

"What are you standing there talkin' to yourself for?" yelled Patterson. "Sayin' your prayers?"

"Might need 'em," said Feathers as he swung into the center cockpit behind the pilot's windscreeen.

Now, you blessed old Stringbag, he thought to his airplane, as he revved the engine and the airedales took away the chocks, *let's not decide to go for a swim*.

Just as he began the takeoff run, *Ark Royal* hit a deep trough that tilted her bow down until her deck was like the steep side of a hill. Feathers could see whitecaps on the sea below as he hurtled right downhill toward it. It took all his willpower not to pull back on the stick before the plane had attained flying speed. At the last instant, when he was sure he was going in the drink, the bow started to lift, tossing him in the air.

Bathed in sweat, he pushed the throttle to full power, feeling the plane begin to mush at the edge of a stall. A short dive let the Swordfish pick up speed and stability. With a surge of excitement, Feathers pulled back on the stick, starting a slow climb to attack altitude. The Stringbag might be old, slow and outmoded, but by God there was no other plane that could have gotten off a carrier in weather like this.

As he circled, climbing, he saw the rest of the torpedo-laden Swordfish leave the deck of the carrier. All fifteen made it safely.

Bomber squirmed inside Feathers' jacket. With the plane trimmed for a climb, he could spare a moment for the cat. He let the stowaway slide out from the bottom of the jacket and stuffed the cat between his knees and the edge of the seat.

"Now stay there and don't get tangled up in the control cables. And if you get airsick, it's your own fault. I don't know what made you decide to come along, but there's no turning back now."

Bomber seemed to understand. He wedged himself into the small space, keeping out of the way. He didn't seem to be frightened by the vibration or the hiss of the wind past the open cockpit. He also, Feathers noted thankfully, had shown no indications of airsickness.

Catching sight of another plane in Subflight Two, Feathers joined it and soon both were twining about each other's paths as they climbed to an altitude just below cloud level. Once aloft, the full squadron assembled in formation and flew over the *Sheffield*. The cruiser gave them a somewhat wary welcome and directions to the *Bismarck*. When the flight was past *Sheffield*, they climbed to attack altitude of nine thousand feet. Crocket, Feathers' forward observer, reported a blip on the radar that couldn't be anything but *Bismarck*.

After a short cruise, word came back from the squadron leader that he had sighted their quarry through a hole in the clouds. Most of the Swordfish would come in on the *Bismarck*'s port side, but Subflight Two was to attack from the starboard.

"Let's go get her, lads," came the voice of the squadron leader over the wireless and the fifteen Swordfish started the hunt.

Rain pelted against the Swordfish's windscreen and Feathers' goggles as he dived the torpedo plane from nine thousand feet. Between the rain squalls, the low clouds and gusty winds, Feathers could hardly keep track of the dark gray silhouette of the enemy ship. She was moving fast, crashing though the force eight gale that blew about her and sending up fountains of spray from her bows.

"What's her heading?" the pilot shouted to the observer in the forward cockpit. The lash of rain and wind coupled with the wavering drone of the Swordfish's engines drowned out Crockett's reply, but the discomfited look on his face told Feathers that the weather was making it impossible to do more than guess the warship's heading. And the radar set aboard the Swordfish was too crude to show anything but the ship's approximate location. He couldn't tell if the battleship was in a turn or running a straight course. God, what he'd give for a look at the *Bismarck*'s compass.

And then something stirred beneath his feet, reminding him that the Swordfish was carrying an extra crew member, whose usefulness was doubtful. As if Bomber had caught the gist of that thought, he crouched on the cockpit floor in the cramped space underneath the pilot's knees. His tail began to shiver in an unmistakable manner.

"Not here! Not in the bloody aircraft!" Feathers yelled, but an appallingly familiar pungency rising from the cat showed that Bomber had already begun his performance.

With both hands on the stick and feet on the rudder pedals, Feathers could only curse impotently. Then the cat wriggled to one side beneath Feathers' right thigh, pointed its ears, rippled its fur, and let loose a crack of miniature lightning from eartips into the center of the damped spot.

Wrestling the Swordfish's control stick with one hand, Feathers caught Bomber by the scruff. He was considering a quick toss over the side, but he realized that he was far too late. Rainbow rings were already blooming in the center of the cockpit floor as they had on the cabin wall.

In fright the pilot pushed back against his seat as a circular gap appeared in the floor and enlarged. Would it spread underneath his seat, dropping him through to God knows where? He began to wish he had been a little more diplomatic toward the cat. And if he disappeared right out of the plane, that would leave the observer and gunner still barreling along in a pilotless craft. Surely Bomber didn't have it in for them, too?

The thoughts sped through his mind as the Swordfish continued in its hurtling dive through the clouds. And then he suddenly noticed that Bomber's hole wasn't getting any bigger, but the haze inside it was clearing. He could see through. And what he could see was the top of a military cap, a pair of uniformed shoulders and two arms whose gloved hands rested on the huge upright steering wheel of a ship. A huge glass-faced compass before the wheel read one hundred and six degrees. East-south-east. Roughly the same direction that the *Bismarck* was heading.

In a rush Feathers realized that Bomber had provided him with exactly what he needed; a view right into the *Bismarck*'s helm control room. He was looking right down on top of the helmsman's head and the ship's great main compass. Abruptly the needle began to slide toward one-twenty as the helmsman's hand bore down on the right side of the wheel. The *Bismarck* was starting a turn to starboard, zig-zagging to avoid torpedoes tracking in on her from other Swordfish.

If she'll stay in that turn, thought Feathers, *I can send that torpedo to hit her aft, in the rudder or screws.*

A banging on the fuselage behind him made the pilot jump. "What the hell are you playing at!" the gunner bellowed into the slipstream. "Do you want to send us into the sea?"

Feathers stared at the onrushing waves below. Too many seconds of inattention had sent the Swordfish into too deep a dive. A surge of adrenaline made him pull back the stick barely in time. He swore that spray from a high-breaking wave splashed the torpedo-plane's undercarriage as the Swordfish pulled out of her dive and roared along at wave-top height. Ack-ack fire spat uselessly over the top wing, for the Swordfish was so low that she was beneath the firing range of the *Bismarck*'s anti-aircraft turrets.

He glanced between his knees at Bomber's viewhole down onto the enemy's helm station. The compass was still swinging steadily as the great warship kept to her same rate of turn. In his head the pilot estimated the trajectory needed to hit the *Bismarck* astern. Keeping his course dead level and his airspeed at 75 knots, he bored in toward the rain-shrouded shape of the German warship. He wanted nine hundred yards, but he knew he couldn't make it. The anti-aircraft fire was missing, but the big ship had taken to shelling the sea around itself, the explosions causing eruptions of water like geysers that could swallow a light aircraft and drag it down into the sea. At twelve hundred yards, Feathers pushed the torpedo release.

The bronze cylinder plummeted from the plane. *Stay in that turn, you bastard. Stay in that turn,* Feathers prayed as he veered away and caught sight of the torpedo's wake making a white trail directly toward the *Bismarck*'s stern.

One quick glance down between his knees through Bomber's viewport onto the enemy helmsman told him the warship had spotted the attack. He heard orders in German barked down the speaking tube to the wheelman. The officer leaned to one side, gathering the momentum needed to bring the great wheel hard to port.

Instantly Feathers knew that if the warship swung her stern aside, the tracking torpedo would miss. He'd launched it from too great a distance. *Bismarck* had already shown amazing maneuverability for so long a ship and great adeptness at dodging torpedoes.

With a yowl, Bomber, who had been poised on the edge of the hole, launched himself right through it. Feathers had the most amazing bird's eye view of the cat tumbling straight down onto the head of the *Bismarck*'s wheelman.

The officer threw both hands up in the air with a hoarse yell as a ten-pound bundle equipped with raking claws, teeth, and its own peculiar brand of chemical weaponry descended upon him. Bomber knocked the man's hat off and delivered a flurry of scratches to the hapless victim's head and shoulders. As a parting shot, the cat gave the flailing officer a final blast in the face as he sprang at the ship's wheel.

He landed, caught and held, his weight dragging the wheel back over and ending the change of course the helmsman was about to make. The *Bismarck* continued her sweeping turn to starboard.

Feathers strained his head over the side. Through the driving wind and rain, he saw the wake of his torpedo driving straight and true for the *Bismarck*'s stern. Water fountained up, mixed with smoke. The aft end lifted for an instant, then slammed back into the sea.

From the rear of the Swordfish came more pounding and a roaring cheer from Patterson. "Hoorah! We got her right in the arse!"

From the gap in the plane's floor that miraculously looked onto the helm of the enemy came an unholy racket. Feathers glanced down at the scene happening between his knees. Bomber was still fighting the helmsman, screeching and spitting while the officer fended off the attack. From the voicetube connected to the *Bismarck*'s bridge came frenzied shouts for the helm to obey. The uproar grew, Prussian bellowing mixed with British caterwauling, until the officer lunged, seized Bomber by the scruff, and hurled him against the wall.

Wild-eyed, the embattled wheelman seized control once again, hauling the wheel sharply to port as his captain had ordered, but it suddenly jammed at a rudder position of twelve degrees and wouldn't budge. The torpedo had done its work.

But what about Bomber? Ignoring Patterson's banging on the fuselage and demands to fly the bloody plane straight, Feathers stared down at the scene below him, searching for the cat. He spotted Bomber on the floor, looking up at him with something near desperation in the gold eyes. But Feathers himself couldn't fit through the gap. It was too small. He grabbed wildly at a coil of rope in the cockpit, hoping to throw a line down for the cat to snag. But before he could even find the rope end, the interstice shivered and popped shut.

For a second, Feathers could only stare numbly at the now-solid floor of the cockpit. There was nothing he could do to rescue Bomber short of trying to land his Swordfish on the *Bismarck*'s decks. And that would be sheer suicide.

"Would you tell me what is so interesting between your bloody knees?" Patterson roared again. "Get your head up and this crate home!"

Feathers pulled himself together. Bomber would have to rescue himself as best he could.

The Swordfish's forward observer, who had been completely forgotten during the wild ride, turned a pale but smiling face to the pilot and handed him a slip of paper.

It read "Hit confirmed. *Bismarck* circling to port. Rudder looks stuck."

Feathers gave him a thumbs up and headed the plane for home. As soon as he was beyond range of the warship's anti-aircraft fire, he started a climb to cruise altitude. Again he looked down over the side and was heartened by the sight of the *Bismarck* making a wide confused circle in the rough sea.

All the way back to the *Ark Royal*, the Swordfish rang with cheers and snatches of song. Feathers joined in, but his enthusiasm was tempered by the thought of Bomber lying on the deck of the enemy ship. The helmsman had thrown the cat hard enough to break his back, Feathers thought. But there wasn't anything he could do about it. And he had to get his plane and crew back to *Ark Royal*.

The carrier's stern was still bucking in fifty-foot heaves when the Swordfish began their fly-on. Feathers concentrated everything he had on getting down in one piece. He was given additional motivation when the plane ahead of him touched the deck during the upward surge, smashing the craft's undercarriage and sending it skidding along on its belly, shedding pieces. The crew scrambled out and the airedales pushed the wreck over the side before it could burst into flame.

When Feathers' turn came, the deck dropped away just as he was starting to settle and he had to make another go-round. But on the second try he landed.

He heaved himself out of the cockpit as the airedales rolled his Swordfish toward the lift.

"That was some of the damned craziest flying I've ever been through in my life," said Patterson to him. "I was beginning to wonder if you'd forgot how to pilot."

Feathers just ducked his head and walked through the driving rain. He knew there was no way he could explain to Patterson what had happened there up in the sky. The gunner hadn't even known that Bomber was aboard.

Shepherd was among those down below, welcoming the aircrews aboard. The news had spread quickly throughout the ship that two Swordfish of the second subflight, coming in on the *Bismarck*'s starboard quarter had got in one torpedo hit amidships and one aft. And the aft strike might have crippled her.

"That was your flight," Shepherd said excitedly to Feathers, amidst the general hubbub. "Which was your shot?"

"He kicked her right in the bum!" howled Patterson over his shoulder. "You should have seen it!"

"How the hell did you do it? And where's Bomber got to? I haven't seen him since you took off."

Feathers took Shepherd aside from the throng of rejoicing men. "Jack, he went with me. And he didn't come back. Come on. I'll tell you the whole story, if you'll believe it."

In Feathers' cabin, he and Shepherd shared what was left of the rum while the pilot told his friend the entire tale.

"You must think I've gone crackers. But I swear, that's the way it happened." Feathers ran his hand through his sandy hair. "Jack, you've read more scientific stuff than I have. Do you think it's possible to make a 'hole' between two different places the way Bomber did?"

Shepherd rubbed the stubble on his chin. "I don't know," he said thoughtfully. "The fellows at Farnborough play around with all sorts of queer ideas. But one thing I do know, Feathers. You're not given to fantasies. If it happened the way you said, I believe you."

"I feel terrible about leaving the little chap behind. But there was just nothing I could do."

"Well, look at it this way. You saved his life when you pulled him in from the sea. I think he just wanted to square the deal."

Feathers sighed, then looked at Shepherd with a wan smile. "Thanks. That helps a bit." He hung his head, his hands between his knees. "You know, I'm really beginning to miss him. I wonder if he really was just a cat. Seemed more like a guardian angel. Aah, I'm going all soppy on you, Jack."

"Well he definitely was a cat as far as one thing was concerned." Shepherd said, with a grin.

"I wish I had him back again," said Feathers.

"Even if he were to . . . ah . . . continue asserting himself?"

"Even if he did," said Feathers.

"Well, if it helps any, I'd suggest we give him an award, in memory of services rendered to king and country and all that," said Shepherd. "I'll get the tin snips from the repair shop. We can cut out a little Victoria Cross from the bottom of that mackerel tin and we'll have a proper posthumous presentation ceremony. How's that?"

Feathers agreed that such an award would be the best thing. He and Shepherd embarked on its construction, during the intervals when he wasn't being debriefed about the mission. In the confusion of the attack, no one could definitely assign which torpedo hit to which pilot. Only Patterson stoutly insisted that the aft hit was theirs, but the other aircrew also claimed it. Feathers took no part in the argument, since he had decided not to reveal Bomber's story to anyone except Shepherd.

Several hours into the evening, new reports came over the wireless. The torpedo hit had indeed done critical damage. After making two aimless circles in the North Atlantic, *Bismarck* was now heading northwest, in a wobbling course that indicated that she no longer had rudder control. She was backtracking helplessly, right into the guns of the oncoming Home Fleet.

Both Swordfish aircrews were decorated by the ship's captain and praised for their part in the battle. After the presentation, Feathers took his ribbon below, put it in a drawer and went back to Bomber's Victoria Cross. Ignoring the cuts on his hands from the jagged metal of the mackerel tin, he worked determinedly.

Shepherd came in just as Feathers was laying the finished piece in a little leather case that had once held someone's cufflinks. He pronounced it a beautiful piece of work given the contrariness of the mackerel can and the awkwardness of making fine cuts with tin snips.

"I think Bomber would approve," Shepherd said softly, laying a hand on the pilot's shoulder. "The news of that hit has gone right up to the Admiralty, to Sir John himself. They're all saying that it was a miracle, a hundred-thousand-to-one chance. It proves to me that your story must be true." He paused. "*Bismarck* is surrounded now. She hasn't got a prayer. And the Germans will fly their colors to the end, so we have to sink her. They're so sure of the end now that some bloke on the BBC has gone and written a bloody song about it."

Feathers looked down at the homemade Victoria Cross.

"I'd give him the proper words to write, I would," he growled.

"If Bomber's alive and still on board," Shepherd said, "he hasn't got much time. Maybe we'd better think about holding that ceremony."

"Just hold off another few hours, Jack. Maybe the little beggar can somehow piss his way home."

Shepherd gave the pilot a light pat on the shoulder and started to leave the cabin.

Abruptly an unholy racket broke forth from the direction of the galley. It sounded like a war was being fought with pots and pans. And then came the indignant tramp of feet along the deckway. Shephard backed inside again, clearing room for the red-faced, indignant cook, who held out a large, meaty fist clenched about the scruff of a very wet, oil-stained, and generally bedraggled cat.

"If this animal is yours, keep it out of the galley or Oi'll complain to the captain, Oi will," the cook bellowed, brandishing a ladle over his captive's head. "Oi don't know 'ow 'e got in, but 'e's made a perfect shambles."

"I think we can cope with him," said Shepherd, smoothly taking the cat from the cook and gently escorting the indignant individual out before pushing the cabin door closed behind him.

Feathers had risen from his bunk, his eyes wide. "Bomber!" He took the cat from Shepherd, held him up and looked at him in disbelief and delight. "It really is him, Jack!" Quickly he sat down with the cat on his lap and gently felt along the little body. "I think he may have a few bruised ribs from the smash against the wall, but he seems pretty fit otherwise. Wait till I dry him off a bit."

"Wonder what he was doing in the galley?" Shepherd asked.

"I imagine he was making for my cabin and missed. Must have been in a bit of a hurry. And that's why he fell in the sea instead of the *Ark Royal*. He must have had to pop off the *Hood* pretty fast, too." Carefully Feathers cleaned and dried the cat. He grinned as he scratched Bomber's head between the ears. "He certainly got his revenge."

"The Nazis should know better than to get a British ship's cat . . . ah, a bit niggled at them."

Feathers broke into chuckles, then laughed until he had to hold his sides. "I wonder if they have any idea what happened?"

"I suggest we have the presentation ceremony right here and now," said Shepherd. "Uh, what title were you planning to give him?"

"Why, there can only be one. To Bomber, ship's cat of the late H.M.S. *Hood*, I proudly bestow this Victoria Cross and name you mascot of Swordfish Sub-flight Two and," Feathers drew breath and presented the cufflink box with its tin medallion, "Bombardier, First Class!"

A PUMA
AND A PANTHER

by Wilanne Schneider Belden

Christine was allowed to choose one kitten, Ian the other. Mother was surprised when Christine insisted that the scrawny all-black kitten with the gold eyes was the one and only cat for her. "He was waiting for me," she explained. So he appeared to have been, for he ran to the door and squalled to be picked up the moment she came in. Ian, not yet three, clutched the rotund, yellow-orange kitty who slept in the nest-box. It yawned with all the animation of a damp towel and showed a mouthful of sharp baby teeth. Mother smiled, shrugged, and agreed. The five of them went home to introduce the newest members of the family to Daddy. Daddy took one look at the kittens and pronounced them Punkin and Bat.

The names stuck, and the kittens answered to them from the first. Christine changed the black kitten's name on an average of three times a month, totally without success. Ian, a late talker, probably had a different name for his. But Punkin lolled through life, lovable, loving, and barely animate. Bat lacked only leathery wings and a penchant for sleeping while hanging head downward by his back feet. Outdoors, he spent most of his time in trees, on high walls, or roofs. Indoors, he could be found on the top of the fridge, the top of the draperies, and the top shelf of the bookcase.

Punkin could have been anybody's cat. Fortunately, Ian was unaware of this lack of discrimination. Thus, when the little boy's attention was riveted to Bert and Ernie and Mr. Rogers, someone else could take care of "his" cat. Bat was Christine's cat, and he allowed no one to forget it. He accepted the children's parents with the regal indifference normal to cats, invariably ignored or eluded Ian, and rarely bestowed favors on visitors.

Bat knew Christine to be his human. He and Punkin had, after all, experienced incarnations in three alternate realities while searching for her and waiting until she showed up. Only Bat's genuine affection for her countered his previous annoyance at her tardiness. Punkin was unaffected: all nine lives had to be lived somewhere/somewhen.

Had the family lived in these other times and places, Christine's instant claim of so unprepossessing a kitten would have confirmed a reasonable conclusion. She was, after all, left-handed, red-haired, and green-eyed. She couldn't be called *pretty*, but her appearance left little doubt that she would be strikingly beautiful as an adult. Her personality, in common with a special category of people, combined independence and sensitivity, intelligence and empathy. In her own world, a description might include that most unfortuante phrase—the child who doesn't quite fit in. Part of this stemmed from her unfettered imagination. She believed things nobody else would—or could—and insisted, to the point of crying herself ill if anyone attempted to convince her otherwise, that her imaginings were fact. Her parents hoped that having a kitten would help to tie her to reality, but Bat's arrival seemed to stimulate her fantasy life. Each evening, Christine regaled the parent who put her to bed with a tale she said Bat had told her about a former life. However, as the family lived in the here and now and were churchgoing Christians, the term *witch* never came up.

Bat knew. Or, it is fairer to say, he knew what she would have been if she had not, unfortunately, been born into *this* world, one essentially inimical to magic. If she had not come for him in kittenhood, he would have, when a bit older, dragged Punkin by an ear and set out to find her. Denied his rightful place as her familiar, he took up the position of her pet.

Punkin knew, too. (Cats do.) But his involvement was with Ian, with whom he shared all kinds of preferences: love and affection, lots of good things to eat and drink, a warm, soft place to sleep, and semi-continuous attention.

As the two cats grew—and they did grow, prodigiously—Bat turned into a large, strong, shiny-sleek beast who reminded one of a black panther. Punkin loomed even larger than Bat, and the red-gold of his coat rivaled new pennies. Were he asleep on one of the children's pillows, one could not tell where their hair stopped and his began.

When Bat was about a year old, Christine insisted that he told her to get him a leash and harness so they could go on walks together. Mother, who usually enjoyed her daughter's vivid imagination, smiled to herself and bought the inexpensive equipment. She did not expect it to be used. She was mistaken. Bat required no training. His leash-manners were impeccable.

Circumstances in the modern world being as they are, neither of the children was ever without adult supervision for a moment. But Christine insisted that as long as Bat was with her, she was always safe and well cared for. Being informed, however, that Bat would be given to the Humane Society if she ever, ever went off with only a cat for company, she accepted the restriction. She never entirely accepted the necessity. However, she decided that her most intensely-defended disagreement with her parents—that she had, once, been left alone in the house for a period of perhaps hours—had, as they always maintained, been a dream. Bat, she admitted to her mother, told her straight out that the incident had been only a very clear nightmare, and Bat was always right. He had also told her that she must apologize to her parents for doubting their word.

Wishing herself believed to be as infallible as the cat, Mother accepted the apology without further comment. She wished, as a matter of fact, that Bat would tell Christine to forget all about the dream. Her own worst nightmare was that Christine might repeat the story to someone who'd believe it.

Punkin did not like to walk on a leash. He did not enjoy riding in automobiles, either. Bat loved cars. Originally, he was a problem because he preferred to sit on the dashboard directly in front of the driver. Only with difficulty was he persuaded that the back window, on the old shag rug, was the proper carseat for a cat. The children's mother permitted Bat to come along on short drives provided he did not have to stay alone in a car. He learned early that if he wanted to take the daily trips to preschool, then to kindergarden, he must not try to get out of the car or behave badly on the way home. Mother even let him accompany her on short errands without the children. She did not mention it to anyone, but if Bat was along, it seemed as if the most demented of the dangerous drivers stayed home. She required his presence if she chauffeured one of the school field trips.

Christine asked Mother please to drive when her class went to the Pumpkin Farm so the children could choose Halloween pumpkins. "Be sure Bat comes," she instructed. "He'll help me pick the right ones." Mother had been looking forward to the trip for almost as long as Christine had, and Bat was on his rug before the door was open far enough for Ian to get in and climb into his carseat.

They found Ian's pumpkin first—a huge, round one that had a definite resemblance to Punkin, or so Christine said Bat said Ian said. Christine's jack-o-lantern-to-be was harder to locate, but, after much effort and consideration, she and Bat were satisfied with their selection. "She put a lot more time and thought into choosing it," Mother told Daddy that evening, "than she did when we went to get the kittens."

Daddy grinned. "It wasn't trying to climb her jeans and yowling to be picked up," he explained. He observed the giant vegetable with some rue. "Not that she could have."

Mother grinned back. "Guess not," she agreed.

When the family got together to carve the faces, Christine insisted that the cats pose for their portraits. Daddy, who was skilled with his hands—and something of an artist, as well—agreed. Punkin was easy to capture. "Yawning Cat," Mother dubbed the result. Sleepy eyes, gaping mouth with too many sharp teeth. Ian giggled. Punkin flowed fatly onto the top of the lantern, arranged himself so that the smoke hole was not covered, and went to sleep. The whole family laughed—and continued to snicker whenever they saw him there. He appeared to be attached.

Bat's jack-o-lantern portrait did not yawn. Its mouth gaped open in a fearsome, silent snarl. Ian screamed and hid his face when Daddy put a lighted candle inside. The head seemed a real and menacing presence on the dark porch. Even Daddy regarded his handiwork with mild unease. Mother thought of several correct titles. She decided not to share them with the children. Christine shuddered, but she would not let her father change a stroke of the knife. "He's guarding us," she insisted. Looked at that way, the carving took on a somewhat less threatening aspect.

Despite their appearance, Christine treated the jack-o-lanterns as if they were alive. She always addressed them by name, showered them with affection, and shared her life with them. She supplied their parts of conversation, changing her voice a little for each personality. One who only overheard her play might have believed the child to be one of triplets. Mother found this mildly amusing, but she did not let on. Why shouldn't her little girl have playmates who always wanted her more than anybody else?

Halloween, that year, was on Friday night. Christine and Ian dressed up in their costumes early in the afternoon and came very close to driving their mother into the nearest asylum. "When can we go trick-or-treating? Can't we go *now*? Isn't it late enough *yet*?"

Trying hard to remember what it was like to be three years old—or six—Mother held on to the last wisps of her temper and assured the children that they would go trick-or-treating after Daddy got home, the moment it got dark.

Daddy arrived about four, but dark took forever and seven days longer. Mother put on her makeshift costume, a mishmash of gypsy skirt and every piece of costume jewelry she could lay hands on, a black cape and hat she'd bought at the theater costume sale, and a particularly gruesome mask that Daddy intended to wear to the costume party they'd be attending later.

The family went out to the porch to watch Daddy light the candles in the jack-o-lanterns. Ian had learned not to look at Bat's lantern. He waited at the foot of the steps, steadfastly staring at the pumpkin Punkin. Punkin followed them out the door. He yawned, then curled himself in the slight hollow in the top of his lantern. He rubbed his head against the little boy's side in a surprisingly reassuring gesture.

Ian wanted Punkin to come along, but Punkin yawned again and was asleep before he exhaled.

"Do you think we should blow out the candle?" Mother asked. "I wouldn't want him to get singed hair."

"Bat says it's all right," Christine informed her parents. "He says Punkin only looks stupid. He's not, really."

Over the children's heads, Daddy mouthed that he'd keep an eye on the cat, and Mother set out with Robin, the Batboy, and Tina the (Bat)Tamer. Bat (the cat) led the way on his leash.

The only other trick or treaters making the rounds this early in the evening were no older than Christine, and everyone had a jolly time. Bat made a great hit as a circus big cat, and Christine's star-status as his trainer was almost enough to make up for the times she'd been left out. Mother stood on the sidewalk with her flashlight, shining its beam to light the children's way up the front walks. Other mothers, doing much the same, struck up conversations.

"We're lucky to live in this neighborhood," one woman said. "Where I used to live, gangs would make things really scary on Halloween. Not the shoot-'em-up kind of gangs, or at least I don't think so. But they got a big kick out of frightening little kids and egging houses and writing on car windows with wax. Got so bad last year that the cops came."

Silently, Mother thanked the combination of their hard work, good fortune, and good planning that meant they could buy a house here. Halloween should be fun, not awful, not for little kids. Not, really, for anyone. Never having been that kind of child, she didn't have much understanding or sympathy for teenagers whose idea of fun was making malicious mischief. It occurred to her to make certain that their cats were locked safely indoors when they got home. Recently, the news had been full of the stomach-turning animal mutilations of Satanists.

Because it was Friday, Christine and Ian got to stay up late enough that they could see the costumes of the elementary school contingent who came by after the Carnival closed. But nine o'clock arrived, and the porch light was turned out, and the costumes had to be taken off and hung up. Ian was asleep before Daddy pulled the covers over him, which was all for the best. He'd come to expect Punkin, his soft, warm, living pillow, to purr him to sleep. But despite the intent and efforts of Mother and Daddy, neither of the cats was indoors. Exactly where they were was not clear, as they weren't on the lanterns, on the porch, or, for that matter, anywhere in the immediate neighborhood.

To her parents' ill-concealed astonishment, Christine was not at all concerned. Where else would Bat be but guarding the house from a hidden vantage point? He'd come in through the cat door after he was sure everything was all right. Mother, who'd been sure she would have a hysterical youngster to deal with, tucked her confusing daughter into bed and kissed her good night. She hoped Christine was correct.

No other sitter would do on Halloween night than Grandmother, and Daddy picked her up, as scheduled, at nine-thirty.

"Both asleep," Mother said. "They're really tired."

"We won't be too late," Daddy told her. "About two."

"Run along, dears. Have a good time. I'll watch TV, then go to sleep on the couch. Don't wake me when you come in."

"Please keep an eye out for the cats. Neither of them is in, and it's no night for a black cat, particularly, to be out."

"Bat can take care of himself," Grandmother said. "But I'll watch for them."

Grandmother was awake whem Mother and Daddy got home, and she told a tale of noises and nastiness up and down the street. "Both children slept through it, I'm glad to say. And the cats came in soon after it got quiet outside."

All seemed well.

In the morning, when every other jack-o-lantern on

the street had been thrown, with much high-strung, overloud laughter, into the middle of the street, smashed, and jumped upon, Christine's and Ian's lanterns stood unharmed, if not in the same positions as they had the night before. "Of course," Christine said. "Bat and Punkin wouldn't let those bad boys hurt our friends."

Fortunately, Daddy was taking Grandmother home, for, thoughtlessly, he might have tried to convince his daughter that no such situation could have occurred. Mother, who got her mouth shut in time, found herself wondering if Christine's belief might not, possibly, have some truth in it, though she couldn't figure out either how or how much.

The next night, she was even more perplexed when Daddy told her that, during her evening out, a very angry man with a pimply-faced teenager in tow had banged on their door and demanded that they get rid of the puma and the panther and pay for all the damage the dangerous beasts had done or he'd call the cops. Introduced to Bat and to the sleeping Punkin and shown the damage and destruction caused by the boy and his friends the night before, the man transferred his irritation to his offspring.

"Good thing," Daddy said. "I'd have called out all the neighbors whose kids had their jack-o-lanterns wrecked." He grinned.

"But how did the boy get the idea we had a puma and a panther?" Mother asked.

"Great story," Daddy said. He sat down and, to both people's slack-jawed astonishment, Bat leaped onto his lap, stretched out, and purred. Daddy stroked, rather as if afraid that if he didn't, he'd regret it. He got his story back into line.

"The guys were taking turns running up onto the porches and grabbing the lanterns, heaving them out into the street, then kicking what was left into slop with their boots. When this kid came onto our porch with a friend, the other guy got Punkin's lantern. He insists that it closed its jaws on his hand, dug in with its teeth, and wouldn't let go. He screamed bloody murder and clubbed with his other fist, but nothing helped. Pimple-puss tried to pull the pumpkin off the other kid's hand, and he couldn't. He swears it growled at him and he could feel hair and hot breath. He turned around and grabbed up Bat's pumpkin—I gather to use as a weapon—and nearly lost his whole arm. Or so he says. I don't know where he got the marks, but they sure do look like cat bites. Five times too big to have been made by our cats, of course. But you have to credit him with a lot of imagination."

"Yes," Mother agreed weakly, "I guess you do."

"Anyway, once the two jerks were really caught, the other guys came over to see what was going on. They are all absolutely positive—according to the one who came here with his dad—that we had a puma and a panther on our front porch."

"Oh, sure," Mother said.

"Well, I guess somebody up there must like us. None of the punks was really a hard case: no guns or knives or bicycle chains. They all ran like rabbits."

"Leaving their friends to be eaten?" Mother asked.

"I guess. They're sure they would have been, too, if they hadn't tried putting the lanterns down and backing off. No problem. Once the pumpkins were safe, the teeth let go. The other kid lashed out with a boot—and I understand he has slashes six inches long right through the leather."

Mother grinned. "Couldn't be our cats, then."

Father stopped petting. He regarded Bat very soberly. Then he shook his head.

Mother was not normally telepathic, but she was almost sure her husband was thinking, "Not *now*, anyway." But, of course, he couldn't be, and if he was, never, never would he admit to having had such a ridiculous thought.

Bat yawned. He'd had more fun last night than he'd had in his three whole lives and one part-life put together. But he was so sleepy he felt melted. Shape changing took energy. Guess he ought to follow Punkin's good example and get some shuteye. He purred.

He'd convince them all, even if it did take solving the problem of a teen gang on Halloween to set the adults on the right track. Christine already knew he was here to take care of her—and the things she cared about, like those silly vegetables with holes in them. Ian talked silently to Punkin all the time, and to Bat, sometimes. He'd soon start speaking aloud in complete sentences. His grown-ups would faint from shock. Even if they convinced him that he really hadn't had conversations with cats, he'd always believe anything Christine told him. Mother was another of the odd ones—left-handed, red-haired, green-eyed, too smart for her own good, and one step to the *reft* (or *lown* or some other direction normal people couldn't enter). Hmm. Perhaps he should see to a "pet" for her, too. And Father? Well, Bat was mildly embarrassed at how long it had taken him to realize that Daddy was a wizard unaware: who else could so easily convince the ordinary populace of this continuum that everything was ascribable to ordinary, reasonable causes?

Even a puma and a panther on the porch.

THE LAST GIFT

by Elizabeth H. Boyer

Upon the day of her sixteenth birthday, Isolf was presented to the jotun as an offering, along with three sheep, five geese, some chickens, two goats, and a cow.

"Will I be killed and eaten outright?" she asked her father the night before. "Or will I be held captive?"

"Skrymir is an old friend to this clan," said her father, Alborg. "You are my firstborn child, the most precious thing I can think of, so he won't destroy such a gift. Sixteen years ago I promised him my firstborn in exchange for a drink of his honey mead. Because of that drink and my promise, I was given the secret of making steel. Our people turned back the savage Utlanders, and we have lived in peace ever since. But a promise is a promise, especially when you make it to a jotun. A jotun's gift always has a price, and you, my precious daughter, are the price I must pay for the freedom of our people."

Isolf took a firm grip on the cow's halter and knocked on the great door leading into the jotun's mountain hall. The earth quivered as heavy steps approached, then the door abruptly fell open with a rusty grating and grumbling.

"Who are you? What do you want?" rumbled the mighty voice of the jotun.

Isolf stepped over the threshold of the jotun's cave, making the appropriate protective sign, and gazed up into the craggy countenance of the jotun, lurking far above in the shadows of the cave. His eyes blazed down at her, casting a faint smoldering sort of light over his massive form and unkempt mane of shaggy beard and hair.

"My name is Isolf, firstborn daughter of the wizard

Alborg. Sixteen years ago you gave him the gift of steel, and he promised to give you his firstborn child."

The great and terrible jotun chuckled a dire chuckle.

"Firstborn children! Beautiful maids! Livestock cluttering my doorstep! What a nuisance you mortals are!"

"Well, you've given us so much, we want to give something in return. Do you mind if we come in?" She gathered up a goose under one arm, a bundle of bound chickens under the other.

"Are you not afraid of the mighty jotun, mortal maid?"

"Not in particular," said Isolf.

"Indeed. Men nowadays fear nothing. Some even make a mock of the jotuns, with masks and costumes." The jotun sighed, a gusty sound made hollow with ancient wisdom and intolerable burdens. "Come in, then. I must make a memorandum about making rash promises with mortals. Sometimes they actually stick to them."

Skrymir diminished himself to a size more appropriate. Standing before Isolf was a craggy-shouldered old man who reminded her of her own grandfather, with white hair and beard streaming over his shoulders in a forgotten tangle.

"Many have not forgotten your gifts," said Isolf, glancing about the dust and gloom of the jotun's hall. "If not for the Elder Race, men would still be wearing skins and throwing rocks. With jotun knowledge we have tamed the metals of the earth, learned to bake and brew and weave and make cheese and husband the earth and its creatures. It is true, many have forgotten, and the Elder Race is derided. I think that is the cause for the rising Chaos around us. Fields are no longer fertile. Our flocks are not as plentiful. Our walls and houses no longer stand as firm and true. If I can do anything to drive back the Chaos by coming here as an offering, then here am I to serve."

The great Skrymir chuckled again. For several centuries, he had watched over the New People, benignly assisting their progress from skin-clad, warfaring scraelings to civilized, warfaring vikings. Their busy antics amused him, as might a disturbed anthill, with their trials, tragedies, and heroic endeavors. Even their epithet for him—

jotun—he found amusing. In stature he was not so much a giant to them; their scalds and legends and folktales served to increase their expectations to a fearful extent, so when they came to him begging favors, as was their wont, he shifted his shape to a larger one, so as not to disappoint them. But of late, their respect was sadly lacking. So many of them came as thieves and tricksters, instead of earnest suppliants for wisdom.

Skrymir gazed down upon the slight figure of Isolf, clad in a blue cloak for health and protection, with a red hood for courage.

"What can you do against the rising tide of Chaos? What use have I for such a tiny thing as you? My needs are not human needs. Everything I require is here." He let a handful of dust sift through his fingers. "I have lived here alone since the dawn of time, and I don't need any looking after by a human creature."

"And no one seems to do much cleaning up," said Isolf, darting a shocked glance around the great hall in the mountain. "My mother and the wise women of the clan taught me that disorder is an affront to nature. It is my duty to put nature back into harmony wherever I find it disordered, so I shall stay where I may do some good against Chaos."

"I shall ponder the matter," said Skrymir. "After I ponder the rise of Chaos and the future of the New People. Wisdom makes thinking such an ordeal." He settled himself in his chair in a pondering pose, with his chin resting upon his fist and his eyes drawn nearly shut in a baggy scowl.

Lost in his weighty ponderings, Skrymir either forgot or simply did not notice the presence of Isolf for at least a fortnight. In that time, she shoveled away the heaps of ash from the hearth, she discovered the scullery under layers of soot and grease, and she discovered smooth and shining floors beneath years of dirt and rubble. Gradually Isolf spread the sphere of her power throughout the underground halls of Skrymir until order prevailed, pushing back the boundaries of encroaching Chaos, rendering the dusty, cluttered halls of Skrymir pleasant and serene.

When Skrymir returned from his contemplation, he

remembered the small female creature Alborg had sent him.

"All your work is splendid and orderly," he greeted her. "But still you are not happy. You are lonely here."

With one crabbed finger he lifted a telltale tear from her cheek.

Isolf shook her head. "I was promised, and nothing binds like a promise freely given and a vow freely taken."

Skrymir beckoned her to follow him to the brewery, the only room to which she was denied access. He illumined it with a gesture of his hand. Another gesture summoned an elegant cushioned seat for Isolf, drawn from nothing but the dust on the floor and Skrymir's imagination.

"You are lonely." There was no denying the truth to one who knew all things as Skrymir knew, from the thoughts in her head to the doings of her father far away in Holm. Skrymir never asked questions that required an answer. A question was a signal for silence and deep scouring thought.

"So I have decided to create a companion for you and all lonely persons of mortalkind. It has been long since any new creatures were created on the face of the earth. All the greater spirits have been taken for the bears and wolves and horses and a host of other fantastical creatures who would astonish you if you saw them. Fortunately they live far away from here, in a hot and dry place, so you'll never see an elephant or a lion or a gazelle. The limitations of mortal flesh are often a nuisance to you, but what a protection."

As he talked, he searched through the impressive clutter of his chamber, choosing pots and kettles in his careful, bumbling way, scratching runes upon them and the floor and in the air, and mumbling over names of elementals.

"It has been a long time since I brewed anything," he said, pressing his finger upon his forehead thoughfully. "My supply of honey mead is down to one small cask. The day of the jotun and his wisdom is nearly done, my child."

"Could you not brew more mead and more knowledge?"

"I am too weary and your people too disbelieving."

As he worked over his brew in the kettle, he invoked names and elementals, all without benefit of the protective runes Isolf had seen her father use. Nor did Skrymir defend himself with guardian rings and pentacles scratched about him on the floor or in the air. She saw the faces of demons and elementals swirling in the air about Skrymir's head, and all were orderly and obedient.

The wizards of her own clan summoned fires and thunders and furies that wreaked terrible havoc before a way was found to banish them once again into the ether from whence they had been brought. Magic for mortals was a perilous business; plenty of aspiring wizards had been destroyed by their own spellcasting, carried away by the elementals they had rashly summoned, shapes shifted and souls cast out without knowing how to bring them back. Watching Skrymir, Isolf knew that they were an amateur, arrogant lot, grasping for dazzling truths with their eyes tight shut and their minds clouded with ignorance.

"A spirit guide, companion, and protector," mused Skrymir through a cloud of vapor rising from the kettle. "A boon to all mankind, a comfort to womankind in her lonely and difficult walks, an augment to her powers. A companion in grace and beauty and mystery and curiosity."

He searched about, examining and discarding several skins of animals. A bag spilled out small scraps of fur of all colors. The jotun studied them and sighed, shaking his head and furrowing up his forehead in consternation.

"None of these are big enough. The guardian of women must be somewhat bigger than the palm of my hand. I wish I could have had the supervision of the lion or the tiger. I would not have summoned such ferocious spirits into them. In the old days, we had limitless materials. Now there's scarcely anything left."

"If I had nothing but scraps to make a thing from, I would sew the scraps together to make a larger piece," said Isolf. "Perhaps I am presuming, but it seems a thrifty way to get rid of scraps."

"So be it." With a shrug Skrymir tossed the scraps of fur into the kettle. "Now for a spirit. It isn't easy to take the same piecemeal approach to fitting a spirit into a creation. I have many small spirits, friendly spirits, malicious spirits, playful spirits, fierce little spirits left over from weasels, foxes, martins, ferrets, and other little hunting creatures, affectionate spirits, sleepy spirits—all are very good spirits, for the most part, but nothing large enough for a creature such as I want to make. So the only thing to do is to lump them all together and hope for the best."

The moment Skrymir added the spirits and their Names, the brew in the kettle gained a voice. Or voices—Isolf heard a chorus of squeaking and mewing and yowling and squalling, as well as some fiery hissing and spitting.

"Nothing of this sort has ever been done before," said Skrymir dubiously, venturing to reach into the smoking kettle, resulting in a flurry of spitting and hissing and growling. When he withdrew his great hand, three small, multicolored furry creatures were clinging to it and glaring around with wild beady eyes.

"Claws! I don't remember adding claws! Or teeth!" said Skrymir in surprise as he attempted to dislodge the small growling creatures from his hand and sleeve. The little brutes climbed up to his shoulders with amazing speed and agility, still hissing and sputtering ferociously.

Three more pointed little faces peered out over the edge of the kettle in wild alarm. When Isolf stooped for a closer look, three pink mouths opened in virulent hissings and spittings. Short fuzzy tails like weasels, enormous batlike ears, legs like little sticks, and a wicked pixie-faced head set on a shapeless blob of a body that seemed more bristling fur than actual substance. When she ventured to advance one hand toward them, the three little fiends scuttled mightily and escaped from the kettle. The last view she had of them was three small shadows disappearing into the heaps of impossible clutter filling the room.

Skrymir beckoned for a basket and managed to unsnag the other three beasties from his shoulders and beard, dropping them one by one, sputtering, into the basket.

"I think," he said thoughtfully, "I must have put too much spirit into such little bodies."

"Never mind," said Isolf. "Perhaps the savage little monsters will be a match for the mice and rats. They don't seem very companionable."

Skrymir examined a large rent in his finger and quickly healed it with a bit of dust and spit. "I don't think they turned out very well. Not at all what I'd intended. When I catch those other three, I'll cast out a few of the wild and malicious spirits and see what we're left with."

"What are they called? All creatures must have a name."

"By naming them, we are claiming them," said Skrymir with a ponderous shake of his head. "We give them a certain power over us with a Name. When you say it, they will come, and they may come whether you want them or not. No, we won't name this creature just yet."

Isolf took the basket and the creatures to the scullery. Almost immediately the little beasts pushed off the lid when she wasn't looking and scuttled across the floor in three different directions. No amount of hunting and chasing recaptured them. Having better things to do, Isolf returned to her work. As she sat plucking a young goose, she saw shadows from the corners of her eyes, slinking around the edges and dark corners of the room. Indeed, the jotun had created company for her but not the sort of company she cared for. When her back was turned, the three creatures hurled themselves upon the goose and dragged it away, off the table and toward the den they had chosen in a cleft in the wall. Isolf saved the goose but not without a great deal of high-pitched growling from the little brutes. From then on she took care to leave no meat lying about unattended; even so, she frequently saw the creatures sniffing around for it on the table top or around the bucket of leavings for the midden heap.

It took only a few days for the other three beasts to join their fellows in the scullery. Now it seemed that everywhere she looked, Isolf saw parti-colored shadows flitting beneath the table, across the sleeping platform, or even creeping across the rafters overhead with larcenous intentions upon the meat curing there in the smoke of the fire. They snatched food straight out of the pot; if she left the lid off a moment, and if she turned her back on the table, whatever was on it immediately went careering toward the niche in the wall where the creatures had denned up. A pan of milk left for the cream to rise disappeared down six furry gullets, even if she weighted the lid down. It made no difference; the little beasts were amazingly strong and determined. Once she managed to grab one, with the idea of flinging it outside, but it twisted and lashed around like a mad thing so that no one could have held it, then shot away from her grasp like an arrow out of a bow.

When her father Alborg came to visit every six or seven days, he brought her a joint of meat or smoked fish, which drove the little beasties wild with its smell. She only left the fish on the table a moment to close the door, but when she turned, there they were, all six of them with their sharp little teeth fastened in the package, eyes glaring with fiendish joy as they bundled it away toward their den.

"Stop!" Isolf stamped her foot with a furious shriek. "You wicked, savage, hateful little kettlingur!"

Kettlingur! She had no idea from when the word had come, but she had named them. They glared at her a moment, a motley patchwork of colored fur, then abandoned the fish and scampered away into their den, with their insolent tails sticking straight up to show their disdain. From the safety of their den, they all stared back at her, wide-eyed, craning their necks to see what pitiful attempt she would make to hide the fish from them.

"Greedy little kettlingur!" she scolded them, shaking her finger in their direction. "At least I have something to call you now. I wonder which of Skrymir's friends or demons put your name into my head."

Watching them suspiciously as she unwrapped the fish, she was suddenly smitten with the comical expressions of their faces. Their random stripes and patches reminded her of little wild flowers growing beside the burn. Their ears were far too large, and their sly little noses were offset on either side by a sprig of mischievous pricking whiskers. One beastie's face was half black and half white, and one wore a mask over his eyes like a bandit.

Feeling her heart soften unexpectedly, Isolf set out a

row of six smoked mackerel and retreated to watch. The kettlingur peered out of their den in astonishment, dividing their attention between Isolf and the fish until they were all squirming with impatience and greed. The one with the bandit mask was the first to fall out of the den and tumble toward the fish in a voracious pounce. The others scuttled after him, ignoring the five other fish. After a brief, hissing, yelling fight, the other kettlingur commenced to notice their scattered feast. It mattered not if any opposition was nearby or not; each kettling clamped down the fish with one clawed paw and gnawed on the rubbery fare to the tune of ferocious growling.

When that revolting display of greed and suspicion was over and the fish was gone, the kettlingur bathed themselves on the warm hearthstones. They not only earnestly licked their paws and rubbed their ears, they forgot their hard feelings over the mackerel and bathed each other until they all became so sleepy they could do nothing else but pile up in a helpless heap and purr themselves to sleep. With their eyes shut, they almost appeared to smile with innocence.

Isolf also smiled, for the first time since she had come to the jotun's hall.

On the following day she fed the kettlingur again. In scarcely any time at all, she had tamed them completely, and they swarmed over her like long-lost and needy relatives becoming reacquainted after a long separation. A parade of kettlingur attended her footsteps, in case she let fall something edible. When she sat, all six of them struggled desperately to crowd onto her lap, fighting for the best positions. Once content, they immediately fell asleep, grinning and sagging limply off her lap like dead things.

When Alborg and her brothers or other guests arrived, their dogs were usually relegated to the scullery. The kettlingur began to take offense at this invasion of their domain by great hairy, smelly beasts, or perhaps they were defending Isolf from imagined threat and insult. With rigid tails and spines, the six of them bristled up like cockleburrs. On stiffened legs they skittered at the dogs with explosive spittings and hissings. After a slash

on its tender nose, any dog would give a frantic howl and
dash for the safety of the main hall.

It was about this time that Isolf suspected that the
kettlingur were indeed getting larger. Beyond a doubt,
they were getting more ferocious as far as dogs and rats
were concerned. Their bunchy little bodies elongated;
their legs and tails lengthened, and their ears grew somewhat more into proportion with their faces. Their scruffy
baby coats turned sleek and glossy, their button eyes
turned into green or golden orbs. If anything, their playful antics became more violent as they grew. Isolf often
nearly lost her feet in a maniac charge of rumbustious
keetlingur, chasing each other for no good reason except
high spirits. When one of them dragged in a dead rat, it
was played with from one end of the scullery to the
other, until an unsportsmanlike kettling ended the game
by eating the ball.

Skrymir was not displeased with his furry inventions.

"Kettlingur," he mused, when Isolf told him what she
had inadvertently named them. "Well, we can do nothing
to change them now."

"We can do nothing at all with them," said Isolf.
"They don't behave like dogs. They might come when I
call them, if they are of a mind to. They usually don't.
But they massacre rats and mice like Grimfang the war-
lord. If they didn't sleep most of the time, there wouldn't
be a rat in all of Skarpsey."

"You are pleased with them," said Skrymir. "I hear
you laugh often now, and I see you are smiling."

"Yes, they are good company, and often useful," said
Isolf. "Thank you, Skrymir, for the kettlingur."

Other guests of Skrymir did not find the kettlingur so
agreeable. One old jotun favored the form of a raggedy
crow for his travels. When the kettlingur spied Hrafnbogi
roosting untidily on the back of Skrymir's chair, they
crouched down, eyes glinting with rapture, jaws chattering as if they were berserkers invoking the protection of
their war gods. Then they hurled themselves to the attack, shinnying right up and over Skrymir and his chair.
With a startled squawk, Hrafnbogi took to the air, barely
sailing out of the reach of the masked rogue Fantur, who

made a heroic and doomed leap into the air, which landed him in the woodbox. The other kettlingur chased poor old Hrafnbogi around the hall until he finally managed to gasp out the words to a shape shifting spell, collapsing breathlessly into a chair just as all six kettlingur pounced upon him. Suspiciously they sniffed over him as if he might be held responsible for hiding the carking crow under his rusty old cloak. Then Fantur discovered a moth to chase, and they launched themselves off Hrafnbogi's meager chest as if he were a springboard.

"What are these horrible little creatures?" he panted, his eyes red and moist with passion.

"Kettlingur," said Skrymir. "I made them for Isolf."

"Do they multiply?" demanded Hrafnbogi, settling his disarrayed cloak and hood with a ruffled sputtering.

"I fear so," said Isolf. "Kisa, the striped one, has five little kettlingur."

"Then we'd better call the big ones kettir," said Skrymir. "Now there's eleven of the creatures."

"And more to follow, I'm afraid," said Isolf. "Silki and Silfur seem awfully fat."

"They multiply like trolls!" Hrafnbogi patted his forehead with a fluttering kerchief. "We're doomed! And they eat birds, don't they?"

"Now then, don't be alarmed," said Skrymir. "We'll give them to the New People to get rid of their rats."

"New People! I wouldn't do them any favors. Do you know what they call us? Giants. Giants, out of their own covetous fear and profound ignorance!" Hrafnbogi shivered his rusty shoulders, reminding Isolf more of an exasperated old rooster than an all-powerful jotun.

"I hardly think giving them kettir and kettlingur is a favor," said Skrymir.

"They have no respect for the old ways. We'll all be forgotten, derided, and turned out." Hrafnbogi snapped his mouth shut, like a beak, and commenced to sulk.

"At least we'll no longer have to answer their questions and settle their feuds," said Skrymir with a long and weary sigh. "They'll have to manage for themselves."

Indeed, Skrymir was tired. Isolf had plenty of occasions to spy upon him unwittingly, and usually saw nothing

more portentous than Skrymir sketching runes, burning
incense, or reiterating a phrase with the aid of a knotted
string. Much of the time he simply sat in his great chair
and pondered, his chin upon his fist, his eyes lost beneath
craggy brows. His shoulders stooped when no one was
about, sagging under the weight of his immense store of
knowledge, beginning far back at the start of time itself.
The last remnants of the Elder People must be fairly
tottering with the burgeoning Past, with no foreseeable
end in sight for beings who would never taste death.
Ofttimes Isolf thought herself of little more consequence
than an ant that lives and toils one summer and dies,
when she compared herself to Skrymir's antiquity and
wisdom.

Nor did the wisdom go uncoveted among mortal men.
Isolf came to dread and resent the visits of heroes from
farflung settlements, in search of wealth and adventure.

"What am I to feed these brutes?" Isolf asked of
Skrymir, when the mountain hall was filled with twenty
or thirty skin-clad power seekers. "I have only a few hens
and geese and three sheep. This lot would eat that much
and look around for the main course!"

Skrymir surveyed the reeking brood with a tolerant
smile, which was easy from his towering vantage point.

"Feed them this. It is what they came from, and what
they will return to, so it should nourish them well." With
one great hand he sifted a handful of dust into Isolf's
outstretched apron.

When she returned to the scullery, she poured the dust
into a large cauldron and filled it with water. One did not
question a jotun's wisdom with puny mortal objections.
When she heated the kettle of dust and water, she discovered that the dust had reorganized itself into boiled
fowls, fish, mutton, cabbage, spices, and other things to
make a feast for their uninvited guests.

Isolf, from then on when company came, wordlessly
accepted a handful of dust and took it to the scullery,
where a pinch of it in the dough trough became bread, or
ale in the ale barrel, or soup in the cauldron, meat on the
hook, or whatsoever she desired to place on the guest
table.

Try as she might to keep them locked up, the kettir always managed to misbehave when visitors arrived. Dogs they would not tolerate a moment, sending them howling back into the cold dark corridors. The kettir then took possession of the hearth in the main hall and the space beneath the table, where guests were always wont to throw bones and scraps when they were done with them, or liable to spill or drop something tasty. The guests laughed when the kettir fought with the dogs, laughed when their boorish laughter frightened the kettir, laughed when an impudent kettir stealthily snagged a toothsome tidbit off someone's plate. The feasting always attracted a horde of rats, and the ferocity of the kettir in killing them never failed to excite the admiration of the travelers. Thus stuffed with food, the kettir posted themselves on the hearthstones like furry, purring hummocks of assorted colors, or showed off their amiability by climbing into the nearest cooperative lap to be petted. Frequently after a feasting, a bristling warrior crept self-consciously into the scullery to inquire if Isolf could spare a couple of kettlingur for a faraway wife or mistress. Though Isolf grieved at parting with her pretty kettlingur, she was pleased to see them carried away to far places to win fame and the admiration of mankind.

There were some guests, however, who would as soon make a kettir into a pair of gloves as look at it. Their hatred of kettir dawned upon them at first glance, much the same as some people loathe snakes.

Raud Airic was one of these kettir-haters, and fancied himself quite the wizard besides.

"What horrid little beasties!" he declared furiously, after the fearless Fantur made off with a well-nigh empty bone from his plate, adroitly dodging a cup Airic threw after him. To show his disdain, Fantur stopped a moment in the middle of the table to sit down and extend one hind foot for a quick licking, as if a few deranged hairs might seriously impair his retreat to the hearth.

"It only shows," continued Airic slyly, as if he thought Isolf could not hear him from her lonely position on the dais at the end of the hall, "that the skill of the Ancient Ones is declining with the rise of the New People. Once they created mountains and oceans and huge beasts with rending tusks and claws. Now we get kettir, sly and slinking little thieves, able to kill nothing larger than a rat. The last gasp of a once-noble race—"

He might have gone on, but his speech was sundered by a series of explosive sneezes. This, too, Isolf had noticed before. Kettir possessed the amazing ability to make some people sneeze and weep at the mere sight of them.

Unfortunately, the sneezing and weeping occasioned by the kettir did nothing to discourage Airic's visits to the mountain hall. Each time he came with more questions and insolence, bringing his warriors and apprentices with him to devour piles of food and generate a mountain of garbage.

"I don't know how you tolerate him!" flared Isolf to Skrymir. "He comes and demands the answers to his questions and scarcely has the manners to thank you for them. And we know he doesn't put his answers to happy uses, Wise One. Yet last time you let him have the secret for predicting the eclipses of sun and moon, as well as the mysteries of the herbs, both good and deadly. Who knows what he wants now?"

Skrymir chuckled. "Airic doesn't even know what it is he ought to be asking for. Herbs and astrology ought to make him feel very important for awhile. We shan't worry about Airic until he learns the right questions."

To Isolf's dismay, it was not half a year before Airic returned, alone this time, and she instinctively knew that he had come with the right questions at last. His elegant wizard's robes were ragged now, his boisterous companions forgotten, and his eye gleamed with the light of dawning meaningfulness.

"What have you come for this time?" Skrymir's question hung in the air, like runes etched with fire, though his voice was soft and gentle. He had not bothered to alter his form to a more impressive one; he still looked like Isolf's grandfather, who had spent his early days as a renowned Viking and his latter days puttering about in the vegetable garden, growing useful plants that no one had ever seen before. He, too, had known the secrets of the jotun race.

"I have come for the honey mead," said Airic.

"I have never been loath to share it before," said Skrymir. "You yourself have tasted it already, many times."

"Yes, but not your oldest and most potent honey mead. This is where your best knowledge lies hidden. All that you have given mankind until now has been merely the stuff of survival. We have come to you seeking to become great, and you have sent us away with simple skills, and we considered them marvelous because we had not seen them before. Brewing, cheesemaking, forging of metals, all this has become ordinary to us now. I have learned, jotun, that humankind can be as great as the Elder Race—maybe greater, since we are destined to rule the world. You have held something back from us. We are entitled to all your knowledge, not just trivial scraps."

"What would this knowledge accomplish in human hands? Would all men have it, or just a chosen few?"

"These powers are not suitable for all men. I have seen you form living creatures from a pinch of dust. I have seen you summon life into them. You can heal the dying, call the life back to the dead, and you are invulnerable to wounds or death. All this is done with the powers of the mind, not of sword or formulae written down in a book. You have pretended to enlighten us, Skrymir, but we are as much in the dark as animals when it comes to real knowledge."

"Mankind is not done with warfaring yet. When he is tired of the sword and the fetter, he will come naturally into the hidden powers of his mind. Be assured, Airic, they are waiting for the right time to blossom."

"This is the right time," said Airic. "We need those powers now to subdue our enemies, to know when they are plotting to attack, to see and hear them from afar for our own protection. Give me the honey mead and I will keep it safe for mankind."

"What are you prepared to give?" asked Skrymir. "Great gifts have high prices. Sometimes they take a great deal of time. Human possessions for the most part are nothing but trash and trouble. And I have no use for any more firstborn children."

"Time to a mortal is the only thing of true value. Let us make a wager, my life against your wisdom. I shall prove my worthiness."

A wager. Isolf sighed and rolled her eyes. For a moment, she had almost believed Airic more clever than the rest who had come swaggering and wagering to Skrymir's mountain. Usually Skrymir feigned defeat, letting them carry away a bellyful of honey mead and some trifling enchanted cup or sword in heroic self-congratulatory zeal. Once the cup or sword was taken out of Skrymir's enchanted presence, it would soon lose its powers and become as uncooperative as any other cup or sword. The mead itself would be pissed against some wall somewhere, but with luck, the pinch of wisdom contained in it might lodge within the bearer's mind and become useful.

"A wager. Very well," said Skrymir. "What do you wish? Three questions? A quest? A challenge to combat?"

Isolf heaved a short impatient sigh and made a disdainful clucking sound. The warriors who challenged Skrymir were perhaps the most pathetic of all, swaggering into the hall, sleek and bulging with muscle, exuding all the confidence and intelligence of an ox being led to the butcher's stall. Tiresome indeed for Skrymir, who tried to meet their furious attacks as creatively as possible, after thousands of years of the same glinty-eyed heroes seeking aggrandizement by killing a being they did not understand. Skrymir obligingly conjured a monster for such characters to fight, and then sent them packing with a trunkful of gold or jewels.

"A quest," said Airic. "Send me in search of treasure and power, and if I return successful, all the honey mead will be mine. I shall supplant you in wisdom. Men shall come to me for a sip of mead."

"And if you fail?"

"Then you get to keep everything you've got, and I shall probably be too dead to trouble you further."

"Well enough. As a jotun, I never lose a serious wager with a mortal, unless it's a mere trifle, or something your race needs anyway. I warn you, mortal, I shall not let you win this time. The gifts you desire are the greatest knowledge I possess."

"You won't need to allow me to win," said Airic. "I shall succeed on the merit of my own skill and wisdom, and I shall have the mead."

"Very well. I shall send you on a journey. Return to me with three magical objects, and you shall have what you wish. Bring to me the diamonds of Borkdukur, the captive princess of Fluga, and the sacred Orb of Ekkert, and then the last secrets of the Elder Race shall be yours."

"Then I shall be off upon my expedition. Would you mind pointing me in the proper direction for Borkdukur?"

"Certainly not. Anything to be of service. You simply go south until you reach the land of giant trees. You must climb up one of them until you reach the land of clouds. You'll know you are there when the landscape turns white, and scarcely anything grows upon the ground."

"Thank you. I shall return quite soon, I'm certain."

"Good day to you, sir."

Airic bowed mockingly low, chuckling in a very superior way. In the midst of his bowing, Skrymir flicked one hand and Airic suddenly vanished with an unsavory-smelling puff of murky smoke. It smelled like hog-rendering days back in Holm. Isolf wrinkled her nose and looked for the greasy spot that must have been Airic. Instead, what she saw was a little creature about the size of a dung beetle tumbling around in a violent tussle with a linty length of worsted thread that must have come unraveled from the hem of Isolf's gown, trailing as it did across the rough flagstones of Skrymir's cave.

A closer look revealed that the beetle-creature was Airic, shrunken down to a less troublesome size.

"Hah, now all that remains is to step upon him and our troubles are over," said Isolf cheerfully.

"No, no, we must allow him his chance to prove himself," said Skrymir tolerantly. "Besides, he's going to have a great adventure, which will be handed down from generation to generation, gathering embellishments each time it's told, until Airic will be quite a hero. Who are we to deny him his moment of fame?"

"Compared to him, we are gods," said Isolf. "We can do anything we please to him. See, now it is nighttime."

She inverted a bowl over him, putting an end to his manful battle with the string. "You shall win, of course," said Isolf.

"There's no way out of it, I fear."

"Why would you wish to lose? Why didn't you just give Airic the mead and the wisdom?"

"Mortals learn best by opposition at every turn and obfuscation of their simplest desires. He would be suspicious and unappreciative of an unearned gift."

Skrymir rose to his feet and stepped over the bowl, treading as carefully as he could. "I've become so weary of my burden, child. Mortalkind is almost ready to carry itself, instead of riding upon my shoulders. I shall welcome the day when no one believes in jotuns. Then I shall take my walking stick and disappear into the mountains. Watch out for him awhile, won't you? Do what you wish to make his journey as uncomfortable as possible, short of killing him outright."

Isolf considered the bowl a moment, then removed it from over Airic. She was amused to discover that he had hacked the string into a hundred pieces, then he had curled up and gone to sleep in a fissure in the floor, with a tiny spark of a fire glinting like a jewel.

For the fun of it, Isolf blew on him, buffeting him around awhile like a grain of wheat on a skillet.

"Wake up and get along your journey, you lazy dolt," she said.

For an hour or more he scuttled around among various obstructions, sticks of firewood, ashes, dead coals. Once he blundered into a dropped glove, and Isolf turned it around to face another direction when he came out, in case he had begun to get his bearings somewhat. True to her suspicions, he wandered out and became lost in a forest of chairs and stool legs. Isolf became tired of him after watching him laboriously climb several chair legs, so she put the bowl over him and went on her way.

Remembering Airic some hours later, she returned

and took off the bowl. After climbing a few more chair legs, he ran into the well-picked skeleton of a chicken in the twilight land beneath the table. It must have seemed a land of death; bones from the table had been tossed under there from the previous night's feasting. The kettir had taken what they wanted, leaving the rest for the mice and rats.

Isolf scraped off a few plates and trenchers. Attracted by a sudden squealing and squeaking, she peered beneath the table and spied a mouse kicking around in death throes, with something like a pin stuck in its throat. The tiny figure of Airic put its foot on the monster's shaggy neck and pulled out his sword. Busily he wiped it on his pants and put it away, drawing out his knife to begin skinning the creature. He worked industriously, skinning a beast that was at least the size of a horse to him. When he had the skin off, he built a fire and carved off some choice steaks, which he cooked over the fire. Using the mouse skin for a small tent, he climbed beneath it and went to sleep probably exhausted, but his troubles were far from over. Attracted by the smell of blood, the rats came out of hiding, lumbering along with twitching whiskers in hope of a fresh meal for once, instead of the usual humble table leavings. One of them made off with the mouse carcass and another set its teeth in the skin, but Airic came charging out in defense of his hard-won property, and stuck his sword into the rat's nose. With a startled squeak, it shook away a drop of blood and rubbed its nose. Gritting its teeth menacingly, the rat charged at this unfamiliar little animal challenging him for his deserved scavenging rights.

Isolf watched the battle with interest. The rat attacked and fell back rebuffed twice. Eyes glaring, it paused to consider its opponent, then it rushed again. This time, a puff of flame engulfed the rat, setting its fur on fire. Isolf blinked, amazed and curious, but Airic was, after all, a wizard of sorts. After a few more puffs and bursts of flame, the rat collapsed upon its back and expired, no doubt a great deal astonished to find itself killed by such a minute opponent.

Next Airic made an assault upon a table leg, which

would have led him to the land of Borkdukur—or Table-cloth, in the old language of the jotuns. However, Airic stopped for the night in a knothole in the table leg, after first evicting a large spider from her nesting place. The spider blindly insisted upon her knothole, until Airic used some spell or other and fried her into a sizzled knot of crisped legs and withered carapace.

Isolf settled down with some sewing while she watched him, with several kettir and kettlingur for company. The kettir went to sleep, too full and lazy to do more than eyeball the occasional rat under the table. The kettlingur romped and wrestled themselves to exhaustion, then fell asleep in Isolf's lap, trusting her to catch them when they were about to slide off on their brainless little heads.

Meanwhile, Airic made it to the top of the table and commenced a perilous journey across the wasteland of eating untensils, crockery, jugs, and the other natural hazards left over after a meal. Once he stepped into a small pool of spilled honey and had a wretched time extricating himself. Then he climbed onto a large slice of bread and nearly broke his leg stepping into unsuspected air pockets. With the worst sort of judgment possible, he discovered the entire loaf and wandered into quite a large tunnel, and finally emerged a few inches away, coughing and sputtering after hacking his way through part of the loaf like a maggot. Obviously feeling out of sorts at the experience, Airic dusted off his cloak and conjured a great sheet of flame that browned the slice of bread as nicely as if it had been done on a toasting fork. Isolf frowned upon this veiled insult to her breadmaking skills. Her mother had always told her she mixed a very fine loaf, with excellent flavor and a dainty crumb.

Presently Airic ran up against the saltcellar, with its accompanying sprinkling of salt crystals surrounding it. For a short while he seemed stunned by his success, holding up the crystals and examining them with reveren-tial awe. Then in a disgusting display of avarice, he scuttled about gathering the salt crystals into heaps. When he was almost done, an ant strolled out from behind the milk jug, waving its antennae curiously. Airic evidently perceived himself endangered by this armored newcomer, and commenced battering the little creature with his sword. The ant had only the most vague notions of defense, and did not imagine itself imperiled until Airic managed to sever its back end from the rest of its body. Enraged, the creature went after him with clashing jaws, until its strength gradually deteriorated into mindless spasms, evidently lacking some vital communications available only from its severed hindquarters. Some last desperate plea for assistance must have escaped the dying ant; no sooner had it beetled away and dropped off the table than half a dozen replacements appeared on the scene. Immediately the ants were fascinated by the salt crystals and commenced carting them off in all directions, running back and forth, seizing and dropping salt with no discernible plan to their activity. The more Airic hacked and slashed and tore off legs and feelers and hinderparts, the more ants came swarming across the table to see what the fuss was, and to get themselves hacked and dismantled until the table-cloth was strewn with ant parts and wounded ants staggering around in headless, legless disarray.

Airic mounted a blistering defense behind a lump of potato, with a heap of salt crystals at his back. One of the ants suddenly discovered the treacherous pool of honey, and before long the rest of the attackers had forsaken Airic completely for the privilege of becoming thoroughly mired in the honey, after first drinking themselves delirious in their final revels before their inevitable and sticky death.

Airic meanwhile gathered up his salt crystals and fell down in an exhausted sleep. Isolf considerately put the bowl over him, in case any more ants felt the call to the battle of the dinner table.

Isolf removed a few more platters and took them to the scullery to be washed. When she returned, she removed the bowl to see what adventures Airic would stumble into next. Busily he gathered up his salt, or diamonds, and set off across the tablecloth, first in the direction of a wet place where Isolf had spilled her ale. Airic forged his way into the heart of the spill, where he bogged down eventually and stopped. Listening closely, Isolf could hear a faint tinny voice uplifted in riotous song. From the looks of him, he had no intention of getting on with anything but getting thoroughly drunk. Isolf shook her head and clucked her tongue in disapproval. Well, if that was all the better he could do, he had done for himself until the tablecloth dried. She took out a basket of mending and measured a length of thread.

Airic might have wallowed there in the pool of ale until he shriveled up, neatly preserved like a dead insect in alcohol, but a small yellow moth happened on the scene, hatched from some forgotten clutch of eggs in a protected niche, left after its progenitors had extincted themselves in the candle flames, or sputtered out in molten wax. For want of a candle to die in, the moth delicately teetered on the edge of the gravy bowl, hovered yearningly over the lip of the milk jug, staggered around the rim of the honey pot, and finally settled on the spilled ale, fanning its dainty wings as it sampled the heady fare.

Airic roused himself from his stupor and wobbled after the little moth, thinking perhaps he was being subjected to a most holy vision. Unheeding, the moth skipped away, with Airic running after it in a frenzy of visionary zeal. Tilting fore and aft, port to starbord, the moth skimmed drunkenly over the table, circling rapturously over a half-smothered candle flame, with Airic in hot pursuit. It had got Airic out of the ale, at least, Isolf noted with satisfaction, as she nipped off her thread between her teeth. Self-indulgence was not seemly in a questing hero.

Somewhat burdened down by his diamonds, Airic pursued the moth through a forest of scattered cutlery, and over a mountain range of crumpled cloth in pursuit of his vision. Next he climbed up into the meat platter, which had just been discovered by a flock of wasps and honeybees. The fickle moth settled down on an island of meat in a swamp of congealing grease, opening and shutting its wings tantalizingly. Airic plunged into the grease, not realizing how deep it was going to get by the time he reached the meat scrap where the moth rested. Considerately, Isolf threw in a raft of bread, which enabled him to reach the island. By this time the wasps and bees had settled on this juicy bit of choice property. One wasp darted at Airic in defense of their meal, buzzing menacingly. Catching it amidships, he exploded it in a sooty conflagration of wing and leg parts. The wasp kited about in a furious, disabled manner before plummeting out of control into a cup, where it flamed out in the last drops of remaining ale. Another mindless battle commenced, and it might have turned out rather badly for Airic if Isolf hadn't tired of wasps and bees falling into the left-over food, which she thriftily planned to feed to Airic when he returned from his adventure. The scraps she calculated to make soup of, and to take a pot of it to old Hrafnbogi's housekeeper, an ancient little crone down with a spring chill. Dead bees and wasps would not enhance the soup, so she scattered the insects by flapping a cloth at them, swatting some of them down and crushing them efficiently with a butter paddle. The charred carcasses she flipped out of the grease, thinking to save it for soap—another skill which Skrymir had taught her people.

Airic captured his moth at last, securing it with a raveled thread from the tablecloth. Hearing a suspicious crash from the scullery, Isolf threw down her mending and hurried to see what mischief the kettir were causing. It was nothing more than Fantur and Silki overturning a pot to see what might be inside; it had been foolish of Isolf to ever have put the lid on, knowing as she did that such a mystery was irresistible to kettir. An open pot would have been investigated or perhaps napped in or hidden in during a play-battle, but a closed kettle invited trouble.

Scolding them gently, she righted the kettle and left the lid off, thereby removing the dread kettir enigma of the unknown.

When she returned to the eating hall, she discovered Airic surrounded by a circle of curious kettlingur. He had taken refuge inside an overturned cup, and the kettlingur took turns poking their paws in after him, adroitly springing away when he popped sparks at them. When they weren't occupied with Airic, they batted about a small glass bead from Isolf's belt, which she intended to mend. Airic also had designs upon the bead, and made heroic forays out to attempt to secure it, a circumstance with delighted the young kettlingur to no end. They reared up and pounced at him, titillated by the sparks he threw and the desperate fluttering of the moth still trapped in the cup by its string tether. Once Airic was seized in two paws and carried aloft toward some very sharp and inquisitive little teeth, but Isolf distracted the kettling from its intended feast by tweaking its stumpy tail. With a hiss, it dropped Airic in the butter and jumped over the water jug, upsetting it and creating a brief but lively flood across the table top. The kettlingur scuttled for safety the moment their feet got wet. Airic slid down off the butter and at once took possession of the glass bead.

"I don't think Airic has learned much from his adventuring," Isolf greeted Skrymir upon his return to the hall. "Not only has he taken afront and slaughtered quite a few innocent creatures who were just doing what nature intended them to do, he has made a captive of that poor yellow moth. It's going to die unless he lets it go. Should I let the kettlingur have him? They're just perishing for a chance to play with him."

Skrymir set down in his chair to watch a moment as Airic chipped away manfully at the gold handle of a knife. Inadvertently he kicked the table leg, creating a considerable earthquake in Airic's world as a cup toppled and the jugs and crockery clattered.

"It's time for him to return for his reward," said Skrymir. "This is the last gift I shall give to the New People. The time has come for me to go away and allow you to find your own way now."

"Alone? But Skrymir, we are helpless little fools, bungling around like Airic on the table top, blind to what's directly in front of us. Simple things are like mountains to us. Tremendous things we climb over without seeing. Without you and the wisdom of the jotuns, all manner of dreadful things will befall us!"

"You won't be completely alone," said Skrymir. "You shall have the likes of Airic to help you and defend you and impart to you what knowledge they see fit."

"Airic!"

As soon as she said it, Airic himself stood before her.

His clothing was nothing but shreds, well-greased and torn and blackened. His handsome fox-colored beard and mane of hair were now streaked with gray, and his face had aged into a map of wrinkles and anxious creases.

"What an adventure I've had!" he exclaimed. "I traveled to strange and wonderful lands! I've returned burdened with the wealth I've discovered! I've rescued a king's daughter from a dread enchantment and I've killed a thousand hideous enemies! You should have seen the flying dragons, the hairy monsters that would have eaten me, the great beasts with enormous teeth! My journey has made me rich and powerful." He slapped about among his belt pouches. "Look at this! I truly discovered the diamonds of Borkdukur! Thousands of them!"

"Yes, indeed you have," said Skrymir. "And I have prepared for you your reward. Isolf, fetch the milk jug. Pour out a draght for our champion."

Isolf obligingly found a clean cup and poured out some milk. Deep in sleep, the kettir recognized one of their favorite sounds and came twining and purring around her legs, rearing up to butt her knees encouragingly.

"That's nothing but milk," said Airic after a quick sniff, disdainfully tossing the milk onto the floor. "Food for those miserable kettir and nothing more. Do you think I can be fooled so easily? I earned the honey mead, and that's what I must have!"

"You refuse to be rewarded? Well, Isolf, bring him the last cask from the cellar. The smallest and oldest one, marked with three crosses."

Isolf brought the cask from the cellar under the kitchen floor. She had no way of guessing how long it had been since it had seen the light of day. Airic's eyes gleamed as he tossed down a cup of the ancient stuff, which filled the room with its acrid perfume.

"Now ends the rule of the jotuns," he said. "Mortal man is now the wisest of all earth's creatures."

"Perhaps now that you've claimed your reward, we'd be wise to examine your trophies," said Skrymir.

Airic upended one pouch, his eyes glittering in expectation, but all that came out was a sifting of salt. His countenance changed from the heady flush of arrogance to a deathly pallor.

"Where are my diamonds?" he gasped. "I had them! They were here right in my hands!"

Skrymir gently tapped the salt cellar with a spoon and shrugged his shoulders. "Nothing in this world is more difficult to hold onto than wealth," he said.

"Wait! I have the chieftain's daughter! She's in a different form, winged, like a bird—" He pulled out another pouch as he talked, opened it, and the little yellow moth fluttered out, tumbling in midair like a fragment of sunlight. With sudden unerring accuracy, the moth took a dive at the table, where a stump of a candle still sputtered and oozed in a pool of wax. Only a wisp of flame remained, but it was enough. The moth expired in a small, silent explosion of flame, like a miniscule funeral ship cast upon the waters, and its charred remains fell into the wax.

"Oh, no! My princess!" Airic gasped. "I could have married her and inherited a tremendous kingdom!"

Skrymir shook his head slowly and made a comforting clucking sound. "Fame among men is as fleeting as a circling candle-moth," he said.

"Never mind," said Airic. "I still have the orb of Ekkert. Unlimited power is mine to command."

He searched about among his pouches, his expression growing strained. Tenatively he peered into one, then upended it with an impatient shake. The lone bead from Isolf's girdle dropped out and bounced into a nearby plate, where it lodged in a spot of congealed fat. Without speaking, Isolf fished it out, wiped it out, and quickly stitched it back into its place in the design on her belt.

"Power is never what it appears," said Skrymir.

Airic slumped into a chair. "Nothing! I've gotten nothing, after all I've been through! All the years I labored—" Suddenly a cunning smile overspread his features. "But at least I have the honey mead. I have beaten you, jotun. Your knowledge is mine."

"Yes, I've been fairly bested," said Skrymir, reaching for an old ragged cloak hanging on a peg. "All I have is now yours, Airic. Mankind will no longer be troubled by

jotuns meddling in their affairs." Taking a walking staff
from the corner, he turned toward the door with a farewell wave to Isolf and a gentle smile of weary peace. He
truly looked much smaller in stature now, a withered
little hobgoblin of a creature.

"Yes! Go! I already foresee—I foresee—" Airic shut
his eyes and stretched out his hand in a compelling gesture.

"What do you foresee?" asked Isolf.

His eyes snapped open. "I foresee nothing! He's given
me hindsight in the mead instead of foresight! The true
gift was in the milk! Stop him before he's gone! Come
back, jotun! You tricked me!"

"You tricked yourself, you arrogant fool!" Isolf said,
turning to look for Skrymir, but the stooped, ragged
figure had vanished, with a chuckle still echoing in the
earthen halls.

Mocking the chuckle, a contented purring sound rose
to Isolf's ears. Kettir and kettlingur were beneath the
table, avidly lapping up the milk and the jotun's last gift
of knowledge along with it. More kettir came scampering
in from the hall and the scullery, guided by the unfailing
kettir instinct for knowing when their fellows have fallen
upon favorable circumstances involving food.

"Kettir!" gasped Airic. "Those horried little beasts will
have the last of the jotun knowledge!"

Their clever little tongues cleaned out every crevice
and polished the floor to a glossy sheen. Fantur had his
head inside the cup, lapping noisily. With a despairing
wail, Airic lunged for the cup. Fantur leaped away as if
scalded, slinging the cup over the stones toward Isolf.
The kettir scattered before Airic, tangling among his
legs. Isolf seized the disdained cup and drained out the
last drops of milk, making scarcely a swallow.

"No! That's mine! It's wasted upon you!" roared Airic,
snatching the cup from her hands. It popped from his
grasp as if it were greased, and shattered on the flagstones. Airic frozen, clenching his fists. For a moment
Isolf feared he would kill her, but Airic sank into a chair
and buried his face with a groan of defeat. The kettir
assembled upon the hearthstone, bathing themselves and
each other after their milky feast. Chancing to open his

eyes and glimpse them, he groaned afresh, with deeper misery.

"Don't despair so," said Isolf. "Surely you've learned something from your travails."

"Nothing except the pain of hindsight. Nothing a man can do is worth anything worthwhile at all," said Airic bitterly. "The moment he thinks he's got wealth or influence or power, he takes a look at it and realizes it's nothing but trash and illusion. My life is nearly over, wasted and foolishly spent on trivialities. I'm old and I've been a fool. There's nothing left for me but to die. I never dreamed he would put the knowledge into something as common and simple as milk, when he's so famous for his honey mead."

"Skrymir offered you his most priceless secrets, and you refused to take them," said Isolf. "Now all of them have gone down the throats of the kettir. At least someone will possess some of the gift. And better womankind and kettir than your sort."

"But what knowledge has the jotun given you and those wretched beasts?" Airic demanded. "Do you feel different, now you've got some of the jotun's knowledge? Can you see the future? Things far off? Do you hear voices?"

Airic's questions went unanswered. Isolf packed up her few possessions and a large basket of young kettlingur. The adult kettir followed her down from the mountain to the settlements, where they very promptly ensconced themselves in nearly every home and byre and fishing shack. No woman walked without a kettir at her heels, and no hearth was long vacant of its kettir protectors.

Travelers from far places carried away many of the attractive and affectionate little beasts without seriously reducing their thriving population. Strangely enough, no matter how far they were carried away, a few kettir with amazing skills of navigation managed to find their way home again, and some of them several times, and even over water to get there. Isolf read the jotun's gift in their eyes and smiled in her quiet way when people marveled.

For many years she went about her business of healing the bodies and woes of mankind, as befit her status as village wisewoman. Cats and cradles always sat upon her hearth, and her daughters grew up as wise and clever as Isolf at seeing beyond the things directly before their eyes. Her sons were fey warriors, knowing when to go to battle and when to stay home with their women and kettir.

Isolf never saw Skrymir again, though she and her favorite kettir often walked the mountain trails looking for a ragged old wanderer with a walking staff. Many times she felt that he was close, giving her warnings and intuitions that saved her and her clan much grief. In times of serious trial she thanked him silently for the small swallow of jotun knowledge he had afforded her. The kettir, with their large alert ears seemed to hear Skrymir's voice far better, and their gleaming eyes that penetrated the dark seemed to see him lurking and watching. What else those green and golden orbs perceived was denied to human eyes.

Kettir cleared the barns and cheered the hearts of many lonely people and imparted their secret knowledge to those who had the skill to hear them. Kettir in the future would be both revered as gods and hated as devils, hunted and destroyed as such by ignorant and devilish humankind. Both a blessing and a cursing had been given to mankind, and all because of a lonely mortal maid and a cup of spilled milk.

PAPERCUT LUCK

by Patricia B. Cirone

Ling Mei crouched so close to the brazier that the rising steam caressed her face. She poked at a bamboo shoot, moving it around, then prodded the chopped cabbage. Her heart was not in her task; even the gentle swaying of the boat failed to soothe her.

The side of the junk scraped against the Guo's, moored next to it. Grandmother Guo peered over. "Why are you cooking all that food, child?" she called harshly. "No sense in it. Your family is gone. They won't be eating supper here, not tonight, not tomorrow, not ever again."

Ling Mei set her chin stubbornly and continued to cook the dinner. "They will be back, honorable grandmother."

"Hunh. What the soldiers take away, they don't bring back." The old woman hunched her shoulders and returned to tending her own family.

Ling Mei looked longingly at the bustle in the other junk: the babies playing, the children helping their grandmother to cook, the parents, aunts, and uncles cleaning the day's catch and mending a patch on the sail. She compared it with the desolate quiet of her own junk. A tear trickled out of the corner of her eye.

Ling Mei stopped poking at the now limp vegetables and emptied them over the rice she had already prepared. She ate and ate and ate until she felt sick. It had been stupid to cook so much—enough for a whole family—but she had hoped cooking as though she expected her family would somehow bring them.

She wished this morning had never happened, that she had never returned from the market to hear all the people calling her and running up to her with the news her

78

family had been arrested by the emperor's soldiers. She wished they'd never taken on that passenger who had paid so well.

The wish seemed very far away as the boat bobbed in the darkness, and Ling Mei tried to hush her aching stomach and drift off to sleep.

She had never slept alone before. It was too quiet.

The next morning she watched, through the slits in the matting, as the Guo's junk pulled away from the swaying docks to do their day's fishing.

HER family didn't do messy, smelly fishing for a living. THEY carried goods, and sometimes passengers, up and down the river. Ling Mei's supple mouth turned down at the corners. That was what had gotten them into this trouble. The soldiers of the Son of Heaven, the boy emperor, had accused her family of carrying one of the barbarous, spying Mongols right into the heart of Canton.

How would her family know who they carried? The man had paid his money, and they had brought him down the river to Canton.

Yen Su-wing, of four boats out, had said she could hear the wails and protests from Ling Mei's family all the way up the dock. The soldiers didn't care; they had taken everyone on the ship, even youngest brother, only ten months old. Grandmother Guo was right. Ling Mei would never see them again. But she didn't know what else to do, except hope.

The day was long. Ling Mei put on the sandals her mother had cut down for her when second oldest sister had worn out their edges, and slapped up the slats of the swaying dock to the shore. She went to the market. Perhaps there she would hear news of what had become of her family.

The market seethed with people and rumors. Some said the Mongols were at the gates of the city. Others scoffed, and said the barbarians would never get that close. The servants of the nobles who had fled here when Hangchow had fallen shoved the common people aside and bought food and cloth as if there would be no tomorrow. Ling Mei looked and listened to all of it, but nowhere did she hear mention of one small family off a junk. The marketplace did not care about one small family. Discouraged, Ling Mei turned and started to trudge back home.

Yesterday the market had been an exciting place, filled with infinite possibilities to spend a birthday coin. Instead of taking care of family business first, she had darted first to one stall, then another, fingering the coin in her pocket and putting off the moment when she would actually spend it. Sweets? A toy? A pretty bit of cloth? Ling Mei had been so excited by all the possibilities, she had still not made up her mind when the sun told her it was time to finish the family errands and run home.

Today, sticky sweets or pretty twists of cloth didn't rouse the slightest bit of interest. The only thing she wanted, her birthday coin couldn't possibly give her. She didn't even want to *remember* her birthday coin and what she had been doing while the soldiers had arrested her entire family.

If she had been there, at least she would have been taken with them. Ling Mei shivered, thinking even that would be better than being so alone.

A block from the marketplace, she passed a small table she didn't remember ever seeing there before. It was covered with papercuts. Papercuts! Ling Mei stopped and turned back.

Her quick eyes darted over the papercuts, trying to recognize the character for "luck." It was hard to remember what one written symbol looked like, when you couldn't really read.

The wrinkled eyes of the thin, old man who sat behind the table smiled at her.

"Do . . . do you have one for luck?" she asked.

He looked over the cuts carefully, then shook his ancient head. "Many people have wanted luck today. I have sold the last one."

Shoulders drooping a little, Ling Mei started to turn away.

"Wait." The wrinkled man opened a small drawer underneath the table and drew out a small papercut. He pressed it into her hand. Ling Mei looked at it, startled.

It looked a bit like the outline of a tiger, which meant courage, but the head was too small. She raised her eyebrows politely.

"Hang it up. Sometimes courage makes luck," he said, his eyes narrowing and the corners of his mouth turning up ever-so-slightly into a smile.

"But . . . this isn't a tiger, honored sir. It's too small."

"You are small also." His eyes stared into hers.

Reluctantly, Ling Mei dug down into her one pocket for her birthday coin and placed it in the old man's hand. She didn't want a cut of something that looked a bit like a tiger and a bit like a street cat, but she couldn't insult someone old enough to be her grandmother's father. She tucked the papercut into her now empty pocket, bowed, and left, trudging back to her family's junk.

The Guo boat was back. Grandmother Guo's black eyes pricked her with their sharp gaze.

"Still here, girl? Can't survive without a family. Nothing for you to do, now, but gather up a bowl and go," she said in her harsh voice.

"I'm no beggar!"

"You think you're father-head of your family's junk? Going to sail it all by yourself?" the old woman cackled.

"I won't have to manage by myself. My family will be back soon."

"Hunh!" was the old woman's disdainful reply.

Ling Mei hunched her shoulders and cooked only a small portion of rice for herself. Her tears flavored it. She squeezed past the matting that covered the family's quarters and perched on the rear of the boat, near the big steering oar. She ate her rice as the colors of sunset filled the sky, but it failed to lift her spirits. She stayed until the moon had risen, full and round and whole. She wished her family's junk was as full, and whole and bright.

Rising, she heard a crackle from her pocket. She had forgotten the papercut. She took it out, crouched back down and carefully smoothed it out on her knee. A tear fell on it. Carefully, she wiped that away, too. It didn't look that funny in the moonlight, she thought with a sigh. The white of the paper almost seemed to glow.

Standing up, she carried it forward and hung it over the door to the family quarters before she crept inside. Perhaps it would give her just a small bit of courage, enough to let her sleep in a quiet so lonely she could hear the stars.

That night, as the odors of jasmine and eucalyptus, bamboo groves and fish mingled with the smells from tens of thousands of braziers, and wafted onto the ship, Ling Mei woke to the feel of a footstep on the deck. She sat upright, her sudden movement rustling the straw in the sack she slept on.

She listened.

Whatever movement the foot had started was now lost in the ripples of the harbor. Ling Mei sat, barely breathing, and waited.

A soft pad, pad, pad started toward her. Ling Mei could feel her heart hammer a matching rhythm at the front of her chest.

A small form cast its shadow on the door matting. Ling Mei gave a choking laugh as she recognized what it was. A cat.

It poked its head under the edge of the matting and peered in at her.

"You silly cat!" Ling Mei said, too loud in her relief. "You're lucky my honored mother isn't here, or she'd throw you into the harbor. Good only for rats and stealing food from babies, she says. Get off, now. Shoo!"

Ling Mei whooshed her hands forward like small brooms.

The cat did not scurry away. It just stared at her, calm and silent.

Ling Mei got up and darted toward the cat, shooing more vigorously.

The cat did not budge. It . . . just stared, its eyes huge, as huge and mysterious as the moon.

Suddenly, it was Ling Mei who was frightened. Those eyes . . . they seemed to glow. And the cat was big, bigger than any scrawny pier cat she'd ever seen, almost . . . half a tiger.

Ling Mei sat down with a thump on oldest sister's mat,

her frightened breath whooshing out of her. The cat just lowered its gaze, and stared at her eye to eye.

His eyes did not glow green, or yellow, or night-red, like a normal cat's. Their eerie shine was blue, with flecks of gold.

Ling Mei felt the small hairs on her arms lift, and her scalp tingle. This was no ordinary cat. Her eyes crept up to where she had hung the papercut cat on the other side of the door matting. They crept back down to the real cat. Perhaps. . . .

With a masterful shrug, the cat pushed the matting aside, strode the rest of the way into the sleeping chamber and turned, looking back over its shoulder at Ling Mei. It meowed sharply, once.

Ling Mei got up. The cat walked out and strode toward the side of the junk nearest the dock. The tip of its tail glowed white in the moonlight. The rest of its body was a silvery gray. Poised on the edge of the junk, it looked back at her once more, its shining blue eyes commanding.

Ling Mei followed.

The cat led her on a twisting path through the streets, treading sure-footed between sleeping chickens and restless dogs, through circles of men engrossed in their play of liu-po, and the money that was changing hands. The cat's passage disturbed no one, although eyes blinked at Ling Mei and disparaging comments about her ancestors were muttered. Ling Mei wondered if perhaps she was dreaming, but the ground was hard beneath her feet, with none of the give and sway of her beloved home, and the night air was cool on her skin. She shivered. The glowing tip of the cat's tail beckoned her on.

The cat led her for many li. Ling Mei's legs started to ache. She was not used to so much walking. The narrow breadth and cluttered length of a junk had been her home since birth. She had never set foot off it until she was five, and since then, the most she'd walked had been back and forth to the markets of the various towns on the river. Still, the silvery sheen of the cat no one but she noticed drew her on.

The cat turned another corner and wove its way down

a twisty street so narrow the flapping laundry overhead nearly blocked the stars. As Ling Mei ducked beneath a pannier of chicken feathers, she thought she could hear shouting up ahead.

It was too far away to know for sure, or to make out any words. The cat led her on, down through more twists of the street. Ling Mei widened her nose, wrapped it around a familiar, comforting scent. Water.

The noise was clearly voices now.

The cat melted close to the side of a building. Ling Mei did likewise. Softly the cat padded forward, then stopped, near a corner. Ling Mei peered around it.

The side street and docks before her were filled with the figures of men, running, jostling each other, carrying huge bundles bound with hemp, then running back for more. Before her, bright from the light of a hundred torches, lay the Imperial Ship. On either side of it was docked an entire fleet of fast, sleek junks: the boats of every Sung noble who had managed to flee to Canton.

They were being provisioned: loaded with food, clothing and luxuries. Chang Shih-chieh, defender of the Sung dynasty, and protector of the emperor's brother and heir, was preparing to flee Canton. *The rumor must have been right; the Mongols are at the gates,* thought Ling Mei.

She felt something brush against her leg. The cat was moving again, backward. *Yes!* thought Ling Mei. *Let's get away from any soldiers and servants to nobles and find our way back home!* Quickly she followed it back up the twisting, narrow path.

But the cat turned again, and plunged down a path that led them right back toward the docks again, toward the nobles, toward the soldiers who would have scant mercy for a peasant girl watching what they did on this moonlit night. A peasant girl whose family had already been taken for supposedly aiding the enemy.

Ling Mei stopped.

The cat turned, stared at her with glowing eyes. The tips of its silvery hairs caught the moonlight in a way that made its outline glow against the dark of the building behind it. The way it was standing, its outline exactly matched the silhouette cut into paper that Ling Mei had hung on her family's junk. The outline of a small tiger, a large cat. Courage.

Reluctantly, Ling Mei put one foot in front of another again, and followed the cat toward the sound, toward the lights, toward the soldiers. Her hands were shaking, but her heart felt full. The two, cat and girl, crept almost to the feet of the sweating workers.

Why was she doing this? Ling Mei wondered.

The cat turned, slipped behind a building. Gratefully, Ling Mei followed it into the darkness. But her relief was short-lived. A few steps beyond, a wall blocked their path. Ling Mei cast a look back toward the light and danger they'd just left. She didn't want to go back, but there was no way past the wall, and it was too high to climb.

When she looked forward again, the cat was walking through the wall. *Through* until only the glowing tip of its tail was visible. Then that, too, vanished. Ling Mei stared at the spot where it had disappeared.

A sharp meow commanded her from the other side of the wall. Ling Mei slithered back a step. She stopped again, stared in dismay at the wall.

The meow commanded again. Soldiers behind her and a wall in front. *Courage can make luck,* the voice whispered in her memory.

Ling Mei crouched down and stretched her hand forward, slowly, toward the spot where the cat had gone through. Instead of stopping at the edge of the wall, her hand slid into it.

Ling Mei snatched her hand back. Her feet ran backward, crabwise, and she fought to keep her balance. Just as she was about to turn and flee, the face of the cat shimmered, a living picture on the wall. The eyes stared at her, commanded her.

Reluctantly, Ling Mei slid her feet forward. The cat still stared. Ling Mei thought she could see its tail now, swishing, dim though the darkness of the wall. She shut her eyes, thought courage, and plunged in . . . to . . . it. . . . The wall felt like breath crushed out of her, like grit carried on the bosom of a typhoon, like the scrape of a thousand barnacles.

She was through.

The cat meowed its pleasure, an astonishingly normal meow, and rubbed its silvery fur against her legs. Then, all business again, it trotted forward.

The next wall was easier.

The third wall took her inside a building. A red-shaded lantern glowed, dimly lighting the darkness. Crouched in the corner of the small room were her grandmother, her honored parents, oldest brother and oldest sister . . . her whole family! With a cry, Ling Mei ran toward them.

"Hush," the cat seemed to sigh, its breath soughing through the entire room.

With tiny gasps and whispers, Ling Mei hugged each one of the family.

"Where did you come from?"

"You've been arrested, too?"

Ling Mei tried to answer.

"Quickly, quickly!" the cat meowed.

"Yes, yes," Ling Mei answered, turning to face its silveriness.

"Who are you talking to, third daughter?" her mother asked.

"The cat, honored mother," Ling Mei replied.

"Cat? What cat?"

Her mother stared right at the spot where the silvery tail with the white-glow-end swished, back and forth, back and forth.

"Never mind," Ling Mei whispered. "Just come. Quickly, quickly."

As her family shuffled to their feet, Ling Mei heard the tramp of men approaching the door to the room.

"Soldiers!" whispered second oldest brother.

"Quickly!" Ling Mei gasped. She herded her family toward the wall. The cat walked ahead, disappearing through it. Second oldest brother gasped, and Ling Mei knew *he* had seen it. "Follow, follow!" she said. She grabbed grandmother's arm and shoved her after second oldest brother. Father and oldest brother snatched up two of the younger children and plunged into the wall. Hurriedly, Ling Mei picked up youngest brother, thrust him into her mother's arms, and pushed both through the wall. She was still herding her three sisters and two other brothers through, when soldiers burst into the room.

"Ai-yi!" the soldiers cried, and raced forward.

With a gasp, Ling Mei threw her arms around all the brothers and sisters she could reach, and they tumbled through the wall together, tripping over each other, landing in a heap on the packed dirt outside.

An arm started to come through the wall after them, a soldier's arm. The cat's tail swished, once. The night was pierced by a bloodcurdling scream, and the arm stopped, frozen in the hard, stone wall.

Shuddering, Ling Mei scrambled to her feet, and pulled oldest sister up with her. She was too rude for her sister's liking.

"No time!" Ling Mei whispered softly back at her, while she pulled fourth younger brother to his feet and urged him forward. Second oldest brother was already leading the rest of her family down the path, following the cat. Ling Mei counted noses in the moonlight, and breathed a sigh of relief. None of them had been left with the soldiers.

A thud vibrated the wall of the building beside them. *They are trying to break down the wall!* thought Ling Mei. She hushed fourth younger sister's tears, and scurried down the path.

The thuds against the wall ceased, and Ling Mei knew the soldiers had stopped trying to go through the wall. They would come after them in the streets. She trotted forward, urging her brothers and sisters faster, faster still.

With a deep breath, honored grandmother, second oldest brother and then mother carrying youngest brother plunged through the second wall. The rest of the family followed. Ling Mei could hear shouts on the streets. She knew the last wall would bring them out practically on top of the soldiers and the men loading the ships.

"No!" she hissed to second oldest brother. "We can't go that way," she apologized to the cat.

"Luck," it wished, seeming to smile, then vanished.

"No! Come back!" she half-whispered, half-cried. But there was no swish of tail or glow of eyes. With a gulp,

Ling Mei realized the cat had helped them all it would. Now the yoke rested on Ling Mei's shoulders. Could she find her way back to their junk, through all the twisting streets, especially if she didn't use the ones the cat had led her down, the ones that would lead them too close to the searching soldiers not once, but twice? "Courage," she whimpered to herself, and plunged uphill, sideways to the last wall. Her family eddied, then hurried after her.

Ling Mei tried to remember what twists and turns the cat had led her through, so she could angle her way back through the city to bring them to their section of the harbor. At first they could hear the shouts and see the glimmer from the torches of the soldiers searching for them. Gradually, that was left behind.

"Third daughter, this makes no sense, her mother hissed. "The soldiers will just come to our junk, and arrest us again."

"I don't think you have to worry, honored mother," Ling Mei whispered back. "The protectors of the Son of Heaven are busy fleeing the Mongols. They will not have too much time to waste, chasing after one small family of peasants."

"Ah-yii, the barbarians," her honored grandmother moaned.

"Yes, honored grandmother," Ling Mei replied respectfully, but urged her on. Eventually the welcome scent of water and fish drew her, and gratefully they made their way down to a less exalted part of the harbor.

"I know where we are, now," second oldest brother whispered. "This is where you sent me once to buy hemp, honored father." He motioned. "Follow me."

Relieved that she no longer had to guess her way through streets she'd never seen before, Ling Mei stepped back to let him lead. Soon they were in sight of their family's junk. All was quiet. No soldiers, no torches: only the soft lap of the waters and the scrape of one junk against another.

"Is it safe, do you suppose?" Ling Mei asked second oldest brother. He shrugged.

Their honored father drew them down into the shadows of the buildings that lined the harbor. They nestled there until the sky blossomed into pale gray. Then, with still no appearance of the soldiers, they crept down the swaying dock, and boarded.

"What's this?" asked Ling Mei's mother, fingering the papercut of the cat hanging over their door to the sleeping quarters.

"That's my luck," Ling Mei replied.

Her honored mother took her hand away from it, and did not protest its presence. Luck was very important, even if it came in a distasteful shape. The family settled back onto their boat, murmuring with the comfort of being back on their home again.

Grandmother Guo's head popped up on the deck of their junk and peered over at the Ling family. Her black eyes opened so far they grew round. Muttering, she dived back down under the matting again.

Ling Mei giggled, hiding her mouth behind her hand.

As the pearly sky brightened into the colors of full dawn, the waters of the harbor swished with the sound of prows cutting through the waves, and Ling Mei and her family watched as the Imperial fleet sailed out of the harbor. Honored grandmother wept in fear of the Mongols, but Ling Mei and her parents just watched carefully. What did it matter to peasants who ruled, as long as you brought no notice down upon yourselves?

With the dawn, a breeze sprang up and flapped the rust red sails of the junk.

"Oh, no!" Ling Mei cried, as her papercut tore loose and flew over the side of the junk. "My luck!" She ran over and peered down into the narrow strip of water that appeared and disappeared between the junks with every wave. But she could see no sign of the little papercut cat. "My luck," she moaned.

The breeze, as usual, brought with it dust from the city. Ling Mei's mother handed her a reed brush. With a sigh, Ling Mei bid the last wisps of her role as savior and leader good-bye, and settled back into her position of third daughter. She swept the deck.

Later that afternoon, while honored father and oldest brother were still discussing whether they should head up the river or stay put in the harbor awhile, as the fishing families had decided, a small, skinny kitten wandered down the dock toward their boat. Its meow was pitiful and its paws stumbled with the sway of the dock. It looked up at Ling Mei. Its small mouth opened, and the pinkness within was as delicate and needy as a baby's.

"Oh!" Ling Mei cried, and clambered over the side of the boat. She dropped down and cradled the kitten.

"Third daughter! What are you thinking of! Put down that scrawny beggar at once. Good for rats and stealing food from a baby, that's all. I won't have one of those on my junk!" exclaimed her mother.

But Ling Mei had noticed its eyes were a pale blue.

"It's payment, honored mother," Ling Mei said respectfully, but more firmly than she ever would have dared before. "All of this most wonderful family would have been lost, and I would have been a beggar, without family and outcast, had the magic cat not led me to where the soldiers had taken you. Caring for this beggar, in turn, will bring us luck."

Her mother's mouth pursed as it had when she had seen the papercut, but she said, "For luck, I suppose I can spare some scraps. Very well, my third daughter who is not a beggar today. Bring this luck on board."

Ling Mei tucked the kitten under her arm and climbed back into the junk.

Luck was the first of many cats to ride on the matting of the Ling family's junk.

SHADO

by Marylois Dunn

Cat slipped under the castle gate and stood surveying the world outside. Fog softened the meadow shrouding the nearby forest with gray robes. There was no breath of breeze, but the cloud shifted, thickened, thinned, captured and released the objects outside the walls. To Cat's disgust, it left a thick residue of moisture over everything. Small beads of water even formed on his whiskers, which he wiped away with an impatient swipe of his forepaw. It was a dreadful morning to hunt.

Cat, however, had learned that while his kind generally chose to remain indoors near the warmth of the kitchen fires, the field mice regarded a foggy day as a Mouse Holiday and ran about fearlessly, not expecting depredations from fox, hawk, or cat on such a day. Perfect weather for a fellow who did not mind getting his paws and tail wet.

Wet grass bent silently under his paws as he made his way toward a slight declivity which had always been productive. He wanted two mice this day, one for himself, of course. He would eat his on the spot. The other was for White Cat who had been somewhat off her feed lately. She was always generous to share with him. A fat, juicy mouse might make her laugh, make her eyes sparkle again.

The trouble was that they were growing older, she somewhat older than himself. Cat was still in his full strength, but White Cat had not brought a litter in more than two cold times. The human closed her door on those days when Cat would most like to enter. No matter how he begged, cajoled, sang his most melodious songs outside, the door remained closed and White Cat barren.

She was depressed and her sadness troubled Cat. He did his best to be amusing, telling her the castle gossip and bringing her his problems to solve. He often acted in kittenish ways which he found embarrassing but as long as it amused her, he did not mind.

A large drop of water from a berry bush struck him on the nose, and he stopped, shook his head, and stepped forward without looking where he stepped.

Several things happened simultaneously which utterly destroyed his dignity and left him frightened, embarrassed, and ready for battle all at the same time. As Cat stepped forward, his paw fell on something which moved under his foot. Unnerved and unbalanced, he hissed, leapt into the air, became entangled in the bush and leapt even higher to escape the new enemy, squalling aloud his fierce battle cry. He came to earth several feet from the spot he had left it, fur erect, back bowed, tail switching furiously. His eyes were wide, flashing green fire, and his growl frightened every mouse in the meadow into its hole.

Nothing moved under the bush.

Cat watched for long moments before he stalked slowly to the bush to see what had so alarmed him. At first he saw nothing, but as his eyes gradually returned to normal he saw one shadow which seemed more solid than the others under the bush. It looked like a living creature, a very still living creature.

Cat hissed and struck at it with a hooded paw. If it was a snake, he did not want to battle with it, merely warn it away.

A tiny, trembling voice said, *Please don't hurt me.*

Cat stepped back astonished. The voice was that of a very young kit, barely able to communicate. He moved closer and nosed the kit lightly. *Why are you here alone? Where is your mother?*

The kit trembled violently and drew back farther into the brush. *Are you going to eat me?*

Of course not. Do I look like a cannibal? Be still. I'm not going to hurt you. Cat sat down.

You frightened me when you flew through the air. I have never seen a cat fly before.

Cat harrumphed. *You are not very old. You'll see many things before you are my age. Where is your mother?* he repeated.

I don't know. She brought me here and told me to wait. She said she would come back, but it's been a long time. Three darks. I'm afraid something has happened to her. The kit seemed frightened to have said such a long speech before this giant stranger. He made himself as small as he could waiting for what might happen next.

Cat thought to himself that the kit was probably right. Either the mother was an irresponsible fool to bring her child out here and leave him, or something had happened to her. In any case, Cat could not leave him out here alone. There were many dangers to a grown cat outside the walls. He was surprised the kit had survived as long as it had.

The kit had to be starving. Three days without food was a long time for a little one. *What have you eaten?* Cat asked.

I found a beetle yesterday, a large beetle. My stomach hurt, but I would have eaten another had I found one. I licked water from the grass.

Cat said, *Don't move from this spot. I will bring you some real food. Wait for me.*

The field mice, not privileged to understand cat communication, had come from their holes when they did not hear any more growls and were going about their business under the grass. Cat quickly selected a small one, killed and brought it back to the hungry kit. He showed the young one how to slice open the belly and draw out the entrails. He bit off the tail, paws, and head himself and left the meaty part for the youngster who fell on it and devoured it with much high-pitched growling and many mock kills.

After the kit had eaten, Cat lay down beside it and began to bathe it gently. The tiny kit's fur was wet and matted and, through the fur, Cat could feel all of its fragile bones. His eyes grew large again, flashing with anger as he thought of the negligent mother who had treated her kit so. *Were you born in the castle?* he asked between licks. *I don't remember a gray kit of your age in any of the litters I have seen this spring.*

I don't know, the kit said. *I was born in the forest a long way from here. What is a castle?*

A feral kit, Cat thought. His mother must be one of those who left the castle for the freedom of the woods. He looked closer at the kit who was so small there was no way to know, but it might be one of those who were combinations of the small wildcats of the forest and the feral cats. If so, it would be an interesting creature when grown. Certainly, it did have enough spunk to speak up to him.

I can't leave it here, he thought. That something has not already eaten it is pure luck. And then Cat began to purr. White Cat might find a kit just the thing to bring back her good spirits.

Would you like to go back to the castle with me? Cat asked. *I fear your mother will not come for you. If she could, she would have come long before this.*

The kit trembled. *That is my thought, too. Oh, I hope she did not fall into one of the traps. What would my sisters do?*

You have sisters?

Two. What will become of my sisters?

Cat stood, switching his tail impatiently. *What do you expect me to do about that? Can you find your way back to them? Isn't it enough that I am taking you to safety?*

I am very grateful to you for rescuing me. But I am concerned about my sisters. They are very beautiful and no larger than I. If Mother was caught in a trap, who will take care of them?

I'm sure I don't know. Rat's eyes. I can't take care of every stray kit in the forest.

The kit did not answer, but its chin began to quiver and a quavering wail came from its mouth.

Now, now. Stop that. What would you have me do?

If you go slow, I think I can direct you back to our birthing place.

If I go slow! Cat muttered to himself. He THINKS he can find the birthing place.

How long did you say it took your mother to bring you here?

The kit, excited by the thought that Cat might take him in search of his sisters, straightened up. *Oh, sir. Not very long at all. From daybreak to the middle of the afternoon. The sun was still up when she left me here and told me to wait.*

Cat switched his tail again looking at the mid-morning sun. "Dawn to middle of the afternoon" would put them at the nesting place after sundown. His ears went back as he considered the journey. The kit was small and helpless. Somewhere in the forest there were two more like it. Two more for White Cat to cuddle. Three is always better than one in mice, in biscuits, perhaps in kits as well. He sat down and washed his front paws, taking care to pull the burrs from between his toes.

All right, he said in a grumpy tone. *We will go looking for your sisters, but you'd best know the way.*

I think I can direct you, the kit said.

You certainly cannot lead the way, Cat said. *I'll carry you.*

Mother carries me by the back of my neck.

I know how to carry kits. Cat's tone was dry. He took several trial nips and, finding the proper hold, picked up the kit and carried him easily.

The kit directed him past two large trees into a rabbit trail which they followed for some time, the kit muttering from time to time when he saw something he remembered. The sun had begun its downward descent when Cat sensed something ahead. He stopped and dropped the kit under a bush, covering it with leaves as he said, *Stay here. I want to investigate ahead. I will be back for you in a little while, and I'll try to find us something to eat.*

Mother said she was coming back, the kit said in a tiny voice.

I am not your mother. If I say I will come back, I will come back.

I'll be here, the kit snuggled down in the leaves, already warm and growing sleepy.

Cat moved with caution through the tall grass until he

found what he feared. Under a trap of the type called "deadfall" he found a gray and white female cat. He could not see for a moment what had triggered the trap that she would allow herself to be caught so. When he came close he heard the squeak of live mice and as he stepped over the log which had broken the back of the female, he found a small box woven of green willow and something he had not seen before, a silvery colored vine and very strong. In the box were three live field mice.

A few bites told Cat he could not chew through the silvery vine any more than the mice could. They were there for the eating, but he could not get to them. What a waste. They would probably starve before the traps were run.

The one thing the tragedy told him was that they were on the right track. The kit had been uncertain in a few turns and crossroads, but when it made a decision it was correct. This had to be the mother cat. He leapt the log again, landing lightly beside her crumpled form. Her head was under the log and when he looked closely, he saw something else.

A small leg extended stiffly from under the log. She must have returned to the birthing place and was bringing a little sister to join her brother. While he sniffed the remains of the kit's family, Cat was alert to the forest around him.

A tree-climbing rodent was chattering angrily at him, running up and down a nearby tree, its tail switching furiously. Cat watched it dispassionately. He had caught one in his youth, but of late, he had not tried for one of the swift rodents. Saliva flooded his tongue, making him swallow. As he remembered, they were delicious.

The rodent grew bolder when Cat lay down beside the dead one. Cat did not look at the rodent directly but faced the trail away from it. He heard the creature make a short run on the ground, then turn and leap for its tree.

Cat did not move an ear.

He heard the creature land on the leafy ground and begin a short run toward the log where he lay.

Cat did not quiver a whisker.

The creature's claws scrabbled up on the log which had smashed the kit's mother as it came forward to see if Cat also was dead.

Cat was not dead. From his prone position, he came up in a leap that took him over the log, almost over the curious creature, but Cat had not intended to pass over it. He grasped it with tooth and claw, carrying it off the log onto the ground on the other side. He was the heavier and, though the creature tried to bite him and did claw him seriously several times, he kept shifting his mouth hold until he reached the position he wanted. In a few moments the creature was as dead as the kit's mother.

Cat dragged the creature across the log and up the trail to the kit. *Wake up, Shado,* for Cat had begun to call the kit by name in his mind. *I have something for us to eat.*

After they feasted, they curled up together and slept.

The edge of the sky was light when they woke. Without mentioning his mother, Cat picked up the kit and carried him around the clearing where the mother lay. He followed the kit's instructions with more assurance now that he knew they were reasonably accurate. Before he had time to tire of carrying the kit in his mouth, they had come to the river. A short way upstream brought them to the rocks the kit had described.

He had been here before. He and the yellow-eyed hound had come this far to find the camp of the magician. That camp lay on the other side of the river. He remembered the shallow crossing, glad this day that he would not have to go to the other side. The birthing place was on this side of the river.

There, the kit said. *Up the hillside is a small cavern. My sisters should be in there. Perhaps Mother, too.*

Cat carried him up the hillside, placing him on the ground just outside the cavern. *I must tell you, Shado, you will not find your mother here. Perhaps not either of the sisters. Far back on the trail, while you were sleeping, I found your mother and one of the sisters in a deadfall trap.*

They were—the kit hesitated, *dead?*

Both, Cat said. He did not know what he expected from the kit. Whatever it was, he didn't get it. The kit

made no expression of sorrow or regret. Instead he got to
his feet and walked as steadily as he could into the
cavern. In a few moments Shado came into the morning
light followed by a beautiful black kit with a bit of white
at her throat and both ears outlined in white as if edged
in frost.

Cat felt an inward tug at the beauty of the sister. For
the first time, he stopped grousing to himself and was
glad they had come the long distance to find Shado's
sister. White Cat would certainly be pleased to have this
pair to raise.

When Cat began to wash his whiskers without saying
anything, Shado sat down in front of him. *My sister has
not eaten for two daylights. Could you find something?
I'm hungry, too.*

*No doubt you could eat a mastiff if I were strong
enough to kill one for you,* Cat said. *Stay here. I'll see
what I can find.*

Before the sun had moved very far in the sky, Cat was
back, dragging a rabbit almost as large as himself. He
chewed the head off and showed the kits how to reach
the meatier parts without swallowing too much fur. He
sat back and watched as they attacked the dead creature,
"killing" it for themselves several times before they settled down to eat.

I suppose it is the way they learn to kill for themselves,
Cat thought as he watched from the top of a nearby rock.
The kits were out in the open and he watched the area
around them for movement. He did not want them to be
endangered by some animal he did not know was coming.

Before they had finished eating, he heard dogs. The
voices were those of hunting dogs on a trail and the
sound was coming from the direction they had taken.
The dogs might have been trailing them and where there
were hunting dogs, there were men with weapons.

At the first distant sound Cat was down off the rock
and beside the kits. *Quickly now, I will have to try to
carry both of you at once, and I am going to move fast.*
He took Shado into his mouth first and then pulled him
close to the black and white kit. She had been carried

before because she allowed herself to go limp to make it easier for him to carry her.

He set off upstream to where he knew there was a shallow ford. Of course, when they reached it, it was not as shallow as he remembered. Although he held the kits as high as he could, they were all soaking wet when he came out of the river on the other side. Both kits mewled miserably and Cat growled, *Silence! We are all wet. We will dry shortly, but you must be silent. The dogs can hear as well as smell.*

The kits fell silent, and Cat turned downstream and began to run. He leapt a log and Shado fell to the ground with an audible thud. Cat turned and tried to grasp both of the kits again. The sound of the hounds was almost directly across the river from them and he was anxious to get far down the river before they followed to the crossing.

A red fox stepped out of the shadows before Cat and he stopped, dropping the kits from his mouth between his front paws. He bowed his back and hissed.

Easy. Easy, friend cat. I thought the dogs were coming for me, but it seems you have the same thought. I have never seen you here before and I know the forest well. Would you trust me to take you away from the dogs?

Cat allowed the fur to lay down along his spine and relaxed slightly. *Do you know the castle on the plain where the sun rises?*

The fox gave a delicate cough. *I have been there. They have good hounds and we have had some interesting chases. Is that your destination?*

Yes, Cat said. *It is on the other side of this river. Is there another shallow ford? I do not swim well.*

Certainly not carrying two kits. I know a good crossing farther down. Allow me to carry one of the kits and we will move faster.

I am not sure I can trust you, Cat said.

The fox sat down facing him, its white paws together, tail curled around them. *I know that. Decide. I will help you, or I will leave you alone. As you choose.*

Is this creature our friend? Shado whispered.

I'm sure I don't know, Cat sat down and licked his aching pads. *But I think I trust him.*

Her, the fox said. *I have had kits of my own. I will take good care of yours.*

They aren't mine exactly, Cat said, *but that is a longer story than we have time for here. All right. We will take your help and be glad of it.*

The fox stood as she said, *Then let us be off. The dogs will soon cross the river and start back on this side. We do not want to lose our lead.*

She reached between Cat's paws and picked up the trembling kit.

Cat picked up Shado and followed the fast moving fox as she slipped into trails he would not have seen had she not been leading. In a little while, they came to a log that lay across half of the river. The fox leapt onto it and walked over to where it ended, waiting until Cat caught up. *Do you mind getting wet?*

Of course, Cat said.

I'm afraid it can't be helped. There is a branch that goes to the other side, but it is under water a couple of inches. I think we can keep the kits dry.

Cat looked at the difference in their heights and growled to Shado, *Curl yourself up as tight as you can. You may get wet anyway.*

I've been wet before, Shado said.

The fox led the way over the slippery branch through the swift water. Cat was almost swept away by the current but quickly learned to walk with claws unsheathed, almost as if climbing a recumbent tree. They reached the other side with the kits only minimally wet.

Better than the first time, Shado murmured.

Hush! Cat said between his teeth and kitten neck. What he wanted most to do was drop Shado, sit down, and give himself a good wash, drying the cold water of the river from his fur as best he could. The fox's tail disappeared into the underbrush beside the river and Cat could do nothing but follow as fast as he could.

In a length of time that seemed much shorter than it should have, they reached the edge of the forest. The fox stopped under a clump of broken conifer limbs, putting the kit down carefully between her paws. She spent the time waiting for Cat to catch up washing the kit, massaging with her large fox tongue to get the circulation flowing again. After awhile, Cat came up and began the same treatment on Shado.

With both kits cleaned and curled together in sleep, Cat began his own long-overdue toilet. He began at the tip of his tail and worked his way methodically toward the final lap, ears and whiskers. Finished, he looked around to find the fox as meticulously grooming herself as he had.

Thank you, Cat said and the fox stopped in mid-lick.

My pleasure, the fox replied. *I like to see a family stay together and I did not think you were going to get far trying to carry two kits at once.*

Cat smoothed his whiskers again with a clean paw. *I'm sure,* he murmured. *But I couldn't come back for the other kit. You heard the hounds.*

I do believe we left them at the river. I haven't heard them in some time.

You really do know these woods. Are you as familiar with the castle?

Goodness, no. I have never been in the castle. The hounds would scent me in a moment. The fox made a sound which could have been taken for amusement. *Wouldn't that stir the stale air inside those walls? Can you manage from here?*

Thank you, Cat said. *I might not have escaped the dogs without your help. What may I do for you in return?*

I don't have a need at the moment, except for dinner. All this excitement has made me hungry. The fox looked at the kits with her mouth open, tongue curled.

Both kits drew back into Cat's shadow. Cat understood that the fox was making a small joke and took no offense. *Do you know the declivity across this meadow where there is a city of mice?*

The fox looked across the meadow. *No, I have not hunted there. A city of mice?*

Holes everywhere. Follow the line of the forest. When you reach a small hill, go carefully as you pass over it. On the other side you will find many fine, fat mice for your dinner. If there is ever anything I can do for you, send word to the castle. I will hear of it and meet you in this spot.

With a final poke of her sharp nose at the kits, the fox disappeared into the forest in the direction of the mouse haven Cat had described to her. Cat was hungry himself and knew the kits were as well, but food would have to wait. First, he must get them into the castle and up to Cat's domain.

The shadows of evening were long across the meadow. Cat picked up the two kits and, following the darker shadows, made his way to the castle gate. He waited until the humans had gone inside to their evening meal before he carried his double burden under the gate and up to the kitchen entrance.

I'm hungry, Shado muttered as they slipped through the kitchen and toward the stairs.

Don't think about it, Cat mumbled. *First, safety. Then, food.*

Cat tried to keep to the shadows and out of sight of the other cats and the stupid dogs. He was not altogether successful. One of his hunting companions, a black and white tom with only half a tail, came out of the kitchen just as Cat started up the stairs. The tom raised his hackles and hissed in mock horror, *What is this? Cat, Lord of the Castle, swinging not one, but two kits. Where are you taking these little beggars? They look like something our companions would toss to the dogs.*

Cat felt the little ones tense with fear. *Be still,* he said to the kits. *You are perfectly safe with me from both the dogs and from cats whose manners are as short as their tails.*

The black and white tom hissed and bowed his back, but he was not close enough for Cat to take a swipe at him, so Cat moved up the curved stairway, the kits swinging as he climbed.

He isn't following us, Shadow stretched his neck to watch the stairs behind them.

I would be surprised if he did, Cat said. *He does all his fighting with speech. Perhaps having part of his tail missing makes him feel inferior. He rarely throws himself into a real fray.*

Do the other cats tease him about his tail? a soft voice asked and Cat realized the little sister had spoken for the first time.

Cat put the kits down at the narrow end of the stairs and sat, with them between his front paws. *Most of the time the castle cats are kind to each other, even to him. I was unkind to speak of his short tail. I will bring him a mouse one day soon.*

Now, we are almost there. I am taking you to the White Cat. She is very wise and will know what to do with you.

The two kits sat obediently, seeming overwhelmed by the castle and the activity in it. From the stairs they could watch people and animals passing below. *Is it always like this?* Shado whispered.

Most of the time, Cat said. *Come, let's finish our journey.*

White Cat said, *My, my.* Then repeated it for the seventh or eighth time, *My, my. Where did you find them, Cat?*

Cat told her the entire tale including the flight through the air which made her laugh. He told her everything that was known about the kit's mother and other sister, about the hounds, and the fox who had helped them escape.

Through all the discourse the kits sat silent, backed up against Cat, watching White Cat with dark luminous eyes. They had never seen a cat of such size or beauty. When she leaned down to sniff them, they shrank closer to Cat, trying to hide behind his front legs.

Ho, now. I have just finished telling what brave kits you are, and you are making a liar of me. Sit up straight. White Cat is the best friend you will ever have.

The kittens straightened and tried to endure White Cat's scrutiny without trembling.

Do the younglings have names? she asked Cat.

Not when I found them. I think Shado is a good name for the gray. I have not thought of anything for the little sister.

Appropriate for him, she sniffed. *The little sister reminds me of the lace Milady wears on her gowns at the edge of the sleeves and hems. Would you answer to Lace, little sister?*

If it pleases you, the smaller kitten answered.

I see your poor mother taught you some manners. How long has it been since you had a bath?

Cat nearly washed my fur off, Shado said, *and the fox washed her.*

The fox! she murmured in surprise as she flattened Lace with one white paw and began at her ears to wash away all traces of the forest and of strangeness. *Hours ago, I am sure.*

Although he needed a wash himself, Cat began to wash Shado to hide his expression of amused satisfaction. White Cat was purring. She had not sighed once since he walked in the door with two kits swinging from his tired jaws.

The journey had been arduous. Even the hair on the tip of his tail ached, but it was worth every step if it made White Cat happy.

Baths over, White Cat pushed the kittens toward her dish of fresh cream and showed them how to lap from the bowl. While they drank, she curled herself around Cat and began to wash his ears. *How do you know, Cat? How do you always know what will make me happy?*

Cat did not answer. He put his weary head down on White Cat's flank and allowed himself to drift off to sleep. The kits were safe and White Cat was happy. What more could any cat want?

IN BASTET'S SERVICE

by P. M. Griffin

He met Bastet's eyes. His mien was respectful, certainly, for she was revered in heart and mind by all his kind, but his gaze was steady and calm, set. He would not yield.

The goddess' platinum-furred body was perfectly still, her tail coiled daintily around her forepaws. She read her companion's determination but felt no anger that his will was set against her command. Pride and courage, independence of thought and strength of will, dignity of being were integral to a feline soul and honored her; abject submission could never do so. It was a glory to all catkind that he had not been broken by the awesome adversity he had endured.

Sadness softened the serene majesty of her exquisitely formed features. He was without choice in this all the same, as was she. The Great One who ruled above all the creatures' gods had set her charges on the Ninefold Path, and every cat must walk it the full distance before rest and reward could at last be claimed.

You have been hard-used, little traveler, she said with infinite gentleness, *but eight more incarnations lie before you, eight more lives in which you must seek to follow and fulfill the Plan as it has been given to us.*

No more Plans and no more Partners, he declared firmly. *All I need to know of those, I have learned already to my great hurt. I cannot refuse to live again, for that is the nature and the fate of a cat, but never, O Divinity, shall I voluntarily approach one of those blood-tainted renegades or open myself at all to their treachery.*

Not all humans use those sharing place with them so, she corrected gently.

The goddess fell silent. She understood his stand and

sympathized with it, but by holding to it, this high and worthy soul was dooming himself to eight more barren lives. He would never know the greatest joy and fulfillment a cat could have before gaining entry into the Wide Realms. He would never experience the Plan as it should be lived, never walk in true partnership with a human in a relationship where each loved and supported the other in accordance with his or her own nature and abilities. Even if the opportunity for such an association should present itself, he would not and could not permit so much as the initial approach to take place. Most assuredly, he would never seek a Partner of his own accord. As a result, his remaining lives would be dim shadows of what they could have been and even the eternity to follow would be less full, less complete, and less satisfying.

Her head raised. That was the fate of all too many of her charges, but this little one had suffered so intensely and had come through so strong. He deserved better than he would permit himself, and she determined to take a hand in his affairs herself.

You need rest and peace before resuming your work. Go now and taste a little of the happiness of my realm. It may be that I shall assign you a place and specific duties within it rather than merely send you forth with my blessing and good wishes to seek your fortune as it falls.

Francie eagerly lifted the statue out of its box and studied it closely. It was thirteen inches high and surprisingly heavy for its size, though she should have anticipated that weight. It was bronze, after all, not something cast in plastic, however cunningly.

The little cat was indeed a lovely thing. It was an exact reproduction, albeit on a smaller scale, of the Egyptian original which always drew and held her when she made one of her frequent visits to the museum. Here was the same realism in the lithe, muscular body, the same serenity. Even the gold, intricately worked collar looked to be identical to that worn by the original. She had paid a hefty price for the piece, but it was money she did not grudge. To her mind, it was more than well spent.

The woman stroked the figurine as she set it on the

table near the closet in her bedroom that she had allotted to receive it. She was pleased to see that it looked as well there as she had hoped.

Her eyes instinctively went to the empty place below the pillow on her bed, and she sighed. Poor little Turtle. If only she were here to appreciate this new acquisition with her. . . .

Francie's home had been catless for three weeks now, ever since the eighteen-year-old had died peacefully in her arms. It was still too soon, but she would not wait too very long before opening her heart and life to another four-footed friend, or maybe to a pair. There were many little creatures in this world in need of the love, care, and respect she wanted to give, beings who would return any offering of hers a thousandfold.

If the need were great but the apparent response were slight?

Francie's heart seemed to jerk out of her breast and then stop altogether. The question had been quite audible, perfectly comprehensible, but it had rung directly in her mind, not in her ears at all.

She whirled to face the statue, from which the thought-words had seemed to come. It was precisely as she had left it.

The human blinked and shook her head emphatically. Of course, it was the same! What was she imagining? Some ancient curse out of a violated tomb? Such things might or might not be, whatever the denial of accredited science, but one had at least to have the misfortune of possessing a genuine artifact to come under their power. Her cat was a wonderful replica, but it was of very recent vintage and had been manufactured by thoroughly modern methods for the most unmystical purpose of making money. It was not even issued by the museum owning the original but by a large, mail order mint specializing in producing such collectibles.

It is a fine piece for all that, a worthy image of me and a suitable focus for my manifestation as well as a guide in leading me to you—though I grant the craftsfolk fashioning it hardly anticipated that their work was destined for such honor and significance.

"What . . . Who . . ." This could not be happening, but with all her senses contradicting reason, she had to try to conduct herself as circumstances seemed to demand.

I am Bastet, of course, the reply came instantly, amusement rippling in it, *she whose image you display.*

"But it's not *real,* Francie protested.

It is real enough, although not old. The original statue was new, too, in its own time. The mental voice became graver. *I do not inhabit it. The figure is merely a focus, as I have said. Folk of your species have always been disconcerted by being addressed, as it were, from out of the air.*

Holding a discussion with an inanimate object was not particularly reassuring, either, the woman thought miserably. Was this insanity, then? She had always imagined the mad to be at ease with their delusions, accepting the reality, the rightness, of them even when they were of an unpleasant nature. . . .

Do not fear for your sanity, child, the soft voice assured her. *Your mind is sound, very sound, as well as uncommonly open and sensitive to the Wide Realms, or I should not have revealed myself to you. You are, in full truth and concrete reality, in the presence of Bastet, who was once worshiped by your own kind even as I am to this day by my fur folk.*

A new thought, and with it sharp fear, filled the human's mind. "I give you welcome, Lady Bastet, as best I can, and respect, but I can't adore you." The words came in a rush before she could be struck down for a seeming lack of courtesy and her failure to display the expected behavior, which she did not even know. "I—I bought the statue because I loved it, not . . ."

I know where your allegiance lies. That is proper, and I do not expect you to waver in it. It is not your worship that I desire but your service, more of that same service you gave me for eighteen of your years in your association with one of my charges.

"Turtle!"

The goddess smiled. Francie could feel it, although she still saw nothing but the immobile figure. *A being rich in love and peace now free to enjoy the bliss of the Wide Realms since this last was her final incarnation. She only awaits reunion with your spirit for her happiness to be complete.*

The woman swallowed. "I'm glad of that. I wouldn't call her back here, though I miss her terribly." She hesitated. "She was so much a part of my life and of this apartment that everything I do or see here brings memories of her. They're happy, but still. . . ."

I know, Francine. You are a true Partner, ever treating one with one with your comrade, equal to equal, despite the differences in species and gifts. That is as it should be, though many even among those who love my little ones fail to achieve it.

Francie's eyes, as green as Bastet's own although of a less intense shade, rested pensively on the goddess' image. "What do you want with me, Lady Bastet, and what made you choose me for your work in the first place? A great many very talented and capable people love cats. I'm in no way extraordinary at all."

Again, that mental smile. *Let others more practiced than your kind in the reading of hearts and souls be the judge of that, Francine of the Partners. I shall answer your second question first. The sensitivity to reality beyond what your people see as the normal pale and your openness of mind were strong factors influencing my choice, as was your proven history as a Partner. Your reasons for acquiring my image sealed my decision. You did not want it for display, for idle show as some sort of proof of culture. You took it into your home because you loved the work and the species it imagined, because you were drawn to the particular vision of my charges, the respect and dignity and beauty, that the ancient artist revealed in his portrayal of me.*

The human's lips tightened. High praise sometimes preceded dark or heavy labor. "The service you want from me?"

There is a cat currently in my realm who was severed from his first incarnation only a week after passing his first natal anniversary. It was a year of unremitting abuse.

"I don't want to hear it!" She caught herself. "I'm sorry, Lady, but don't tell me the details. They'll only torment me. I can't do anything about them, not even try to avenge him. Such stories bother me terribly," she finished lamely.

Very well. It is not necessary for you to know. Let it suffice to say that never in that year did he know a tender word or gentle touch, yet he came forth with mind and spirit unbroken, though with heart heavily scarred. Soon, he must begin his second incarnation following the nature of his kind. The scars he carries within him will prevent him from seeking, much less attaining, a partnership such as Turtle enjoyed throughout her thrice-blessed life, not in his new incarnation or in any of those to follow it, unless an active and constant effort is made to undo the damage he has sustained.

"You believe I can help?" Francie asked doubtfully. She would not have dared to adopt a human child so troubled, recognizing that she was not qualified to handle the challenge, and she doubted that a member of the feline race was any less complex.

Without question, Bastet responded, *but the full benefit may not blossom until the incarnation to follow. The cat died young. It is my belief and hope that he will heal quickly under consistent love and care, but you must face the possibility that you shall never receive from him any part of the open affection and trust that you enjoyed in your time with Turtle even should he be with you as long or longer still.*

Francie's eyes closed. The image of Turtle's loving little face filled her mind, Turtle, who had almost lived for her. . . .

I do not expect you to go on for years without the warmth of a true Partner. There is no reason why you should not share your life with a kitten of happier birth as well once this troubled companion is settled. All three of you would benefit from her presence. I do need to know now if you will accept my commission. Choose freely. Refusal will bring no penalty since I know it will spring from your doubt of your ability to meet the small one's needs.

"Of course, I'll take him!" The woman paused. "He won't actually attack me, will he?" A cat's teeth and claws were no mean weapons when wielded in earnest.

No, neither your person nor your property will suffer, nor will he violate your sanitary arrangements.

"He'll be real? A normal kitten, I mean. If I start buying food for a ghost or even just talking to one, people're going to see me as pretty odd, maybe strange enough to cost me my job. No one's going to want to buy a house from a head case."

Bastet laughed. *He will be a very live and visible cat.*

"Cat? Not a kitten?"

"Cat. Those who have been badly used, unless they died as infants, cannot return in that state. They are no longer capable of the wonder and innocent trust of life's early spring.

The human squared her shoulders. "When will you bring him, or how do I go about getting him?"

I shall give him to you now.

A thought struck Francie. "Could you let me have half an hour, Lady Bastet? I have Turtle's things clean and ready since I'd planned on adopting another cat fairly quickly, but food's perishable, and I don't have any of that in the house. It'd probably be best if he could be assured from the start that he'll always have access to that."

A wise and thoughtful suggestion. So let it be, Francine of the Partners. We can wait that long, he and I.

Francie had not known what to expect in the emotionally injured waif, but even after six months had gone by, she was still a little stunned by the magnificence of the cat. Bast's Gift, for so she had called him, was beautiful. His short coat was a gleaming black with no white hair upon it, broken only by the enormous copper eyes. He was also big, fourteen pounds of muscle rippling in a body long enough to allow him to stand on the floor and sweep objects off a table or dresser.

At first, he had spent most of his time beneath the bed or chaise when she was in the apartment, but that open fear of her passed after a couple of weeks. Now, he absented himself only during the rare times when some of her friends were visiting her.

His behavior was exemplary even as Bastet had promised, but he remained cold and aloof, sleeping alone and barely tolerating an occasional caress of his silky head or back.

Gift considered it a major concession that he permitted that much contact. The care and consideration he received were excellent, in keeping with the divinity's assurance. He had to admit that in basic feline honesty, and common politeness required that some recompense be given for it, but chiefly, he was moved by the promise the transfigured Turtle had wrung from him. They had spoken together at length before his return, and she had pleaded so earnestly that he not be cruel to her Partner—cruel! him!—that he had in the end agreed to allow limited physical approach.

No trouble followed that lessening of his guard. Certainly, no blows came from the human's small hand, and she made no attempt to force further intimacy from him, though it was easy enough to read her desire for a great deal more. He began to feel guilty about that but steeled himself with the knowledge that she had been fully warned about what she might expect from him and had agreed to shelter him on those terms. If the human was not satisfied, well, let her bring in a kitten as she and Bastet had discussed.

Matters drifted on thus for some time, and Francie could see no sign that their relationship might better soon or at a future point. Despite her foreknowledge, her frustration grew in proportion to her deepening love for the beautiful animal.

Her heart came to close to breaking the evening she unexpectedly lost the very large sale she had hoped to close that same week. The woman sat wearily on the end of the chaise as Gift jerked away from her hand. Her head lowered, and the memory of her first sight of Turtle swept over her, a minute, orphaned kitten sprawled in a shoe box, her head and legs extended, her tiny tail sticking out behind, for all the world like the little turtles Francie and her sister had kept as children. She was sincerely glad her friend had found the happy place Bastet had described and would not wrench her away from it again for anything, but how she longed for the warmth of the little tortoiseshell's company right now. One simply could not feel like an utter failure while hugging a cat.

A failure she was, too, or so it seemed at the moment. She had let a seemingly sure sale slide through her fingers, losing the finest commission she had ever yet been in a position to earn and drawing her boss' well-merited anger down on her. As if that were not bad enough, she then had to come home only to be faced by her inability to reach the heart and gain the trust of one poor, formerly abused little animal. . . .

Suddenly, a warm, furry cheek rubbed against hers followed by the quick rasp of a tongue.

Francie almost jerked away in her surprise but managed to control her response and raised her eyes to meet the somber, knowing ones of the black cat. "Oh, Gift," she whispered, stroking him timidly with two gently wielded fingers. "Thank you, my little friend. I did need you just now."

A rumbling purr, the first she had ever heard from him, answered that, and she stroked him again. "I don't expect you to be another Turtle. I love you for yourself, and none the less because I also loved and still love her."

The purring continued, this time a genuine rather than a forced response. Bast's Gift knew misery and unhappiness, none better, and he would indeed be cruel if he did not help Francie. She was good and certainly not worthless like she had felt herself to be. It was a pleasure for him and an honor to use his power to comfort in her cause.

If the cat did not greet his human at the door each evening after that, he did rouse himself to rub against her legs, and he gradually took to sleeping at the foot of her bed.

He also began to play, or work out, rather, with her, an advance she particularly welcomed. She had feared he might lose his sleek form and fine muscle tone if he maintained too sedentary an existence. Francie would wrap her arm in a towel or sweat shirt and wrestle with Gift, allowing him to release both energy and aggressive tension. To the black's credit, although he rabbit punched with his hind legs and used both claws and teeth to grapple with the padded arm, he never forgot himself and either scratched or bit in earnest.

For still more active sport, she used a device consisting of a short fishing rod with a string attached to its tip and a small piece of cloth tied to the cord. It provided a lively, moving target, and they battled it around the apartment several times a week in very vigorous sessions lasting half an hour or more.

Of the other toys that had intrigued and occupied Turtle for nearly all of her long life, he took no notice. Only one type of plaything drew and held him, life-sized mice fashioned of real fur. Ordinarily, Francie would have refused to have anything to do with the things, but when her sister Anna had brought one of them on her last visit to the city and Gift had reacted so favorably to it, she had swallowed her scruples and bought more of them.

She soon discovered that several were necessary. No sooner did she give Bast's Gift one than it would vanish beneath some dresser or chest from which she would then be summoned to retrieve it. When this happened for the third time in the space of an hour one Saturday morning, she gave her innocent-looking comrade a quick look. Was this the stirring of the playful mischief that should be so basic a part of a young cat's personality but which had been entirely absent from his behavior thus far?

Bast's Gift came to enjoy their time together, although he was not as yet willing to ease up any further on the guards he had set about himself. Francie seemed to be everything Turtle had said, but humans were humans. She was far the bigger and stronger of them, and there was little he could do to protect himself from her if she went into a rage against him, nothing except try to keep his heart from breaking along with his body.

It happened in the end, as he had been telling himself it must. The woman flung open the door of the apartment, and he cowered down, sick with the terror of the fury he could read and smell on her.

Francie saw the cat's body shrink in upon itself and realized what had happened. She dropped her bag and tote on the table and went to her knees near him. "It's not you, baby. You're about the brightest, best thing in this whole city, at least as it impacts on me. I was just furious with something I'd read in the paper."

Because he had never unleashed his claws on her, she braced herself and swept him into her arms despite her uncertainty as to what he might be driven to do in his fear.

The cat merely lay against her as she held him close, listening to her voice more than to her words and to that which lay behind it. His dread faded under the magic of it.

"I'd never intentionally hurt you or be mad at you, my own little friend. It's this 'Jaws-of-Life Burglar' that's got me going." Her mouth hardened. "Only now, it's 'Jaws of Death.' "

Francie did not think it strange to be explaining herself thus to an animal. She had always done that with Turtle as well. She refused to walk around in dead silence like some sort of zombie except when she uttered a command or endearment just because there was no other member of her own species present. Humans were articulate beings. They spoke in sentences, put their thoughts into words, and she felt no constraint against doing precisely that when the occasion arose, whatever her company. Indeed, since her interview with Bastet, she felt courtesy required no less from her, that she was dealing with a creature of sensitivity and intelligence, albeit of abilities and gifts very different from her own.

The cat understood her way of talking by then, her meaning if not all her words. He knew what the paper was. Every evening after supper, or earlier in the day on holidays, his care giver went through a ritual of sitting down with the thing to the nearly inevitable souring of her mood.

It was a mystery he could not comprehend. When a cat encountered an unpleasant situation, he endeavored to avoid future contact with it, but Francie continued to court distress day after day. It was an astonishing display of idiocy on the part of a normally highly sensible individual.

The woman continued to stroke him, but her thoughts drifted back to the story that had so aroused her. For the better part of a month, the Jaws-of-Life Burglar had been in the news on and off. He normally struck moderately prosperous middle-class neighborhoods, cutting screens or glass or jimmying insecure locks in the manner of most of those engaged in his profession. He apparently preferred these easier targets even as did his peers to judge by the number of dwellings ransacked in the manner characteristic of his work in his signature raids, but every once in a while, he would strike a more efficiently guarded place. The bars and gates thwarting most of his kind posed no barrier to him. He cut right through them using a Forcible Entry Tool, the implement made famous by fire and police rescue units throughout the country, or something closely modeled upon it.

Anger rose in her as it did every time she heard the case mentioned. Those tools, or the Jaws of Life as they were more commonly known, had saved countless people trapped in fires and in the twisted wreckage of vehicle accidents. It infuriated her that an invention created to bring aid in time of crisis and dire peril should be used instead by the vermin infesting the great city to wreak still more misery upon its decent inhabitants, misery and now something more dreadful.

Always in the past, the violated houses and apartments had been empty, but last night, that part of the pattern had been broken. The burglar had found the occupant at home, perhaps by his intention.

There had been no bars to delay him or to arouse anyone inside with the noise of their breaking, just a screen over a window left open to admit the pleasant evening breeze. The intruder had sliced through that without difficulty and slipped into the living room from his perch on the fire escape.

Marian Sayer, the apartment's tenant, had been sleeping in her bedroom. The police either had not known at the time of the writing or had not divulged the sequence of events that followed, but when a neighbor had investigated the door boldly left ajar by the culprit when he had gone out that way, she had found the bedroom literally coated in blood, its unfortunate resident terribly dead, dismembered, her body completely severed at the waist, by the powerful cutter. The reporter had been careful to note that no one could say at what point death had ended the nightmare for her.

At least, his sympathy was clearly with the victim, Francie thought bitterly. That was more than could be said for his associate whose editorial followed the account. That individual dwelled instead on the killer, on the inner anguish and pressures and perhaps the early physical sufferings which might have driven him to strike against either woman or society in general in so brutal a manner.

Her eyes glittered coldly. If that butcher was sick, well and good. Let him be treated medically instead of jailed if he was caught alive, but she would save her sympathy until he was either dead or otherwise so confined that he was no longer a threat. A rabid beast was not responsible for its actions, either, but it still had to be prevented from spreading its infection to other creatures.

A case without apparent motive or significant clues had to be slow in the solving, and other tragedies, other scandals, soon replaced it in the headlines and in people's minds, Francie's along with the rest as she turned her attention and energies to the living of her own life with its specific demands and interests.

The woman woke out of a fitful sleep. By the bonging of her clock in the living room, she knew it was just three, and she sighed. It was still villainously hot. There would be no relief tonight now, she thought unhappily, and none at all tomorrow according to the weatherman. That meant no relief for her. The technician would not be coming until the day after that to fix the air conditioner, if it could be repaired at all.

She heard it then, a muffled scratching sound. There was a simultaneous hiss from Bast's Gift, and the cat leapt from the foot of the bed to the stacked boxes on top of the wardrobe which formed his favorite retreat when strangers were present.

Another noise, soft in reality but clear as a trumpet call to her straining ears.

Francie's heart beat so fast and hard that it seemed louder to her than the rattle that had set it racing. She slipped off the bed and crouched in the deeper shadow near the table by the closet.

A figure loomed in the doorway, a man, nearly as big in fact as he appeared to be to her terrified eyes. The features were clear enough, but she could make no hand of reading them save that he seemed annoyed at finding the bed empty.

He spotted her, and his mouth curved. It was more like a spasm than a smile. Certainly, any pleasure it mirrored had nothing to do with joy as she knew it.

Her own lips parted in a scream that would not become audible. The intruder held something in his hands, both hands. She recognized it all too readily and stared at it with fascinated horror. The tool was the smallest of its line, but it was still enormous even without the gas generator powering it harnessed to its wielder's back. It reminded her of a great pair of pliers. . . .

The man took a step toward her. He said nothing, and he did not take his eyes off her to look about the room. He had not come for cash or property but for another person, another woman, to rend in response to the irresistible demand of the compulsion swelling inside him. He fondled the handles of his weapon in anticipation as the Jaws spread wider.

An ebony streak shot from the wardrobe to the back of his neck. Claw-clad paws tore forward, raking face and the left eye, gouging deeply so that blood that looked black in the lace-filtered moonlight poured from the ravaged cheeks and the shredded pulp in the socket.

The killer seemed unaware of pain, at least to the extent that it did not appear to affect either his purpose or his ability to carry it through. He shook his head violently to dislodge his tormentor, and when he failed to do so, he hafted the big cutter to strike backward with it.

A second challenger hit him in that moment, a small, tortoiseshell spirit of fury who rent his hands with teeth and claws that did not merely look like fire in the dim light but seemed actually to be fire.

This time, the man gasped, the first sound he had uttered, and the Jaws clattered to the floor.

With a tremendous, jerking effort, he flung Turtle from him, tossing her hard against the wall beside them. She should have been smashed, or dazed at best, but her reactions were sharper in her new nature. She braced herself for the strike, used the energy of the blow to fire a run up the wall, thus dissipating rather than absorbing its force. The spirit cat dropped to the ground in a battle crouch, hissing fiercely, her eyes aglow with a light of their own making that would have told any sane witness the nature of the creature he faced.

Bast's Gift did not waste those precious seconds. He continued to punish the killer's head, so ripping forehead and scalp that in two places, thin strips of flesh hung from the bone. Periodically, he scored the back of the hand instinctively raised to defend the remaining eye.

Turtle sprang back into the fray, this time joining the black in going for the vulnerable head.

Francie watched in dread. The attack was definitely affecting their enemy, but he was not defeated. His hands were free, and he was lashing at his small assailants. They were both so positioned as to make difficult targets, but he would not be long in throwing them off and finishing them if he could land a solid blow, as he inevitably must soon do.

She had to stop him! Desperately, the woman groped for some weapon that could put the madman out of the battle, but only Bastet's bronze image came to hand.

She caught up the heavy little statue, suddenly deadly calm. She would have once chance, only one. Her first blow had to fall true, and it must strike with such force that it would bring and keep the big man down. It was pointless to question her ability or the ability of her weapon to accomplish that. She was without any other choice.

In that moment, Francie was filled with knowledge and the strength and control of body to translate it into action. Setting the figurine aside, she flowed to her feet.

The man's functioning eye dilated. He shook his head to clear the blood half blinding it, but the apparition before him still did not resolve itself back into his cowering intended victim. Tall, female, clad in platinum fur, it took a single step toward him.

A cat's whisper-soft paws concealed a defense of no small import, witness the work Francie's two defenders had already wrought on the intruder. Her own claws were something more, every bit as sharp as the animals' but strong and deadly in proportion to her new size. Her arm slashed out, and two scarlet geysers struck the ceiling, pumping wildly from the severed arteries of what had been his throat.

Francie sunk to her knees as the eldritch strength left her again as abruptly as it had come. Two little bodies, both trembling violently, came to her and pressed against her, seeking comfort. Fighting the shaking of her own limbs, she closed them tightly in her arms, whispering that everything was fine now, trying to ascertain all the while that they were indeed both whole.

Do not fear for our charges, Sister. They are unscathed.

The human's head turned to the statue. The shock and horror of those few, ghastly minutes just gone was beginning to grip her, numbing her so that she did not start at the sound of the familiar mental voice.

I must crave pardon, Francine, for possessing you as I did without first seeking your leave, but it was essential that I act at once. Your weapon was inadequate. Had I not seized the offensive, you might have felled him in the end, for your determination would have bought you more than one blow, but you yourself would have been gravely injured, probably to the death, and maybe these valiant ones with you.

"I—am grateful for your help." Francie made herself look at the corpse, at the gaping hole that remained of the throat, and she gripped herself with every shred of will she had left. "What—what about him? Is he being . . ."

The judging of human souls is not mine, yet I can state that his mind was hopelessly awry. He had no knowledge of wrong, no ability to comprehend the pain of others.

"I hope his judgment will be mild, then," she replied with a genuine charity she had not known she could muster, "milder and more just than I may receive."

She could feel the invisible entity frown. *What do you say, Sister?*

"You—you've saved me, Lady Bastet, and I'm truly grateful, but it may be only to face another kind of dying."

Francie shivered. "I don't know how I'm going to explain all of this. The police'll see that nothing in here could've made that kind of wound. Even if I claim I don't remember a thing, I'll be in trouble." Her eyes closed. "You must know something of humans, Lady. All it needs is one lawyer, one man or woman looking for notoriety, and I could be in jail or be subjected to an ordeal that'll strip me of everything—job, home, name."

There were others to think about beside herself. "Turtle'll be all right. She'll be going back to her new place, but there could be long stretches when I won't be able to take care of Gift. He might be caged somewhere or actually suffer physical as well as emotional neglect."

The woman's face, already nearly colorless, turned as white as if she lay dead beside the one the goddess had killed through her. "Lady Bastet, take him! You have to take Gift! The death weapon may be impossible to identify, but not the rest. They might put him down, slaughter him, because he attacked a human, even though it was to defend me. —Please. I know this may not follow the laws or customs ruling you and your charges, but none of what happened here's normal, either. Gift overcame all his terror of strangers to do this for me. You can't let him suffer!"

She took hold of herself before hysteria shattered her completely. "I'm human, and this was a human matter initially. I can work my way through whatever's to come of it, but, please, please, don't let my brave little friend be punished for his love of me!"

You truly believe that will happen, Sister, to you or to him?

Francie's head lowered. "It could happen. It . . ." She groped for words. "Our society seems more comfortable with victims, statistics, than with successful survivors. It too often punishes them as a result."

Can you imagine that I am unaware of the ways of those among whom my charges must live or that I would inter-vene only to leave you and yours in a state worse in its way than that from which I saved you? I questioned you merely to see if you yourself were aware of your continued peril. Close your eyes, Francine, for you have witnessed too much that is strange already this day.

The human obeyed. There was no sound for what seemed like many minutes, but she did not look again until Bastet told her to do so. The body, the weapon, the blood, all sign of the intrusion and battle, were gone from the bedroom, as she had no doubt they were gone from the living room and the entry window as well.

"Thank you," she whispered.

It was a service I was pleased to render, my Sister. Know, too, that I do not call you that in courtesy but in fact, and few there are in all your species' history who have borne that title. Your behavior this night has gained it for you, coupled with your deep and true partnership with my little ones.

"I didn't do anything!" Francie exclaimed. "You were the one who . . ."

I do not grant kinship for bringing death! the other snapped. *You rightly feared what would become of you as a result, and you knew I was possessed of many powers—I surely had given ample proof of that—yet your plea was only for Bast's Gift. That, Francine of the Partners, is the measure of your greatness.*

"He's done so much for me," she murmured, stroking the black.

Are you still willing to do my work?

"I am, of course," she replied, surprised that the question should be posed.

Then it is time for you to bring a kitten into your life. One has just returned to me who had been so used in her first incarnation that she has lost the power to play or seek. That a kitten should be so crippled is an obscenity before nature and Those who rule her.

"You believe I can help her, too?"

I do, with the assistance of Bast's Gift and Turtle.

"Turtle?"

She refuses to leave you again.

Francie sighed to herself. Three cats, and she knew full well that this would not be the end of it. The need was simply too great. Every doctor of worth, and she, it seemed, was slated to be a healer of sorts, was doomed to be swamped with patients. She sighed again. She had never craved the unenviable title of 'Cat Lady'. . . .

Bastet laughed. *You are too much a lover of a normal life to allow yourself to become an eccentric, nor would I inflict that fate on you since it would be so unwelcome. The kitten will seem to be Turtle's young one, as if you took both in together as a result of her supposed resemblance to your old companion. Any others whom I send to you will remain only the relatively brief span of time required for their needs to be met and will not be perceptible to those with senses less acute than yours.*

"Ghosts?"

You would term them that. I would rather describe them as spirits finished with one incarnation and awaiting the next.

"Is Turtle . . ."

Turtle is a special case. She has completed the Ninefold Path. You are most fortunate in her. She will serve as your familiar and should be helpful to you in dealing both with your own kind and with others sharing this realm with you.

Francie stroked and then cuddled the tortoiseshell in delight and welcome but immediately turned to the cat snuggled in the crook of her other arm. "What about it, Gift? I'm not the only one living here. I can see that you accept Turtle, but what do you think of the rest of this proposed invasion of our peaceful quarters?"

In answer, a pink tongue rasped across her chin, and the copper eyes slitted in pleasure as the black cat purred his complete assent.

SHADOWS

by Caralyn Inks

Jariel Belldancer ranged ahead of Wizard Sanja and the guardsmen spread out behind him, looking for signs easily missed from horseback. For two days his small band had searched the hills north of Fort Duval for Scholar Tabler and his twelve-year-old apprentice Marian.

Pacer, he subvocalized, *have you found anything?*

I might have.

Past experience with the camilacat had taught him to trust her hunches. Jariel increased his pace, then half stumbled over a grassy hillock.

"Blast it all to sea!" Behind him he heard the other men laugh. Sanja rode up, the reins of Jariel's horse in his fist. With a grin, he held them out, saying,

"I think it's time you rode for a while. Your feet are objecting to the work you're putting them to."

Jariel laughed, took the reins, and mounted. "To look at the foothills of Bramare Duval all appears smooth grass. What a deception!"

Sanja nodded, hitched his cape back over his shoulders. "By the One, how any could so pursue the study of bats as to get themselves lost is beyond me."

"Quiet!" Jariel held up his hand. "Pacer's talking to me."

I've found them, Minddancer.

Are they alive?

Yes. But they are imprisoned by a magical force. You'll find them behind the hill shaped like a crooked finger.

Jariel shouted to the men behind, "They're found." He glanced at Sanja. "It's a good thing you decided to come along. Pacer says they're trapped by magic."

"Magic? Out here?" With a flick of his fingers Sanja

124

indicated the land about them, the vast dip and roll of
the foothills of Bramare Duval. Except for an occasional
outcrop of stone and clusters of trees, the land appeared
empty of human habitation.

"As Pacer says, 'the unexpected is always found in the
least likely places.' " He laughed to himself when Pacer's
voice slid into his thoughts.

*It's good to hear some of what I taught you has stuck in
that selective memory of yours!*

The hill shaped like a crooked finger loomed ahead.
They slowed their pace, stopped on seeing Pacer. She sat
before a ragged opening in the earthen mound. In the
cave mouth Tabler and Marian could be seen supporting
one another. Apprentice Marian's arm was in a sling. As
they all dismounted, Tabler shouted, "Don't come any
further!"

Belldancer stopped beside Pacer, lightly touching the
cat's head. He could see no barrier preventing their escape, but did not doubt Tabler's warning.

"What happened here, Tabler?"

"We followed the bats to this cave. Once inside we
couldn't get out."

Marian interrupted. "Please, have you any food or
water?"

Jariel tossed them a water bag and a packet of dried
fruit. As they helped one another sit down, Jariel himself
matched the wizard's slow approach to the cave mouth.
Sanja's hands were stretched forth, eyes closed in concentration. Jariel clasped the seer's elbow to guide him
around a large rock. They were both within inches of
Marian and Tabler when there came an explosion of
light. Akin to lightning, it flashed across the opening.

Dazed, Jariel staggered and rubbed his eyes to rid
them of the afterimage seared on his inner eyelids. Tears
streamed down his cheeks as he hurried to Sanja. The
force had thrown the wizard a good ten feet from the
cave. As Jariel knelt down to raise his friend, Pacer said,
He's fine, Minddancer. Even so, relief coursed through
him when the man moaned. Jariel helped him sit up.

"The power sealing that cave is old," Sanja said, blinking his eyes. "So old it makes my back teeth ache.

Here," he grabbed Jariel's arm. "Help me up." Together
they walked back to the cave.

"If it's as old as you say, how can it still retain such
force?" asked Jariel.

"If I'm not mistaken, and I doubt that I am, this is the
work of the Wizardess Baltaz."

"Baltaz! How can that be possible? She's been dead
two hundred years."

"Even so. She was the most powerful mage of her
time. Her delight was creating intricate traps and puzzles
with spells made to last beyond her lifetime." Sanja turned
from him, a look of utmost concentration on his face,
and slowly began to pace back and forth before the cave
mouth. Jariel left him to join Pacer. She rested, out of
the hot sunlight, in the shade of a tree.

What do you make of all this?

She yawned, pink tongue curling up to shield her front
teeth. *If I had removed the bells the Healers placed in
your body would you have learned how to dance without
making a single bell chime?*

No.

*Then the answers to the questions you pose you must
seek yourself.*

With an inner sigh he hoped Pacer did not hear, Jariel
examined the area around the hill. Clumps of tough grass
thrust up from among the stone riddled ground, still
green though it was mid-autumn. He knelt down, fingering the earth. As he wiped the damp soil from his fingers
onto the grass, Jariel sniffed the air. Close by, there was
a source of water.

On the eastern edge of the hill he discovered a small
disturbance in the ground. Circling it, Jariel noted the
dried dung, only partially covered in dirt, the freshest
about three days old. There was also a tuft of reddish fur
snagged on a rock. Near the dung he saw a paw print.
Fox. Jariel turned back to Pacer.

*A fox has used this cave as a dwelling place. It has not
returned because the cave is now occupied by humans.
Tabler and Marian could enter but not leave. When the
mage tried to walk through, it repulsed him.*

And, she prompted.

If this wizardess was as powerful as history tells us, she could have set wards to allow only animals the freedom to come and go.

Why?

Jariel paused to review. *I think to hide her real purpose it was necessary that the cave appear normal. That is why ordinary humans cannot leave. They would carry the tale of a strange cave and someone Gifted would eventually investigate.*

Very good. But, my heart spirit tells me we only scratch the surface here. Come, let's talk with Tabler.

A chill slipped down Jariel's spine as Pacer mentioned her heart spirit. Over the years she had chosen to become his teacher and friend, he had developed a healthy respect for the times when her inner voice spoke. It usually called them to action, dangerous action.

Sanja met them, shaking his head and saying, "I can't find a weak point anywhere. I even tried to walk through without calling on my powers. It repulsed me, though not as violently. It's as if the barrier can tell I have the gift."

Jariel clasped the wizard's shoulder, turning him. "Let's see what Tabler can tell us."

The scholar looked exhausted. He held a wet cloth above Marian's hand so the moisture dropped gently on her injury. Her fingers were red, puffy, blistered. In several places, cracked skin oozed a bloody pus.

Jariel asked, "How was Marian injured?"

Tabler did not look up. "Foolish curiosity, Belldancer."

Jariel studied the bent head, the muscles across the scholar's shoulders tight with fear. "Tabler, look at me." In the old man's eyes were fear, exhaustion, and guilt. He conveyed all the distress of his position as Belldancer spoke.

"Is Duval in jeopardy?"

"I do not know."

Jariel motioned to the ten guardsmen that accompanied him. "Come forward. You and the Wizard Sanja will bear witness to Tabler's words." When they were settled about him, Jariel said, "Speak with truth before these witnesses."

At Jariel's nod, Tabler continued, grateful Belldancer

wore no warrior's knot in his hair. Had that been so, he and Marian would have to face the young man in a judgment dance for bringing either shame or peril upon Duval and its people. Peril they might bring, but only through foolish, not deliberate actions. "We followed the bats into the cave. We used the night lanterns Sanja made us. . . ."

Sanja eagerly interrupted. "Did they work?"

"Very well. Once our eyes were adjusted, we could see just fine. The dim light didn't bother the bats at all. In the course of studying them, we discovered something odd. This cave is quite large, larger than the hill containing it. In fact it seems to lead into a maze of caves and stone grottoes." He shook his head. "Strange, very strange. I'd like to make a study of it."

Jariel commented dryly, "If we can't get you out of there, you might just have the opportunity."

"Sorry, Belldancer." Tabler shook out the cloth he used to wet Marian's arm and laid it again gently over her injury. She moaned. "Does anyone have anything for pain?"

One of the guard leaned forward. "I have some brandy."

"Thank you, Marcan," Jariel said, taking the flask which he tossed to Tabler.

The scholar supported Marian and tipped the flask. She gagged. "I know it's awful, but it will help. There, that's enough. Now, lie down beside me." Tabler covered her with a cloak. "Try to sleep, brave one."

Jariel saw the fatigue on the old man's face. He hated to push Tabler, but he had to have more information. "You were saying?"

"My apprentice and I got turned around in the caves. As we were trying to find our way out, we saw a dim orange light. At first I thought it was moonlight shining in through the cave mouth. I became concerned, though, when the light brightened, stronger than any moon glow, the closer we approached." Excitement tinged his voice. He looked at Sanja. "We found a large cave. The walls were smooth, covered by a strange orange substance that glowed. The place reeked with magic, the very air was tinged with the scent of spent lightning. But the true wonder was the woman. She stood on a plinth in the center of the stone room."

"A woman!" Sanja leaned forward. "Is she alive? Where is she?" Not waiting for an answer he turned to Jariel.

"By the One! What if she is from Baltaz's time? What I—we could learn from her."

Tabler shook his head sadly. "Don't hold any hopes, Wizard. We ruined all."

"What do you mean," asked Jariel.

"She stood encased in a substance that rose up from the edges of the plinth. It had the appearance of flames carved from ice." Tabler cleared his throat, shifted on the ground. "Marian reached through a gap between the flames, to touch the woman's hand. At that moment, the woman opened her eyes. When she tried to speak to us, the flames burst into life, whipping to strike Marian." Tabler shuddered. "I can't get out of my mind the look in the woman's eyes and. . . ."

"What?" urged Jariel when Tabler did not continue.

Horror tinged the scholar's voice. "The flames began to consume the woman, though she tried to keep out of their reach. She screamed. Screamed for such a long time." Tabler covered his face with his hands. "We were responsible. Our presence had broken some balance of power. We could do nothing to save her. Unable to watch her destruction, we ran. Eventually we found our way back here, only to discover we couldn't leave." Exhausted, Tabler leaned back on his elbows. "Since then we've waited, hoping for rescue."

Minddancer, we must go see for ourselves.

Heart spirit calls?

Come, she commanded, in a voice he knew full well not to question. Jariel obediently moved with Pacer. Just before they passed the unseen barrier, Sanja grabbed his arm.

"By the One! What do you think you're doing?"

Jariel looked from the wizard's hand to his eyes. When Sanja released him, he said, "I am doing my job. You forget I represent Duval's Honor. What threatens our homeland must be faced by the current Belldancer. I must see if the magic centered here poses threat to our people."

Sanja released Jariel. "I'm sorry. You're my friend. Sometimes I forget you are more. What would you have us do?" He gestured to the guardsmen.

Belldancer thought a moment. "Send a messenger back to tell Lord Davan what has occurred. Have him bring supplies and a Healer for Marian. On the chance Pacer and I can win them free, have them bring a litter also. There's no way they could ride."

Minddancer!

"I come," he said aloud so all could hear. Just as he crossed the barrier, Sanja called,

"Take one of the lanterns. It'll be dark in those caves."

Jariel nodded, picked one up, and followed Pacer into the dim interior. Pacer caught the scent of Marian and Tabler. It seemed that hours passed as they moved from one cave to the next, often having to backtrack. From above came a constant scraping of wings and claws. Once the lantern light struck just right and Jariel saw a mother bat cradling her young while it nursed at her breast. He found it odd that such an alien beast cared for its young as humans did. No wonder Scholar Tabler studied them.

Minddancer, I smell burnt flesh.

Though he strained to catch the odor, they had to walk several paces more before he picked it up. In the distance the dim orange light Tabler had described broke the darkness. Jariel wanted his hands free to meet any danger, so outside the chamber he set down the lantern. As they crossed into the cave, Pacer murmured, her mind voice a whisper,

My heart spirit pounds with the residue of power just released here. She padded over to the plinth and sniffed at its base.

Beware! She turned suddenly and leaped, knocking Jariel to the stone floor.

The walls flared with orange light. Whiplike flames of icy white curled up from the edges of the plinth. Behind the white fire the ashes of the dead woman stirred and became a miniature whirlwind.

About them sounded a hum, a deep bass note that

vibrated through Jariel. Through his touch on Pacer's body he could feel that thrumming. The light flaked away from walls and ceiling. Each sun-tinged mote spun in independent motion, casting its own light. Those gathered above the plinth formed an orange whirlwind. The tip of that sparkling mass spun down into the swirling body ashes, merging with them. Now the white-ice flames, edging the plinth, curved back from the magic storm, arching down like petals to almost touch the floor.

Jariel was aware of Pacer's claws piercing his leather breeks, but the pain did not distract him from what he saw forming from the mixture of body ashes and orange sparks.

Bones. With each rotation of the magic force, muscles, organs, breasts, then skin were layered on that skeletal foundation.

The sound changed, turned into the pulsating beat of a heart. Now the chest wall of the re-formed woman heaved, then the rhythm grew steady. The last of the sparks and ashes drifted down over her, leaving behind sun-silver body hair. Her eyes opened and focused on him.

Jariel leapt to his feet and raced toward her. For perhaps a count of three breaths no flames showed and she was free. She ventured to move, to speak. Like striking snakes the petals of flame curled back into place, fire dancing about her. She screamed.

Pacer! We must do something. Jariel stretched his hands out to wrench her from the plinth.

With a leap Pacer grabbed the back of the man's leather vest and jerked. *No! Don't touch her.* Pacer reared to set both paws on Jariel's chest, knocking him from his feet. Grief tinged her mind voice. *There is nothing we can do. The cycle has begun again.*

Dazed, Jariel asked, *Cycle?*

She'll be consumed, then reformed repeatedly. Pacer sat back, tail flicking back and forth. Her gray-gold eyes met his. *There is more at stake here than just the woman.*

Jariel tried to concentrate, but the woman's screams ripped through him. *More important than preventing the death of a human being?*

Pacer touched his face with her nose. That rare sign of

affection comforted him. He breathed deeply and rolled on his side away from the plinth, refusing to look up. *What are you trying to tell me?*

What did she say before the fire struck?

Jariel suppressed the urge to wring Pacer's neck. How could she answer him with a question now? *It didn't make much sense. She said to bring her her shadow.*

Pacer turned. *Look behind you.*

He stood. Turned. Then froze. A shadow had formed on the wall, but not a human one. Across the rough stone the shadow's contortions were painful to behold. A great rack of antlers nearly touched its back and dark wings fought to fly from the torment consuming it. *What's the shadow of an immortal Pierdon doing here?* Memory stirred—what did he know—not enough! Jariel all but growled when Pacer spoke.

What is its source?

Belldancer studied it. The Pierdon reared, shadow hooves slashing. From its back legs a fainter streak of darkness crossed the cave floor, flowed up the plinth to the woman! He cringed at the sight of her blackened flesh. *Pacer, isn't there anything we can do?*

At this moment, no. Now, what is the shadow's source?

She is. But why doesn't she cast her own? At that moment memory clicked in and he knew.

No. It's not possible. He knelt down, eyes level with Pacer's. *Is this the lost one the Pierdon have searched for all these years?*

It is. One of their own has carried the burden of the woman's shadow all this time. Now that the balance of power is broken Baltaz's doom is upon them both. Their eyes met with perfect understanding. Jariel quoted one of her teachings back to her. *The one who sees a problem is responsible for its solution.* Pacer butted his shoulder,

Come on, let's go.

Wait. I want to check something. Jariel walked over to the wall where the Pierdon's shadow crawled. *This whole thing is odd, but should a shadow be so thick?*

Don't touch it! Pacer sniffed the wall, nose almost touching the shadow. She growled. *This is the outer shell*

of an evil more foul than you can imagine. Look at the hind legs.

A wave rippled up the shadow legs and on throughout the dark body. Where it moved, the shadow thickened. The wave then reversed its course, traveling back to the ashy remains from which it came. *What does it mean?*

It's her life force. Now let's get out of here.

Jariel paused long enough to pick up Tabler's lantern. Quickly he followed Pacer. She was difficult to see in this light. Because she was a camilacat, Pacer's fur took on the coloration of the objects nearest her. Now she was all shades of gray. Tiny threads of red coursed up and down her guard hairs where the lantern light touched her.

Jariel came to a complete stop. *By the great sea, Pacer, how am I to get past the barrier?*

Pacer slowed, looked at him over her shoulder. *It's not as difficult a problem as you think.*

I don't understand, he said, walking beside her. *There's no difficulty in your passing through, but like Tabler and Marian, I won't make it.*

They hold no magic in their bones. That is why they're bound.

Pacer, you're not implying I'm like Wizard Sanja, are you? I cannot perform feats of power. He flinched at the tone of her reply.

No. But you are more like him than the Tablers of this world. Think, Jariel. What are you?

I am Duval's Belldancer. I represent the honor of all her people, her justice and pride.

I am relieved to know your brain still works, she said dryly. Pacer let a few heartbeats pass, then said with a sigh. *Haven't you realized, yet, that as you move through the phases of the dance you bring to it what no other Belldancer in Duval's history has?*

Shaken by what she implied, Jariel paused. He rested his hand on her shoulder until she faced him. *No. How could I? My training differed in no respect with those others who competed for Cavis Belldancer's place when she retired.*

Jariel, your lack of knowledge is the fault of this teacher. Forgive me. I assumed you knew.

Knew what? he asked, and sighed when Pacer cocked her head quizzically. *No. Not another question.*

In dance practice you only reach Warrior level by first moving through all the phases which come before it. Why?

You know all that, he said in exasperation.

Even so, repeat it.

If I didn't, I would injure my body. But more importantly, my mind wouldn't be prepared. Each movement, from first to last, has a corresponding mental and emotional exercise. If I've done it correctly, my body, mind and emotions function as one—in tune with and an extension of my surroundings. I am unified, whole. Only when I reach that state can I function as Belldancer, make the judgments so Duval's Honor is maintained.

Pacer reared up, hooking her claws over the edge of his sword belt. *Why else do I call you Minddancer, been willing to teach you the movements and thought patterns of the camilacats? No other Belldancer has reached this state of oneness with self and the world around you.*

But we all were taught from childhood the dance would bring us to that point.

She freed him. *Yes. A goal of perfection which broke the hearts of many who reached for it and found themselves lacking. Now, come. Begin such exercises as you can do walking. It's late and the doom Baltaz placed on the Pierdon and the woman will not wait for us.*

Pacer passed through the barrier. The setting sun etched her body with gold-red light. She turned to face him. *Dance.*

Jariel nodded. Needing room to dance he motioned Tabler, Marian, and the Healer now with them aside. Beyond the barrier he saw Lord Davan, Sanja, and several guardsmen. On the way back he had done the mental exercises, increased his pace to the point his muscles were loosened. Hands at his sides, he bowed his head, honoring the One. Slow in the beginning, he directed the muscles along his spine to move. Then he flexed the large muscles in first one leg, opposite arm, then the other leg and arm. The pattern must be whole.

In a distant part of his mind, Jariel monitored each

flowing movement as if he still wore bells. Not a one must chime. Defeat was not an option.

He tested finger tendons, let the horror of the burning woman slide out of his mind onto the slick bones forming his hands. With slow grace he released that painful memory through fingertips. Relief, in the form of increased energy, suffused him.

The welcome voice/presence of Pacer intertwined with the flow of mind and body patterns he was creating.

Good. Will you join with me and dance the dance of mind and body?

Jariel merged with the wild, arrogant, yet loving personality of the camilacat. In his mind came the mental image he had of her, a spiral of brightness, awe inspiring in its grace and power. He followed—joining body, mind, and emotions in the pattern she created until he mirrored each movement.

All unknowing he surpassed her, became in truth Belldancer and led the way.

Pain! He staggered. The unity of the dance shattered. Jariel moaned at the loss. Pacer's voice broke through the agony. *Open your eyes.* Immediately following her words, hands gripped his shoulders, then he was embraced.

"By the One," shouted Sanja, "I'd like to know how you did that!"

Jariel leaned heavily on his friend, then pushed away. "Oh, it was just something my teacher suggested I try." He was surprised to see full darkness, relieved only by firelight and the rising moons. The aroma of stew was like a lance point in his belly. "My lord," he said, ignoring his hunger. He bowed to Davan standing a little beyond the wizard. "We have a problem." In a few words he told what they had learned in the cave.

Awe tinged Davan's voice, "All these many years the lost pair were only a two-day ride from Fort Duval." He shook his head, then turned, calling out in his usual crisp, decisive manner,

"Marcan, bring our horses. Belldancer and I ride to the Pierdon's valley."

A beautiful voice interrupted. "That won't be necessary, my lord. We are here." Three Pierdon came into the firelight, two supporting a third between them. None were amazed they had not heard the Pierdon's approaching hoof beats or sensed their presence. These immortals were the embodiment of pure magic and could pass unseen among a crowd. Their deer-shaped bodies bore the wings and tails of great birds and were as beautiful as their voices.

Pacer, why didn't you warn me they were near? he asked, hurrying to meet them.

She laughed. *I do not hold the power to know when they are near. I'm as head blind as the rest of you two-footers where the Pierdon are concerned.*

Jariel bowed deeply before the trio. He had no idea that the color brown came in so many shades. Some of their feathers were even tinged with a bronzy green-brown. But when he met their eyes, he faltered. They were a blue so bright that it seemed to him he was pierced by three pairs of swords.

"Belldancer, I am the speaker Myatin. Indeed, you can help us, but for now may we bring our companion to the fire? Nytira needs warmth."

Jariel stepped aside, gestured for them to precede him and saw on the ground three shadows, one a woman writhing in torment. Instinctively he called to Pacer. *Look, the shadow.*

I see, Minddancer.

It's thick, the weight's so great the Pierdon can hardly walk.

And it will grow heaver, gaining more substance until. . . .

Jariel was surprised to hear hesitancy in her voice. He had never known her to be unsure about anything. *Until?* Instead of answering him, she headed toward the fire. Not pushing the issue, he followed her.

Lord Davan crouched down by Nytira, who lay near the fire. "Is there anything we can do for him?" he asked.

"Yes. You can lend us your Belldancer." said Myatin.

Davan met Jariel's eyes and at the slight nod said, "He's yours."

Myatin asked, "Jariel, would you introduce me to your teacher?"

Jariel touched the big cat lightly, wondering how the Pierdon knew. "This is Pacer, much more than teacher."

"It is good you know that." Myatin touched noses with the camilacat, then reached out and nuzzled Jariel's forehead. "Pacer agrees to help us, too. But you are both tired. Eat while we tell you what we know."

Sanja brought them both food and drink, then sat down beside them. He leaned over and whispered, "Why do you get all the excitement?"

"Its my nose." Jariel said, pulling on it. "It's so long, it's always getting me into things."

You can say that again, said Pacer.

It's my no. . . .

Enough! The Pierdon waits.

Jariel apologized, "I'm sorry, Myatin."

"No, do not. Laughter causes even fear to flee for a space of time."

"Please," said Lord Davan, "We'd like to hear what you can tell us of the problem facing us."

"When Baltaz was defeated in the War of Sorrows, she was forced to free the Pierdon she had imprisoned along with their human counterparts. It was not until too late that we realized one of our kind was still missing. Many years after the war we found him wandering in the Hills of Bramare Duval. He had lost all memory of where he had been and only knew his shadow-mate was somewhere here in the North." Myatin nodded in Davan's direction. "The lord of that time gave us Blue Valley for our own. The Pierdon who made their home there continued the search. For two hundred years Nytira's human shadow remained a light burden."

"Until," Sanja exclaimed, "Tabler and Marian broke the balance of power."

"You are correct, Wizard."

"Will you," Sanja asked with great humility, "allow me to watch you unravel Baltaz's spell?"

"I am sorry, that will not be possible. We cannot break it, for it is warded against us. If we should get too close to the barrier, the spell will unleash its full doom. Look at it. See, it already knows we are near."

With the rest of the group, Jariel looked. The barrier

now glowed with a nacreous yellow light. He subvocalized to Pacer, *Who sees the problem gets it. Shall we?*

Yes.

"Myatin, what would you have us do?"

"First tell me all you know." The Pierdon listened intently to all Jariel said. "The wave you saw travel both ways was not just her life force, but Nytira's as well. Her rebirth is at the price of his life. When she burns, he suffers. When she dies, Nytira learns of death. If she and his shadow are ever retrieved, the human and the Pierdon will be forever changed. She will experience a touch of immortality, he humanity, and ultimately death.

"But that is not what is important here and now. If they are not rescued and soon, there will be let loose on this land indestructible entities."

Lord Davan leaned forward. "Just what threatens my land."

"Baltaz's doom." Myatin looked at each of them in turn. "Pierdon are immortal. We are a living form of pure magic. Baltaz wanted this for herself. When she could not get it, she set this trap. The power in the woman, the Pierdon, and that which Baltaz bound into the spell, will bleed into the shadows until they take on life themselves. Soon it will reach a saturation point and they will break free of their hosts. These shadow entities will not have the ability to reason, they will experience only one thing, hunger. And to live they must feed. Their food is the life energy given off by all creatures. Even the earth itself will be stripped. There is no known power that can defeat them once they are free."

"How can Pacer and I stop this?"

"I am sorry, Belldancer, I do not know. But if you can bring the woman to us, whole, I think we can return to them their own shadows. In the process we hope to dissipate Baltaz's spell causing the life force exchange happening between them."

Jariel knelt down before Nytira, Pacer sat so close to his side he could feel her side rise and fall with her breathing. It was even, strong, just the opposite of the spellbound Pierdon's. The velvet skin around the creature's mouth was turning gray. Jariel leaned forward and spoke softly. "May I touch the shadow?" then he nearly wept when he heard the Pierdon's broken whisper in reply. The beauty was destroyed, he was sure, by screaming.

"Yes. It is safe at this moment."

Jariel gently laid his hand on the woman's shadow. It felt sticky, and icy-hot, both at the same time. The fine hairs on his body rose in response. *Pacer?*

No use waiting. Let's go. No one stopped them.

This time it did not take so long to reach the orange cave. Jariel paused, *Pacer, I'll wager anything you want that Baltaz bespelled the plinth. The moment I pull the woman off, poof! goes Baltaz's Doom.*

What are you going to put in her place?

If I thought I could get away with using a rock I'd do it. There's too much at stake to make the wrong choice and Baltaz loved traps. It'll have to be flesh—mine.

The silence between them was filled with unspoken thoughts and feelings. Finally Pacer said,

So, it is to be the Warrior's dance.

In answer Jariel loosened his hair, pulled a bone comb and a leather thong from his belt pouch. He combed his hair, making sure each strand was free of tangles, then bent over. The silky mass nearly swept the floor. Deftly he smoothed it from nape to ends. He gathered it up, twisting it into a warrior's knot, tying it off with the thong. *Friend. Teacher. Be with me in my mind as I prepare.*

I am here, Pacer reassured.

Jariel moved through the phases of the dance. The disciplined action merged into grim joy as fatigue gave way and strength sang along tendons, bones, and muscles. He shook from his fingers the anger he felt for Nytira's broken voice, the woman's pain, the need to save his world.

He felt Pacer's love, her total acceptance of him—faults and all. But he could not give up the thought of the real possibility his own blackened flesh might adorn the plinth. He cried out.

Help me. I can't let go of my fear!

Minddancer, give it to me. Let me carry it for awhile.

With a sob he let go, felt her draw his imprisoning emotion into herself. He danced lighter, faster. Jariel had no idea what a heavy burden his fear had been until he gave it away. Then, with a last movement, he flicked even that relief away. The Warrior state settled deep into his mind. Purpose and calm assurance and clarity of mind filled him. Jariel whirled on into the orange cave, now his battleground.

Though he kept close to the inner wall he was careful to let no part of his body touch it. *You keep an eye on the body ashes. I have an idea I want to check out.* He touched the shadow. It felt the same as the one weighing down Nytira. He pulled out his comb and lightly touched the orange wall. When nothing happened, he pressed harder.

What are you doing? Pacer demanded. *Trying to get snarls out of stone?*

Are you asking ME questions? He reached down and scratched behind her ears, knowing she spoke as she did to hide the fear she felt for him. *You know the fruit jerky the cooks make at harvest time?*

Now's a fine time to be talking about food. She glanced up at him. *Wait. Isn't that the stuff you peel off oiled paper? Jariel, you can't mean to. . . .*

He nodded, slowly sliding the comb beneath the thickened shadow. *Are the ashes moving?*

No.

Good. He continued to move the comb under the shadow until he reached its highest point; the antlers. He lifted the comb. The shadow peeled away from the wall, curling down upon itself.

His hands were shaking so much his knuckles had almost touched the wall. Frightened that an inadvertent action would trigger Baltaz's Doom, Jariel minddanced until thinking and body responses were again calm. Pretending the shadow was nothing more than a large piece of fruit jerky, he pulled the last remnants of Nytira's shadow from the wall. Pacer stayed close by his side as he rolled it toward the plinth. Two feet away he stopped.

Do you think you and the woman can drag it out of the cave?

Pacer nudged it with her nose. It did not budge. *We will just have to.* She reared up, putting her paws on his shoulders, *Minddancer. Look at the flames. There are spaces between them. When you dance, think of them as bells that must not chime.* Then she did something she had never done before. With the tip of her tongue, she kissed him.

Moved, he grabbed her ears and rested his head against hers before he stepped back. Without another word Pacer touched the plinth. From the walls came the hum and orange sparks flaked away, reforming above the now spinning body ashes.

Jariel crouched, ready to leap. He watched flesh encase the woman's bones. When the last of the ashes drifted down over her, he grabbed her hand and jerked. He leapt as she passed him. He heard her cry out when she slammed onto the stone floor. As the white petals of fire curled up to surround him, Jariel yelled, "Grab your shadow and run."

Pacer's voice came to him as if from a great distance. *We have the shadow. Remember . . . bells. . . .*

The flames were like ice. So cold they burned. Jariel danced. Flowed in a counter movement to the magic. A touch, akin to boiling ice, skimmed his back. He wanted to scream but contained the cry and thrust the pain out through the soles of his feet. Nothing must break the Warrior state of mind.

In the corner of his mind he heard a single bell chime when the flame touched him again. No! There will be no more! I am Duval's Belldancer. Baltaz's wizardry will not take that from me. I dance and no bells chime.

Jariel reached within himself, called up the memory of Pacer leading him through the barrier. He had followed her. What if he followed the flames?

With renewed determination he slowed the dance to observe the flames. Sanja had taught him that all magic, high or low, had to have a pattern or it did not work. Then he saw it. Every fourth flame moved widdershins, the two in between arched outward, then in a one count of his breathing, they moved inward, but with a drift to the left.

Keeping the pattern fixed in his mind, Jariel danced. Danced till the sweat so burned his eyes that he closed them only to discover the same pattern in his mind, but clearer. In between the flames were gaps, ragged about their edges. Instinctively he knew it was caused by the fraying of a spell two hundred years old. He wondered if he could widen the gaps. Keeping his eyes tightly closed, concentrating only on the image in his mind, Jariel danced into a gap.

Pain lashed him. He pulled back, stifling a moan. Then he wanted to shout in joy. There, the space where he danced was now wider, more frayed. For a moment he faltered, knowing full well when he danced into each gap, the flames would reach him. By the One, he did not want to die like the woman.

Pacer, he cried out, but there was no reply. For the first time in their relationship she was not there, a secure presence in his mind. But just the thought of her calmed him. He remembered who he was and who he represented. He was a Belldancer in the service of the people of Duval. Committed to them and to the land, he accepted that he must face this danger alone.

He danced. Ice-fire etched his body. Still Jariel Belldancer moved in a rhythm counter to the magic, turning pain into power.

In and out of the spaces between the flames he dipped, turned, retreated only to repeat the dance in a new place. The gaps widened. Beneath his feet the plinth trembled as if shaken by a giant fist. Heartened, he increased speed. The flames were shoulder high, then waist high. They whipped about his legs and feet and his clothing burst into flame, then whirled into ashes. Jariel danced, though he could no longer rise above the pain. The leather soles of his shoes began to smolder when the plinth violently shook, knocking him to his knees. The icy flames grew smaller, flickering like a candle flame in a draft, then died. Huge cracks formed in the plinth. Jariel rolled off, only to be struck on the head. He looked up. Fissures were forming in the ceiling and walls of the cave as parts of the stone fell. He had to get out of here!

Jariel struggled to stand, caught a glimpse of his legs, and was sickened. In places he could see bone. The ground shook. He fell. Agony. A wall of blackness threatened to engulf him. At the last moment he cried out.

Pacer! She answered with her body as well as her mind voice. He tried to speak as she ran toward him.

Hush. Be still. She nuzzled him. *All is well.*

He felt her mental touch course over his mind, then press hard. Pain faded—was gone. Over her head he saw Sanja and Duval.

There, she said with satisfaction, *that should hold you until we get you to the healers.*

Lord Davan crouched down, covering him with his cape. "It's over, Belldancer. No. Don't try to talk. The woman and Nytira are recovering. The shadows are bound. More can wait. I want to get you out of here." Jariel knew better than to argue when his lord spoke in that tone of voice. Carefully Davan and Sanja rolled him over, then lifted him by the edges of the cape.

Sanja grasped the improvised litter at Jariel's shoulders. "Next time," he leaned down to half-whisper, "let me have some of the fun."

Jariel answered from the very edge of consciousness, "Your nose isn't long enough."

THE EXECUTION

by A. R. Major

Having recently come across the archives of one of catdom's noblest kings, it has become my rare privilege to share with the public one of the written records of none other than Greywhiskers IV. It is not generally known that this royal representative of the feline race was one of the first in catdom to make use of the mechanical devices of the inferior humans to assist us where strict brute force is needed. All through recorded history our race has used the inferior humans by the simple device of offering them our limited love, and the poor, love-starved beings have been putty in our paws. But we must admit, this royal king found another way to make humans work for us!

This, then, is the tale as translated from Greywhisker's Chronicles.

It came to pass on a certain day at two in the morning, human time, that Greywhiskers IV was holding court. He chose this time as it was when most of the bothersome humans were asleep. His courtroom was situated in the alley known as Fish Head Lane, right behind the local shop where the humans printed their device called "newspapers."

From the top of the empty oil drum that served His Highness as the throne of his kingdom of Catasia, Greywhiskers ruled a kingdom of definite borders. On the north was the catdom of the Blue-eyes. The south ended at the local waterfront. It extended east to west from Fifty-third to Sixty-first Streets. In this area of Catasia, Greywhiskers' word was absolute, final, divine-right-of-kings-law, and he was constantly coming up with new ways to prove this truth.

144

He closed his eyes to almost slits in that disconcerting way of his as he observed the faces of the three visiting Blue-eyes in front of him. How long, he mused, had it been since that certain Siamese Tom had left his Park Avenue home to establish the catdom in the north, one based on the distinct citizenship of having blue eyes? Probably during the reign of Greywhiskers II.

Those visitors in front of him were glancing around his court nervously, in spite of being offered diplomatic immunity. Well, let the visitors sweat a little, it would keep them properly humble!

The cats that made up his royal court that night, in contrast to the visitors, were sitting around in a loose circle in a completely relaxed atmosphere. They sat on boxes or crates the careless humans had cast aside. The fence behind Greywhiskers was reserved for his five loyal advisors.

"And how is my brother ruler, Blue-eyes II's health these days?" inquired his majesty, after first permitting himself the luxury of a wide yawn.

"Excellent, Your Grace," intoned the guard standing to the right of the frightened female that he and another tomcat guard had escorted to the courtyard between them.

"That delights me exceedingly," replied the king of Catasia, wrinkling his ruff in displeasure at the harsh Siamese note in the visitor's voice. Then studying his visitor shrewdly, his exhalted majesty added, "And how may we be of service to one of the Blue-eyes' citizens?"

Taking this question as an invitation, the young female in her crouching position eased a little forward and said, "A boon, O mighty King. I crave revenge for my poor, dead kitten."

Humph, mused Greywhiskers, does she *really* want revenge or is this just a clever trick by her king to test my power and ability to rule? Is Blue-eyes II planning a territorial expansion, and are these really three clever spies? He must be certain that whatever report they took back to *their* king would bring honor to himself as king of Catasia! Long experience in intercat diplomacy had taught him to look beneath the surface of appearances to locate hidden meanings. He brought his right hind leg to the front, examined it critically, gave it a few licks of grooming, then permitted himself a soft purr of consolation.

"My heart goes out to a mother in her moment of sorrow," the king replied in a manner completely devoid of emotion. "And, now, feel free to give us the sad details. Then, if it so pleases us, we will pass judgment."

"It was one of your territory's citizens," interrupted one of the visiting bodyguard cats. "A certain boxer dog named Flintface killed the Lady Fluffa's child, your majesty!"

The king's reply was a rumbling yowl of displeasure. This was followed by a moment of tense silence, broken by the large cat on the king's right who spoke tersely.

"The king was speaking to *her,* not you! Be advised that in *this* court you will speak only when spoken to, or when you ask permission. Since you are apparently untaught in court procedure, this infraction will be overlooked *this* time, but if it occurs again, it could get your tail cut off . . . right behind your ears!"

There was another impressive silence, then the offending cat bobbed his head and said, "Permission to speak." After receiving the king's nod, he continued, "I wish to apologize for the interruption. No offense was intended."

"Apology accepted. Flintface, you say? Harump! I seem to remember something very recent and unpleasant concerning that name. Refresh our memory, Lady Scribe."

Of course he remembered every detail of the Flintface episode, but he would not miss a chance to demonstrate to these upstart strangers how excellent were the records this court kept.

A small striped female moved to the king's right, carefully licked an immaculate paw and intoned: "One moon and three nights ago, it was brought to our noble lord's attention that the organ grinder's monkey, one Peppo by name, had been chased away from his place of honest employment by a member of the canine tribe, one Flintface by name. It was further noted that this canine was only living here by your majesty's tolerance. It was this court's judgment to give said canine one fair warning, to wit: such conduct would not be tolerated in your majesty's catdom. Said warning was given the following day by the king's own knights, Sir Strongheart and Sir Fairhowl. End of record."

King Greywhiskers put on a show of feline fury aimed at impressing his foreign visitors. He succeeded admirably; never would they forget the picture of flattened ear anger that was frightful to behold. His voice became a sibilant hiss of rage, forgotten were his courtly manners.

"Sssso! That rebel thinks he can avoid *my* edict by going to a *friendly* neighborhood to commit his catacide, does he? He refuses to show remorse for his gangsterlike behavior, does he? Why, that obscenity on the face of this earth deserves to be cut up and used as fishbait! I swear by my royal kingship, that the only answer is his death! How votes the council?"

By this time the king had left his throne and was pacing back and forth in an angry crouch before the five royal advisors, his tail flicking back and forth in rage.

One by one the five cats on the fence nodded to their king, each giving a murderous yowl of assent and exposing the claws in the right forepaw like flashing sabers. The affirming vote was unanimous! Flintface was as good as dead!

The Royal Chamberlain, the cat who had corrected the visiting bodyguard's bad court manners, now placed himself between the Lady Fluffa and Greywhiskers' royal throne. He paused to impress his visitors with the seriousness of the moment, then gravely he spoke in measured tones.

"Be it noted by our visitors from the land of the Blue-eyes: King Greywhiskers the Fourth has heard and passed judgment on your request. We have condemned the gangster Flintface and will carry out his execution in such time as the Royal Executioner chooses."

Then, feeling the puzzled response of the visitors to the courtly language his king insisted upon using on formal occasions, he lowered his voice until only the visitors could hear and added, "Relax doll-face. You put the finger on the mutt, now the boys will be happy to bump him off!"

Resuming his courtly dignity, the Lord Chamberlain

yowled, "Will the Royal Executioner come forth and face his king?"

The circle of court cats moved aside to allow a wide lane for the king's chosen to enter. Even the visitors found themselves slinking backward to place as much distance as possible between themselves and that terrifying presence. Greywhiskers never batted an eyelash but thought gleefully to himself that he bet they did not have anything like that in *their* kingdom!

The approaching cat looked like death incarnate. He was a good six inches longer than the average adult Tom, and at least four pounds heavier. The tufts of hair on the tips of his ears showed that somewhere in his ancestors there had been a bobcat, which was further confirmed by his twitching stub of a tail. His coat suited his court position, for it was solid black from his nose to his tail. As he strutted slowly toward his king, massive muscles could be seen rippling under his glossy hide.

"Sir Ex," as he was known to the court, was a Tom without the slightest twinge of mercy. It was hard to believe he was the same bedraggled kitten that their king had saved from a storm sewer at the risk of his own life. that had been two years ago, and "Sir Ex" had rewarded his king with a devotion unparalled in catdom.

"How can I serve my lord?" the big cat murmured with a voice like an idling diesel engine.

"You know what the boss wants," responded the Chamberlain. "How soon can we get some action against this glorified fleabag?"

"I should be ready to lower the boom on the mark by 5:45 Wednesday morning, on the execution field. Will this be soon enough to please my king, or would he prefer I cut him to ribbons tonight while he sleeps?"

"I prefer the formal execution. It will better impress other members of the canine tribe that might become troublesome."

Two days, mused the king, his mind racing like a calculator. Two days will give sufficient time for the visitors to report back to their king, and then . . . he decided on a bold stroke of diplomacy.

He waved a regal paw to an elderly cat at the head of

his loyal advisors. It was evident from the elder's arthritic walk and the white hairs on his muzzle, that this was one of the oldest dwellers in Catasia. After consulting with him in subdued tones, the king nodded to his hit man in satisfaction.

"The Royal Astrologer informs me the stars are right and the weather should be good on the day you have chosen. I trust your judgment in this matter, for you have never failed me."

Then turning his attention to his visitors, he continued, "Return to your king, most welcome visitors, and inform him that he is invited to send a detail to observe this execution, or if he should choose, to even come himself to observe our royal justice!"

We'll teach that upstart not to doubt *our* ability to cope with any situation! His entire contingent of body-guards could not polish off a dog the size of Flintface! Wait until he sees Sir Ex in action, his whiskers will have a permanent curl!

Now if they had been human beings, the entire court would have gasped aloud at their king's audacity. Suppose Sir Ex failed to bring it off? But being well-mannered cats, they merely squinted their eyes and flicked the tips of their tails in anticipation of the great event.

The court broke up and the citizens went their various ways. Soon all Catasia would be buzzing with the king's daring invitation, but it was tacitly understood that no information would be leaked to anyone friendly with the intended victim; for cats know well the value of guarding secrets, and in all the animal world, no one can keep a secret better than they.

Sir Ex passed the word: he had an urgent message for the Sirs Fairhowl and Strongheart, they were to report to him at once. They knew better than to keep him waiting.

The message was simple; the "mark" was to be placed under constant observation. It was urgent that he know Flintface's personal status by 5:30 Wednesday morning. In the meantime, Sir Ex had some work to do on the important matter of checking out the execution machine.

So saying, he moved over to his favorite "scratching post," a nearby telephone pole, and proceeded to peel

off great splinters of wood while he exercised his powerful back muscles. Without a sound the other two knights
melted away into the morning darkness.

His two scouts came back and reported to Sir Ex the
following evening, but their report was not good. Their
target was in bad with his owners. They had caught
Flintface chasing cars and had chained him in his yard for
an indefinite time.

"That's it, boss. You will have to postpone the action
until the 'mark' serves his time and gets out of the clink!"

In the stream of cat profanity that followed this suggestion the two royal knights gathered the following information: Sir Ex felt that dog couldn't do anything right,
not even to keeping an appointment to depart this life;
he was saddled down with two asinine helpers who did
not know that you simply did not put off affairs of state;
and by the cat-god's headdress, *he* for one was going to
make the deadline if he had to do everything all by
himself!

Then Sir Ex resumed the calm, probing air that all
catdom had come to fear and respect. Was the mark on a
leash, rope, or chain? Were they certain? How long was
it? Where was it fastened, to the fence or a peg in the
ground? Were they *positive?*

Over and over the questions were asked until Sir Ex
had an accurate picture of the situation. Flintface was in
his backyard, chained to a wrought iron fence about six
feet long, and the chain had a snap lock on it. Clearly the
cats would have to enlist outside help. And he knew
where that help was going to have to come from.

"Where does this monkey Peppo live?" he snarled at
the other two knights. Silently they led him over rooftops
to the home of some sleeping humans only fifteen minutes away form the dog's home. There, sleeping in a
basket on the back porch of this house lay their future
partner, Peppo, sound asleep.

Peppo awoke to face the meanest looking cat he had
ever seen. It was watching him from the other side of the
back porch screen.

"Be silent, little one, and listen and you won't get

hurt," hissed the terrible face. "Our king has honored you by permitting you to aid us in carrying out his orders. Do you remember the big boxer dog named Flintface that chased you down the street a moon ago?"

The little monkey hissed and bared his teeth to show that he remembered the humiliating incident.

"He was warned for that, then committed an even more evil crime. The king has put out a contract on him, and we intend to collect it tomorrow morning. It must be done in a very public way to be a warning to other mutts not to step out of line, get the picture?"

The little monkey jumped up and down to show his excitement.

"I'm glad you approve," the big black cat said sarcastically, while the two other knights smirked to themselves in the shadows.

Then he continued, "You will come along with my two aides tomorrow morning early. Can you get out, or will I have to slash this screen for you?"

Peppo assured them he could open the simple screen door without any trouble.

"Good. You will go with them to Flintface's house, but be sure to stay *outside* the fence. If he is asleep, you will reach through the fence and unsnap his chain, understand?"

"You want to unleash *that creature* in our community?" the little monkey whispered with terror in his voice.

"Only long enough, little one, to take him to his place of execution. Do you remember what happened to the bulldog Ironjaw several moons ago?"

The monkey nodded affirmatively. "But that was an *accident,* or was it. . . ?" and here his voice trailed off as he looked at the black cat's unblinking eyes. "What happens if he's awake?"

"Then my two knights will keep his attention until you can do your job, and little friend, *do not fail us* or the next time we see you . . ." He made a knifelike movement of one extended claw across his throat. If it had been possible for a monkey to turn pale, Peppo at that moment would have turned snow white!

*   *   *

If any humans had paid attention at 5:00 on Wednesday morning they would have seen an amazing sight, for every cat in Catasia surrounded the square in front of the local printshop. And each one moved into their chosen position without making a sound. The few humans moving about were too concerned with their early morning tasks to pay attention to the affairs of cats!

And though the visiting cortege of cats was burning up with curiosity about the method of execution of a beast so large, the host animals offered not the least bit of information. "Keep them in the dark until the last minute," had been their king's final order.

Greywhiskers led the visiting king to the second floor flower box of the house of the people who claimed to "own" him. He, with the wisdom of his race, merely permitted them the honor of feeding him, or providing shelter when the weather was bad, and he paid for that with a few purrs or an occasional dead mouse left on their doorstep. The box had a perfect view of the pavement in front of the printshop facing them.

"Nice view," King Blue-eyes remarked politely.

"Thank you," replied Greywhiskers equally politely. "The large warehouse to the right is my private game preserve. If you'd like, we can go in there after the execution and have a hand at a rat killing."

Blue-eyes permitted a deep purr of anticipation and replied with gleaming eyes, "Why, thank you, now you are talking *my* language. I'd be delighted to accept your invitation!"

Talking your language indeed, fumed the host king! Why I'd drop dead before I spoke the sacred tongue with that Siamese accent!

Five-thirty sharp arrived, and right on schedule two large, powerful trucks backed up to the printshop doors. Few words were spoken by the humans as they began loading the large bundles of freshly printed newspapers onto the trucks. Unnoticed by the humans, a large black cat with a twitching stub of a tail stalked slowly down the center of the street. He looked like an old time western gunslinger about to "call out" an opponent. He was the picture of poise, confidence and . . . murder.

"My Royal Executioner," purred Greywhiskers proudly. "I taught him everything he knows. You are about to see poetry in action, and he *never* misses."

Blue-eyes kept his thoughts to himself. True, he had never seen a cat quite like the one below, but polishing off a dog the size of a boxer was not an easy task for a dozen cats! No, let the old goat brag, I'll try not to laugh in his face when this is all over!

But Sir Ex was not as confident as he appeared. As he heard the first truck pull away from the loading dock, he was wondering what was stopping his fellow knights.

Sir Fairhowl and Sir Strongheart *did* have a problem. While Peppo was safely protected outside the wrought iron fence, the dog was crowding close to it making it impossible for the little monkey to unsnap the chain. Further, the violent barking and growling of the dog might bring an irate human being into the picture at any moment.

With their natural inborn sense of timing, both knights realized now was *the time* to get the big dog moving. Both thought about having to explain their failure to Sir Ex. No way!

"Flank attack! Draw sabers, ho!" snarled Sir Fairhowl.

Both cats flashed in toward the dog's unprotected backside, both struck a flank simultaneously, their sharp claws cutting red trails of blood down his rear legs.

With a howl of rage and pain, Flintface spun to meet his attackers. This was the opening the little monkey was looking for; he rapidly reached through the fence and unsnapped the chain. He never looked back, for his job was done. Quickly Peppo leaped into a tree and sped for home.

There was a strangled roar from the dog as he dashed after the two cats. In his rage, he sounded just like he was strangling. Never questioning his sudden freedom, he dashed down the street pursuing his fleeing adversaries, his length of chain bouncing behind and kicking up sparks from the pavement. It never occurred to the stupid beast that the two fleeing felines *could* have escaped easily up a post or over a fence. This was war! Death to catdom!

Back at the king's observation box, the sound of the back doors on the second truck being slammed almost drowned out the distant sound of a very angry, baying dog chasing two fleeing cats. This was going to be close, Sir Ex reasoned.

As the truck slowly moved away from the loading dock, its headlights picked up the sight of two large alley cats racing across the road in front of them. They did not pick up the form of the larger black cat crouched facing the side road from which the other cats had just emerged. Sir Ex rose to his full height and moved gracefully to the center of the road.

The truck's headlights illuminated the scene like a stage production. There was Sir Ex in the classic feline challenge pose: mouth open, back arched, stub of a tail pointed skyward, right forepaw extended with claws shining, ears flattened close to the skull, and mouth issuing the insult no red-blooded dog could ignore.

"Mangy kitten killer! You who would run from the shadow of an adult cat! Come face the anger of Sir Ex!"

The enraged dog forgot the other knights and turned to face the challenger. At a normal time he would have thought twice about taking on *this* cat, but in the heat of the recent chase, all sanity seemed to have left him. He spun in his tracks and raced after the black cat fleeing directly into the path of the approaching truck.

At the last instant, with split second timing, Sir Ex pivoted and aimed himself at the exact center of the truck. He crouched just in time for the big machine to rumble safely over him. The pursuing dog, being taller, did not have that option.

The heavy truck bumper struck the boxer with a re-sounding crunch. He did not even whimper as he went spinning through the air, to land as a bloody mass of bones and fur beside the road.

Greywhiskers smirked contentedly. "My Royal Executioner never disappoints me," he gloated.

Blue-eyes looked as shocked as it is possible for a cat to do and just nodded his head in admiration. The many cats watching in the shadows melted silently into the pre-dawn darkness. Their feeling was one of complete confidence; as long as Greywhiskers IV was on the throne, Catasia would be secure.

The following conversation was reported to the chronicler by one Inkdevil, mascot cat of the printshop, who liked to ride the newspaper truck on its daily rounds dropping off papers.

"Hey Jack," the truck driver said to his helper, "did you see *that?* That's the *third* time this year that ol' bob-tailed alley cat has gotten a dog killed by a truck. D'you think he planned it that-a-way?"

"Naw," Jack replied. "Cats 'r dumb animals. Jes' one of them coincidences if ya ask me!"

HERMIONE AT MOON HOUSE

by Ardath Mayhar

FROM THE JOURNAL OF HERMIONE:
The Grange (Moon House)
Oxbridge
June, 1884

For the past Years, these Journal Entries have been quiet—even dull, for the Tastes of some. However, following my former Position, with its disastrous Ending, that has come as a welcome Relief. Dullness, when one is a Familiar to Adepts, equates with Peace, and that is desirable to lone Females engaged in doing their Duty and rearing their Young in a conventional Manner.

Sir Athelstan Girby is, by and large, a very pleasant Gentleman. His astronomical Investigations tend to be most convenient, taking place as they do by Night. The Calculations that he performs by Day in his Study are not likely to cause unexpected Consequences of the sort that Sorcerers tend to create.

In addition, he is partial to Kits, which is most gratifying to their proud Mama. My new Litter is at this Moment at Play about his Feet and rolling on his Lap as he absently fondles their furry Ears. The Opportunity this gives me to write in my Journal is advantageous, for in my past Employment it often fell out that my Master kept me so occupied that I became remiss in my monthly Reports to the Coven of Familiars.

Sir Athelstan's Work, I must admit, is not something that I Understand, even after two Years of constant Attention. The Astrolabe, the Mathematical Calculations, the measurings upon Charts of the Heavens, all those are

156

a Mystery to one trained in the more Occult Practices of Magicians.

However, as he does not need my Presence or my Skills in the Practice of his Art, that is of no Consequence. This has become most gratifying, as I was never one to court closer Acquaintance with Demons and suchlike Conjurations. The Stars, the Moon, and the Planets keep their proper Distance, as well they should, leaving our quiet Household to its own Devices.

My Reports to the Coven are, of course, invariably Dull and without Substance. It has occurred to more than One of my Peers that an Astronomer, who is no true Magician, should need no Familiar.

Being one who has always tried industriously to perform her Duty, I have also suggested to my Master that he might easily dispense with the Presence of so many Feline Persons within his Household. But Sir Athelstan became most Disturbed at the Suggestion, rising to his Feet and pacing to and fro in a most unsettled Manner.

"I am a lonely Man," he said to me in Reply. "And while an ordinary Cat, content to keep the Mice in order and to sit by the Fire and Purr, might suffice for Some, I require a more responsive Companion. Perhaps I do not use your special Abilities to their Fullest—indeed, I regret that you may feel somewhat Frustrated at the lack of such Exercise. Yet after enjoying the Company of Hortense, your lamented Predecessor, I could not find it in my Heart to return to more ordinary Domestic Pets."

At that Point he stopped and bent to look into my Eyes (which I must admit are a fetching Shade of Green), and to set his Hand lightly upon my Head. "You are my Friend, Hermione. After that, a mere Pet would just not Do."

Once, of course, I had thought over his Explanation, I could only agree. The Coven, after being apprised of his Needs, granted an extension of his special Privilege, and so we continue as we were, a Family in every Sense of the Word.

The Kits, of course, adore their large Playmate. Often I feel that they disrupt his Work, but when I call them to Order, Sir Athelstan almost always objects and keeps them Nearby. That pleases me, as a Mother, and yet I could only feel that it might lead to Disaster. However, I felt at the time that might be only a Reflection of the Culmination of my former Position.

Having one's Kit devour a mouse that happens to be one's Charge, however understandable such an Error might be, can only leave Scars upon the Memory of the Familiar involved. It has left me more Cautious than before, you may rest Assured.

Perhaps the Matter that most engages Sir Athelstan's regard is the Literacy of my Kind. He has interested Himself closely in the Education of my new Litter, which has now reached a Point at which all are scribbling away for an Hour each Day, using pinfeather-quill Pen and small Thimbles of Ink. They must prepare for their own Futures, and of course I am Teaching them all that I may.

Their tiny Copybooks litter the Space about the Master's Table, and he takes Care to place his Feet so as to avoid damaging any Work in Progress. I found him, some Days ago, with Rufus, the most precocious Tom in the Litter, sitting upon his Desk. The Kit was Writing busily, and Sir Athelstan was helping him to form his Letters with the Copperplate Swirls and Curlicues that he uses Himself in his Correspondence with other Astronomers about the Realm.

I was upset at the Time, although I could find no immediate Reason. Was that the Intuition common to my Kind? I can only feel that to be True, for Misfortune came of it, and very soon.

Being young and flexible of Mind, the Kits seem to have absorbed Much of the Esoteric Detail concerning Sir Athelstan's Work. Rufus in particular loved to work the Astrolabe, when it was not in use, and he has also learned, much to my Astonishment, quite a Lot of the Mathematical Calculation necessary for plotting the Orbits of Stars and Planets.

Finding his Copybook filled with this Lore, I felt some Pride at his Accomplishment. Foolish Hermione! I have been taught, as have all my Kind, that Pride goeth before a Fall, and such has proven to be the Case.

That became obvious two Days past, when there came a Knock at the Door. Musgrave, Sir Athelstan's Manservant, upon receiving the Communication handed in by the Servant outside, brought it directly to the Study. I watched my Charge's Face as he read, and I knew at once that something had gone Amiss.

His Cheeks went quite Scarlet, and his white Beard seemed almost to Bristle with Outrage. "What Audacity!" he shouted, ringing for Musgrave with unaccustomed Vigor. "Some Charlatan is endeavoring to sully my spotless Reputation! A Letter must be sent at once, Musgrave (for that Individual had arrived promptly)."

He turned to his Table and his Quills, but when he thrust the first into the Silver Inkwell, so disturbed was he that he broke its Nib against the Bottom. Ink splashed onto the Calculations laid ready for Work, and he looked as if he might burst into Tears.

"If I might be of Service," I told him in the Private Speech used between Familiar and Charge, "I will be Happy to Inscribe the Message for you."

He lifted me onto the Table with much Gratitude and sent Musgrave from the Room on a Pretext. We try never to disturb Servants with our Association, for many of those become Fearful when faced with our Abilities.

My Kit had left his small Pen on a Corner of the Table, and I managed to make my Letters large enough for easy Reading by Humankind. Slowly, my Master dictated his Missive, and as I copied his Words, I felt a Chill in my Heart. This was Mischief, not Conspiracy, and I had a dreadful Intuition as to its Cause.

Learned Sirs: the letter began,

It was with Dismay that I received your Communication of two Hours past. A Comet that threatens to destroy the Terrestrial Globe? I have found no trace of such a Matter, though I have scanned the Sky each clear Night through the best Telescope within my Means.

The Letter sent to you over my Signature is obviously a Forgery of the rankest Sort. I had not supposed that Jealousy existed among our Fellowship,

*and I refuse to believe that any of our Trusted Peers
are involved in this Conspiracy. I can only suppose
that Others, unknown to the Society of Amateur
Astronomers, have decided to disrupt our Cooperative Endeavors and misguide our Investigations of
the Heavens.*

*You have my deepest Apologies for the Unease
this unfounded Report must have caused within the
Group. I will, rest assured, look into the Matter with
all possible Assiduity, and if the Culprit is discovered, I will reveal his Name to the Society, that he
may be called to account.*

Your Friend and Servant,

Athelstan Grisby,
Brt.

As Sir Athelstan read the Letter, sprinkled Sand on
the ink, and appended his Signature, I was investigating
for myself. Beside the Spot on which Rufus's Pen had
rested Lay his Copybook. I strolled to sit beside it and
washed my Face daintily, managing while so doing to
Read what was Inscribed there.

He had, as I suspected, been Writing in Sir Athelstan's
distinctive Hand, making the Letters large enough to
convince anyone that they had been formed by a Human
Being. Additionally, those Letters were intermixed with
Calculations resembling Those on my Master's unfinished
Pages.

Without any Doubt, I was looking at the Practice Sheet
that was the Forerunner of the Forged Letter sent to the
Society. How? That was, of course, instantly Apparent.
Sir Athelstan's Secretary, who came each Morning to
tidy his Correspondence, must have seen this Missive
lying on the Table, ready for the Post, and he had Sealed
it and placed it with the outgoing Packet.

Musgrave entered the Room, took the new Letter, and
left again. With my most beguiling Purr, I settled onto
Sir Athelstan's Lap, the Kits at the moment being engaged in being Fed in the Scullery.

I stared up at him, my Eyes pleading. "I know the
Culprit," I conveyed to my Charge. "And it is no Enemy

of yours, but instead a great Admirer. He meant no Harm, rest assured. I do hope that you will not be Angry with him!"

He stared down, his eyes wide. "But—but how could You possibly know who did this Outrageous thing?"

I sighed and licked one Paw reflectively. Then I rubbed my Chin against his Knee. "Because it was Rufus. Look at his Copybook, there on the farther Side of the Table."

He reached and found the Item in question. When he began Perusing it, I felt his Stomach begin to quiver with Chuckles.

"That little Devil!" he said. Now he was beginning to Laugh aloud. "Would you believe that a mere Kit could comprehend my Discipline well enough to mislead an entire Society of Astronomers, if only for a short While?"

"Rufus is not your ordinary Kit," I responded, feeling great Relief that he was reacting with Amusement rather than Fury.

"But why did he imitate my Style and my Handwriting?" asked Sir Athelstan, rereading the scribbled Page.

"Admiration? Emulation? Who can say what motivates a Child?" I asked. "But you do need to Caution your Secretary, when you find the Opportunity. Unless you have outgoing Letters in a certain Spot, he should never send them out without asking you."

"I will see to it." His Stomach was still joggling gently. He stroked my Head with his free Hand as he read the Page yet a third Time.

As one might suppose, I had Words of my own with my Precocious Kit. Rufus was suitably Subdued when I was done, for not only the Society was misled for a Time. The News had been sent to the Newspapers, before the Recipients of the Letter thought to verify the Information therein. This led to considerable Excitement and Distress among the Readership of the Publications involved.

So respected was Sir Athelstan that his Name (which was admirably forged) was enough to convince the most Skeptical of the Authenticity of the Danger. By the time Corrections were made, the Damage was done.

It was not an easy Matter to correct this Mishap. Some unnamed Villain is still blamed, for not even one so Secure in his own Skill as Sir Athelstan could possibly admit that this sort of Deception could be managed by a Domestic Animal.

However, nowadays when my Charge is busy with his Mathematics, Rufus is usually at his Elbow. The Kit has a Gift for this, and Sir Athelstan plans to Work with him in Future, using his unusual Skills to Augment his own.

As the Child's Mother, I am, of course, extremely Proud and Grateful. But as Sir Athelstan's Familiar, I keep a very close Watch upon them Both. Neither is as Mature as one would Wish, and both tend to be Daring in the Extreme.

I have no wish to deal with another such near Catastrophe as the last might have become. And though I have Worked extremely hard, I still cannot comprehend the Calculations needed for charting the Courses of the Stars. It is difficult enough to keep an Eye upon my pair of Astronomers.

QUEST OF SOULS

by Ann Miller and Karen Rigley

"Prosh! Where are you?" Rasson called, running from room to room as his voice echoed through the huge stone dwelling.

The boy heard an annoyed "meow" in answer and skidded to a stop in front of a stretching gray cat. "Cat Prosh, I can't wake the Master!"

Then let him sleep. Prosh licked his left paw to express disinterest.

"You don't understand. My master cannot wake. He lies white as morning snow and still, so still. Come see!"

Rasson raced through the main chamber into Master's bedroom with the cat darting past him. Prosh hopped upon the bed, using nose, whiskers and very keen cat eyes to examine the pale master.

You're right. Master cannot wake—his soul is gone. Cat Prosh gazed unblinkingly at the boy.

"Gone?" Rasson leaned over the bed to poke at his master's cheek. "You mean he's dead?"

No, but he will die, Prosh warned, *if you do not rescue his soul by the next new moon.*

"How can I do that?"

Get help from the village witch. Prosh leapt off the bed. *Now I must find Cook and get my meal.*

"Cat Prosh," called Rasson. "Come back!"

The cat ignored Rasson and shot away toward the kitchen with the pleading boy trailing behind. They found no one in the kitchen and the black stove had not been lit. No aroma of baking bread greeted them, no hearty good morning from Cook, and no breakfast for cat or boy.

"Maybe Cook is in her room behind the pantry," Rasson

suggested. The cat and the boy found her door unlocked and cautiously entered Cook's chambers. No snores sounded from the huge lump in bed. Still, the boy stayed back fearing Cook's temper, and allowed Cat Prosh to investigate.

Her soul has been stolen, too, Prosh announced.

The boy crept forward. "Why?"

Prosh sniffed and stared at the human boy. *Soul robbers steal souls and imprison them in the Dark Fortress until the seventh new moon. Then they drain the kidnapped souls, using that essence to increase their evil power.*

"I thought soul robbers things of legend only—stories told to frighten children. If you knew about them, why didn't you protect Master?" Rasson cried in anger and fear.

Who knows when soul robbers will attack? A long time has passed since they last ventured forth—longer than either of our memories. Soul robbers strike at random, after dark. Cat Prosh leaped down and pattered back into the kitchen. *Last night I was outside exercising Hound. He needs it.*

"I should've been here—*I* would've saved them."

Where were you? Prosh's ears perked.

"In the woods catching glowflies," Rasson answered, hanging his head down in remorse and feeling as if he wanted to cry.

Did you catch any? The boy nodded, and Prosh added, *Good. Put the glowflies in a lantern and take them with you on your quest. Their light will guide you at night.*

"Please, Prosh, I need *you* to help me free Master and Cook," Rasson said. A thought struck him. He stopped and blinked down at the big gray cat. "Oh, no! Do you think they got Mistress?"

"Meooow!" screeched Prosh.

Prosh darted up the stairs with the boy scrambling after, Rasson reaching Mistress Sunlee's chambers seconds behind the cat.

Rasson knocked lightly. No response. He cracked the door open and Cat Prosh swished past to pounce upon the bed. There, stretched out like exquisitely carved ivory, lay Mistress, her golden hair spread out over the pillow. She slept deeply as if she had abandoned the living world.

Prosh wailed so loudly, Rasson jumped. Though aware Cat Prosh adored Mistress, it still startled the boy to hear such deep anguish from the normally aloof feline. "Don't grieve, Prosh. We shall free their souls and bring our people back to life." The boy picked up Prosh and carried the trembling cat away from Mistress and back toward the kitchen. "I'll find us something to eat, then we can plan the rescue."

Prosh emitted a weak meow as Rasson put him down by an empty bowl and disappeared into the pantry. Soon the boy came out with Cook's prize cream instead of plain milk. He poured most of the cream into the bowl, then gulped down the remainder from the bottle. He divided a chunk of smoked fish between himself and the cat, glad to see Prosh eating and acting normal again.

As their fish disappeared, the boy began to chatter. "Once I told Koge that you talk to me. He didn't believe me. Why can't Koge hear you like I can?" Rasson said, remembering how the older boy had laughed and ridiculed him.

I don't wish to talk to that ruffian. Cat Prosh finished off the cream, then sat back to lick his whiskers. *Why you speak to Koge, I'll never understand.*

"Koge says I'm crazy if I think cats talk. I told him you don't say words out loud, you say them into my head, but he just called me stupid."

If you were stupid, boy, I would not bother talking to you. Prosh turned attention back to the fish, nibbling delicately at a small chunk of it. *Is there more of this?*

"Yes, but you'll get sick if I feed you too much."

No, boy. Store it in your pack with water and foodstuffs that humans eat. Don't forget the glowfly lantern and a blanket. Prosh began licking his fur with his rough pink tongue. *Also you need to gather dahi blossoms, wild fluta, and bloka leaves from the woods before we go.*

"Does this mean you're coming with me?"

Of course. Mistress Sunlee needs me and we might as well save the other souls, too.

"I'm ready," Rasson announced breathlessly, a short

time later. He stood by the door, clutching a knapsack bulging with supplies, determined to rescue the people who, in great kindness, had taken in the small orphan boy. He could not fail them.

About time. Prosh swished his tail. *Did you pick the herbs?*

"Yes, here they are." The boy touched a leather pouch hanging from his belt. "But why do we need them?"

Just a little cat magic. You'll learn when it's time. Come, let us go before more of the day passes.

They journeyed west, using the ascending sun as a compass. Sometimes the cat trotted ahead, making Rasson break into a run to catch up to Prosh. After a few hours, the boy took the lead. He darted past ferns and wild berry bushes, calling, "I see something shiny and bright in that clump of olla flowers. Maybe it's a jewel that someone dropped."

No, boy, don't touch it! Prosh admonished, reaching Rasson as the boy stretched a hand toward the shimmering gold spot among pink flowers.

"I found it, so it's mine," Rasson replied, annoyed at the cat for trying to keep him from his treasure.

SSsSsst!

The gold spot undulated with shiny scales as a hooded head raised up hissing, a forked tongue darting from the snake's mouth.

Horror flooded Rasson as he heard Prosh caution, *Do not move. Stay completely still. Glimmer snakes are poison.*

The boy held his breath, too terrified to move. From the corner of his eye he saw Cat Prosh circle in closer while the snake held Rasson prisoner with a cold black gaze. The snake reared back its head, preparing to strike. "I'm doomed," Rasson whispered.

At that moment a cat paw knocked the snake's head. Before the serpent could recoil, the cat snapped jaws over its midsection and pulled it from the flowers. Prosh swung the squirming snake, whipping its head against a boulder until he beat all life out of the golden serpent. The cat dropped the dead snake to the ground.

You are greedy and impulsive like all of your kind, Cat Prosh told Rasson, before moving away to wash the snake scent from his fur. *I should have let the snake bite you.*

"But you need me," pleaded Rasson, ashamed of himself. He offered the cat some water in a small cup and placed a piece of smoked fish next to the cup. "Forgive me for being so foolish. Next time I shall help you, Cat Prosh."

The cat regally accepted the boy's offering, but as he nibbled the fish he replied, *I do not need you. A cat does not need a human.*

"Wait and see," Rasson promised. "I will prove useful and you will be glad you saved me." He tried hard to think of something he could do for Prosh besides the offering of food. Nothing came to mind, but Rasson vowed he would find something during their journey.

The afternoon wore on as they traveled westward, the countryside changing from flat wooded ground to hills strewn with boulders and fallen rock. The sun blazed hot, sometimes glaring right into Rasson's eyes and he couldn't help wonder how Prosh felt under all that fur. The boy stopped to sip from his flask and watch the cat trot ahead. Rasson gazed around the strange countryside, thinking how different it was so far from home. The next hill looked more like a mountain and he wanted to explore it. Up the trail, he noticed the cat slowing down.

Cat Prosh surveyed the rugged terrain, glancing back at Rasson. The feline stretched and yawned under the shade of a waala bush where fern leaves fanned the air. *Boy, you scout a ways up the mountain and I'll keep watch here.*

With a hop and a skip Rasson started off to hike up the rocky trail until he stood by a big boulder at the cliff top. "Look, Prosh! I can move this big rock."

The dozing cat meowed a protest before opening green eyes to stare as the boy teetered the precarious boulder to and fro. *Be careful, it may roll off the edge,* Prosh warned, then curled himself in the other direction and closed his eyes again.

"On my way up I passed a cave, not far from you," Rasson yelled down at the cat. "Can we sleep there tonight?"

Prosh snoozed under the bush, ignoring Rasson. The boy began tossing pebbles off the cliff to land in front of the cave, several yards from the cat.

Stop that racket and come down, Prosh commanded.

The boy shinnied down the mountain side, but just as he reached the bottom, a ferocious growl thundered from the cave. Rasson glanced over to see a huge gray beast standing at the entrance. He blinked disbelieving eyes at the giant wolf-dog, blood dripping from its fangs and a half-eaten zincod clenched in its teeth.

"Yeowl-hiss!" Prosh stood with back arched and fur on end and for a second Rasson froze in horror. Would the beast attack Cat Prosh? He couldn't bear to lose anyone else.

He scrambled back up to the cliff top. "Stand clear!" he hollered at Prosh. Then with a great shove, he pushed the boulder over the edge. Plop! Crash! Crunch.

Heart pounding, Rasson peeked over the edge. "Did it squash him?"

Cat Prosh relaxed. *Probably not, but it blocked the entrance. Let's get out of here in case there's another way out of the cave.*

"Wait for me," Rasson said, scurrying down with a final glance at the stone blocked cave, happy he finally did something to help the cat.

After they put distance between themselves and the cave, Rasson began to laugh. "This time I saved you," he said.

I was in no danger. Prosh padded forward through a sloping meadow toward the forest.

"What? That wolf-dog could have gobbled you in three bites," Rasson protested, hurt that Prosh did not appreciate his efforts.

I only needed to climb a tree to be safe. You saved yourself, not me.

Rasson charged into an angry run to dash past the cat into the forest. The trees blotted out the lowering sun as if it turned to night. A chilly breeze swept by, making the boy shiver. He paused to wait for Prosh.

"I can't see," Rasson complained, as the cat brushed by his ankles.

Then take the glowfly lantern from your knapsack. Cat Prosh sat and fluffed his fur as the boy obeyed, soon a twinkling glow radiated from the old lantern.

The boy held it up to illuminate the path, spilling light across sprawling roots and green fleshy vines strung from the trees. The canopy of leaves, branches, and vines completely obliterated the sky, making Rasson shiver again. "I don't like this place. Can we go another way?"

We're only cutting across a narrow strip of the forest here. Be patient and we will be through it soon.

True to the cat's prediction, they soon emerged into the slanted rays of a sinking sun. Once beyond the forest, Rasson carefully replaced his glowfly lantern into his knapsack and strapped the pack over his shoulders. He felt he had been walking forever and his back was stiff from the weight of his pack. So when they reached low marshy ground, he slipped his pack off again and carried it in his hand, slinging it to the ground the first opportunity he found.

"What's that horrid smell?" Rasson asked, as they stopped by a fallen log to rest.

The swamp is not far from here. You sit for a spell while I hunt for a tasty morsel. Prosh disappeared into the willows, leaving a rustling trail in his wake.

"I'm so tired," Rasson said to himself, then he stretched out on the flattened log. It felt good to be off his feet; he hadn't slept much last night and they had been traveling all day. His eyes drifted shut. He listened to the soft hum of a flitterwing, letting the sound lull him to sleep.

Sensing something staring at him, Rasson awoke to see the red slit eyes and twitching nose of a giant rodent, a creature as big as Cat Prosh. The boy couldn't move. Sweat beaded across his forehead and all he could think about was the swamp rat drooling inches from his face. Swamp rats carried a disease fatal to humans and Rasson knew one bite from this creature would kill him—a painful, slow death. He had heard stories and they'd given him nightmares. Should he scream? Or would a scream spur the rodent to attack? What could he do?

"Meeow!"

The rat turned from boy to cat. Rasson rolled behind

the log and peeked over the top to watch as Prosh threateningly approached a rat as large as the cat himself. What could a cat do against a rodent his own size? The cat sprang forward. The boy saw a tangle of fur, claws, and teeth accompanied by hisses and growls.

Rasson felt terrible—now Cat Prosh would die because of him. Tears pricked his eyes, blurring his sight as the fur and teeth rolled to a stop and gray separated from brown. He swiped the tears away with his sleeve to clear his vision.

For you. Prosh released the rat's throat from his teeth and the rodent lay limp and bloody.

"How did you kill it? It's as big as you are," Rasson gasped in astonishment.

Size isn't important. To a cat, a rat is a rat.

"Did he bite you? Will you die?" the boy asked, afraid to hear the cat's reply.

Prosh sniffed. *Of course not, human. I am a cat.* With that he pranced away down the trail, obviously expecting the boy to follow.

Rasson hurried along behind, too wound up to feel tired any longer. Soon they left the willows, reeds, and swamp stench behind to enter what appeared another section of the thick, pungent forest, but trees here grew thinner and allowed in more light.

"How much longer before we reach the Dark Fortress? What do soul robbers look like?" Rasson asked. "Can we stop and eat yet?" He hopped on one foot trying to get the cat's attention. "Do you really know where we're going?"

Humans talk too much. Prosh curled up in a downy patch of wild grass. *You eat and I'll doze awhile. Maybe food will keep your mouth quiet, boy.*

Rasson found a comfortable rock and sat down. First he sipped from his flask, the water cooling his parched throat. Then the boy wiped off his knife before cutting a chunk of cheese and a slice of bread. He gazed around him as he munched on the strong goat cheese and wondered again if they were lost. He no longer had any sense of direction and the forest closed around them like a maze.

"Wake up," Rasson coaxed, stroking Prosh's silky fur and tickling the cat's ears.

One green eye opened. *Rest, boy, you'll need all your strength in a short while.*

Rasson tried, but couldn't rest. He thought about the swamp rat, the snake, and the wolf-dog, and how he wanted to reach the fortress and save Master, Mistress, and Cook. Then he could rest. Only then. He played with the pouch of herbs hanging from his belt. Opening it, he looked inside to see the dahi blossoms, wild fluta, and bloka leaves that he had picked in the woods that morning. It seemed so long ago. He drew the pouch closed just as Cat Prosh yawned and stretched.

When we reach the edge of the forest, leave your knapsack behind a tree. When we arrive at the fortress, you can move faster if you only carry your knife—and the herbs, of course. Prosh trotted away.

Rasson trudged along behind, wondering what would happen at the fortress. How did Prosh plan to battle the soul robbers? Could they save the imprisoned souls? Or would they lose their own? The boy's pulse quickened with his stride. Whatever would happen, he wanted it over.

They paused between trees before leaving the forest. Ahead, silhouetted against a violet-smudged evening sky loomed a stone fortress, dark and forbidding, rimmed by a high wall that looked impossible to scale. Cat Prosh streaked through the meadow grass. The boy began running after Prosh, not daring to call out "Wait for me!" Instead, he followed in silence, his gaze drawn by the fortress appearing larger as he drew closer.

The cat stopped so abruptly that Rasson nearly tripped over him. "Why stop now? We've finally reached the fortress," the boy said, regaining his balance.

A moat. I won't get in that water—not even to save Mistress Sunlee. The cat drooped from his ears to his head to his tail.

Rasson had never before seen Prosh appear defeated. "I won't let some water stop us," he declared, watching the cat.

Cat Prosh gazed down at the murky swirling waters and shook. *I cannot enter the moat. It's impossible.*

"Nothing impossible!" Rasson protested in alarm. "After the dangers we've survived on our quest, we can't give up now."

It's no use. I cannot cross this water. It is cursed. Things live within it which will devour us. Prosh circled around to begin the journey home, looking so dejected and forlorn that it tore Rasson's heart.

"I will swim across alone," Rasson said. "You can wait for me here while I rescue the souls." The boy felt his body tremble as he spoke, but he bit his lip against the icy fear seeping through him.

Even if you survive the moat, you cannot fight the soul robbers without my magic. They will steal your soul and imprison it with the others. Come, let us return home. Prosh would not look up at the human boy, as if he could not bear the shame of his decision.

"Wait! I can make us a bridge. See that towering balta tree? It's very skinny and if I cut it here . . ." the boy dashed over to the tree and pointed to the far base of the trunk, ". . . it will fall across the moat and land near the top of the wall."

What will you use to chop it down?

"My hunting knife is very strong," Rasson answered. "What do you think, Cat Prosh?"

Humans are good for some things. Prosh stared through desperate green eyes at the boy, who grinned smugly.

Whack, whack, whack. Rasson chopped at the slim tree with his heavy knife until his arms ached. "Why won't it fall?" he grumbled.

You need to make the cut wider.

"What does a cat know about chopping down a tree?" Rasson snapped, wishing he could just wake up and discover this had all been a bad dream.

Cats know everything. Prosh looked his old arrogant self and so Rasson chose not to argue.

The boy hacked away at the tree to widen the deep cut as Prosh suggested.

Crack, rumble, crash! Finally the towering tree fell, snagging the top of the wall with a shower of leaves.

"Do you think the soul robbers heard it?" Rasson asked, startled by the noise.

Hide! Prosh commanded. *We must wait and watch.*

Together they dove back into the cover of the deep woods and peered out from behind a bush to view the fortress. Nothing happened. They watched in silence until Rasson felt the cat's claws kneading his arm.

Now it is time. We must go before darkness falls. Ready, boy?

Rasson nodded. Cat Prosh ran to the fallen tree, jumped onto the trunk, and began scaling the boy-made bridge. Once Rasson thought he saw Prosh pause and stare down into the moat, but the cat moved ahead quickly, leaving the boy to wonder if he had imagined the hesitation.

Rasson had more difficulty climbing the tree. Under his weight the trunk shifted slightly and limbs caught at his feet. Sometimes, he could only grab twigs which snapped and threw him off balance, but the sight of Cat Prosh watching and waiting for him from the top of the wall kept him going until he finally hauled himself up beside the cat.

"What now?" Rasson whispered, trying to catch his breath.

Enter the fortress. Prosh leaped off the wall to land neatly upon the rock sill of a deep window. *Come.*

Rasson glanced down at the cobblestone ground far below, then across at the window sill. He felt sick. How could a boy jump across here? He was no surefooted cat; if he could not exactly reach the window, he would plummet to his death. No human could survive such a fall.

Boy, I've seen you jump farther playing with Koge at the creek. Prosh gazed at him through bright green eyes. *Now jump!*

The boy took a deep breath, focused on the window and dove into the air. For a moment he stayed airborne, then as he began to drop he stretched frantically for the window. He felt the rough stone edge hit solid beneath his fingers and grabbed. His torso and legs slammed against the wall, knocking his breath out, but he held tight. Using his arms, he pulled himself up onto the sill.

When his heartbeat stabilized, Rasson let out a slow breath. "I made it."

Of course. Prosh had hopped to the floor of the upper chamber and stood twitching his whiskers and sniffing. *We must find the soul prison. I think it is below.* The cat dashed through a doorway and Rasson followed.

The boy moved as quietly as possible, but when he saw Cat Prosh slinking down a spiral stairway of stone, he hesitated. The cat paused to glance up at him. *Hurry, before the soul robbers awake.*

"They're sleeping?" Rasson whispered in relief.

Yes, only until darkness. We haven't much time. Prosh continued down the winding steps.

Try as he might, Rasson couldn't keep his feet from clattering as he descended the narrow uneven stairs. They went down to the bottom level, then the cat scurried through a long hall and disappeared into an adjoining chamber.

The boy entered the chamber, aware of a foul odor as a prison of crystallized ice drew his attention to the center of the room. There, trapped within the frozen walls, an iridescence glowed and flickered with the essence of life. Excitement and wonder throbbed through Rasson. Souls!

SQUAWK!

At the cry, Rasson whipped around to see the sharp-hooked beak and midnight black feathers of a bird swooping at him in attack.

Protect your throat! Prosh ordered.

The boy cowered, trying to obey. He felt a sharp sting as the bird grazed his forehead. Instinctively raising a hand to the wound, Rasson drew it back, sticky with blood. Prosh meowed in warning and the boy glanced up in time to see the bird dive again.

The cat pounced but missed the bird. Too late, Rasson turned to run as the bird delivered a stunning blow to his upper left arm. A stabbing pain shot through him, making him stagger. The boy fell, collapsing onto the cold stone floor, his throat exposed as he landed. He saw the bird dip back toward him.

Cat Prosh sprang, catching the bird in midair and bringing it down. Rasson struggled to his feet as he watched cat battle bird. Feathers flew, screeches filled the air, and then there was silence.

"Prosh!" Rasson cried, relieved as the cat shook free of the bird. "You're amazing!"

Tear off your sleeve and use it to bandage your wounds. You're bleeding all over. With raised tail Prosh trotted over to the prison.

Rasson followed the cat's orders, wrapping cloth from his sleeve around his head to cover the gash, then binding another strip of the fabric around his arm to effectively stop the flow of blood. It was awkward to do it himself, his head ached and his arm hurt, but he worked as quickly as possible.

He could hear Prosh scratching at the crystal prison. "What are you doing?" he asked, stepping closer.

Drawing ancient symbols to summon forces beyond your human world. The cat stopped scratching. *Done. Now rub the bag of herbs over these symbols. Keep the bag closed and hold on tight to it. Don't let go—no matter what happens.*

"Yes, Cat Prosh." Rasson removed the bag from his belt, cinched it shut as best he could, and placed it against the first row of symbols. As he rubbed round and round, touching every symbol, he saw sparks. The bag got warm, then hot, then hotter.

Suddenly the crystal fortress exploded, the blast flinging Rasson against the wall. He slid to the ground still grasping the bag and sat watching with bewildered amazement as the ice cracked and shattered, showering pieces of crumbling fortress. For a moment the spirit flames hovered, shimmering, flickering so intensely, that the boy could barely stand the brightness. He shielded his eyes with his hand just as the flames billowed together, ascending upward to vanish through a window.

A meow startled Rasson as the cat wove between his legs. *Mistress Sunlee is saved.*

The boy bent to stroke Prosh. "Are the souls returning to their bodies?" he asked, his fingers drawing comfort from the cat's soft fur. "And shall Master, Mistress, and Cook live now?"

Yes, they will wake from dreamless sleep and know nothing of our quest or their imprisonment. Now we must go.

The boy started up the stairs, but halted as Prosh declared, *No time. Unbar the door. Quickly!*

The cat led Rasson to a wide wooden door. The boy tried to raise the board barring the door, but it stuck. His left arm was sore and he dared not let go of the herb bag, but he tried again. He shoved hard, finally jamming the bar upward to unlatch the door.

Just as the boy pushed the heavy door open to let in a rush of sweet fresh air, a terrible wail echoed through the fortress, shaking the walls, and jolting Rasson with sheer terror. He wanted to race out the door into the night, but a yowl from Prosh spun him around as a pointed shaft of ice penetrated the cat's paw, spearing it to the floor.

Throw me the bag of herbs and run. Save yourself, Prosh advised, unable to free his skewered paw.

"I won't leave you." Rasson grabbed the ice spear; it burned his palms with cold, but he held on until he wrenched it free.

Horror gripped Rasson as he looked up to see shadowy, cavern-eyed figures floating down the stairs. He aimed the ice shaft at them and threw with all his might.

The spear passed right through the leader, who just kept coming. Behind them the ice hit a stair and broke into pieces. The soul robbers neared Rasson, emitting an evil that sucked at his strength and cloaked him in heavy dread. Teeth chattering, death moving ever closer, the boy drew his knife.

No, throw the herbs at them. Prosh nipped open the bag. *Make sure you get everyone. Or we're doomed.*

With frantic desperation, Rasson scooped a handful of herbs from the bag and tossed them at the spectral robbers. The herbs sprayed into arrows of fire, piercing the front three soul robbers with a kaleidoscope of sparks. Banshee wails shook the walls as the figures burst into flames.

Two more robbers charged forward. The boy threw another handful of herbs, leaving the bag nearly empty. The herbs flew through the air, transforming into burning arrows to bombard the moving targets. An unholy shriek ricocheted through the fortress as the figures exploded with magic fire.

Another shadow advanced.

Fighting down fear, Rasson emptied out the herbs. One chance. He watched the sinister figure approach, held his breath, and took aim. The herbs sparked and points of colored flame shot out. They hit their target to extinguish the robber with fiery death as a resounding wail echoed through the fortress.

All that remained of the soul robbers were red wisps of foul-smelling smoke. The boy watched the smoke dissipate. It blew away on a breeze gusting through the open door.

"We did it!" Rasson cried, turning back to the cat, who was licking the injured paw. There would be no walking on that foot, Rasson knew. The boy swept Prosh up with his good arm and cuddled the cat close. "I shall carry you home, brave cat."

I'll be fine, as soon as you bandage my wound the way you did yours. The boy could see Prosh was shaken but attempting to hide it.

Rasson ripped off the end of the cloth on his arm and very gently bound the cat's paw. "Are you strong enough to travel home tonight?"

Together we can do anything. Prosh butted the boy's cheek, making Rasson feel important, happy, and needed.

"You're so remarkable, Prosh," Rasson said, stroking the feline. "Sometimes it's hard to believe you're only a cat."

Cat Prosh purred and nuzzled against Rasson's shoulder. *Sometimes, boy, it's hard to believe you're only a human.*

EDE'S EARRINGS

by Sasha Miller

The magician's house was not a happy place these days. The air fairly quivered with misunderstandings, hurt feelings, and—not the least of it—downright stubbornness on the parts of both the magician and his cat.

"Don't you clatter those things at me," Ferdon said. "Not another time! You're wrong, and there's an end to it."

Ede glared at him and shook her head, causing the jeweled rings in her ears to jangle even more defiantly. Then she stalked off, head high, tip of tail twitching in annoyance.

"I'm going to do it anyway," Ferdon called after Ede. "There's no reason not to! There's no harm in it—" But he was talking to the air. With a last clinking of jewels, Ede had leapt to the window sill and vanished. "Right. Go outside and sulk, you ridiculous cat. Who needs your help, let alone your interference? Next time I'll have a frog or an owl for a Companion, just you mark me well."

But it was an empty threat, and Ferdon knew it even before the words were out of his mouth. Ede had come to him—as magicians' Companions always did—of her own will, already versed in Companion lore and already wearing the jewels in her ears. At first, appalled at what he conceived to have been cruelty to the cat, he had tried to remove the earrings only to find that there was no way to take them off, short of destroying them, and that method of removal he was instinctively loath to try. Nor was there a discernible weld in the two thin gold rings. They would have fit loosely on his thumb, and were strung with gold, emerald, and sapphire beads that clinked softly with every movement, and simply were there, as

178

much a part of Ede as her blue-green eyes. She had a
most unusual ruddy brown coat, each hair banded and
tipped with black; a dark stripe accentuated her back
while her belly and the undersides of her legs were creamy
in color. Bands of dark tipping circled her throat like
necklaces and the capital letter "M" on her forehead—
the mark of cats the world over—stood out vividly.

Ferdon was young, as magicians go, and Ede was his
first Companion. Only when he had done some research
in his extensive and as yet largely unread library had he
discovered how lucky he was. He had bought the books
complete with the house, from the elderly physician-
mage whose practice he had taken over when the old
man retired. Magister Grinden had accumulated a number of volumes over the years, and among them was a
small book, bound in purple leather, a book he had not
encountered at the Academy. The very finest Companions, according to the chapter he read in "Arkane Magick
et Jewells et Cattes" were cats from Egypt. This Ede
undeniably was, for there were many colored drawings in
the book and one, entitled "Aegypttian Catte," could
have been a portrait of her. Furthermore, the best Companions always had rings in their ears. Sometimes the
cats even had some magical powers of their own.

Ferdon discovered that Ede was a Companion with a
strong sense of what was wrong and what was right.
When he seemed on the brink of doing something of
which Ede did not approve, she jangled the rings as a
warning. She had saved him from several blunders in the
past, such as the time one townwife wanted him to wither
her neighbor's flowers. Considering what the neighbor's
lapdog had done to his client's begonias, he had been
ready to oblige her. Ede's even disposition changed; she
became terribly agitated, shaking her head and pawing at
her earrings to make the beads jingle. He had to delay
working the spell until she was in a more cooperative
mood. Then he had learned how his client's son had
unmercifully tormented the dog. Another incident, involving a farmer and the size of the litter he wanted from
the sow bred to the local baron's prize boar, would
certainly have had serious repercussions had he agreed to

the farmer's wishes. But Ede had shaken her head, jangling her earrings, and he had turned the man away at once. Later, when the baron took reprisal, Ferdon learned that the farmer had bred his sow without prior approval. The farmer lost everything he thought to have gained by the sale of a large number of pigs of choice lineage; his family deserted him, and he wound up in the baron's prison. With a cold sinking in the pit of his stomach, Ferdon realized that if he had become involved to the least degree, he might have been thrown in prison as well.

This disagreement he and Ede had been having lately, however—well, there was no reason for it that Ferdon could see, other than plain jealousy and stubbornness on Ede's part.

He had met someone. How simply it had happened, and how profoundly it had changed his life. On the first market day after he had taken up residence in the town, Ferdon had visited the square, thinking only to acquaint himself with his new neighbors and potential clients as he walked among the stalls and booths. The sight of a woman's magnificent shape outlined against the sun stopped him in mid stride; a thunderbolt could not have affected him more. Instantly smitten, he hurried over to introduce himself. Then he had seen her face. Her features were pretty enough, but her skin— Pity swept through him and the man stepped aside in favor of the physician.

"I am Ferdon," he said to her. "Please. Forgive me, but—"

She nodded. "I know. The new mage. You want to know what is wrong with me, why I look the way I do." Her voice was incredibly rich and deep, full of promise, and he could have lost himself forever in the brownish green of her eyes.

"Mine is not idle curiosity."

"Very well. It is a tale that has grown worn in the telling. One more time doesn't matter."

As long as she could remember, both she and her mother had had red, scaly patches that itched abominably at wrists, ankles and around their hairlines. During the time when she started to change from a girl to a

woman, however, something even worse had happened
to her skin. Her face, shoulders and back began to be
disfigured by pustular eruptions and now she was seldom
free of them. Both her parents had died; these days she
wove fabric and embroidered fine garments for a living,
and occasionally sold vegetables, when she had some to
spare, on market day. She had no money to rent a stall
but found a spot on the cobblestones where she could
spread her wares.

"I am poor because people don't want to buy from me,"
she told him in conclusion. "I think they are afraid they
will catch something, the way I caught it from my mother."

"Has this ever happened?"

She shook her head. "Not yet."

"And did your father catch it?"

"No. It was very strange. But he was a strong man." In
the current fashion—or as close as she could come to
it—she wore a shift serving as underdress and petticoat
in one under a tightly laced bodice and had a fold of
overskirt tucked up in her waistband. An empty purse
dangled from her belt. She sighed, and absently fingered
the tie of the threadbare shift. "How I would love to
have a few coins to spare. And to be pretty."

"You are," he said. He almost stumbled over the
words. "Believe me, you are. I think you are very pretty
indeed."

But she remained unconvinced, shaking her head and
sighing even more deeply. He found it difficult to concentrate, enthralled by the thought of the warm, soft
bosom inside that bodice. And more than that, he found
himself wanting to, well, to *do* things for her, to make
life easier for her, to make her smile. With difficulty, he
tried to think like a physician once more. "Have you
sought medical help?"

"Magister Grinden could do nothing to help me," she
said. "But he was old, and, I fear, somewhat behind the
times. Whereas, you—"

She left the thought unspoken, but Ferdon could read
the rest of it in her eyes, in the flattering way she looked
at him, as if he were the most attractive, virile man in the

universe, the one for whom she had been searching all her life. . . .

"Ah, er, yes," he had said. He stopped and cleared his throat. "I will undertake your cure, Mistress—"

"Dala."

"Dala. I will undertake your cure, but you must realize it will take some time. I have never done anything like this before. I must study. We will be forced to meet often and, and perhaps experiment with several techniques. Methods of treatment."

"That would be wonderful." She stood up straight, arching her back and accidentally showing off the proud profile of her breasts through the thin shift she wore. "When shall we begin?"

"Oh, as soon as possible. You understand that it would be preferable if we can work out a cure by natural means, rather than magical. It is much easier on both the patient and the practitioner."

"You are the master."

But all the herbal remedies he had tried proved incapable of healing her. The scaly red patches, unvanquished, merely retreated into Dala's hairline along with the eruptions. This wen on her temple was only the latest in a long series of torments she endured. Ferdon was ready to resort to magical means of attempting a cure. The problem was that the ingredients were both rare and costly and he was far from being wealthy himself. Doing everything he wanted to do could ruin him financially.

Privately, Ferdon entertained the picture of Dala in his house, Dala preparing his meals and embroidering fine garments for him alone, Dala in his life and in his bed. He was a fine young mage—none better in his class at the academy. It could be argued that it was his responsibility to settle down while he was young and sire a new generation of magicians. No sense in letting them go unborn, the way too many did, until centuries and virility had passed and his talent died with him.

"Despite the cost, I will remove the wen on Dala's left temple, using magic," Ferdon said aloud, "and you will help me do it. That is an act you should approve of, my stiff-necked Companion. And we will do it tomorrow

morning!" Then he began to smile, thinking of how he
would slip in at least one extra spell, the one he knew
Dala wanted in her heart of hearts. Not that Dala had
ever asked for such a thing. But he could afford it.
During their conferences together he had become aware,
when she caught sight of her reflection, of the faint sigh
of disappointment every time she beheld herself. How
much easier her life would be if she had the beautiful,
clear skin she dreamed of. If another part of what he
wanted to do for her also involved casting a certain aura
over the goods she brought to market day, well, what
harm was there in it? And how grateful she would be to
him. . . .

If only Ede could get over this ridiculous antipathy.
The first time Dala had come into the workroom where
Ede lay dozing, Dala had begun to sneeze. Rubbing her
eyes, she stumbled and accidentally brushed the cat from
the table. Startled and taken unaware, Ede had landed
heavily on the floor. Then she jumped straight up, fur
bristling, eyes ablaze, and dashed from the room.

"I'm sorry," Dala said. "I always sneeze when I'm
around a cat. Poor little thing."

Though Ferdon had tried to coax her back, Ede wouldn't
return to the workroom that day. However, on subse-
quent occasions when Dala came in, Ede stayed put in
her favorite spot on the worktable, refusing to leave and
watching with great interest as Dala sneezed with pro-
gressively greater violence. Ferdon had been forced to
put Ede out of the room each time so he could complete
the treatment. At first, Ede stalked back and forth outside, yowling and scratching at the door; later, she simply
hid when Dala was due for an appointment. Now, every
time anything even remotely connected with Dala came
up, Ede jangled her earrings in the most emphatic manner possible. Ferdon could only surmise that dislike had
become jealousy over his attentions to Dala when Ede
was excluded. He hoped Ede would get over it in time.
No, more than that. Ede *would* learn to endure Dala's
presence, and do it politely, or—

No use in dwelling on that subject. It fogged the mind,

when clear thinking was required. He went to the window. "Ede," he called. "Eeeeeede!"

The cat materialized on the window ledge and rubbed the entire length of her body against him. He gathered her into his arms and she responded with a full-throated purr that made both of them vibrate. Despite everything, they loved each other dearly.

"Ede, Ede, whatever am I going to do with you?" He rubbed her silken chin; she nuzzled his fingers. "Can't you see that I am only trying to heal someone who is ill? Will you help me? Please?"

Ede tensed in his arms and the purring ceased. He wondered if she could sense his very small, well-intentioned deception. But she didn't struggle to get down, nor did she jangle her earrings. Instead, she closed her eyes and pushed her head against Ferdon's chest.

"Thank you, Ede. I knew I could count on you."

Treatment day was also market day; but even though Dala was likely to miss getting her favorite spot where she put out her wares for sale, she came to Ferdon's house in answer to his summons. Ferdon habitually left the kitchen door unlatched, so that any who needed his services might enter. He heard her when she came in, dropping the bundle of embroidery and the basket of early summer squash just inside before going directly to the magician's workroom which he had left unlocked for her.

Today, however, there was no scent of herbs or goose fat in the air, no decoction of bark or roots simmering over the fire. He had neatly put away all the medicines and heal-craft implements, and in their place on the table had laid out the emblems of magery. Dala's eyes widened. She looked up at Ferdon. She put her fingers to her chapped lips.

"Yes," he said, answering her unspoken question. "I can do nothing more for you by ordinary means, so I have decided to work a spell." He indicated a stool placed in the center of a maze of chalk lines drawn on the floor. "Sit here. We'll start simply— Ede? Where are you? I need you now."

"The cat? Is it necessary? She doesn't like me."

"That's just a misunderstanding. She'll learn better. As I was saying, we'll start with something small, like taking away that wen on your temple."

Self-consciously, Dala touched the angry swelling. "And then?" she said.

He smiled. "All in good time." He slipped into the robe with the magic symbols painted on it, thinking as he did so how superior a robe would be if it were embroidered by loving, grateful hands. Then he lit the brazier, and took up the wand of *lignum vitae*. Dala sneezed. Ede appeared out of nowhere and wound around Ferdon's legs, miaowing plaintively. "Here you are," he said, picking her up. "Let us begin."

He cast the proper ingredients into the fire. Smoke began filling the air. Unhappy though she was at the process and at Dala's presence, Ede allowed Ferdon to hold her while he followed, counter-sunwise, the inwardly spiraling path of the chalk marks. In a high, nasal tone of voice he began to chant: *"Rignus, sallivus, quantum facterium. Placus, fortunatus—"*

The Power throbbed through him, magnified and channeled by the Companion's presence. The very air trembled, crackling with the enormous energy he was tapping into, almost drowning out the occasional sounds of sneezing. With each circuit he made of the seated figure in the center of the maze, the pustular lump at the temple was diminishing under the great forces being directed against it. Ede lay in the crook of his arm, tense and alert, now a part of the thing being done, a willing participant. At just the right instant, as he took the last steps that would bring him face-to-face with the subject of the spell, he threw the pinch of magic dust into the air to drift down upon this subject, and inserted the additional words he had looked up the night before. *"adque, pulque—veritum est!"*

A clap of thunder reverberated through the room. Ede, every hair bristling, screamed in outrage, tore herself from Ferdon's arms and vanished. Dala just sat there, stunned and dazed, until Ferdon knelt at her feet. "Here," he said, holding out a silver mirror. "Look at yourself."

The expense had been worth it. With satisfaction he watched Dala seeing for the first time what he had always known she could become. Hesitantly, she touched the clear, unmarked skin, running her fingers over features that were, and at the same time, were not, those with which she had been born.

Ede's last-second refusal and rejection had spoiled the spell a little. Dala's hair had been dull red; now it was just a shade short of russet, the highlights not as bright as he had envisioned. Her eyes were the same hazel as before, not the golden brown he had been aiming for. But her skin was flawless, stretching smooth over remodeled, aristocratic bones, all redness gone except for the faintest blush high on her cheeks. Her nose was small and straight, her lips now the color and texture of tea-rose petals. Her teeth were very white, though, alas, still a little crooked. While not the shattering beauty he had planned, the one who could have empires at her feet, she was still a woman who could grace the hall of any noble in the land, even that of the king. If he had not been infatuated before, he certainly was now; wholeheartedly, he fell in love with his own creation.

"Do you like what you see?" he asked, still at her feet. "If you do, then perhaps you will grant me the favor of—I mean, perhaps you will do me the honor—I mean, I want to—"

"In a minute, Ferdon," Dala said, still engrossed with her image in the polished silver. She wiped her nose on her sleeve. "This is so unreal. I—I have to have some time to get used to, to what I look like now."

"Of course." He arose and helped her to her feet. "Of course you do. Go home. Or go to the marketplace and sell your wares if you like. I think you will find that you have more customers this day than you ever dreamed of." He closed her hands over the mirror. "Keep this, the first gift of many, and remember who gave it to you."

"Thank you," she said. "Thank you." She wandered out of the workroom, still in a daze, unable to tear herself away from the vision she beheld in the silver surface.

Ferdon smiled at her pleasure. Then, remembering, he

hurried after her, just in time to see her pick up her
bundle of goods and open the kitchen door. "Will you
return to me this evening, after the market?"

"What?"

"This evening. Will you come back?"

"Yes. Perhaps. I—I have to think."

She went through the door, almost stumbling, trying to
balance the packages and still look at herself in the
mirror. Ferdon laughed aloud. She would be back. He
knew it.

Suddenly and ferociously hungry, he opened a cupboard and began setting out dishes. Some porridge, perhaps. Ede would be hungry as well. Magic-making always
did that to one, drained all the reserves of energy, and
one had to cast spells on an empty stomach to begin
with—

"Ede!" he called, rattling the dishes. Usually this was
enough to bring her running; porridge was one of their
favorite breakfasts.

But she stayed hidden, still sulking, until he had the
porridge cooked and poured, with her bowl all nicely
prepared with milk and a dusting of expensive cinnamon—a
very special treat. Only then did a faint clink of jeweled
earrings tell him that she was in the same room with him.
Yet she did not jump up onto the table to eat with him,
as was their wont. Stubbornly, she sat at his feet and
glared at him out of blue-green eyes; stubbornly, he
refused to set her dish on the floor. Only when he had
finished his portion and had taken his bowl to the side-
board did she climb, with great dignity, to the tabletop
and begin eating the now-cold porridge.

Dala did not return to the magician's house that evening nor the next day, nor the day after that. She almost
stopped coming there altogether. Ferdon went calling on
her instead, any time his duties took him near the farm
where she lived, just beyond the town walls. This happened not nearly as often as he would have liked. As a
physician-mage, he needed to be available for anyone
who needed him, and in the good-sized country town
where he lived, there were many who did, and those

sometimes at very odd hours. It interfered with his courting, but there was no help for it. He began to long for a
servant, to help him keep track of appointments and
messages. He purchased a slate and kept it propped over
the kitchen fireplace for those who had missed him, but
few in the town knew how to read or write.

Courtship it had become, and no mistake. Every time
they met, Ferdon asked Dala to marry him; and every
time he did, she turned him aside in such a way that it
was no refusal at all. She needed more time. She was just
now beginning to enjoy her life. Why did he want her to
give it up so soon?

The main trouble was, Ferdon was not alone in his
attentions to Dala—or Doucette, as she called herself
these days, saying that "Dala" was an ugly name fit only
for the ugly creature she had once been. It seemed that
half the eligible young men in town were now paying
court to her, including, if rumor was to be believed, the
son of the ruling baron.

Doucette only laughed whenever Ferdon objected.
"They mean nothing to me!" she told him, over and
over. "I hated myself for far too long and they make me
feel good. Do you think I could forget who I have to
thank, the wonderful man who was responsible for all my
good fortune?"

At such times, she would take his hand in both of hers,
and sometimes press it to the warmth of her breasts. But
Ferdon could not help noticing that he was not the only
person who gave Doucette presents these days. At least,
he knew he hadn't given her the locket hanging from the
fine chain around her neck. And surely her new-found
success in the marketplace didn't account for the beautiful clothes she now wore every day, nor the various
improvements to the farm, the house, and its furnishings.
He could have discovered where all these things had
come from if Ede had been there to help him, but Ede
always knew when his rounds were going to take him to
Doucette's house and refused to accompany him then.
Ede's anger had become unhappiness. He grew used to
the sight of a brown cat-lump sitting in the window,
watching him as he walked away, her blue-green eyes

glowing with disapproval. They were both miserable these days, but it seemed to him she might be coming around, if slowly. At least, since that day when she had knocked his books all over the workroom, she didn't jangle her earrings at him any more.

Ede had a lot of time for contemplation while Ferdon was away. She took to leaving the house as well, sometimes for a week at a time. When she was home, she hunkered in the window or near the fireplace, brooding. Sometimes she threw herself into a mood of play and mischief, batting a toy around and leaving destruction in her wake for Ferdon to clean up when he returned.

On one of these occasions, by accident she knocked a book off the shelf and it opened when it landed on the floor. Flinging herself on the pages, she danced madly, scrabbling at the expensive paper with her paws, delighting in wrinkling the pages as she turned them. The marks on the paper meant little to her and she quickly grew bored with this volume. Leaping to the shelf, she selected another and then a third, and a fourth, according them the same treatment. Methodically, she worked her way along the shelf until she came to a small, leather-bound one, hidden between two larger books. This one contained many pictures and it caught her interest. If Ferdon could have seen her then, he would have observed the cat crouched over the book for all the world like a schoolboy studying his lessons. From time to time she raked at a page, turning it, absorbed in what the pictures were showing her. When she finished looking through the book, she sat very still, tail wrapped around her paws, staring at nothing. Then, with great care and deliberation, she shoved all the rest of the books off the shelf until that particular volume was quite lost in the welter.

A few weeks later, when the summer was beginning to draw to an end and the evenings to grow cool, Doucette came to the magician's house, letting herself in the kitchen door. She wore a new shift of creamy linen and her skirt and bodice were of rich velvet; now she went shod in red leather, all in all looking nothing like the disfigured farmgirl she had once been.

"Ferdon?" she called. "Are you home? I have something to tell you— Oh." Ede trotted through the open door. Doucette eyed the cat sourly. "You. Where's your master? Can't talk, can you? Or won't, is more like it, at least to me. Who knows what little chats the two of you have when you're alone." Her lips lifted in a smile that didn't touch her eyes. She stifled a sneeze. "We've never liked each other, but at least I was smart enough to try to hide it. No sense in pretending now, is there? I've got a message for your master."

She took the slate from over the fireplace and sat down at the table and began to write. Because the art had come late to her—the lessons another present from an admirer—she unconsciously spoke the words aloud as she wrote.

"Fare you welle, frend Ferdon. I am getting wed. To Rikkar, the barron's sonne. Thank you aginne. Your frend Doucette."

She propped the slate against a bowl on the table. "There. He ought to see it when he returns." Ede jumped up onto the table and stared at the woman. "It's a good thing for both of us that you and I didn't get along. I might have married Ferdon out of sheer gratitude, except for you, and then where would I have been? Not as well off as I'm going to be." She laughed out loud. Ede walked toward her, miaowing. "I would have kicked you out of the house the instant the bans were read and no mistake. But that's all past. Might as well be friends now, eh? No harm in that, I suppose." She sneezed and wiped her watering eyes on a cambric handkerchief.

With a luxuriously sinuous movement, Ede stropped herself against Doucette. The earring on that side fell clattering to the table. The cat turned and stropped back in the other direction and the second earring fell off.

Doucette recoiled from the contact, and then saw the jewels lying on the table. "How nice!" she exclaimed. "A wedding present!"

She took the earrings, admiring the gleam of the sapphire and emerald beads, the glitter of the gold, and put them in her own ears. . . .

Ferdon let himself in, wearily unslinging the carry-sack of medicinal and magical supplies from his shoulder. It had begun to rain outside and he was tired and cold. To his surprise and pleasure, the lamps were lit and the good smell of supper cooking filled the air. There was a woman at the fireplace, bending over, but not to tend the cookpot. Rather, the woman appeared to be doing something with the poker—stirring the fire to make it burn brighter, perhaps. The wife of a rich, ailing townsman, come to fetch him and preparing a hot meal while she waited? She was certainly dressed well enough, in velvet and red leather shoes. He dropped the sack beside the door. "Can I help you?" he said.

The woman—girl, really—started, as if caught in the act of doing something questionable. "You are the physician-mage, Ferdon?" There was a lilting quality to her speech, almost like an accent, hard to identify. "I have a message from Doucette."

"What message?" He moved toward the cookpot, sniffing appreciatively. His stomach growled; he had not eaten since that morning. Something flared up, a flash of purple in the depths of the flame, then died away. He caught a whiff of another odor from the fire itself, as if the girl were burning an old shoe. From force of habit he glanced up at the slate, but it was as clean as it had been when he had left that morning—cleaner, even. "You know Doucette?"

"Oh, yes." The color rose in the girl's cheeks. "I know her well. There is news, unpleasant for you, I fear. She—she could not stay to tell you herself."

Ferdon sighed. "Well, out with it. It won't grow any better for being postponed."

"Doucette has gone away, for good. She's never coming back."

There was silence in the magician's kitchen, broken only by the crackle of the fire and the faint sound of the stew bubbling in the pot. Ferdon sat down heavily at the table. "Gone. . . ."

The girl stirred the kettle and spooned some of the contents into a bowl. A curl of half-burned paper drifted out onto the hearth and she stepped on it, sweeping it back into the fire. The fingers of one hand moved in a curious gesture as she set the food before him. "Here, eat," she said. "You will feel better for it."

"Did she say why?" Automatically, he put a spoonful of the stew into his mouth. It was very good.

The girl shook her head. "I believe she felt this town was unworthy of a woman of her immense beauty. There were larger worlds waiting for her."

"So she sent you to tell me."

"Actually, it was my idea to come." The girl's cheeks grew redder. "Please, forgive my forwardness. But she never cared for you, not after she got what she wanted from you. And I—" She bit her lip.

Ferdon put down his spoon. Frowning, he studied the girl's face, trying to remember where—or even if—he had seen her before. There was something, though he couldn't put his finger on it. She had a heart-shaped face, brown hair, a slender figure—the velvet dress, laced to its tightest, was loose on her—and, he now noticed, the loveliest blue-green eyes tilted at the corners. "No," he said. "I have never seen you before. If I had, I would have remembered."

The girl smiled a bit sadly. "How could you know? You never even looked at anyone but Doucette."

He had to smile with her. "That's true. Ede— Where is she? Have you seen anything of an Egyptian cat? She's not been around much lately, but the smell of this stew ought to bring her hurrying back—"

"Doucette said to tell you she'd taken Ede with her."

Ferdon lurched to his feet, almost upsetting the table. "She took Ede? That's impossible! Ede detested her!" He paced angrily across the room, calming himself by an act of will. His infatuation with Doucette evaporated as abruptly as it had begun. He bowed his head. "I never thought she would steal my Companion. She must have done it for spite. I will miss Ede. I—I loved her a great deal." He drifted off into thought, remembering.

With an effort, Ferdon brought himself back to the

moment. The girl stood quite still in the firelight, only her fingers moving in the folds of her skirt. She swallowed hard. "Though I know you, you don't know me. I am called Edanne."

Ferdon opened his mouth and closed it again, unsure of what he wanted to say. At that moment, something thumped against the window. He hurried to open the shutter and see what the trouble was. A ginger-colored cat squirmed through immediately and landed with a heavy thud on the floor. It shook drops of water off its fur, then stood up and snagged its claws in Ferdon's leggings, miaowing loudly and showing its sharp white teeth, as if it wanted to tell the magician something.

"Hello, yourself," he said. He knelt and picked the cat up in his arms. The lamplight caught points of green and blue fire from the jewels on the rings in its ears. Ferdon stared in disbelief. Then, slowly, he began to laugh.

"What does this mean?" Edanne said.

"It means that I am lucky beyond measure!" Ferdon exclaimed. "In the space of one hour I have lost a treasured Companion, regained my senses, another Companion has come to me—not as fine a one as Ede nor as well-trained or clever I daresay, but a Companion nonetheless—and I have found you." He set the cat down and folded Edanne in his embrace. "I have found you, haven't I?"

"Yes. I love you. I always have."

Outside, the rain began pelting down in earnest. The cat, an unfathomable expression in its greenish-brown eyes, stared and stared at the two of them. Then it sneezed.

CLARA'S CAT

by Elizabeth Moon

The old lady was almost helpless. She had never been large, and her once-red hair had faded to dingy gray. Behind thick glasses, necessary since the surgery for cataracts, her eyes were as colorless as a dead oyster. She had always had a redhead's white skin that freckled first, then burned at the least touch of the sun. Now the duller brown spots of age speckled her knotted hands.

It was going to be easy. Jeannie had a blood-claim—the only claim, she reminded herself. Her mother had been the old lady's niece; the old lady had never had children. So it was simple, and no court could deny it. Besides, she was going to spend a while convincing everyone that she had the old lady's best interests at heart. Of course she did. They knew that already. She had come to take care of dear old Great-aunt Clara, left her job in the city—a pretty good job, too, she had explained to everyone who asked. But blood being thicker than water, and her the old lady's last blood relative, well, of course she had come to help out.

"Did I ever tell you about Snowball?" The soft, insistent voice from the bed broke into her fierce reverie. *Yes,* the old lady had told her about Snowball . . . every white cat in creation was probably called Snowball, at least by senile old ladies like Great-aunt Clara. Jeannie controlled herself; there would be time enough later.

"I think so, Aunt Clara." Just a little dig, that implication of careful patience.

"He was so sweet." A vague sound meant to be a chuckle, Jeannie was sure, then . . . "Did I tell you about the time he clawed Mrs. Minister Jenkins on the ankle, when she scolded me about wearing my skirts too short?"

Oh, god. Jeannie had heard that story on every visit—every reluctant, restless visit—since childhood. It was disgusting, that someone of Great-aunt Clara's age remembered the juicy side of youth, remembered rolling her stockings and flirting with a skirt just a bit short . . . that she could still enjoy the memory of a minister's wife's clawed ankle, that she still thought a stupid cat had defended her. But there were visitors in the house, Clara's friends, people Jeannie had not yet won over completely. Clara's lawyer, Sam Benson, stocky and grave and not quite old enough to fall for any tricks. Clara's old friend Pearl, still up and walking around—though Jeannie thought it was disgusting for anyone her age to wear sleeveless knit shirts and short skirts which left knobby tanned knees all too visible.

Jeannie let out a consciously indulgent laugh. "Was that when you were courting Ben, Aunt Clara?"

Again that feeble attempt at a chuckle. "I wasn't courting *him*, dear; we weren't like you girls today. He was courting me. Very dashing, Ben was. All the girls thought so, too." Clara's eyes shifted to her friend Pearl, and the two of them exchanged fatuous grins. Jeannie could feel the smile stiffening on her own face. *Dashing.* And did this mean Pearl had been one of the girls who thought so, too? Had they been rivals?

"I didn't," said Pearl, in the deep voice Jeannie found so strange. Little old ladies had thin, wispy voices, or high querulous voices, or cross rough voices . . . not this combination of bassoon and cello, like a cat's purr. "I thought he was a lot more than dashing, but you, you minx, you wanted him to play off against Larry."

"Ah . . . Larry." Clara's head shifted on the pillow. "I hadn't thought of him in . . ."

"Five minutes?" Pearl conveyed amusement without malice.

"He was so . . ." Clara's voice trailed off, and a tear slipped down her cheek. Jeannie was quick to blot it away. "The War . . ." said Clara faintly. Pearl nodded. The War they meant was the first of the great wars, the one to end wars, and Jeannie was not entirely sure which century it had been in. History was a bore. Everything before her own birth merged into a confused hash of dates and names she could never untangle, and why bother? The lawyer cleared his throat.

"Clara, I hate to rush you, but . . ."

The old lady stared at him as if she couldn't remember his name or business; Jeannie was just about to remind her when she brightened. "Oh—yes, Sam, of course. The power of attorney. Now what I thought was, since Jeannie's come to stay, and take care of me, that she will need to write checks and things. You know how the bank is these days . . . and the people at the power company and so on don't seem to remember me as well. . . ." What she meant was lost bills, checks she never wrote, and a lifetime's honesty ignored by strangers and their computers. But it had never been her habit to accuse anyone of unfairness. "Jeannie can take care of all that," she said finally.

In the face of the lawyer's obvious doubts, Jeannie's attempt at an expression that would convey absolute honesty, searing self-sacrifice for her nearest relative, and steadfast devotion to duty slipped awry; she could feel her lower lip beginning to pout, and the tension in the muscles of her jaw. Silence held the room for a long moment. Then Pearl, carefully not looking at Jeannie, said, "But Sam's been doing all that, hasn't he, Clara?"

"Well . . . yes. . . ." Clara's voice now was the trembling that meant a lapse into confusion, into dismay and fear, as the edges of her known world crumbled. "I mean . . . I know . . . but he is a lawyer, and lawyers do have to make a living . . . and anyway, Jeannie's *family*. . . ." In that rush of broken phrases, in that soft old voice, the arguments Jeannie had tried to teach her aunt to say sounded as silly and implausible as they might printed on a paper. Jeannie knew—as Clara would remember in a moment, if she calmed down—that Sam had not charged her a penny for managing her money since he'd taken it over. Jeannie thought it was stupid; Clara claimed to know the reason, but would never explain.

The lawyer's face stiffened at the mention of money, and Jeannie wished she had not put those words in her aunt's mouth. Yet that seemed to do what she had wished of the whole conversation; his warm voice chilled, and he said "If that's how you feel, Clara—Mrs. Timmons— then of course there's no question of not doing exactly as you wish. I brought the papers, as you asked." Jeannie left the room on a pretext of making iced tea for every- one, while Clara signed and Pearl witnessed; she was not surprised, when she returned, to find them on the point of leaving. The lawyer's glance raked her up and down like an edged blade, but his voice, in deference to Clara, was gentle.

"I'm quite sure you'll take excellent care of your aunt, Mrs. Becker. She's one of our town's favorites, you know—if you need help, you have only to ask."

"Thank you," said Jeannie softly, in her best manner. Great-aunt Clara must have told him she'd been married. She herself liked the modern fashion of "Ms." which left her marital status handily obscured. Keith had been a mistake, and the divorce had been messy, what with the battle over the kids. He had custody, on account of her drinking—not that she was really an alcoholic, it was just that one time and unlucky for her that the roads were wet. But she could trust Great-aunt Clara not to have told anyone about that; she had too much family pride.

Pearl shook hands with her firmly. "I'll be dropping by every day, you know," she said, with her big old teeth showing in a fierce grin. "If you need a few minutes to go downtown, that kind of thing."

The old lady. Clara. She had a heart condition, for which she was supposed to take two of these little pills (morning and evening) and three of those (with each meal.) There were pills for the chest pain that came on unexpectedly, and pills for the bloating. She could just get out of bed, with help, to use the toilet and sit for a few minutes while Jeannie changed her bed. Jeannie was very careful and very conscientious, those first weeks. She kept the rasping whine out of her voice, the note Keith had told the judge was his first sign that something was really wrong.

And in return, Great-aunt Clara talked. She had had no full-time companion for years, not since her last sister

died, and she had a life's stored memories to share.
Jeannie gritted her teeth through the interminable tales
of Clara's childhood: the pony her brother had had, the
rides in the buggy, the first automobile, the first electric
light in the town. And endlessly repetitive, the stories of
Clara's favorite cat, Snowball.

"He looked *just* like that," Clara would say, waving
feebly at the cheap print of a sentimental painting on the
wall, the picture of a huge fluffy white cat with a blue
bow around its neck, sitting beside a pot of improbable
flowers on a stone wall. It was a hideous picture, and
Jeannie was sure Snowball must have been a hideous cat.
The picture was not the only reminder of Snowball. Clara
had an old, yellowing photograph of the animal himself
(he looked *nothing* like the cat in the painting . . . merely
a white blur beneath a chair), several white china cats of
various sizes, and a cat-shaped pillow covered with rabbit
fur. At least Jeannie hoped it was rabbit-fur, and not the
cat himself, stuffed.

She did not care enough to ask. She was sick and tired
of Snowball stories, from the time he caught the mouse
in the kitchen ("And carried it outside without making
any mess on the floor at all. . . .") to the time he hid in
the car and startled Clara's father by leaping on his
shoulder as they were driving to church, and the car
swerved, and everyone thought her father had been . . .
indulging, you know . . . until the cat leapt out. The
town had laughed for days. Jeannie felt *she* had been
trying to laugh for days, a stiff grin stretched across a dry
mouth.

She wanted a drink. She needed a drink. But she
would not drink yet, not while Pearl came by once a day
or more, and the lawyer stopped her on the street to see
how things were coming. First they must see what good
care she took of Clara; first they must believe she was
what she appeared.

Day after dull day passed by. Summer in a small town,
to one used to a large city, is largely a matter of endur-
ance. Jeannie didn't know any of the faces that fit the
names in Clara's stories. She tried harder to follow them
when Pearl was there, but the women had been close for

over seventy years, and their talk came in quick, short-hand bursts that meant little to an outsider. Pearl, quick to notice Jeannie's confusion, tried to explain once or twice, but gave it up when Clara insisted "Of course she knews who we mean—she's family." The two women giggled, chattered briefly, giggled, shed tears, and to Jeannie it was all both boring and slightly disgusting. All that had happened years ago—before she herself was born—and what did it matter if some long-dead husband had thought his wife was in love with a Chinese druggest two towns away? Why cry over the death of someone else's child in a fire forty years ago? They should have more dignity, she thought, coming in with the tray of iced tea and cookies to find them giggling again.

Grimly, with a smile pasted to her face, she cooked the old-fashioned food Clara liked, washed the old plates and silver (*real* silver: she didn't mind that), and dusted the innumerable figurines on the shelves that seemed to crawl all over the walls. Not just white china cats, but shepherds and shepherdesses, barking dogs, fat-bellied ponies in lavender and cream, unbearably coy children being bashful with each other in costumes that reminded Jeannie of the more sickening children's books of her past. Blown-glass birds and ships and fish, decorative tiles with flowers hand-painted, Clara explained carefully, by the girls of her senior class. Pearl's tile had a wicked-looking yellow rose, thorns very sharp, on pale green. Jeannie thought it was typical of her . . . sallow and sharp, that's what she was. She dusted the old photographs Clara had on every wall surface not covered by shelves of knickknacks: hand-colored mezzotints of a slender girl in a high-necked blouse with leg-o-mutton sleeves . . . "your great-grand-mother, dear" . . . and a class portrait from Clara's high school days. Ben and Larry, the boys Clara and Pearl had loved (or whatever it was) were two stiff, sober-faced lads with slicked-down hair in the upper right and upper left-hand corners. Jeannie tried to imagine them in ordinary clothes and hair, and failed. All the faces were sober, even frightened; it had been the class of '17.

In August, Jeannie first began to notice the smell. No one had ever said Jeannie was slovenly; the one thing she

truly prided herself on was cleanliness. She hated the feel
of Clara's flesh when she bathed her—that white, loose
skin over obscene softness—but she would keep her great-
aunt clean until her dying day. The smell of age she
found unpleasant, but not as bad as in a nursing home.
No, the smell she noticed was another smell, a sharper,
acrid smell, which her great-aunt tried to tell her was
from the bachelor's buttons under the window.

Jeannie did not argue. If she argued, if someone heard
her arguing with her great-aunt, it would be hard to
present herself as the angel of mercy she knew she was.
She did say she thought bachelor's buttons had no smell,
but with a wistful questioning intonation that let her aunt
explain that *those* bachelor's buttons smelled like that
every summer, and she liked the smell because it reminded her of Snowball.

Of course, Jeannie thought, it's a cat. A tomcat smell,
the smell of marked territory. Odd that it came through a
closed window, in spite of air-conditioning, but smells
would do things like that. Since Clara said she liked it,
Jeannie tried to endure it, but it was stronger in *her*
bedroom, as if the miserable cat had marked the bed
itself. She looked, finding no evidence, and vacuumed
vigorously.

Outside, on the white clapboard skirting of the old
house, she found the marks she sought. Hot sun baked
the bachelor's buttons, the cracked soil around them (she
had not watered for more than a week), and the streaked
places on the skirting that gave off that memorable smell.
On the pretext of watering the flowers (they did need
watering, and she picked some to arrange inside) she
hosed down the offending streaks. And a few days later,
dragging the hose around to water another of the
flowerbeds (when she had this house, she would forget
the flowerbeds), she saw a white blurred shape up near
the house, and splashed water at it. A furious streak sped
away, yowling. *Gotcha*, thought Jeannie, *that'll teach you*,
and forgot about it.

Clara had another small stroke in September, that left
her with one drooping eyelid and halting speech, now as
ragged as soft. Jeannie had driven her (in Clara's old car)

to the hospital in the county seat, and Jeannie drove her home, with a list of instructions for diet and care. In between those two trips, in the hours when the hospital discouraged visitors, she explored Clara's little town. The square with its bandstand had been paved, parking for the stores around it. She remembered, with an unexpected pang of nostalgia, climbing into the empty bandstand and pretending to be a singer. A hardware store had vanished, replaced by a supermarket which had already swallowed a small grocery store the last time she'd visited. The farm supply and implement company had moved out of town, as had the lumberyard; a used car dealer had one lot, and the other was covered with rows of tiny boxlike rental storage units. A few people recognized her; she hurried past the door that opened onto a narrow stair—upstairs was the lawyer's office, with its view over the town square and out back across a vacant lot to the rest of town.

It was stiflingly hot. Jeannie got back in Clara's car and drove out of town toward the county seat and its hospital, well aware of watching eyes. But the county seat had more than a hospital, and it was larger, and she was less known, Clara's car less noticeable. She parked in the big courthouse lot, walked a block to a sign she'd noticed, and glanced around. Midafternoon: the lawyer would be in his office, or in court.

She came out two hours later. Not drunk at all—no one could say she was drunk. A lady, worried to death about her old great-aunt, needing a cool place to spend a few hours before the hospital would let her back in . . . that's all. She knew her limits well, and she knew exactly what she wanted. She had the name and number she had expected to find, and would not need to visit the Blue Suite again.

That night, alone in the house (Clara would be in the hospital another two days, the doctor had said), she lounged in the parlor as she never did when Clara was there. She had remembered to call Pearl, had said she didn't need any help with anything, and now she relaxed, safe, wearing the short lacy nightshirt she'd bought in the county seat, enjoying the first cold beer she'd ever had in

this house. She smirked up at the shelves of figurines.
Clara's monthly allowance wouldn't exactly cover what
she wanted, but she knew there were places to sell some
of this trash, and if Clara were bedfast she'd never know.

Clara came home more fragile than before. She never
left the bedroom now, and rarely managed to sit up in
the armchair; Jeannie had to learn to make the bed with
her in it. She had to learn other, more intimate services
when Clara could not get out of bed at all. But she
persisted, through the rest of September and October,
until even thorny Pearl admitted (to the supermarket
clerk, from whom Jeannie heard it) that she seemed to
be genuinely fond of Clara, and taking excellent care of
her. When the first November storm slashed the town
with cold rain and wind, Pearl called to apologize for not
visiting that day. Jeannie answered the phone in the hall.

"It's all right," she told Pearl. "Do you want me to
wake her, so you can talk?"

"Not if she's sleeping," said Pearl. "Just tell her."

"She sleeps a lot more now," said Jeannie, in a voice
that she hoped conveyed delicate sadness.

Clara was not asleep, but her voice no longer had the
resonance to carry from room to room . . . and certainly
not enough to be overheard on the phone. "Who was it,
dear?" she asked when Jeannie came back to her.

"Nothing," said Jeannie. She knew Clara's hearing was
going. "Some salesman about aluminum siding." She felt
a rising excitement; it had taken months, but here was
her chance. A day or so without Pearl, another inevitable
stroke—it would work. It would be easy. "Do you think
Pearl will try to come out in this storm?"

Clara moved her head a little on the pillow. "I hope
not . . . but she'll call. Tell me if she calls, dear, won't
you?"

"Of course."

Two days later, it was possible to tell Pearl that Clara
had forgotten being told—of course she had told her
about the calls, but since this latest stroke, and with the
new medications . . . Jeannie delivered this information
in a low voice, just inside the front door. Pearl herself
looked sick, her wisps of white hair standing out in disar-

ray, her deep voice more hoarse than musical. If Jeannie
had been capable of it, she would have felt pity for Pearl
then—she knew she ought to, an old woman whose oldest friend was fading into senility—but what she felt was
coarse triumphant glee. *Old cow,* she thought, *I should
try* you *next.* Pearl was nodding, showing no suspicion;
perhaps she was too tired.

She left them alone, and went to fix them tea; she
could just hear Pearl's deep voice, and a wisp of plaintive
trembling treble that must be Clara. When she came in
with the tray, Clara's hands were shaking so that she
could not hold the cup.

"Are you *sure* you told me, dear?" she asked Jeannie.
"You couldn't have forgotten?"

"I'm sure, Aunt Clara. I'm sorry—maybe you were
still sleepy, or maybe the medicine . . ." She held the cup
to Clara's lips, waited for her to slurp a little—no longer
so ladylike in her sips—and set it down.

Pearl, leaning back in her chair, suddenly sniffed. Jeannie stiffened; she had bathed Clara carefully (*that* duty
she would always perform) and instantly suspected Pearl
of trying to make her feel inferior. But Pearl merely
looked puzzled.

"Do you have a cat again, Clara?" she asked. Jeannie
relaxed, relieved. She answer for her aunt.

"No, but there's a stray, and he . . . uh . . . he . . .
you know."

"He sprays the house? It must be, to smell that strong
on a chilly day. I thought perhaps indoors—"

"Did I ever tell you about the time Snowball clawed
the minister's wife?" asked Clara brightly. Jeannie glanced
at Pearl, and met a wistful and knowing glance. She
accepted that silent offer of alliance as silently, and told
her aunt no.

After that it was as easy as she'd hoped. November
continued cold and damp; Clara's friends came rarely,
and readily believed Jeannie's excuses on the telephone.
Once or twice she let a call go through, when Clara was
drowsy with medicine and not making much sense. Soon
the calls dwindled, except on sunny bright days when
they asked if they could come see her. This Jeannie

always encouraged so eagerly that everyone knew how hard it was on her, poor dear, all alone with dying Clara.

When they came, Clara would be exquisitely clean and neat, arrayed in her best bedjacket; Jeannie, in something somber and workmanlike. They never smelled alcohol on her breath; they never saw bottles or cans in the house. They never came without calling, because, as Jeannie had explained, "Sometimes I'm up most of the night with her, you know, and I do nap in the day sometimes. . . ." That was only fair; no one could fault her for that, or wanted to bring her out, sleepy and rumpled, to answer the doorbell.

It was true that Clara's monthly allowance from the trust would not buy Jeannie what she wanted. She began in the cedar chests which were full of a long lifetime's accumulation: old handpainted china tea sets, antique dolls and doll clothes, handmade quilts and crocheted afghans. She would not risk the county seat, but it was less than fifty miles to the big city, where no one knew anyone else, and handcrafted items brought a good price.

Gradually, week by week, she pilfered more: an old microscope that had belonged to Clara's dead husband, a set of ruby glass that they never used, a pair of silver candlesticks she found in the bottom cupboard in the dining room. Clara had jewelry that had been her mother's and her older sisters', jumbled together in a collection of old jewelry boxes, white and red and green padded leather, hidden in bureau drawers all over the house, under linens and stationery and faded nightgowns from Clara's youth and brief marriage. With one eye on the bed, where Clara lay dozing, Jeannie plucked first one then another of the salable items: a ruby ring, a gold brooch, a platinum ring with diamond chips, a pair of delicate gold filigree earrings.

Autumn passed into winter, a gray, nasty December followed by a bleak and bitter January. Jeannie felt the cold less, with her secret cache of favorite beverages and pills. Pearl came once a week or so, on good days, but Jeannie always had plenty of warning . . . and Clara now knew better than to complain. Jeannie had used no force (she had read about it), but threats of the nursing home sufficed. And it was not like real cruelty. As she'd told Clara, "What if it does take me a little while sometimes . . . at least you got a nurse to yourself, on call day and night, and that's more than you'd get there. They let people like you lie in a wet bed . . . they don't come running. You ought to be glad you've got me to take care of you—because you don't have no place else." She felt good about that, really, even using bad grammar on purpose. The world was not the bright, shiny gold ring Clara had told her about when she was a child; using good grammar didn't get you anywhere she wanted to go.

She intended it to be over before spring. She could not possibly stand another summer in this dump. But picking a time, and a precise method—that was harder. Clara slept most of the day now, helped by liberal doses of medicine; the doctor was understanding when Jeannie explained that she needed her own sleep, and couldn't be up and down all the time when her aunt was agitated. Jeannie watched her, half-hoping she'd quit breathing on her own. But the old lady kept breathing, kept opening her eyes every morning and several times a day, kept wanting to talk, in that breathy and staggering voice, about the old days.

And especially, to Jeannie's disgust, about cats. Snowball, of course, first and always. But she sent Jeannie out to find and bring into the bedroom the other cats, the china ones and glass ones and the elegant woodcarving of a Siamese that Jeannie had not noticed in a corner cabinet until Clara told her which shelf. Clara not only talked about cats, she seemed to talk *to* them: to the picture ("Snowball, you beauty, you dear . . .") and the china cats ("You're so sleek, so darling . . .") It made Jeannie gag. So did the tang of tomcat, which remained even in cold weather. Had the cat hit a hot-water pipe, Jeannie wondered? Was it living under the house, in the crawl space?

In the middle of January, Pearl came one day without calling first. Jeannie wakened suddenly in midmorning, aware of the doorbell's dying twang. Her mouth was furry and tasted horrible; she knew her eyes were bleary. She popped two breath mints, put on her hooded robe, and peered out the spyhole. Pearl, muffled in layers of brilliant knitting, stood hunched over a walker on the front porch, holding a folded newspaper in her hand. Jeannie opened the door, backing quickly away from the gust of cold air. "Sorry," she said vaguely. "I've had a sort of cold, and I was up last night. . . ."

"That's all right, dear, and I won't disturb Clara—" Pearl handed her the paper. "I just thought you should know, to break it gently—our other classmate, May, died yesterday in the nursing home."

"Oh, how terrible." She knew what to say, but felt the morning after lassitude dragging at her mind. "Sit down?"

"No." Pearl glanced at Clara's shut bedroom door. "I don't think I—I mean, I might cry . . . I *would* cry . . . and she'd be more upset. Pick your time, dear." And shaking her head to Jeannie's offers of a cup of tea or a few minutes of rest, she edged her way back out and down the walk in careful steps behind the walker. Jeannie watched through the window, then glanced at the paper. "May Ellen Freeman, graduated high school in '17, one of the last few . . ." The newspaper writer had let herself go, wallowing in sentimentality.

It was, in fact, the perfect excuse. Everyone knew that old people were more fragile, could fall apart when their friends died. Pearl was using a walker—Pearl, who two weeks ago had climbed the front steps on her own. So if she told Clara, and Clara's heart stopped, who would question it? And she would choose her time carefully.

Clara, of course, was awake, and had heard the doorbell. Another mistake, Jeannie told her. She hurried Clara though the morning routine—after all, they were late—rushing her through the bedpan part, bathing her as quickly as she could, changing the bed with quick, jerking tugs at the sheets. She even apologized, with the vague feeling that she ought to be polite to someone she was going to kill in a few minutes, for being late. She'd felt a cold coming on, she'd had a headache last night, she'd taken more aspirin than she should. Clara said nothing; her tiny face had crumpled even further.

"I'll get your breakfast," said Jeannie, carrying away the used bed linens. Her head was beginning to pound with the effort of thought. She glanced at the clock as she pushed the sheets into the washer. After ten already! Suppose they did an autopsy . . . Clara would have nothing in her stomach, and she should have had breakfast. Could Jeannie say she had refused her breakfast? Sometimes she did. A snack now? The thought of cooking turned Jeannie's stomach, but she put a kettle on the stove and turned on the back burner. Tea, perhaps, and something warmed in the microwave. She went to her room and brushed her hair vigorously, slapped her face to get the color in it. In her mind she was explaining to the doctor how Clara had seemed weaker that morning, hadn't eaten, and she'd taken her a roll, wondering whether to tell her yet, and Clara had . . . had what? Should Clara eat the roll first, and then be told, or . . . the kettle whistled to her.

Rolls, cups of tea, the pretty enameled tray she might sell at the flea market for a few dollars. She carried it into Clara's bedroom with a bright smile, and said, "Here you are, dear."

"Wish I could have eggs." Clara fumbled for one of the rolls, and Jeannie helped her. It was stupid, the doctor saying she couldn't have eggs, when she was over ninety and couldn't live long anyway, but it saved Jeannie from having to smell them cooking when she had a hangover. She sipped tea from her own cup, meditatively, wondering just when to do it. She felt someone staring at her, that unmistakable feeling, and turned around to see nothing at the window at all. No one could see through the blinds and curtains anyway. Her neck itched. She glared at the picture on the wall, the fake fluffy cat Clara called Snowball. Two glowing golden eyes stared back at her, brighter than she remembered. Hangover, she told herself firmly; comes from mixing pills and booze. So did the stench of tomcat.

What it really did was remind her of the perfect method. She cleared away the tray, gently wiped Clara's streaked chin and brushed away the crumbs, then carried the tray to the kitchen. She was a little hungry now, and fixed herself a bowl of Clara's cereal. The right bowl would be in the sink, later, if anyone looked. They would look; it was that kind of town.

Then she carried in the morning paper, and the white cat-shaped pillow, fixing her face in its fake smile for the last time. She would have a fake sad look later, but this was the last fake smile, and that thought almost made it real.

"I'm sorry, Aunt Clara," she said, as sorrowfully as she could. "I've got bad news—"

"Pearl?" Clara's face went white; she was staring at the paper. Jeannie almost wished she'd thought of that lie. It would have done the trick. But in her own way she was honest. She shook her head.

"No," she said gently. "May Ellen." Clara's face flushed pink again.

"Law! You scared me!" Her breath came fast and shallow. "May's been loony this five years—I expected *her*—" But her chin had started to tremble, and her voice shook even more than usual.

"I thought you'd be upset," said Jeannie, holding out the cat pillow, as if for comfort. "Pearl said—"

Clara's good eye looked remarkably alive this morning, a clear unclouded gray. "I thought I heard you two whispering out there. She here?"

"No, Aunt Clara. She didn't want to disturb you, and she said she'd start crying—"

"S'pose she would. May was her maid of honor, after all." Jeannie had not realized that Pearl had ever been married. Clara's voice faded again. "It was a long time ago. . . ." Now she was crying, grabbing for the cat-shaped pillow as Jeannie had hoped she would, burying her face in that white fur, her swollen knuckles locked onto it. Weak sobs shook her body, as disorganized as her speech.

"There, there," Jeannie said, as soothingly as if she expected it to go on tape. "There, there." She slipped an arm under Clara's head, cradling her, and pushed the pillow more firmly onto her face. It didn't take long, and the bony hands clung to the pillow, as if to help.

Jeannie "discovered" her an hour later. By then she had bathed, dressed, downed two cups of strong coffee, and made her own bed. She checked her appearance in the mirror. Slightly reddened eyes and nose could be grief; she left off her usual makeup. When she called the doctor, he was unsurprised, and quickly agreed to sign the certificate. She let her own voice tremble when she admitted she'd told Clara of May's death. He soothed her, insisted it was not her fault. "But it's so awful!" she heard herself say. "She started crying, into that old fur pillow . . . she wanted to be left alone, she said, so I went to take my bath, and she's . . . it's like she's holding it to her—" Sounding a little bored, the doctor asked if she wanted him to come by and see . . . she could tell he thought it was silly: old ladies do not commit suicide by smothering themselves with fur pillows. "I guess not," she said, hoping he hadn't overdone it.

"You're all right yourself?" he asked, more briskly.

"Yes . . . I'll be fine."

"Call if you want a sedative later," he said.

Jeannie removed the pillow from Clara's face, unclenching the dead fingers, surprised to feel nothing much at all when she touched that cooling flesh. Clara's face looked normal, as normal as a dead face could look. Jeannie called the funeral home Clara had always said she wanted ("give the condemned their choice"), and then, nervous as she was, called Pearl. It was a replay of the doctor's reaction. Jeannie lashed herself with guilt, admitted she had chosen the time badly, explained at length why it had seemed safe, and let Pearl comfort her. The irony of it almost made her lose character and laugh—that Pearl, now twice bereft, and sole survivor, would comfort the murderer—but she managed to choke instead. Pearl wanted to come, right away, and Jeannie agreed—even asked her to call Mr. Benson, the lawyer. "I feel so guilty," she finished, and Pearl replied, wearily enough, "You mustn't."

Everything went according to plan. Pearl arrived just before the funeral home men; she had her moment alone with Clara, and came out saying how peaceful Clara looked. She herself looked exhausted and sick, and Jeannie insisted on giving her a cup of tea and a roll. The funeral home men were swift and efficient, swathing Clara's body in dark blue velvet, and removing it discreetly by the back door, rather than wheeling the gurney past Pearl in the living room. "So thoughtful," Jeannie murmured, signing the forms they handed her, and they murmured soothing phrases in return. She wondered if they would be so soothing to someone who felt real grief. The lawyer arrived; she sensed a renewed alertness in his glance around the living room, but she had been careful. None of the conspicuous ornaments was missing. He murmured about the will filed in his office; Jeannie tried to look exhausted and confused.

"Will? I don't suppose she has much, does she? I thought—if I can just stay here a week or so, I'll go back to my job in the city—" In point of fact, Clara had to have been rich; she'd been married to a rich man—or so Jeannie had always been told—and he'd left her everything. And Mr. Benson had always spoken of her monthly income as allowance from a trust; trusts were for rich people. Jeannie had not come to a small town to work herself to the bone for nothing. But she knew she must not say so. The lawyer relaxed slightly.

"Of course you're free to stay here as long as you need; we all know you've put a lot into nursing Clara. The funeral, now—?"

"I thought Tuesday," said Jeannie,.

"Excellent. We'll talk about the will afterward."

A steady stream of visitors came by that afternoon; Jeannie had no time for the relaxing drink she desperately wanted. Someone middle-aged stripped the bed, made it from linens taken from a bureau drawer. The woman seemed to know Jeannie, and where everything was, which made Jeannie very nervous, but the woman said nothing. She slipped away after restoring Clara's bedroom to perfect order. Several people brought food: a ham, a bean casserole, two cakes, and a pie. Two of the women walked into the kitchen as if they owned it, and put the food away in the refrigerator without asking Jeannie anything. But she survived it all, and at last they left. She was alone, and safe, and about to be richer than she'd ever been in her life.

She was also deadly tired. She thought of pouring

herself a drink, but it seemed like too much trouble. Her own bed beckoned, a bed from which she need not rise until she felt like it. No more answering Clara's bell (in her memory, already blurring, she had always answered Clara's bell.) No more getting up each morning to help an old lady use a bedpan and give her a bath. No more cooking tasteless food for a sick old fool. She stretched, feeling the ease of a house empty of anyone else's needs, with plenty to satisfy her own, and settled into her bed with a tired grunt. Beside her, the bedside table held what she needed if she woke suddenly: the pills, the flat-sided bottle that would send her straight back to lovely oblivion. She turned out the light, and yawned, and fell heavily asleep in the midst of it.

She woke with stabbing pains in her legs: literally stabbing as if someone had stuck hatpins into her. Before her eyes were open, she was aware of the rank smell of tomcat somewhere nearby. She kicked out, finding nothing, and reached down under the bedclothes to feel her legs. Something clinked, across the room, in the darkness. It sounded like beercans. The rattle came again, followed by the unmistakable sound of someone rummaging through tightly packed bottles.

Something was in the room with her, and had found her cache, her secret store of liquor hidden in the back of her closet. Furious, she reached for the bedside table lamp. Something raked her arm, painfully. *Claws* she thought, as her hand found the switch and light sprang out, blinding her. A waifish ginger kitten crouched on the bedside table, one paw extended. Its wistful eyes were pale gray, an unusual color she had never seen on any cat. A dull clank came from the closet, and the smell of whiskey joined the smell of tomcat. A yowl, and another clank and the tinkle of broken glass. Something white streaked across the floor; Jeannie shivered. It slowed, stopped, turned to look at her. A small, sleek, white cat, hardly larger than the china cats on the shelf in Clara's bedroom. Her stomach roiled. Another small white cat joined the first, just enough larger to look like one of a set.

She wanted to scream, to say that this was impossible, but no sound came when she tried. She stared at the open door, where an impossibly fluffy white tail showed now, as an enormous white cat, a blue satin bow tied around its neck, backed out of the closet with something in its mouth. A beer can, one of the silver ones. Her mind chattered crazily, reminding her that cats are not dogs; they do not fetch things that way. The cat turned, gave her a long yellow stare, and dropped the beer can, which rolled across the floor. The two small white cats batted it with their paws as it went by.

Her voice returned enough for her to ask "Snowball. . . ?"

The white cat grinned at her, showing many sharp teeth, and ran its claws out and in. It was as big as the cat-shaped pillow, as big as the cat in the painting. She felt something land on the bed, and looked to see the ginger kitten bound across to jump off the far side and go to the big white cat. They touched noses, rubbed cheeks, and then sat down facing her.

Her mind went blank for a few minutes. It could not be what it looked like, yet she had seen pictures of young Clara, a slight ginger-haired girl with wide, waifish gray eyes. And in the huge white—tomcat, it must be—she saw the protective stance of the acknowledged mate. *Cats aren't like that,* she told herself, as both of them jumped onto the bed, as the sleek smaller cats jumped onto the bed, as she batted helplessly at mouths full of sharp teeth and paws edged with sharp claws, as the massive white fur body of the tomcat settled over her face, and the light went out. *Snowball* she could hear Clara saying in a meditative tone *was not just an ordinary cat.* Jeannie had time to worry about what the broken whiskey bottles, the rolling beer cans, the unmarked packet of pills, would say to those who found her, before she realized that she didn't have to worry about that after all.

HOB'S POT

by Andre Norton

In the old days before Papa came home, no one used the big drawing room since Great-Aunt Amelie had stopped entertaining, saying she was too old for company. However, this afternoon it had been turned into a treasure cave and Emmy, sitting on a footstool beside Great-Aunt Amelie's chair, looked about her very wide-eyed. There was a picture in one of the books Miss Lansdall had brought when she had come to be Emmy's new governess which looked a little like this wealth of color and strange objects, some amusing and some simply beautiful, like the pendant Great-Aunt Amelie was now holding. There had been a boy called Aladdin who had found such treasure as this that Papa's Hindu servant and both of the footmen were busy unpacking from wicker baskets which looked more like chests, pulling back layers of oiled cloth which had kept the sea air out, before taking carefully from the depths one marvel after another.

"Rrrrrowwww!" A cream and brown shape slipped between two of the chests and stopped to try claws on the invitingly rough side of one.

"Feel right at home, Noble Warrior, is that it?" Papa was laughing. "Well, it is true you've seen some of this before. Does this suit your fancy, perhaps?" Papa picked up from a table top a shiny green carved figure. It might have the body of a man wearing a long robe of ceremony but the head was that of a rat!

"Your birth year, Thragun Neklop." Papa laughed again, catching sight of Emmy's bewildered face. "It is true, Emmy. Our Noble Warrior was born in the Year of The Rat. And he will have a very notable series of adventures, too.

213

"Ali San read the sand table for him and the Princess Suphoron before he left the palace. It's all written out somewhere in my day book, I'll find it for you. The princess wanted to be sure that Thragun was indeed the proper guard for *MY* princess. And here, my dear, is your robe, so you will look as if you belong in a palace."

He reached over Lasha's shoulder and picked out of the trunk a bundle of something which was both blue and green, like the gemmed feathers of Great-Aunt Amelie's pendant. There were scrolls of silver up and down, and when Papa shook it out to show Emmy that it was a coat, she also could see that the silver lines made pictures of flowers and birds and—yes, there was a cat!

"Ohhhhh!" Papa put it around her shoulders and she was smoothing it. Never in her life had she seen anything so wonderful.

"A little big, but you'll grow into it—" Papa did not have a chance to say anything else, for there came a loud snarl and then a series of deep-throated growls from floor level.

Thragun Neklop had left off his scratching to swing around and face a much smaller container of wood very sturdily fastened by a number of loops of rough rope. Slow, stiff-legged, he approached the box until his nose just did not quite touch its side, and there, with flattened ears, he crouched. One paw flashed out in a lightning-stiff strike and the extended claws caught in the rope, jerking the box so it fell toward the cat.

With another yowl he leapt up and away before crouching again, eyes slitted and a war cry rumbling in his throat.

"Here, now," Captain Wexley said, "did you find your rat after all and is he in there?" He reached down and picked up the chest, standing it on the table.

At first, to Emmy, it looked just like any other box, but with Thragun Neklop snarling that way she began to feel more and more uneasy.

Papa was examining it closely. He looked puzzled.

"That's odd. I don't remember this."

"Captain Sahib," Lasha said, "that was of the sending

by the rajah. It came just before we sailed and must have been stowed before you could examine it."

"The rajah—" Papa stood very still looking at it. "But he would have no wish to send me a gift, unless," he was smiling again, "he wished to celebrate my leaving. We were always far less than friends. All right, let's see what he thought was due me."

Lasha arose easily from his kneeling position. In his hand he held the knife which usually rode in his sash. "Captain Sahib, the warrior cat warns, let it be my hands that deal with this." He moved swiftly to slash at the rope.

"Some trick, you think?" Papa looked very sober now. "Wait!"

The rope had fallen halfway off the box, but it was still tightly shut. Papa caught it up to carry it into the middle of the room, away from the group by the fire. Thragun Neklop sprang after him and both the footmen and Lasha drew nearer. Emmy bit her lip. Her splendid new coat slipped from her shoulders as she clasped her hands tightly together. There was something—something very wrong now.

Lasha knelt and forced his knife blade into the crack outlining the lid and then very slowly he eased it up. Thragon Neklop, ears back, sleek tail bushed, watched the action unblinkingly.

Once the lid was off, there was an outward puffing of thick grayish fibers. Lasha stirred with the point of his knife.

"Cotton, Captain Sahib." He went on pulling out the stuff carefully until there showed a colored bundle. It was dark red and it also had a great many cords around it which crossed and crisscrossed like a spider's web. Once more Lasha used his knife on the roundish package. The cords fell away and so did the wrapping.

"A teapot!" Papa laughed. "Nothing but a teapot!"

Thragun Neklop snarled. This was his palace, he was the guard. Such a thing as this had no right here. He could smell vile evil—a Khon, truly a Khon. Evil and with power. It had been asleep—now it was waking.

With a yowl Thragun leaped for the top of the table, ready to send this monstrosity crashing on the floor. Then he stopped, so suddenly that he skidded and his claws tangled in the brocade of the table cloth so that he nearly lost his balance. Captain Wexley had picked up the-thing-which-was-eye-hidden, and still laughing, held it closer so Emmy and Great-Aunt Amelie could see it better.

A teapot it was, but not like any Emmy had ever thought could exist. At first it seemed to be a monkey such as Papa had drawn a picture of in one of his letters. Then she saw the lid and she jerked back on her seat, her hand going out for a safe hold on a fold of Great-Aunt Amelie's shawl.

For the nasty face of the thing was twisted up as if it were laughing also, but a mean, sly laugh. Two knobby arms were held out, coming together at their wrists to form a double spout which ended in a fringe of bright red claws.

It had red eyes as well as claws, but the rest of it was a dull yellow color like mud. As it squatted between the Captain's hands, Emmy felt it was looking straight at her. But it was Aunt Amelie who protested.

"Richard—that is a nasty thing. Who would ever give cupboard room to such? Certainly no one would USE it!"

The Captain was examining it closely. He caught at the top of the creature's head and lifted it, peering into the body of the pot.

"Nasty perhaps, Aunt Amelie, but it is a treasure of sorts. It is carved of yellow jade—an unusually large piece, I must say, and these," he placed the head back in position and now tapped one of the eyes, "are, unless I am very much mistaken, rubies, the claws are set with the same. It is worth a great deal—" He was frowning again.

"Why would the rajah give such to me?" he said after a pause.

Lasha spoke in a language Thragun could understand if the rest did not. "For no purpose of good, Sahib."

"Precious stones or not," Great-Aunt Amelie sat up straighter in her chair, "I would say that did *not* belong in any Christian home, Richard." Suddenly she shivered and drew her shawl closer about her. "Gift or no, I would get rid of it if I were you."

The Captain gathered up the red cloth which had been wrapped around it. "Very well. When I go to London next Friday, I shall take it. Hubbard has a liking for curiosities and certainly this is curious enough to suit him. I'll pass it to him with my blessing and agreement that he can put it to auction if he thinks best."

He passed the enshrouded teapot to Lasha who put it back into the box, though the cords which had kept it so well fastened were now cut past use. But he pushed the raw cotton back and hammered the top into place with the hilt of his knife.

Though Papa had other things which might have enchanted Emmy earlier, she kept glancing at the box. Something had spoiled all the fun of unpacking. And Thragun had taken up a post right beside that box as if he were on guard.

He yowled when Hastings, the footman, came to pick it up after they had seen each of the basket chests emptied, his tail moving in a sharp sweep.

"This, sir," Hastings stepped back prudently, one eye on the cat as if he expected to be the goal of any attack, "where does it go?"

"Oh, in the library, I guess. On the side table there for now."

Thragun followed the footman, saw the box put on the table. As soon as the man left the room, he jumped on the bench and leaned forward for a long sniff. His lips curled back in disgust. Khon right enough, though there was a touch of something else. He sat back, his tail curled over his paws, to think. There was just a trace of scent left, but one he had smelled before. Once in the time of rains, when the Princess Suphoron had been ill, they had brought to her an old woman who had burned leaves in a brazier by the princess' bed and fanned the smoke across her so that the princess had breathed it in. She had had a violent fit of sneezing which had pleased the old woman who said then that the princess had so expelled the Khon who had entered into her when she had visited an old shrine. For the lesser Khons were sometimes spirit servants of some god or goddess and lingered on in deserted temples long after those they served had departed.

The very faint smell was indeed that of the smoke which had been raised to banish that Khon. Yet it certainly had not banished that which still was snuggly housed within the teapot. Perhaps the smoke had been used to keep the thing in the pot under control until it was completely uncovered.

Thragun snarled and spat at the box. He did not know if the Khon was free to do anything now, he was simply very sure that, as a guardian for Emmy, he must keep alert.

Thragun hunkered down, his legs drawn under him. It was cold here. There had been a fire earlier, but that had been allowed to go out. Though the window draperies were not closed, twilight outside made the room thick with gloom. He could see fairly well. Certainly the box was not opening again by any power of the thing within it, nor could his keen ears pick up any sound. The Captain would take this away—he had said so. Only not at once and Thragun rumbled another small growl at that thought. No good lay ahead for any of them, he was as sure of that as he was that he had a tail to switch in irritation.

However, just to sit and await upon the pleasure of any Khon was not the way of a Noble Warrior. Thragun never had had a great deal of patience. He preferred things to move into action as soon as possible. They had once before in this house—

Thragun's blue eyes became slits as he remembered the time when Emmy herself had been in a danger which he had sensed quickly but others apparently had not known. Then Cook had taken a hand in the game—

Cook, and someone else who had a jealous need to keep this house peaceful.

A Khon was a Khon he knew. In his own land there would have been ways of forcing the creature out of cover. Thragun's paws reached out and he pushed the box a little. Somewhat to his surprise, it actually did move a fraction. He snatched that paw back with a yowl of rage. The thing had dared to burn him!

The cat arose and walked slowly around the box, keeping his distance but with his head out as he drew deep sniffs in spite of the disgust that the foulness he could scent was decidedly growing stronger. Hot—fire—but the only fire he should smell now was the faint smoky exhaustion of the last live coals in the fireplace.

However, the heat he sensed did not come from any innocent coals or bits of smoldering wood. What was the Khon trying?

Magic—to fight that which sheltered this thing would take magic. Magic spread from a source like a plant grew from a grounded root. Only here, Thragun Neklop considered the matter carefully; there was no root for HIS magic, nothing to serve him as that pot served the intruder. He needed magic which was at home right here, in this other land. And he knew exactly where to find it.

After a last careful survey of the box Thragun jumped to the floor and padded purposefully to the door. It was close to tea time, he knew, when these who rightly valued him provided excellent food on his own dish. His tongue curved over his lips and he paused for a moment by the half opened door of the drawing room, scenting the feast waiting within. However, there was a time for one's taking one's ease and enjoying one's rightful food, and there was a time when duty called elsewhere.

Thragun walked on firmly and then, possessed by the need to do something needful, he flashed down the hall. Hastings was coming with a tray, Jennie holding open the door for him. It was easy enough to slip through and get down to the kitchen.

The smells wafted from well-filled tea stands were as nothing compared with the fragrance here. Cook was working at dinner already. As she moved ponderously from table to stove, she caught sight of Thragun.

"Got a bit o' what's right for th' likes of you, my fine gentleman. Give yourself a taste of this 'ere. 'Twill only be a foretaste—but Christmas if a-comin' an' you won't be sayin' no to a bite or two of goose then. We have 'im already a-hangin' in the larder."

She dipped something out of a large pan into a bowl.

"Now then, you'll be a-takin' that outside of 'ere—I got me too much to do to go dodgin' you this hour."

She carried the bowl to a second door and set it on the floor, closing the door behind her.

Thragun considered a new problem now. The creature whose help might be well needed had first appeared on a flight of stairs not too far away. There was no way for a cat to transfer this treat to that place. Very delicately he pushed at the bowl and it scraped across the stone flooring. It took three more efforts to get it to the top of the stairs, but there was no way of taking it down. He sat down, eyes half closed to consider the point.

There were no secrets in Hob's Green which were unknown to Thragun by now. He always began the night curled up by Emmy. But if she chose to sleep away the more interesting hours, he did not. When the house was quiet, he would go prowling on his own. He had met Hob when Mrs. Cobb, the cook, had set out a bowl of cream to entice the house luck. That had been several months ago when there had been need of all the help one could summon. When another sort of Khon had commanded ill services in this house.

He and Hob had come to an agreement then and had acted together to dispose of she-who-was-black-of-thought. Thragun's lips drew back a little and his fangs showed. Yes, he and Hob had done together what must be done, and most efficiently also.

Since then he had seen Hob once or twice on his midnight trips of discovery. Whether Mrs. Cobb did or did not believe that the fortunate fall of Miss Wyker down the staircase had anything to do with Hob or not, she had since left out a bowl of cream each Saturday night and that was always drained dry in the morning.

However, Hob was not one who yearned for companionship and had not ever sought out Thragun—which was right and proper—a noble guard and a house thewada had really very little to do with one another, as long as the safety of what they were responsible for was not threatened—

Thragun gave a very small growl. His head came higher and he sniffed an earthy, dried grass smell, whiffing up the stairs.

There was the faintest of scuttling sounds and something which might have been a ball of shadow detached itself from the wall on the right-hand side of the stairs. It landed beside the bowl with a plump and yellow eyes regarded Thragun slyly. Small but broad flat feet shuffled on the stone and Thragun saw Hob throw up his long thin arms, his fingers clawed as if in threat. Not that that meant anything—it was Hob's first line of defense to try to frighten.

"Hob's Hole—Hob's own—" The voice was high and cracked. "From the roasting to the bone.

Them as sees, shall not look
Them's as blind, they shall be shook,
Sweep it up and sweep it down—
Hob shall clear it all around."

Whether Hob could read thoughts the cat had no way of telling, but certainly he had grasped ideas quickly enough before. So now Thragun wasted no time in coming straight to the point.

"There is a Khon of great evil now under this roof."

Hob had reached out with both hands for the bowl of offering, but he did not lift it from the floor. Instead he turned his head to one side, his face toward the kitchen door and partly from the cat. It was very wrinkled that face, with eyes far too large, a pair of slits for a nose, and a sharply pointed chin as if he shared a bill with a bird. His eyes, which appeared to give forth a glow of their own, blinked slowly and then swung back to the cat.

Thragun nodded. Hob had forgotten his usual greed, at least long enough to give heed to the cat.

"The master of this household," the cat continued, "has been gifted by an enemy with the source of great evil. Should it escape under this roof, we shall know trouble, and that heavy and soon."

Hob blinked again and then looked down at the bowl. He snatched it up as if Thragun might dispute his ownership and gulped down its contents without even stopping to chew the tender chunks of meat.

Thragun's quiver of tail signaled his impatience. If this were another of his own kind, they would not be wasting time in this fashion. Hob's tongue was out and he held the bowl at an angle where he could run that around the sides to catch the last drop.

Then his voice grated again:

"Hob's Hole!" He stamped one foot to emphasize his claim of ownership.

"Not while the Khon lingers here," the cat answered. "This is a Khon of power and it will take magic well rooted to send him forth again."

The distant sounds of servants' voices reached them and Hob shook his head violently. Thragun knew that refusal to venture far from the portion of the house which the thewada considered its own would hold as long as there was any bustle in the kitchen or the hallways. To impress Hob with the seriousness of this, he must wait until the lower floor of the house was quiet and deserted in the night and he could guide the other to see for himself what kind of darkness had come to trouble them.

Thragun slipped down the hall twice during the evening to see if anything had changed in the library. The box remained as it was. Yet as he marched around it each time, he became more and more uneasy. There was always a bad smell to Khon magic, and to the cat that seemed to grow stronger every time he made that circuit. Yet there was nothing he could do as yet.

He took his night guard position at last on the wide pillow beside Emmy and stretched out purring as he had for every night since he had assumed his rightful position in the household. Emmy stroked him.

"I am glad Papa is home," she said. "Nothing bad can happen when Papa is here—and you!"

Thragun waited until she was asleep and then slipped off the bed and out of the room. He sped at a gallop down hall and stairs. There were still people awake in the house and he could smell the scent of the Captain's cigar from the library. So warned, he crept in with the same care as when he was stalking and took up a position behind one of the long window drapes, hooking it a little aside with one paw so he could watch.

He had no more than taken up his position when the Captain got up and went to the table, pried open the box again, and shook off cotton covering to unveil the enemy, turning the teapot around in his hands and studying it carefully.

"You *are* ugly, aren't you?" Again he lifted the head lid and peered inside. "I don't think anyone would fancy drinking anything which had been brewed in you. The rajah might have had it in mind to frighten us when he sent this. You'd be better off in a case where you'd be locked away from mischief."

He put down the pot on the table beside the box, making no effort to rewrap it. Then he shrugged, ground out his cigar in a copper tray, and made for the door, not giving the thing another look, as if he had forgotten it already.

Thragun growled deep in his throat. Khon magic—now it started. He was certain that the Captain had not unpacked the miserable pot just to look at it—no, he had been moved to do it by some power beyond his own curiosity.

With the Captain gone, and the lamp turned down, the room took on another and more ominous look. Thragun crept from one bit of concealment offered by a piece of furniture to another. The darkness was certainly not complete—growing stronger by the moment was a sickly yellowish light which issued from the misshapen pot.

He sat up and was watching that with such intensity that at first he did not see the thing which scuttled over from the gap which was the fireplace. But the smell of moldy straw awoke him to the fact that he had been joined by Hob.

The thewada of the house came to an abrupt halt. He had to lean far back so that his head was up far enough for him to see the now glowing pot. One broad foot came down with a stamp which narrowly missed Thragun's swinging tail. So, Hob also knew it for what it was. But the cat was not prepared for the next move made by his companion.

Hob leapt, clutched the edge of the table, and drew himself up to approach the pot closer. Thragun moved uneasily, though he thought it prudent not to follow.

"This is a thing of evil." He did not suppress his warning.

Hob reached for the pot which was nearly as large as his own pointed head. In the strange light his wizened face took on a somewhat sinister look. Hob was no quiet spirit when it came to that which aroused any threat of ownership of all within these walls.

Before Thragun could move or protest, he swung the pot around and hurled it straight at the wide hearthstone. There was a loud noise which sounded almost like an exultant cry. The pot, in spite of its substance, shattered and with such force that the many pieces appeared to go on crumbling untili there was nothing but dust.

Thragun cried out, bared his fangs, hunched his back. In that moment of breakage something had reached out to touch him—something evil. He held against it.

Hob reached behind him on the table and caught up an object which glistened. He leapt toward the cat. That evil yellowish glow lingered enough to show that what the attacker held was a paper knife, a begemmed dagger also part of the curiosities Captain Wexley had brought home. Thragun moved with the swiftness of his kind when facing danger. However, Hob had already dropped the dagger. He was now dancing, holding the hand which had grasped its hilt to his mouth. From the hearthstone the yellow glow arose and circled the house spirit, clung to his whole body. Then it was gone as if it had sunk into Hob's wrinkled brown skin.

Hob—the Khon had taken possession of Hob!

Thragun could not suppress a yowl. But there was a shrill cry even louder. Hob swung around and jumped back toward the fireplace. A moment later he had scrambled into the opening and was gone. Thragun shook his head from side to side as if someone had flung some blinding dust in his eyes. He was as cold as if his slender body was encased in that white stuff Emmy called snow.

What had Hob done—what had HE done? Whatever was now loose in the house was the worst danger Thragun could imagine.

There was no use trying to track Hob through his own private runways, many of which were only open to a body which could become unsubstantial at its owner's will. Thragun sped from the library, made his way as a pale streak through the dark up the stairway until he reached Emmy's room again. He was thinking fiercely as he went.

Were he back in his own land once more, those who knew of such things would speedily beware of the Khon by instinct alone and would take steps to separate Hob from his new master. But in this country Thragun had no idea of who might be approached.

Mrs. Cobb, who had first made him aware of Hob's existence? Somehow Thragun believed that she would not be able to handle Hob as a Khon. And he knew that most of the other servants were afraid of even mentioning Hob himself. He was a legend within these walls but also something to be feared.

Thragun headed for his place on Emmy's bed. In all his time he had never seen a one with the old knowledge such as could stand against a Khon.

"No!" Emmy twisted, her face showed fear and she cried out again, even louder, "No!"

Then her eyes opened and she looked at Thragun as if he were the Khon in person.

"It—" she began when there resounded through the house, loud enough to reach them in spite of the thickness of the walls, a heavy crash. Emmy screamed.

"It'll get me—it'll get me!"

"Emmy!" Miss Lansdall had come so quickly from her own bedchamber next door that her dressing gown was half off her shoulders, dragging on the floor. "Emmy—what is—"

She had no chance to finish her question. From behind the half open door of her own room sounded a second crash which certainly was that of broken glass.

Emmy cowered down in the bed and held fast to Thragun in a way he would have speedily resented if conditions were as usual.

Miss Lansdall looked back into her own room. She swayed and nearly dropped the candle she had brought with her.

"No!" she echoed Emmy's cry of a moment earlier. An object hurtled out of the bedroom, to smash against Emmy's door and fall to the floor with a crackle of

broken china. There followed a heavy scent of violets.
Thragun realized that Miss Lansdall had just been deprived of one of her most prized possessions—something
Emmy had always regarded with delight—a slender bottle painted with the violets whose perfume sheltered within.

There came a second crash and again something flew
through the air. Miss Lansdall cried out in pain, the candle
fell from her grip and hit the carpet, its hot grease spatter-
ing, and then flame flickered in the floor covering itself.

Miss Lansdall threw herself forward. Awkwardly she
grabbed one-handed for the pitcher of water on the wash-
stand and threw it at the beginning blaze. Her other arm
hung by her side and in the limited light from the window, Thragun could see a spreading splotch of blood
seeping through her dressing gown sleeve.

Emmy screamed again. Now there were answering noises
from down the hall.

The gleam of another candle gave better light to the
scene. Miss Lansdall had not risen from her knees though
the small flame on the carpet was quenched. She nursed
her arm against her and her eyes were wide with fear.

Captain Wexley paused a moment at the door, then
strode to her.

"What's all this?" he asked sharply, and then, seeing
the blood on Miss Lansdall's arm, he looked to his
daughter.

"Ring for help, Emmy. Miss Lansdall has been hurt."
He helped the governess to a chair and then took up one
of Emmy's own petticoats laid out for morning wearing
to loop it around the bloody arm.

Miss Lansdall was shaking as she looked up at her
employer.

"Sir—it flew at me and—"

Before she could explain further, there came a loud
clap of noise as if a door had been opened with such fury
that it had struck the wall. That was followed moments
later by an explosion.

"What—" Captain Wexley turned as there came a
scream and some cries from down the hall. "What in the
name of—" he bit off what he was about to say and
ended— "is happening."

"My room," Miss Lansdall had reached out her good hand and taken a tight hold of the rich brocade sleeve of the Captain's dressing robe. "Everything—smashed!"

"Captain, sir—!" Lasha came into view, carrying a candelabra with four candles lit. "In your chamber—your pistol—it is in the fireplace and there is much damage—a mirror, your small horse from China—"

Hastings reached them next and then Jennie and Meggy, with quilts pulled around their shoulders. Both of them let out startled cries as there were muffled sounds of more destruction sounding down the length of the hall.

Thragun listened closely. It certainly seemed that the Khon was taking Hob through a rampage of damage, striking at every room.

Strike at most of the chambers he had. China lay smashed, mirrors were shattered, draperies were pulled from their rods, even small chairs and tables were turned upside down. Miss Lansdall was not the only one who suffered personal attack either. Mrs. Cobb, drawn by the uproar, swore that something had caught her by the ankle so that she lost her footing and pitched down the stairs, doing such harm to one of her ankles she could not get to her feet again unaided.

Emmy and Miss Lansdall, once the deep cut in the governess' arm was bandaged, went to Great-Aunt Amelie who was sitting up in her huge curtained bed listening to the tale Jennie was pouring out.

She held out her arms to Emmy and motioned Miss Lansdall to sit down in a comfortable chair near the fire which Jennie must have built up again. There was a look of deep concern on her face as she settled Emmy in the warmth of undercovers.

" 'Tis *HIM* for sure, m'lady," Jennie dragged her own blanket tighter around her, but that did not seem able to keep her from shivering. "*HE* has taken a spite 'gainst us. 'E 'as!"

Great-Aunt Amelie listened, but for a moment she did not reply. Before she could, Miss Lansdall cried out, for a large piece of burning wood apparently leapt from the fire. Luckily the screen had been set up, but it struck against that with force enough to make it shake.

There was such a howl come down the chimney that Thragun yowled militantly in answer and jumped from the bed to run to the hearthstone. If Hob was planning on more mischief and truly aimed at those here, he would do what he could. Though if he might be able to actually attack Hob he was not sure. A thewada was apt to change into thin air under one's paws, and a Khon's reply might be even worse. This trouble was of his own making. If he had not brought Hob into the affair, the Khon, still fast in his pot, might well have been taken safely out of the house even as Captain Wexley had promised.

There were more crashes and Emmy was crying. Miss Lansdall's face was very white. Jennie had dropped on her knees by the bed, her hand a little out as if she reached for comfort to Great-Aunt Amelie.

However, Lady Ashley pulled herself even higher on the pillows and now her expression was one of intent study as if she were trying to remember something of importance.

"The still room," she said as if to herself. "Surely Mrs. Cobb has some in keeping there. Jennie, I will not order you to go there—"

"M'lady," Jennie sat up, "iffen there is something as will answer HIM—" her voice trailed off.

"Rowan," Great-Aunt Amelie said sharply. "Get my robe, Jennie, and my furred slippers. Emmy, you are a brave girl, I know. Remember how you aided *me* when it was necessary. You must come, too."

Emmy's lower lip trembled, but she obediently slipped out of the bed and put on her own slippers.

"My dear," Lady Ashley was speaking now to Miss Lansdall who had started to rise, her face plainly showing that she was about to protest, "I am a very old woman, and there is much which you younger people dismiss as impossible these days. But Hob's Green is a house very much older than I. Some man well-learned in history once told my father that parts of it were standing even before the Norman Lord to which William granted it came here. There are many queer tales. Hob is supposed to be the spirit of the house. Sometimes for generations of time all goes well and there are no disturbances, then again there are happenings which no one can explain. When I was several years younger than Emmy, there was a footman my father dismissed when he found him mistreating one of the village boys who helped with the fruit harvest.

"The man was very angry, but he was too fearful of my father who was a justice of the peace to strike at him openly. Instead, he waited for fair time and stole into the house, meaning to steal the silver. When the servants returned from the fair, he was found lying in the hall, his head badly hurt and a leg broken. His story was he had been deliberately tripped on the stair.

"But this present disorder seems to be aimed at us within the house and not some intruders. Thank you, Jennie. Emmy, do you think you can carry that lamp? It is a small one and it gives us better light than a candle.

"No, Jennie, I must do this. We shall not have our home troubled in this fashion. There was an old woman who looked after the hens in my father's time—" Great-Aunt had taken the shawl Jennie handed her as she finished tying the sash of her warm quilted robe and pulled it about her shoulders. "Now just give me my cane and let me steady myself against your shoulder, girl. Emmy, you can go ahead and light our way. And—" she looked over to where Thragun waited by the door, "you may just have a part in this, I think, for they say that cats can sometimes see much more than we do, and I believe that you are such a one. Now—let us go."

"What about the hen woman, Great-Aunt," asked Emmy. She held the lamp in a tight grip and tried to concentrate on what Great-Aunt had started to say rather than think of what might be waiting outside in the hall, or at the bottom of the stairs, or in the dark ways into the kitchen quarters.

"She was what the villagers call a wisewoman, Emmy. Like a cat, she might have seen further than the rest of us. Mrs. Jordan, who was cook in that day, had a respect for some of her ways and called her in after the footman was hurt. There were strange noises to be heard then but none of this wanton destruction, at least. The woman brought some sprigs of rowan and put them around. After that, things were quiet again. Rowan is supposed to keep off all dark influences and to close doors against their entrance. From that time on, it was customary to keep some rowan to hand—fresh if possible, dried if there was no other way."

Their descent was slow. Great-Aunt held on to the stair rail with one hand and to Jennie, who kept step with her, with the other, while she pushed her cane through her sash to keep it ready. Thragun flowed down into the dark, once or twice looking back so his eyes were red balls in the reflected light.

Lady Ashley said no more, perhaps saving her breath for her exertions. However, there was noise enough in the house. Emmy heard her father calling for water and smelled what might be singed carpet. Two of the portraits on the walls of the lower hallway had fallen facedown on the floor, spraying fragments of glass from under them.

The clock boomed as they turned toward the kitchen wing and Emmy counted the tolls to five. The night was going. It was already time for the servants to be about. Yet this morning no one had time to think of regular duties.

Even the fire in the big range had not been built up and there were no kettles waiting for early morning tea. Spread across the floor was a clutter of utensils, as well as a welter of knives, forks, ladles, and large stirring spoons. There had been a clear sweep made of the many shelves and storage places.

"Be careful, milady." Jennie kicked, sending some of the debris out of their path. "Now you sit here and tell me what you want."

Great-Aunt was moving more and more slowly and breathing heavily. She let Jennie steer her to Mrs. Cobb's own chair and sat down, resting her head against its tall back. Her eyes closed for a moment and then opened.

"Keys—"

Her voice sounded very weak, hardly above a whisper.

"Yes, milady—" Jennie picked up a crock which was the only thing left on a shelf near the stove and felt behind it, to bring out a set of large old keys. "Luckily Cook leaves the spare ones here of a night when she plans to start early in the morning."

"Still room—rowan—"

Jennie nodded. She had busied herself lighting one of the lanterns waiting to be used for anyone needing to venture out into the stableyard after nightfall.

For a moment she stood looking at one of the doors which led from the other side of the kitchen. Then she stooped and caught up a toasting fork, its handle long enough to make it a formidable weapon. With this in one hand, the keys and the lantern in the other, she advanced toward the door, Thragun already ahead of her.

The key turned in the lock and they were able to look into a room whose walls were composed of shelves, each of those loaded with jars and bottles. There was a scent of spice, of herbs, a large stock of the small bottled jams and jellies.

Jennie paid no attention to any of those and luckily Hob-Khon had not yet carried his program of breakage this far. The maid hunted out a bunch of leafed stems which had been hanging from the ceiling on a cord and swiftly made her way back to the kitchen, taking time only to lock the door behind her.

She laid her trophy on the well-scrubbed table and Thragun did what he had never dared do here before, jumped up beside it, sniffing inquisitively. He sneezed and raised his head. There was indeed a strong strange odor, but it had nothing of the dark about it.

"*HE* won't come just to be laid, milady," Jennie observed.

"Probably not, Jennie. But what do they say tempts Hob's famous appetite? Cream, is it not? And surely something quite out of the ordinary to be added on this occasion. Hmmm—"

She looked about as if waiting for a suggestion.

Jennie had gone to fetch the cream. The only other object on the table was a covered bowl. Thragun sniffed that—spices— Great-Aunt Amelie took the cover off.

"Why, it is a Christmas pudding! I thought that Mrs. Cobb had not yet begun to make such! And this one has

been steamed ready for the table, though it is cold."
Lady Ashley pulled the bowl closer.

"Oh, milady." Jennie was back with another bowl, the
contents of which made Thragun's whiskers twitch a fraction. Certainly its contents were more to be desired than
this Christmas pudding. "That was sent up from th' village just this evenin'. Thomas brought it in on th' cart
from Windall. Cook, she an' Mis' Davis over at th' Jolly
Boy 'as been for years now a-talkin' 'bout which Christmas pudding be the best—them with brandy or them with
rum. So this year Mis' Davis up an' sent one of her'n
over for to give us a taste like."

"Bring a plate, Jennie." Great Aunt sat up straighter.
"And then turn the pudding out. We'll just see if Hob
has a taste for a seasonal dainty."

So the table was set, the bowl of cream, the pudding
on a plate. Under Lady Ashley's direction, the bits of
rowan were placed around three sides of the offering
allowing only the fourth to be open.

"Now we shall have to leave it to Hob. He has no
desire to be seen, or so I was always told. Come—"

With Emmy before her with the lamp and Jennie still
holding the toasting fork at ready to help her, Lady Ashley
went slowly out. They had left Jennie's lantern sitting on
the ledge of the cupboard shelf and Thragun remained
where he was, on the table well away from the rowan.

With slitted eyes he looked to the fireplace. There had
been more noise from the forepart of the house, not
muffled by the length of passages and rooms in between.
He thought that Hob was still busy at his destruction and
that he was doing more than ever to cause all the damage
he could as he went.

But after the others had left there was silence. What
new mischief was the Khon about?

Out of the fireplace sped a shadow and Thragun subdued the hiss he had almost voiced. He did not know
how the preparations Lady Ashley had made would act.
But he sat up on his haunches and with his forepaws
made signs in the air, following as best he could his
memories of what was done to discourage a Khon in his
old home.

It was Hob in form who squatted on the table top, grabbed the bowl of cream in both hands and held it high, drinking its contents in a single slurping gulp. Then he swung about to look at the pudding.

There was a crinkling of Hob's wrinkled face as if he were in pain and his two claw hands at the end of spider thin arms patted his protruding belly which looked as if he had already swallowed the bowl along with what it held.

Thragun did not hesitate:

"You are Hob, the thewada of this house—"

· Hob's head was cocked to one side as if he did hear and understand, but his eyes were all for the pudding.

"Hob's Hole—Hob's own
From the roasting to the bone.
Them as sees, shall not look,
Them as blind, they shall be shook.
Sweep it up and stamp it down—
Hob shall clear it all around.
So Mote this be!"

Hob's one hand went out to the pudding, though his other still rubbed his middle as if to subdue some pain there.

"Hob's Hole alone—Hob shall hold it!"

Thragun snapped at a piece of the rowan in spite of the fact that it scratched his lips. With a jerk of his head as if he were disposing of a rat, he tossed that.

Hob threw up an arm but, by fortune, the rowan sped true, striking against that round ball of a stomach nor did it fall away.

With a screech Hob leapt up. One big foot touched rowan and he screeched again. Then he began to shake as if some giant hand had caught him and was determined to subdue all struggles.

Hob's mouth opened to the full extent as if half his jaw had become unhinged. Out from between his small fangs of teeth came a puff of sickly yellow as if somewhere within him there burned a fire and this was smoke. His head, flying back and forth from the violence of that shaking, sent a second puff and both struck full upon the top of the pudding.

Now that shivered and rocked. Thragun, not knowing just why he did it, threw a second sprig of rowan and that touched, not Hob, but the pudding.

There was a howl of dismay and defeat. Hob was loosed from the shaking, to crouch on the table. The pudding was gone. A shimmer of the yellow Hob had been made to disgorge hid it completely. That faded, seeming to sink into the ball of dried fruit and flour.

Hob, his head now in his hands, rocked back and forth. But Thragun pressed closer with a third sprig of rowan which he laid on the top of that ball. Only what stood there now was a teapot—a fine brown teapot, its lid crowned by a sprig of rowan also frozen in time and place.

The cat gave it two long sniffs. He could smell none of the evil that other pot had cloaked itself in. It must be true that the magic of this land was indeed more than even a Khon could fight.

Hob straightened, rubbed his stomach, and there was no longer any sign of pain on his withered face. With a swift bound he reached the fireplace and was gone into his own hidden ways again.

Thragun regarded the teapot critically. It was certainly far more innocent looking than it had been in its other existence, and by what all his senses told him its evil will was firmly and eternally confined. He yawned, feeling all the fatigue of the night, and jumped from the table.

The lantern flickered and went out. But the pudding pot remained to mystify Mrs. Cobb later that morning and many mornings to come.

THE QUEEN'S CAT'S TALE

by Elizabeth Ann Scarborough

I've held my silence long enough and see no reason why my story cannot now be told. My children are grown, everyone concerned save only my lady and me has passed beyond, and though you'd never know it by looking at me, I'm getting on in years. So is my lady, drowsing now beside the fire. Her hair—that smelled so like wild violets that I delighted to roll in its spring-bright strands during those long months when her lord was campaigning and we lay together for comfort. Ah her hair—where was I? Oh yes, (how one does *wander* as one gets on in years) her hair is now white as that cold stuff—snow, it's called—that sticks to the paw pads and inevitably comes around whether it's wanted or not.

Just like some people I could mention. But more about them later.

As I was saying, it's peaceful here in this simple, quiet place, and although it is drafty, my lady always has a nice fire. Of course, the idea is that we live here with the sisters because my lady has been humbled, you see, and they, she and the sisters, are supposed to be all the same, but snobbery springs eternal and my lady's rank gets us our little fire and the choicest morsels and never a cross word about me even if I choose to sleep in the chapel. A queen—even a former queen, even a disgraced queen, is still top cat.

Not that we haven't made many sacrifices. This is *not* as nice as the palace with its lovely fresh rushes twice a day and the delicious fur coverlets to nuzzle and knead and that little velvet cushion just for me. Not that I ever actually *used* the thing, mind you, but I appreciated having it reserved for my exclusive occupation nonetheless.

But those days have long since passed away, as soon shall I and my lady as well, though not necessarily in that order. Just in case I'm some day left alone I've taken as my protégée Sister Mary Immaculata the cook's mouser, a common but cheerful young calico who loves to hear of life among the quality. As well she might. For who came closer to any of them than me? Who knows better the truth behind the dreadful events that preceded the fall of Camelot, and who else fully realizes why anything or anyone worthwhile was salvaged from the entire mess? Who knows with more claw-baring conviction than I the true villain of the piece?

And who besides myself and my lady knows the deepest, darkest, most private secret of the great and fearless Sir Lancelot DuLac himself? No one, that's who. And so of course no one else is aware that this weakness in the great warrior is the crux of the entire matter. Ordinarily I would never cast aspersions on such a seemingly flawless reputation, but willy nilly there's no tampering with the plain and simple fact that Sir Lancelot was allergic to cats and it was that weakness that was both the undoing of Camelot and the salvation of my lady.

When I say allergic, I do not mean dislike leading to the genteelly martyred sniffles some affect in my presence. Oh, no. Blew up like a toad, he did. Broke out in spots as big as mouse droppings. Got so itchy he looked like he was trying to dance a pavane in a seated position. Sneezed loud enough to be heard halfway to Cornwall. And his eyes, usually so clear, swelled shut as if encased in two red pillows.

And me? I was crazy about him. He was like catnip and cream to me. Something about his scent, I expect. But particularly when I was younger, I simply could not stop myself. No sooner did he walk into the room than I twined about his ankles. No sooner did he drop his hand to the arm of a chair than I began grooming his fingers. No sooner was he seated at the Round Table than I leapt upon his shoulders and ran my tail beneath his nostrils, rubbing my face against his hair, purring like a chit of a kitten.

The other knights laughed at us and my lord the king

looked rather sad that I had never so favored him, for he
was very fond of cats and had given me as a kitten into
my lady's service, but I was shameless. My mother always told me it is a wise creature who knows her own
mind and I knew that I wanted to be with Lancelot. Not
that I ever got to spend a great deal of time with him. My
lady would always come to pluck me away, though often
I managed to bring with me a bit of fabric or a strand of
hair for a souvenir, to purr over at some later time. Lady
Elaine, my lady's minion, once tried removing me and all
I will say about that is that she never tried again. Lancelot
himself was too polite and too afraid of offending my
lady to swat at me. Also, I am quite sure he admired me
from afar, for as events revealed, at one time he was
fond of cats, despite his malady, and my fur is very soft
and my purr is very soothing, as my lady has so often
said. I used to hope that one day his iron will would
overcome his unfortunate reactions to my presence.

Alas, we never had the chance to find out, for my lady,
at the instigation of that beastly Elaine, shut me up in the
privy tower whenever Lancelot was in the vicinity. After
the time when I almost fell into the hole and had to be
rescued after hanging on by a clawtip and screaming for
hours before anyone heard me, I decided that my attrac-
tion to Lancelot was merely a superficial one, and whatever silly problems Lancelot had to overcome, he would
simply have to find some other cat to train him out of
them.

Never let it be said that I am anything but generous
and patient to a fault, but I had my position to think of
and my lady could not be expected to do without my
services for long periods of time just because a mere
knight, no matter how worthy, had what was really a
rather comical reaction to cats.

So I hid. I hid in the little hollow of the crown at the
top of Arthur's throne, under the Round Table, and on
nice days in one of the arrow slits overlooking the moat.
I particularly liked the top of the canopied beds because I
couldn't be got down before I made sure the tapestries,
as well as arms and faces, suffered, and I knew very well
how much Lady Elaine hated mending. After awhile,

they forgot to look for me, and I once again assumed my rightful duties as my lady's chief confidante of overseeing the business of the castle.

I could have told them never to let those two in. Mordred and that so-called cat of his. Any cat worth the water to drown her in could have told them that Mordred was the sort of boy who torments cats with unspeakable indignities (and I should know), not the sort to share a morsel and pillow and a bit of companionship with one of us. That alone should have warned them, as I could not, but since it did not, they should have realized what those two were up to at once when that so-called cat snuggled up to Lancelot and he didn't so much as sniffle.

That should have told the humans, poor things, that something distinctly fishy was brewing and it wasn't chowder. I knew at once, of course. The creature's accent was dreadful and her manners worse.

I was in the garden when they arrived, Mordred riding his golden steed, the creature in a basket in front of him. I was paying no attention whatsoever to traffic but was efficiently rearranging the piled leaves the gardeners had gathered. My lady, His Majesty, and Sir Lancelot were playing dominoes on a nearby bench. Mordred, sweet as pie, dismounted, lifting down the basket more tenderly, I swear, than he ever did anything. To no avail. The nasty creature hopped out, landing with a plop in the middle of my leaves, where she sat as if she belonged. Naturally, I hissed at her and told her whose territory she was invading before giving her a pawful across the nose. She did not even do me the courtesy of hissing back. She did not raise a hair, did not arch her back. She merely flipped her tail as she deftly avoided my paw, rose, and sprang straight onto Lancelot's lap.

I crouched expectantly, quick thumps of my tail sending the leaves flying like so many gold and orange birds flushed from the flock. Soon she would get *her* comeuppance as he sneezed and swelled. I was not greatly surprised that no one else stirred themselves to remove her. It had been some months since I had made my private, privy-bound decision to leave the man to his own devices. I've noticed people have very short memories when it comes to who suffers what ailments, and a good thing that is, too, I suppose. But when, after several minutes, the knight's long fingers strayed to stroke her sleek black-and-red mottled fur, and his eyes didn't swell and he did not cough or sneeze, I confess I was quite insulted. To all appearances, he was unperturbed by the newcomer. To all appearances, therefore, he was not allergic to cats in general, but to myself in particular.

Not that I cared, mind you. I'd given up on the man as hopeless already. I sat washing the fur of my stomach with disdainful licks, so that he should see my indifference when he glanced my way. But he did not glance my way. While Mordred charmed Their Majesties with soft words, the tortoiseshell slitted her sly gold eyes at my lady's Champion and purred in a disgustingly ingratiating manner. And Lancelot, normally so intelligent and perceptive, called her *la petite minou* and fondled her ears and smiled like a complete ninny.

I entertained myself listening to Mordred, who was attempting to convey greetings from the exiled witch, Morgan le Fay, the King's sister. His Majesty did not want to hear about it. I have heard rumors that the witch was exiled for plotting the King's murder. I have also heard rumors that she once stole Excaliber and arranged for the disappearance of the king's old tutor, the wizard Merlin. Whatever the king's true reason for her banishment, to him it was an urgent one: that brave and kind man's brow sweated at the mere mention of her name.

My lady the queen nodded politely at eveything Mordred said, but stretched out her hand to the newcomer in Lancelot's lap, who arched so that her head butted my lady's palm. Well! That was enough for me. I bounded from my leaf pile, not that anyone noticed, and twined about my lady's ankles, plaintively reminding her who was her trusted associate and who was not. I was poised to jump up when Lancelot, the traitor, began sneezing and snotting and, though I couldn't see for my lady's skirts, swelling, I am sure. To my great satisfaction the tortoiseshell horror was dumped from his lap and I did a bit of swelling myself and lashed for her with my front paws. Bat-a-bat-bat! I would give her, mincing her nose, which would teach her to bring it interfering into the business of others.

But once more she neither cowered nor raised a hair to attack. She simply sat there and then, as I was poised to strike, emitted the most unfeline meow. Well! Really! I halted in mid-swipe, amazed at her dreadful shredding of our mutual language. Not even her apparent origin in the country could account for such noise. Before I could administer the chastisement due such a creature, a pair of rough hands grabbed me up, nearly breaking my ribs, and flung me into the fish pond.

If I had had any delusions that Mordred contained a scrap of decency, they would have vanished at that moment.

I dashed back into the kitchen to complain to cook's mouser, who laughed at my soaked and bedraggled condition as heartily as ever did his mistress but allowed me a place by the fire. I make it a point to be always on good terms with the kitchen cat, as I may have mentioned.

From this inauspicious entrance, Mordred and his familiar, as I believed her to be, continued to ever more dastardly deeds. Mordred kept the King constantly upset, though he was outwardly polite to everyone else, especially smarmy to my lady and Lancelot. And that beast never let Lancelot alone while he was in the castle. And he *tolerated* her. He even seemed to like her. He never swelled at her, or sneezed at her, or broke out in spots from her. He was quite pleased with himself and with her, looking at her as if he had composed her himself.

I lay atop the canopy and watched them, mourning the ignorance of men. I knew something was wrong but I wasn't sure what until I stalked her, one night, to Mordred's lair in the east tower room.

Even as I stalked, I realized my instincts were correct and the beast was not what she seemed.

It was her scent, you see. She smelled not of honest cat musk, but of bitter herbs and nightblooming cereus.

And once behind the door, Mordred bolting it safely after her, she spoke. I knew it was her. I recognized where the accent had come from at once. Her mews were the sort made mockingly to a cat by a woman who does not care for cats. Her new voice was like this too, nasty-sweet as the smell of a rotting carcass.

"This is rather fun," she said, "But I hope you remembered my tray. I'm not about to actually eat one of those birds I've been catching for sport unless it's properly marinated, spitted, basted, and served."

"Oh, well said," Mordred answered. "And I take it I must wait until our other quarry is likewise prepared before I may begin planning my coronation?"

"Certainly, my dear. As we cats might say—patience."

I confronted her the first time I caught her alone. "See here, you, you, whatever you are. I'm onto you. And let me tell you, dearie, the pecking order is well established around here. My master is king, my mistress is queen, and Sir Lancelot their champion. He may be taken in by your mincing ways now, but if you and that pimple-faced princeling try anything with Their Majesties, he'll make stew meat of you in a thrice, make no mistake."

"What hideous noises you make. I can't understand a word," she said, and sashayed off. I sprang for her back, feeling her tail in my teeth as I leapt. But at the last moment, she was twenty flagstones away and I in midair before I landed—and not on my paws.

It was perfectly obvious to me then who she was, of course. Any cat who could escape my claws had to be using witchcraft. And the witch most closely associated with Mordred was none other than my lord's chiefest bane, his sister Morgan le Fay.

Unfortunately, though I understand the human tongue quite well, my people are more limited when it comes to my own language and were woefully dense.

"Look at Gray Jane!" my lady laughed. "She is so jealous of Mordred's little cat she cries all the time now for attention."

Lancelot laughed and kept his distance, but the king very kindly knelt and stroked my ears. I tried even harder to tell him, and badly wished that the old wizard was there so that I might warn my good master that his old foe stalked him in a new guise.

But Merlin was long gone and I had only my own wits and skills upon which to depend, so I stalked the witch myself. Lurking silent as dust in the shadows, I stalked her, through the rushes of the chambers to the flagstones of the halls, sliding along the walls and darting into corners if she stopped and turned. Once I let her see me, but she summoned Mordred. Fortunately, he was not quick enough to catch me and I always made sure to stay well out of range of her tail. When I saw how the waving of that tail stilled a bird in flight so that it dropped so stonelike into the yard I half-expected it to clatter, I knew that the tail was her wand.

By the waving of it, and the long gaze of her eyes, she hypnotized Lancelot. I scooted in behind her as she padded through the half-open door into his chamber where he sat on the edge of his bed, his head bowed from the weariness of the day's labor and the heavy responsibilities of being the king's most trusted advisor. I dared not draw too near lest his allergies betray me, but I watched as she sprang onto the bed beside him, wriggled herself under his elbow and onto his knee, and sat gazing raptly up at him, the tail describing magic patterns in the air as she held his gaze. His hand, which had moved to stroke her back, hung in the air above her as she purred, sounding less like a real cat than like a Scotsman gargling.

But Lancelot did not know the difference. Nor, for a time, did he know anything else. When at last the witch jumped from his knee to the floor, he stood, belted on his sword, and sleepwalked to the door of the royal chamber.

The king answered. "Yes?"

"My lord, I—" he said. I darted past him into the chamber where my lady was brushing her hair. He sneezed abruptly and said. "I suppose, my Liege, I came to bid you and Queen Guinevere *bon nuit* and a well-deserved rest." But he was covering up. He had no idea why he was there.

I got some hint the next day of what the two malefactors were scheming when I followed the beast and Mordred to the Great Hall where the knights gathered to brag about their latest good deeds. Most of the knights never quite got the hang of virtue being its own reward—they enjoyed topping each other with stories of who was the most modest and selfless, but usually the knight talking finished, as did Sir Geraint that day, by proclaiming, "So honest and humble was I when I accepted the purse that poor clothier begged me to take for rescuing his daughter from the dragon that I'm sure God will notice my goodness and let me find the treasure first."

"Poppycock! The treasure will be mine! I have the most calluses on my knees from praying," Sir Gawain said.

"You can show them to us all if you like, sir," Mordred said. "But I doubt you'll have as many as Sir Lancelot, who will surely have the treasure as he has the confidence of the king and queen. He is so good, in fact, it's a wonder he isn't the king."

Normally, such disloyalty would have been overridden, but with the witch sitting on Mordred's shoulder, waving her tail, gargling Rs, and gazing into the middle space among the knights, the louts didn't seem to understand that anyone was being insulted.

"In fact," Mordred said, languidly stroking the witch's tail where it hung down over his shoulder, "I shouldn't be at all surprised, you know, if he didn't try to do something about it sometime. Really, the tradition *is* that the strongest and most infallible should lead, you know. I wonder if anyone, even the queen, would really object. Certainly Papa—I mean, the king—doesn't seem to guard his own reputation that zealously. He practically allows Lancelot to run things as it is. And the queen seems to agree. But then, may the best man win as they always say."

Someone should have said, "Nonsense, boy. The king has already won and no one could be happier than Lancelot and the queen." Someone should have said, "How dare you sully the name of our gracious queen by even hinting that she is other than perfectly loyal to King Arthur." Someone certainly should have said, "Who does this fool think he is anyway? Throw him in the dungeon and that bedraggled piece of fur with him. Let her try to keep the rats from nibbling him." But no one did.

My position as advisor and confidante of the queen has always been a more personal than a political one for the most part, but even I know treason and accusations of treason when I hear them. Mordred and his accomplice were casting a sticky net indeed to catch the three people who ruled the kingdom. *My* three people.

I could not but emit a hiss of indignation at the whole scene but remembered myself in time and slunk quietly away, resisting the urge to give that mealy-mouthed Mordred such a slash across the legs he'd be hamstrung.

By keeping my peace, I permitted them to underestimate me. Their mistake, of course, for it allowed me to continue my investigations.

I skulked ever so stealthily, shadowing Morgan as she bewitched that poor noble knight, using his thwarted affection for feline-kind to lure him into her clutches (well, actually, she insinuated herself into *his* clutches but the effect was much the same) where she mesmerized him into performing suspicious-seeming actions while Mordred continued to use his poison tongue and his sneaky charm to pollute the minds of the knights of the Round Table.

He pointed out that the Round Table, supposedly so democratic, made conversation with any but those right next to one very difficult—and Sir Lancelot always sat on the king's right hand, Sir Cay to the left, so who, after all, had a chance to talk to the king and share *his* good ideas? No wonder Lancelot had taken virtual control of the kingdom! And the queen, he intimated, spent too much on her wardrobe and had too many relatives in high positions and wasn't it she who had dreamed up the abysmal Round Table anyway, tables being women's stuff, and might she not be secretly in control of the kingdom and with Lancelot to provide the brawn to her brains, what did they need poor King Arthur for? And more drivel of that ilk.

The king remained suspicious of Mordred, but since the conversation always changed when he entered the room, he had no idea of the infamy perpetrated by his guest. Mordred took advantage of his befuddlement by fawning over him, the fawning looking very much like pity to the other knights.

Meanwhile, Morgan La Chat would jump down from

Mordred's shoulder and go find Lancelot, who was always absent during these little character assassinating sessions, of course.

While I watched fuming, she purred in his ear and in a moment, he would rise and walk to the royal chambers or to wherever my lady happened to be, for all the world, to suspicious eyes, as if he was conspiring treason with her. Even though, once he got there, he stammered and stuttered and seemed to have very little to say while she asked his opinion on whether to use the carmine thread or the scarlet in the latest tapestry or if Sir Cay would get the most use out of a linen shirt with wool embroidery or a wool shirt with linen embroidery for his Christmas gift.

From my perch in the window or atop the canopy I would have tried to warn them, but even if it had not been futile, Lady Elaine, who had something of a crush on Lancelot (most unseemly since she was a good five years his elder and of much lower rank besides), would glare at me and I would set to grooming my paws as if I would not dream of approaching while Lancelot was present.

In the same way, of course, Morgan and Mordred couldn't truly approach while the king was present. And so, with Morgan wrapped around his neck, one day Lancelot urged the king to take a break and go hunting. He and the knights could handle any crisis that might come up.

"Yes," Mordred said sweetly. "You're looking a little tired these days, sire. And of course, you needn't worry about the queen with her champion right here to protect her." The king didn't see the broad wink the nasty boy directed at the Round Table in general.

The next morning the king set out for his hunt, carefully selecting the three best hounds. He wanted to be alone. I think his instincts were telling him what his friends were keeping from him and he was very worried, without knowing precisely what worried him.

I was worried, too. I kept close to my lady's side all the day, sprawled across her feet when she sewed and curled up in her lap when she read. Neither Mordred nor Morgan La Chat came near us, but if one of the knights passed by, he would duck his head and look away, as if ashamed to face my lady.

As Lady Elaine readied her for retirement, I grew restless and went in search of a flower pot so that I might ease myself without leaving the premises. My favorite was the captive palm from Palestine a foreign emissary had brought the king. It was kept near the fireplace in the Great Hall. A drunken party was in progress there, however. The king did not approve of drunken revelry and the knights, like mice, were playing in his absence. I would simply have to find somewhere else. I couldn't go in there now without getting stepped upon. But as I fled toward the kitchen and cook's indoor herb garden, I heard familiar hateful voices whispering.

"I still think you should come along and put them under a bit before you go to Lancelot," Mordred whined. "They don't really like me, you know. They're very snobbish about anyone who hasn't bested them in battle at least once. I'm not sure I can convince them to play peeping tom without a little magical urging along."

"I made sure a potion went into the wine," she said, and I heard the staccato beat of her tail impatiently drumming the floor. "They'll do the highland fling from the crenellation with the slightest suggestion. Lancelot's tougher. He is really such an impossible prig. So afraid of appearances. Good thing for me he is so very fond of cats and so very unable to tolerate any others but me. I'd scare him to death in my true form, but he is so delighted with his itty bitty kitty cat he just can't get enough of me."

"Hah!" Mordred commented, and swaggered off toward the Great Hall. I slunk behind Morgan La Chat and followed her to where Lancelot knelt in the chapel, praying, his sword by his side. Lately he had been troubled by his own odd behavior, going to the king's room at odd hours and seeking out the queen's company when in truth he had no interest in the colors of embroidery thread whatsoever.

Most of all, I think he was troubled by the way the other knights had been avoiding him. Like most toms, he valued the goodwill and camaraderie of his brothers-in-

arms more than any other sort of relationship. Little did
he think that had he spent more time with them and less
with that phony feline he could have continued to lead a
happy life indefinitely.

But it was not to be.

Morgan sat upright in front of him, staring straight into
his face, her tail curled like a beckoning finger. Slowly,
Lancelot rose and slowly she sidled away from him toward
the door, the tail all the time beckoning. Lancelot, his
sword at his side, followed.

Why did he need his sword to be captured "conspiring" with the queen? And then I knew. He was not to
conspire with my lady: he was to slay her! I bounded
ahead of them back to the Royal Chamber, making use
of the private entrance the carpenter had devised for me
at the foot of the bolted door.

My lady was asleep already, her golden hair fanned out
across the satin pillow, her fingers curled against her
cheek. I leapt onto her chest and roared my battle cry, so
that she would know I required her immediate and undi-
vided attention. Nevertheless, the effect was somewhat
more dramatic than I anticipated. She sat bolt upright,
flinging me away from her so that I hit the bedcurtains,
where I clung to avoid tumbling off the bed.

At that moment a loud knock thudded against the
timbers of the door.

"Good heavens," my lady yawned, "what on earth is
all this commotion about? Who on earth can that be?
And what in heaven's name can have gotten into you,
Gray Jane?"

She swung her legs over the side of the bed and I did
the unforgivable, had it not been for the dire circumstances. I grabbed her feet with my front claws and
would not let go until she picked me up by the scruff of
the neck and flung me away again.

"Who is it?" she called. "What's the matter? Is the
palace on fire? Is there a dragon in the courtyard? This
had better not be a false alarm."

"C'est moi, madame la reine. C'est Lancelot. I have a
matter of the utmost urgency on which I must speak to
you."

"Oh, very well. But it had better be a matter of an invading army at the very least or I shall never forgive you."

I heard all this human chitchat through a bit of a daze since my lady, in her drowsy state, had tossed me against the stone wall and my head was somewhat the worse for wear. I rose on trembling paws and watched helplessly as she trudged on bleeding feet to the door and opened it. Lancelot stood there with his hand on his sword, the wretched tortoiseshell smirking on the floor beside him.

"Oh, my. It must be at least one invading army for you to come to my chamber armed," the queen said. "You'd better step inside to make your report.

The tortoiseshell came in, too, glancing around the chamber. I scuttled up the bed curtains and peered down at them from the canopy.

Lancelot drew his sword. "Madame, my regrets—" he began, and I sprang for his head, landing on his shoulder when he moved to raise the sword. He threw back his head and sneezed six times, during which the sword clattered harmlessly to the floor—harmlessly, that is, except that the heavy hilt landed on Morgan La Chat's tail and she let out a hideous yowl and sprinted back out the cat door, her tail dragging after her in a rather dashing forked lightning shape.

"Mon dieu!" Lancelot exclaimed. "My Lady, my apologies. The hour—my sword—what am I contemplat— Ahhhchoo!" He was breaking out in spots already and I was twining desperately around his face. The spell was well and truly broken, I was convinced, but I did not want to take any chances.

At that moment, the door banged open and a throng of Camelot's finest flooded in, brandishing weapons and perfuming the chamber with the stench of a cheap tavern. I jumped clear of Lancelot to let him retrieve his sword as Mordred yelled. "You see! You see! They're conspiring." I sprang for Mordred's face, at great personal peril to myself, and jumped from pate to pate of the bareheaded and in some cases balding knights, giving them something to think about besides harassing innocent queens and their hapless cat-enchanted champions.

The queen huddled against the bed curtains, but Lancelot sneezed, scratched, swelled and sneezed again, then fled to the window, gasping for air, in his pain casting only a cursory glance through red-pillowed eyes at the scene in the room. At last he was realizing that Mordred had turned his friends against him. I sprang from a shiny head, belonging, I believe, to Sir Lionel, freshly incised with a random pattern of scarlet ribbons, courtesy of my claws. In one light leap I pounced upon Lancelot's back, giving him one more good sneeze which sent the two of us out the window and, I am sorry to say, into the moat.

He swam manfully out and jumped onto the back of a golden horse conveniently saddled and tethered and let out into the outer paddock for grazing. I, on the other hand, had to crawl and climb, sopping wet, onto the shore and sit out in the freezing rain, hearing my lady's indignant cries.

After a very long interval, the drawbridge thudded down and a black and red streak ran across the bridge and stopped, no doubt wondering where that grazing horse could have gone. She was bleeding about the tail-wand and bedraggled and I was mad as—as a wet cat. I jumped on her and throttled her, giving no quarter to that injured tail, so that when she changed back into human form, she limped away from me, still kicking me off, while trying to protect her eyes and her bleeding nose while I clung to her knee.

We had barely entered the woods when she changed into a giant raven and I crashed to the ground. She dove for me, dripping feathers and gore, but thudding hooves distracted us both and in a heartbeat, I saw the horse and rider and heard the baying of hounds.

I jumped into the nearest tree as she flew away, and as the rider approached, I saw it was the king. With a last mad leap I landed upon his shoulders. Startled, he swore and shook himself, then I meowed plaintively in his face.

"God's blood, 'tis wee Gray Jane! Whatever has happened to you, you poor puss?"

Of course, he was to find out soon enough and even his wisdom could not convince the knights that Lancelot's apparent treachery with the queen had all been a great misunderstanding. He was forced to try the queen in his new courts of justice, where she was found by the jury of knights to be guilty of treason. I could never tell him about Mordred's treachery with Morgan La Chat and could do nothing but sneak into my lady's cell to comfort her as she waited to die.

The morning of her execution they led her outdoors into a chill and drizzling halflight, the dawn so troubled it was black and blue as a bruise and gray as cold iron.

I followed, jumping from one muddy footprint to the other behind the former friends who were now my lady's guards. More than once I was almost squashed or kicked by heavy boots as I looked up past robes and tunics and into grim faces, searching for allies, all the while listening for hoofbeats.

Arthur's face was averted and wet with more than mist and rain, his hair gone silver-white in the week since the queen's trial, his carriage that of a broken man. Lady Elaine, in her usual useful fashion, cried and cried and cried. The knights looked both truculent and shamefaced and more than one would have called the execution off if he could have, I think. Only Mordred glowed and gloated, though without his magical accomplice, he seemed skittish as a kitten in a kennel. Like all of us, he seemed to be listening, waiting.

My ears swiveling to the west, where Lancelot had ridden, I watched as they bound my lady to the stake with the cross in her hands. Mordred himself lit the pyre. It was slow to catch in the wind and damp and the first lit piece blew away. I squatted over it, warming my tail as I wet the flame into oblivion.

The toe of Mordred's boot caught me in the stomach and flung me onto the pyre, at my lady's feet. Mordred poked the torch at me and I sprang for the well-loved safety of my lady's shoulder as he set afire the straw at her soles.

But from there I saw them, Lancelot and his men, soldiers who loved and trusted him and would believe of him no wickedness. They battled the halfhearted knights of the Round Table, who got no leadership from Arthur or from Mordred, who fled before Lancelot's men. Lancelot rescued us with a slash of his sword that broke my Lady's bonds and set her free to jump on behind him.

Of course, he couldn't ride far with us, because of me. But when he would have flung me down, my Lady cried, "No. I will not go without Jane. She would have given her life for me and I will not let her die out here to save myself."

"Oh, very well," Lancelot said, dismounting. "There is a convent some eight miles away."

"I know," she said. "I endowed it."

"You and your cat may find refuge there. I must return to my men and lead them. There will be a great battle, you know—perhaps a war, I cannot imagine how we all fell into such a muddle but it can-can-c-c-c-fare—choo!-well."

"Farewell, Sir Lancelot," she cried.

All of those tedious historians have decried the sorry end of the lovely kingdom that was our home. And it was a tragedy to be sure that all the friendship and love and good intentions were laid to waste and came to such a sad end. But the end was far better than it might have been without my vigilance and intervention.

Some claim there was a last battle, but I have it on good authority that the battle at the pyre was the last one of any consequence, despite Mordred's best effort to stir up more trouble. Oh, there were a few skirmishes, to be sure, but since Lancelot refused to fight the king, any other conflict was purely anticlimactic. The king was broken-hearted not only because he was deprived of my lady and his kingdom, but also because his own noble ideals of law and justice had been turned against him by Mordred's attempt to destroy those he loved. He left Camelot and after a long illness retired to the magical island of Avalon, to have a good long think about what might have been if only he had done this or that otherwise.

Mordred meanwhile sat on the throne in the castle and played at being king, but everyone else went home and didn't pay any attention to his edicts and, being thoroughly ashamed of themselves, tried from then on to conduct themselves as they thought King Arthur would have liked. Since they now believed him dead, his ideas were thought to be far better than they had been when he was still believed to be alive.

Sir Lancelot implored the queen to return with him to his old estates and live as befitted her station with his family. I think she would have done it, too, but by now Lancelot was not only violently allergic to me but, thanks to the witch, had also developed a totally unfair bias against all cats.

And my lady would not, of course, be parted from me. Though I've never been able to give her the details, of course, I believe she may have been leaning out the window, looking to escape herself, as Morgan La Chat changed back into her true form as a human witch. Of course, we never talk about it. Mostly we pray and sing, work in the garden, she with her little spade and I with my paws, we sleep and we read scripture and lead a quiet life, minding our own business, modest and faithful to one another as once we were to the king and our subjects.

So naturally, I can't be sure exactly how much she has guessed, but I do know of all of the fabled participants in the fall of Camelot, only my lady and I, and now you too, gentle readers, know who really kept that sad historical incident from turning into a true and quite literal catastrophe.

THE KEEP-SHAPE SPELL

by Mary H. Schaub

Although spring's first growth eruption had brought a rush of tender greenery, the drenching rain that had been falling for hours numbed the landscape with a near-winter chill. Weary and reeling with pain from his injured paw, the cat dragged himself toward the one spark of light in the pouring darkness. Dim kitten-memories associated the light ahead with a warm bed near a fireside. There had been a soft human hand that fed him and stroked him . . . but that had been long ago. A gust of wind snapped a leafy branch across his face, and he cried out at the impact. Had he ever been dry? Pain gnawed up his foreleg from the paw crushed between rocks earlier that night when a soft stream bank he was crossing had dissolved in a treacherous mudslide. Unable now to bear any weight on the paw, he was forced to limp along on three legs. So cold . . . so *wet*.

Blinking the rain from his eyes, the cat gazed up at a large, chunky shape looming before him. Flaring lightning illuminated a thatch-roofed cottage with corners jutting out in all directions. The yellow lamplight that had drawn him spilled from one small window. The cat lurched nearer, his strength almost spent. So cold . . . wet . . . *hurt*.

Within, an old man sat muffled in layered robes, reading at a cluttered desk. At first, he assumed that the thin, keening wail from outside was simply the storm wind blowing through loose thatch. During an obvious lull in the wind, however, the moaning persisted. With a sigh, the old man set aside his parchment and rose from his chair.

"I suspected that it was too much to ask for a quiet

evening without interruptions," he grumbled to the large
white owl perched on a nearby crowded bookshelf. The
owl, a rare albino specimen, briefly opened one pink eye,
then shut it.

The old man rummaged in an alcove, emerging with a
cloak of shiny waxed fabric. "Little use taking a lamp out
in this rain," he muttered. "What I need is that small
lantern. I know I had it out in the stable last week, but
then I brought it back here and put it . . . aha, under the
shelf with that crystal globe that old Botford sent me. I
shan't be long," he assured the dozing owl. "It's probably only wind in the thatch, but on the other hand, one
never can tell about noises in the nighttime."

The owl remained motionless. Only an occasional rustling of feathers betrayed that it wasn't merely another of
the many mounted specimens tucked away on shelves or
tabletops.

After a few moments, the old man returned, his cloak
streaming with rain. He set down his lantern and cradled
a sodden, dark lump in both dripping hands. "You see?"
he exclaimed enthusiastically. "It's a cat!"

Startled, the owl emitted a complaining hoot and hopped
to a higher shelf.

"It's been injured," the old man continued. "That's
why it was crying. I must clear a space on my desk.
Where did I put that knitted scarf from the shepherd's
wife? It would be just the proper thing to set you upon,
cat. My, you are *wet*. Are you a black cat? No, I do
believe you're gray. There, let me shed this cloak of mine
so I can see to drying us both."

The cat shivered as the old man stroked him gently
with a soft rag, gradually fluffing out the water-soaked
fur.

"I don't think I've ever seen fur quite like this before,"
mused the old man. "Dark gray, but silver-tipped, a bit
like a badger's . . . and your eyes are as blue as the sky
after a rain. Ha! There's a good thought for a name. I
shall call you 'Raindrop.' You were certainly wet enough
to qualify. I trust you feel much drier now. Let me see
that paw. Hmm—mud, grit, and some sluggish bleeding
still. Let me dip it in a cup of water with a little wine to

clean it. Bones broken, I'm afraid. The foot must have been crushed. You fell, perhaps? Or did you squeeze it between rocks?"

The cat mewed pitifully.

"Remiss of me—that paw must be distinctly painful. I should be able to relieve it somewhat." The old man pronounced a series of curious sounds, and lightly touched the paw.

To the cat's amazement, a cool numbness spread through the paw and part of the way up his leg.

The old man smiled. "Better, eh? That is one advantage of being a wizard, you know. Provided," he added, with disarming honesty, "you can remember the proper spell at the proper time. It is most annoying to want a spell for a night light, say, and all that comes to mind is the one for changing the color of a sheep. Now then, what we need is something to protect that paw while the bones knit back. If you were a human, I could use splints or plaster, but your paw is so small and delicate . . . aha, I think this lump of beeswax might serve. If I warm it by the lamp and mold it into a sort of mitten, it should hold your paw steady. How's that? You can't walk on it, but you shouldn't walk for a time as it is. Why don't you lie down on this scarf and rest? I shall be close by, here in my chair." The wizard yawned, and leaned his bald head against the high padded chairback. "I had no idea it was so late. I'll just rest a moment myself before I finish reading that interesting spell. . . ." His head drooped to one side, and he began to snore.

Relieved of his major pain, the cat relaxed into the warm nest of knitted wool. *Dry*, he thought, then slept.

In the morning, the cat woke to a miscellany of sounds—rattles, clunks, whisks, and bangs. The wizard was busily engaged in what he fondly considered his daily tidying. Since the jumble in his cottage remained equally multitudinous and obstructive after his rearrangings, it was hard to distinguish any real progress.

While the wizard puttered about, the cat surveyed the room. The large white owl he'd noticed briefly the previous night was still apparently asleep on a high bookshelf. Beginning with that distinctive owl scent, an entire intriguing array of smells jostled for the cat's attention. He had never before been in a place with so many nose-tingling sensations. Closest to him came the wizard's human scent, tinged with hints of dust, ink, and some puzzling accents for which the cat had no name. Also from nearby wafted a strong metallic tang of copper and brass from a set of scales and weights on an upper shelf of the desk. Mingling with these, he could detect whiffs of musk, amber, and oil of cloves. A faint odor of snake was temporarily disquieting until the cat saw a dried snakeskin rolled up and stored in a cubbyhole. The concentrated sweetness of dried fruits hanging in nets from the ceiling beams roused the cat's hunger.

Famished by his ordeal, the cat scanned the desktop for anything edible. Various nooks above his head were jammed with bundles of dried herbs, packets with powders sifting from their corners, and countless twists of leather and parchment. Close by his shoulder was a squat, tawny glass bottle sealed with dark wax over a cork stopper. Judging from its dusty surface, the cat concluded it must have been undisturbed for a long time. During the previous night's activity, however, the bottle had tumbled over on one side. Over time, the sealing wax had cracked, and the cork stopper had split, so that some of the bottle's contents had spilled out on the desk. The cat idly noted the amber-red pellets, then his nose twitched. Were those pellets the source of that tantalizing minty scent? He stretched out his forepaw and batted a pellet closer. It smelled delicious, and he *was* hungry. He lapped it into his mouth, where it melted at once, like a cool, flavored snowflake. But, but . . . cold—hot—COLD going down! The cat tried to arch his body and spit, but something was suddenly awfully wrong with his body. He was *growing*, much too large to fit on the desk. With a terrified yelp, he fell off the desk onto the floor.

The noise attracted the immediate attention of both the owl and the wizard. "Oh, my," said the wizard. "What have we here? I left a cat on my desk, and now I see no cat, but instead a boy. No, wait—there is a strong feeling of magic here."

The wizard peered at his desk, noticing the opened

bottle. He then carefully surveyed the boy, who stared back, speechless, from the floor.

"Most interesting," observed the wizard. "I see before me a boy of ten or so years, with unusual dark gray hair edged with silver, and—yes, azure eyes in a rather triangular face. Can you speak, lad?"

The cat—now boy—tried to yowl his dismay, but produced only a wretched croaking sound.

"I thought so!" exclaimed the wizard. "You *are* the cat! That is to say, you *were* the cat; you are now a boy. Oh, I do feel most keenly responsible for this, you understand. I could have sworn I'd given those shape-changing lozenges to Otwill ages ago . . . or was it Otwill who gave them to me? There was supposed to be a parchment attached to the bottle. . . ." He sorted unsuccessfully amid the clutter for a moment, then sighed. "I shall seek it later, but I do fear . . . well, no need to borrow trouble. Quite likely I am recalling the wrong strictures entirely. What should we do first? Arrange for you to speak, I should think; most frustrating otherwise for us both. I have a spell for speech tucked away here somewhere —aha! Here, in fact. Now, pay attention." He intoned more sounds unintelligible to the cat/boy, but suddenly the sounds *were* intelligible.

The wizard watched expectantly. "Can you say my name, boy? My name is 'Flax.' "

His mind whirling from all the unimaginable changes that had befallen him, the cat/boy opened his mouth, producing a grating sound. "Fflleeckss?"

"Not at all bad for a first try," said the wizard, nodding encouragingly. "Take a moment to settle yourself. You might be more comfortable sitting in a chair . . . or then again, perhaps not."

The cat/boy swallowed, and tried to move his paws. But they weren't paws any more . . . and he was so LARGE. His whole viewing perspective seemed horridly wrong, shifted dizzyingly far up in the air above where it should be. And . . . and he had no fur—except for that on his head—and no whiskers, and—he gazed frantically down at himself—no *tail!* However could he walk, or jump? With a low moan, he tried to extend his claws . . .

but he had no proper claws, either. Instead of his formerly elegant paws, he now had great long finger-things, with blunt, flat nails that wouldn't extend or retract. Apprehensively, he tried to stand on his four legs . . . but he now had only two—great LONG legs, with peculiar bent feet. He fell over with a resounding thump.

The wizard hurried to assist him. "I know," he said kindly. "Your balance must feel quite askew, but then your body proportions have altered significantly. Before you harm yourself falling, try sitting in this chair. Yes, the rump goes there, and you must bend your legs—what were your back legs—at the knees. Those joints are knees, you know, although they must seem oddly placed. The feet stay flat on the floor, by the way. That position will be different to you as well, I fear, for cats' feet are more like our human fingertips and toetips. At the moment, you are quite frankly clumsy, but you'll soon adapt. We must call you something. I had named you 'Raindrop' last night while you were a cat, but that seems a trifle poetical for a lad's name."

The wizard paused, regarding his shivering guest. "And there you sit, naked. I must find you some clothes before you suffer a chill. Weren't there some lad-sized clothes in this chest? Ha, try on this sleeved jerkin. It fits on over the head. No, no—arms through those holes, and head out the top hole. Never mind, I'll pick it up. Try again, a bit less vigorously. Much better. Not 'Raindrop,'—no. 'Drop.' That should do admirably for the present. I shall call you 'Drop.' Can you say it? Very good. Anything else you care to say—no? In my experience, cats usually aren't loquacious creatures. So much more restful to have about the house than parrots. I once treated a parrot with an eye ailment. I finally had to settle a dumbness spell on the wretched bird. He wouldn't give a person peace to think in—always prattling on and on. Ah, here are some breeches of a reasonable size, and some soft slippers that should fit your feet. When you have dressed, you might try moving about a bit. Yes, the breeches fit over the legs. While you're finishing, I shall search for Otwill's parchment. I know I saw it quite recently. The cord around the bottle had frayed, you see, so I slipped the parchment into one of these cubbyholes for safekeeping.''

Drop wrestled with the hideously uncooperative clothing, then subsided into the chair, breathing hard. His exquisite sense of cat-balance was asserting itself, adjusting to his new body shape. He flexed his curiously divided fingers, pondering the other changes that intruded into his awareness. Scents, for one thing, were now much less keen and distinct. That was discouraging, but perhaps compensated for to some degree by the enormous expansion of his color vision. Before, as a cat, he could tell a difference between blue-to-green colors and orange-to-red ones, but only in bright light. Now the world was a riot of colors, for which the wizard's speech spell obligingly provided him names. He wondered briefly about his night sight—so important to a hunting cat; his loss or gain there would be revealed later. The humans he remembered seemed to take shelter at night. Perhaps, he reasoned, they couldn't see as well in dim light as in full sun.

Drop looked curiously at the preoccupied wizard. Although the old man had initially appeared bulky because he was swathed in so many layers of cloth, it was now clear that he wasn't actually much larger than the cat/boy's own body size. His head was completely bald and beardless; frost-white eyebrows shaded a pair of bright blue eyes flanking a beak of a nose.

"Aha!" The wizard triumphantly waved a dusty scrap of parchment, then brought it near the lamp to read the faded writing. "I thought so—it *was* Otwill's, for here's his rune. I don't know what possessed him to create this spell.'' The wizard frowned at the scrap as he read aloud, " 'Reveals the true character of the user: what his spirit might otherwise have been but for the accident of birth.' Meddlesome—I always said Otwill was a meddler, although generally well-intentioned. I remember now . . . he sent me these lozenges shortly after they had turned his servant into a toad. Most unfortunate. Still, the fellow really *was* rather toadlike, and Otwill did take good care of him afterward. Put him in a walled garden, I believe. Hmm.''

The wizard read on, then paused and sighed. "I must be honest with you, Drop. This Keep-Shape Spell of Otwill's is not, I fear, reversible . . . at least, that is, he neglected to specify how to reverse it." For an instant, his face brightened, then fell back into an apologetic expression. "I was about to say that I could transmit a query to Otwill concerning this spell, but I just recalled that he has been missing for some time—went on a quest for phoenix feathers or some such rare thing. Bother. I shall simply have to puzzle it out by myself." He stopped and gazed thoughtfully at Drop. "Until I can return you to your proper cathood, you are most welcome to stay here and lend a hand." He waved vaguely at their muddled surroundings. "Would you care to learn a bit of magic? First, of course, you'd have to learn to read. I've never before taught a cat to read, but I feel sure you should be quite capable of learning. Oh, do speak up! I hate talking to myself all the time."

"P . . . paw?" asked Drop, extending his injured hand, which had swollen and was darkening with bruises.

"Forgive me," exclaimed the wizard. "That little beeswax mitten I made for you last night couldn't possibly contain the mass of a human hand." He bustled around the room, collecting materials. "My numbing spell should still be in full effect. Now I can attend properly to those broken bones. I shall need some dry plaster, water, strips of cloth, and perhaps some light wooden splints."

Working briskly, the wizard soon constructed a damp, but quickly stiffening bandage immobilizing Drop's swollen hand. As he tied the last knot and dabbed it down with a glob of plaster, he observed, "There—that should serve. Once those bones mend, your hand ought to be perfectly usable. A bit awkward, I expect, but then having hands will seem awkward to you for a time until you get used to them. Now that you're presentably dressed and bandaged, what should we do next?"

"Food?" suggested Drop, in a hopeful tone.

"Food!" The wizard's eyes widened. "My word—haven't we had any? Of course there's food. The cowherd left me some milk and cheese, and I have bread in the larder . . . and some dried herring. You should quite fancy that."

They had almost finished their breakfast when they were interrupted by a shy tapping at the door. By the time the wizard opened it, no one was in sight, but a basket of brown eggs had been left on the doorstep.

"It's because of the pig, you know," said the wizard, shaking his head. "I can't imagine why they still feel obliged."

"Pig?" prompted Drop.

"I worked a magical cure for it, you see," explained the wizard. "The poor creature had a palsy . . . or was that the farmer's aunt? Perhaps it was colic. In any case, they're grateful for my help, the nearby folk, but most of them are mistrustful of magic." He sighed. "I've always had a talent for magic, ever since I was a child. It quite upset my parents. They expected me to become a wool merchant. I can't think of any other excuse for the name they gave me."

Puzzled, Drop said, "Flax?"

"Er, no." The wizard hesitated. "Woostrom," he confided, making a sour face. "What sort of name is that for a wizard? Still," he conceded, "they didn't know that I was to become a wizard. Fortunately, everyone soon began calling me 'Flax,' for the obvious reason."

"Reason?" Drop could perceive no reason to relate the wizard to a vegetable fiber which the speech spell informed him could be spun into linen.

"My hair, of course," retorted the wizard, then added with a rueful smile, "when I had some, that is. It was just the color of flax."

"Ah," said Drop, enlightened.

"Before I forget," the wizard continued, "do let me introduce you to the others who share my cottage. You will have noticed Ghost, our resident owl." Flax pointed toward the pale puff of feathers on the high shelf. At the sound of its name, Ghost briefly opened both pink eyes. "After I mended his broken wing, he chose to stay on. Very keen hearing, owls," the wizard observed, then added in a low tone, "I try not to disturb Ghost by speaking loudly, and most especially avoid shouting his name. For some reason, that agitates him unduly, and he tends to fly to one's head and . . . er, um . . . pull one's hair." Flax patted his own bald head reminiscently. "In my present condition, I do *not* welcome such aggressive attention. And there is, of course, Cyril, who had a most dreadful injury to his tail. I feared for some time that he could not recover, but he has assumed his place under the table, and nowadays I seldom even see a mouse. Most satisfactory."

Drop stared under the table, seeing nothing but bare wooden legs and the wizard's own buskined feet.

"No, not this table," said Flax, following his glance. "The side table."

What Drop had previously dismissed as ornamental rings of carved wood now slowly uncoiled into a sizable snake, albeit a snake with a much truncated tail.

Flax bent down to rub Cyril's head. "So few people recognize the real virtues of snakes. I'll wager there's not another snake in the kingdom who can rival Cyril for learning. Not scholarly learning, you understand," he hastened to add. "No, I can't claim that, but Cyril responds famously to patterns of taps on his head. I rather suspect that snakes may well be deaf; certainly Cyril doesn't appear to hear at all. You can imagine how long I bellowed at him with absolutely no result—except to agitate Ghost. Then I thought he might possibly feel vibrations, so I tried the tapping. Cyril now knows that two taps mean 'come,' three mean 'food,' and four mean 'danger.' Most accomplished of him."

Drop warily watched Cyril's blunt head approach his slippered foot, but apart from flicking out a forked tongue, Cyril politely refrained from touching Drop. In his cat form, Drop had usually avoided snakes. He had definitely never seen a snake as large in girth as Cyril, whose broadest dimension rivaled Drop's own wrist.

"Large," Drop observed, looking from his own forearm to the snake.

"Oh, yes, Cyril's size," the wizard replied. "I was given Cyril by a traveler who had acquired him in a distant, warmer land. Cyril dozes a good deal in cold weather, and, for that matter, he also frequently basks in the garden in the summer. While indoors, he generally curls around that table base. He doesn't care to be trodden upon, you know—much better to stay out of the way of people's feet. Now, let us carry these dishes to the kitchen, and I shall show you how to wash them."

"Why?" asked Drop, carefully balancing his plate between his uninjured fingers.

"Because we shall want to use them again," the wizard explained. "When you were a cat, you washed yourself, to stay tidy. We humans have to use soap and water instead of our tongues, but the object is the same. Come along."

Over the next few days, Drop gradually became accustomed to the shape and uses of his new body. Learning how to grasp objects took some practice, but soon he could brace things against the hard bandage protecting his broken hand, and was able to fetch most of what the wizard needed. As his natural feline grace of movement emerged, he stopped blundering into things, to Ghost's considerable relief. The owl much preferred a quiet, steady household, without the crash of shattering dishes or items cascading from jostled shelves.

Drop discovered anew that humans were creatures of habit, insisting upon three meals a day, and sleeping most of the night. Fortunately for Drop's cat nature, the wizard tended to indulge in frequent naps during the day, and often worked far into the night. The wizard patiently answered Drop's questions, and encouraged the lad in his efforts to decipher the curious marks called "writing."

"Until your hand heals," the wizard said, "I don't think I shall trouble you with a stylus or quill, but you can learn the shapes of the letters and how words are made from them."

They were somewhat impeded in their activities by the wizard's explosive fits of sneezing.

"I must have become overly chilled the night I brought you inside," Flax remarked, dabbing at his reddened nose. "Bother—most frustrating when one is trying to weigh something small like this mustard seed . . . a-choo!"

It was late that afternoon when they were startled by a volley of thuds on the front door.

"My hat," complained Flax as he hurried to open the

door. "There's no need to batter your way in. Well, what can I do for you?"

A stocky figure enveloped in a black cloak was just raising his cudgel for another thump. "At last!" he exclaimed in a rasping voice. "Am I in the presence of the illustrious Woostrom?"

The wizard sneezed convulsively. "Yes, I am Woostrom, although I prefer being called 'Flax.' Come in, come in, before the draft sets me to . . . a-choo!"

The unexpected visitor strode past Flax, pausing in the main room to pivot on a burnished boot heel. "A splendid house—for, if I may say so, a splendid wizard. Your fame, Master Woostrom, has spread over considerable distances."

The wizard blinked in surprise. "I can't imagine why," he said. "I exchange a few spells now and then with some colleagues, but chiefly I am occupied here, in this rather isolated cottage."

"You are entirely too modest," declared the visitor. "I have traveled far, and always when potent magic was being discussed, the name of Woostrom arose. But allow me to introduce myself." With a flourish of his cloak, he bowed imperiously. "I am Skarn, a humble apprentice at the noble craft of wizardry."

"Indeed. I am *Flax*," the wizard asserted, "and this is Drop, my assistant."

Skarn scarcely glanced at the silent lad, who was pondering a growing sense of instant dislike to the stranger. His face seemed unremarkable—he had a rather narrow, pointed nose, long, dark red hair, and beady eyes the color of grimy green bottleglass. But there was *something* about Skarn . . . Drop's human nose twitched. Skarn exuded a curiously peppery scent that made Drop's nose tingle. Surely Master Flax was aware of it—but one look at the wizard's swollen nose confirmed that in his congested state, he likely could not distinguish catnip from turnips. There was, however, one other of the cottage's inhabitants who appeared to be disquieted by Skarn's arrival. The humans didn't notice, but from the corner of his eye, Drop saw that Ghost was sidling quietly along his bookshelf toward the corner near an interior door. In a moment, he glided soundlessly away down the hall.

Meanwhile, Skarn was continuing in a wheedling tone, extending a gloved hand importunately toward Flax. "I have searched for you for such a time. Could you permit me to bide here for the night? It would be a great honor to confer with you, at your leisure, of course."

Had Drop been a dog, his mounting distrust would have made him growl; instead, Skarn's pungent scent made him sneeze.

"Bless you," said Flax, instantly concerned. "I do hope that you have not contracted my own difficulty."

Skarn harrumphed loudly, displeased that the wizard's attention had been distracted. "I should not require much room," he persisted. "Any small space where I might roll up in a blanket. . . ."

"Eh? Oh, a place to sleep," said Flax. "We have a number of spare rooms here—no problem at all. Take off your cloak, then, Master Skarn, if you are staying. Drop, put on the kettle, if you will, and we shall offer our guest some herbal tea. He can use the back room two doors down from my study . . . I believe that its bed is made."

"So warmly hospitable." Skarn grimaced, showing narrow, rather sharp teeth that reminded Drop of a wharf rat he had once chased on a dockside. Unaccountably, the hair stirred at the back of Drop's neck.

Skarn whipped off his cloak, and tossed it at Drop without any word of thanks. Drop hurried to fold the cloak across a chair in the small guest room. Wrongness, he thought—there was something unnatural about Master Skarn, something besides his unmistakable reek of pepper.

During the evening meal, Skarn withdrew an ornamental metal shaker from his vest and liberally dusted his plate of stew. "A weakness of mine," he confided. "I don't invite you to try this spice blend, Master Woostrom, since most folk find it exceedingly strong. I encountered the ingredients in far Druzan years ago, and plain food now seems insipid without it."

Drop and Flax sneezed simultaneously as a faint whiff of the spice mixture reached them.

"I'm sure that would be too lively for my simple tastes," commented the wizard. "Pray tell me, is it true as I have read, that Druzan is much afflicted by sorcerors?"

Skarn airily waved a sharp-nailed hand. "I did not find it so. The Druzanians seemed most willing, even eager to share their knowledge. But doubtless I have bored you with my lengthy traveler's tales." His mouth gaped in a vast yawn. "Forgive me—I find I am wearier than I thought. If I might retire for the night?"

"Of course. Drop, light a lamp for Master Skarn. Thank you. Let me show you to your room. This way." With a final sneeze, Flax bade his guest good night, and shortly afterward, the household settled into peaceful slumber.

It seemed peaceful until Drop roused—sharply, suddenly wide awake. What had caught his ear? Some unusual sound? Not waiting to tug on his slippers, Drop padded barefooted along the twisting hallway toward the wizard's study. Furtive sounds were emanating from that direction, and even Drop's now woefully inadequate night vision could distinguish glimmers of light around the closed study door.

Closed? Master Flax *never* closed his study door. Drop crept silently to the threshold and listened. Something or someone was definitely moving about inside. Spreading his fingers wide, Drop gently pressed his unbandaged hand against the door. The rough wooden surface eased back until Drop could see into the study. Fitfully illuminated by a yellow-greenish witchlight, Skarn was rummaging through the cubbyholes and drawers of Flax's desk.

A surge of anger swept through Drop. Taking a deep breath, he cried out loudly, "Thief! Flax—Come!"

Skarn spun around at the call, gesturing at the door, which slammed violently open, revealing his accuser. "Be quiet!" Skarn snarled, but both of them could hear the sneezes of the awakened, approaching wizard.

Flax stopped behind Drop, and peered over his head into the study. In a deceptively mild tone, the wizard observed, "Why, Master Skarn . . . if you couldn't sleep, I would gladly have recommended a soothing spell—

although surely a man of your talents could have managed that on his own." With a quiet word, Flax gestured, and the candles in the study kindled. Skarn's witchlight contracted to a point, then vanished.

"Bah!" Skarn bared his teeth in a thoroughly unpleasant smile. "The time for acting is past. I mean to have Kryppen's potion. Where have you concealed it?"

Flax appeared genuinely puzzled. "Kryppen's potion? I do assure you that I have no idea what that might be. I frequently make up Kraffen's poultice for drawing out boils, and of course, there's Warpin's pitch for sealing leaky vessels, but as for Kryppen's. . . ."

"Silence, you garrulous old fool!" bellowed Skarn. "Do you realize how much trouble you have caused me? So far, I have had to kill four men and one demon to trace the path of this precious potion to your door."

"*My* door?" Flax shook his head. "I fear you must have been misled. I have no such item."

"Ha! You can't deceive me. Master Kryppen created it twenty years ago, and I have sought it for ten. You have hidden it!" Skarn glared at the jumble of items he had already disarranged. "I know it is somewhere here, and I intend to find it."

"But I have never heard of Master Kryppen," Flax objected.

Skarn ignored the assertion as he impatiently scrabbled through a file of dusty bottles on a desk shelf. "He sold some of it to Nementh of Goor, whose lackwitted nephew gambled it away. Never mind its trail over the years—it came to you after you performed some service for Mistress Wryfern, who, not knowing what she had, gave it to you."

"Dear Mistress Wryfern," exclaimed the wizard with genuine warmth. "I do hope she fares well nowadays."

"She's as hard to pry news from as a clam embedded in stone," rasped Skarn. "Still, I determined what she had done, and I have come to claim my prize."

"Why?" inquired Flax.

"What do you mean, 'why'?" retorted Skarn.

The wizard sighed, employing his most patient tone, familiar to Drop from his reading instruction. "I mean, why do you consider it *your* prize? If this particular potion had been given to me as a token of gratitude, why should you claim it as yours?"

"Because I know how it should be used," snapped Skarn. "In my hands," he added with gleeful satisfaction, "it could slay hundreds . . . thousands."

"Nonsense!" said Flax stoutly. "I distinctly recall that particular potion now. Mistress Wryfern described it to me clearly as a mere entertainment for parties—a prank potion."

Skarn guffawed. "No doubt that was as far as that fool Kryppen could envision a use for it. But consider the possibilities on a battlefield or against the crowded populace of an enemy city—when I applied my mind to that aspect, I was quite inspired. I thought of the rot-flesh fungus almost at once."

Drop saw all trace of color drain from the wizard's face.

Evidently appalled, Flax blurted in a strained voice, "Skarn—you would not. You *could* not!"

Skarn rubbed his hands together. "Oh, but I could, and I did. Just ponder the glorious combination—start with an innocent potion that spreads your intended effect from person to person by touch. What merriment at a party to have first one guest brush another, who touches a third, and each one commences to sneeze or laugh or twitch—most amusing, wouldn't you say? Picture that multiplying effect transferring the activity of the rot-flesh fungus. You will have seen what happens to any luckless animal who brushes against those fungal growths from the far southern swamps? Something like the action of quicklime, or general corruption, only much accelerated."

"You could not loose such a plague," said Flex hoarsely. "You would yourself be caught up in the contamination."

Skarn bobbed his head, smirking as if pleased by his listener's insight. "And so I would, should I be demented enough to be present—but I do not intend to *be* present. Someone else will be my agent. They will necessarily perish, of course, but then every great plan has its minor costs."

The wizard's pale face seemed stricken, but he also

appeared to have come to a decision. "Drop," he said quietly, "you did well to summon me. This is far worse than a case of mere thievery." His voice hardened with resolve. "Skarn—if that be your true name—you are contemplating murder on a hideous scale. You shall *not* have that potion."

"Ah, but I do have it within my very grasp," purred Skarn. "Is that not the private seal of Mistress Wryfern on that quaint little blue glass bottle I have just uncovered at the back of your desk?"

Throughout this confrontation between Skarn and the wizard, Drop's sense of unease and alarm had been mounting. It was clear to him that Skarn was a dangerous creature who must be prevented from stealing Master Flax's property. Giving no advance warning sound, Drop leaped toward Skarn, hoping to bear him to the floor, away from the desk.

Skarn, however, whirled at the initial movement, and pronounced some harsh sounds. Instantly, Drop found his forward thrust jolted to a stop, and his limbs immovable.

"Relying on a one-handed lad to defend you, eh, Woostrom?" crowed Skarn. "My binding spell will deal with him."

"Deal then with me!" roared Flax, raising both hands. As he intoned a spate of awesome sounds, great thick ropes formed in the air and spiraled around Skarn, pinning his arms to his sides.

Drop felt greatly relieved, until Skarn spat other sounds, at which the ropes withered away to mere threads he cast contemptuously to the floor.

"You dare to oppose me?" he sneered. "I am Skarn the sorcerer! No man stands before my wrath." Flinging up his hands, he conjured a gust of murky flame that blasted toward Flax, but it was quenched in mid-flight by an equally fierce geyser of conjured water sent by the wizard. Spells and counterspells erupted in the quivering cottage, clashing between the magical combatants.

Literally spellbound, Drop watched, his mind racing. There had to be some way he could aid Master Flax . . . but first he had to be able to move. Skarn had mistakenly assumed that Drop was a normal human lad; but Drop was not merely that. A binding spell meant to restrain a lad might not necessarily fully bind a magically transformed cat. Drop cautiously endeavored to move his toes . . . they responded slowly, leadenly, but they did move. Now for one arm, then the other . . . very slowly. He could not afford to attract Skarn's attention. Fortunately, Skarn's attention was most fully engaged by Flax's magical assaults.

As light-bolts blazed, sounds crashed, and weird smells curdled the air of the study, Drop realized that he might possibly call on two other allies for Flax. The very floor boards had been shuddering beneath their feet for some time, and Drop now distinguished one particularly broad bar of shadow near his own feet. It was Cyril the snake, understandably disturbed by the bizarre lights and upheaval, who had abandoned his table base to seek the cause. Drop eased his bandaged hand down until he could tap on Cyril's questing head. One, two, three, four—there. Cyril should now be alerted to the danger to Flax.

For the last short while, Drop had also become dimly aware of a persistent clicking sound. In a brief lull between spells, he suddenly located the source: Ghost, who had been dozing as usual on a high shelf, had been awakened by the wild activity below, and was snapping his beak in decided disapproval. Drop recalled what Flax had said about Ghost and loud noises. His desperate plan lacked only one other element.

While Skarn and Flax were totally absorbed in their duel by magic, Drop edged quietly toward the desk. At first, he couldn't locate the tawny bottle he sought, then he recognized it over to one side, where Skarn had thrust it during his search. Extending his free hand, Drop extracted a Keep-Shape lozenge. He succeeded just in time, for Skarn produced a wave of force that flung Flax bodily against a bookcase, temporarily dazing the wizard.

Skarn stepped forward, gloating. "So much for you, you feeble old fool. I have dawdled with you long enough. Feel now my Death Spell, you and your useless apprentice!"

Unluckily for Skarn, he had earlier discarded his fancy riding boots in order to pursue his thievery quietly. When he now strode forward, he planted one stockinged foot flatly on Cyril's back, prompting the offended snake to rear up and sink his fangs into Skarn's unprotected leg.

Seizing this splendid opportunity, Drop yelled as loudly as he could, "Ho! Ghost! GHOST!"

The owl, driven to frenzy by all the blinding lights, swooped down from his shelf, talons extended. He landed on Skarn's head, buffeting the sorceror with his great soft wings, while yanking cruelly at the man's long red hair.

Skarn, understandably, yowled under this multiple, totally unexpected attack. As his mouth gaped open, Drop lunged toward the floundering sorcerer and popped the lozenge between his lips.

There was a frozen instant of startled silence, a gasp from Skarn, then a gulp. The tormented sorceror wrenched Ghost from his head, and would have dashed the owl to the floor had it not twisted from his hands and flown safely to its ceiling shelf.

Skarn gibbered, shuddered, and slowly shrank in size. Drop watched with keen interest to see just what Skarn's True Shape might be. It was momentarily concealed by the heap of Skarn's human clothing, then there was a jerky stirring, and tearing aside the fabric, a rather warty yellow-brown demon emerged from the folds.

Flax, by now recovered from his breathless impact against the bookcase, pointed at the demon, pronouncing a stern magical order.

The demon shook its claws defiantly at him, but was summarily vanished, leaving behind a cloud of foul smoke.

"Faugh!" exclaimed Flax, gesturing open all the adjacent doors and windows. "A cleansing breeze should suffice to disperse this. Ah—much better. And there is one more item that needs to be destroyed—Mistress Wryfern's gift potion. Although it was intended only to be an innocent diversion, I now perceive what a deadly threat it could pose in wicked hands." Snatching up the blue glass bottle, the wizard vaporized it in a flash of white light.

From his lofty perch, Ghost emitted a loud hoot of protest.

"My dear Ghost," said Flax, "and Cyril, and above all,

Drop! I thank each of you for your valiant efforts. Had you not assisted when you did, I fear that we all should have perished. You must all be fairly rewarded. Let me see—some nice brown eggs for Cyril, I think, and pickled herring for Ghost and Drop. How does that sound? Where did I put that jar of herring? Was it in the kitchen, or the back storeroom?"

As Drop followed the wizard to aid in the search, he privately regretted only one thing. He had not had the chance to try a bite of the demon, which had smelled most deliciously of *mouse*.

OF AGE AND WISDOM

by Roger C. Schlobin

There are few tales that remain of the ancient times when dragons and cats ruled the Earth and humanity was no more than a stirring in the genes of screeching monkeys. Of these times—when cats chose to use their enduring power of speech to talk with only the most interesting of dragons and when the two races were united by the Bond of Talon and Claw, Fire and Fur—the foremost remaining epic is of Mei-Chou, the wise silver-mackerel tabby, and Ao Rue, the last of the blue-eyed sorcerer dragons, and how the two fared when the dragons ill-advisedly terraformed the Gobi from its native sea to a desert with the fell power of the Northern Lights. Together, the two battled the vampirism of the mindless Azghun Demons and the power-mad tyranny of Lei-kung and his demented cohort, Han Chung-li. Prominent too of the stories of this forgotten age is that of Ao Rue's great, undying love for the stunning Nü-kua.

Yet, despite Mei-Chou's great fame and courage, should she be asked for her favorite tales of these long-forgotten days and if she found someone worthy of her speech, she would humbly tell of the greatness of her aging mentor and father, Lord Chu, affectionately known to her as Chu-Chu. This is her favorite, the one she told the most.

Mei-chou cut through a wide, high-walled canyon as she descended the Mount of God, known as the Bogdo-ola in the old speech. Normally, the chilled air might draw her to thinking of the unknown, remote heights and how cold it was at the twenty-two-thousand-foot summit. No one knew what lived there or how cold it was; the cloud-draped heights defied even the mightiest dragon's wings. But, at this dark hour, her thoughts were filled with her beloved Chu-Chu, the cats' shaman, who lay dying in his cave. Despite his matted fur and hollow flanks, her love's eye always remembered him in the glory of his youth. His dark-blue eyes were almost black. They still shone within the lush fur of his ebony mask. His face and ears were framed by a creamy, camel-colored mane that circled to his full jowls. At least, Chu-Chu liked to call it a mane; Mei-chou thought of it more as a ruff. He'd say ruffs were prissy. But he'd also say that jowls had nothing to do with weight and everything to do with dignity. His mane blended back and down through rich, thick shades of chestnut and sable to black legs, paws, and tail. No color quite separated. They all moved in harmony, one into the other. The changes were so subtle that, when the light changed, there were moments of tan, chestnut, chocolate, and charcoal on his body. His most arresting feature was the oversized fangs that extended down over his lower jaw into the velvet of his chin. He thought they made him look fierce; Mei-chou knew it was only overbite. A Himalayan Sealpoint, Lord Chu insisted he was one of the few felines indigenous to the Gobi. But Mei-chou had heard enough to suspect that he was the product of a momentary lingering between a Black Persian and a Siamese. Cats, for all their proclamations of civilized demeanor, were erotically prone to random couplings, to spontaneous trysts. Perhaps, these passing matings had something to do with their complete immunity to guilt, their absolute freedom from embarrassment.

But now even the wonder of the unassailable Bogdoola and Lord Chu's beauty could not take her mind from her sorrowful thoughts: *So old. My Woolly-Bully. Senile, I guess. So fat. Hardly moves at all. His latest mate, Pita, makes his last days soft. Good! More and more he tells his strange, rambling stories, especially the one about the great tom who slew a dragon. Mind wanders more each day. Dragon slaying, indeed! That a cat ever could or would fight a dragon! Such nonsense! Still I wonder if there ever was such a tomcat? Nonsense! As much chance of that as a smart ape!*

If Mei-chou had not been so preoccupied, she probably would have heard the raver that waited for her. She was both surprised and annoyed at her lack of vigilance when the demented dragon lurched out from behind a large outcropping of rock. Mei-chou looked right and left. The canyon walls were too far away for her to run. She couldn't outrace his fire despite his obvious clumsiness. There was nowhere to go. So she sat down, began to wash her paws, and acted like he wasn't there at all.

"Now you are mine, fur turd!"

"Oh, hello, did you say something? Who are you?" Of course, Mei-chou recognized Han Chung-li, but she had decided that the best tactic was to keep him off balance. *This one is deep dumb. He shouldn't be too hard to handle.*

"I am General Han Chung-li. The rightful and blesséd successor to the glorious Lei-kung, you stupid cat!"

"Oh, you're a general now. Who appointed you?"

"That's dragon business. Nothing for you sub-creatures to worry about." Smoke began to rise from his nostrils as his flame brewed. Mei-chou remained calm. Dragons rarely frighten cats. It was considered bad form. Moreover, cats are indifferent to any dragon's magic, much less this one's poor excuse for anything, and they fully enjoy the dragons' narcotic smoke.

"So, what can I do for you, General?" She shifted slightly to try to catch the full effect of the smoke.

Han Chung-li paused for a moment to remember what he was doing on this cold mountain. "I am here to complete Lei-kung's majestic work, to serve the great power of the Northern Lights, to lead the Azghun Demons to bring dragonkind to its full potential! And Lei-kung had special plans for you cats. You have a place in the master plan. You will serve!"

"Are you sure that's what you're here for? I remember you saying something else when I called you and told you to come here." Now Han Chung-li was doubly puzzled. She was right. He'd come with some other purpose. And now he couldn't remember her calling him either. "Well, General, while you're trying to get yourself together, I'll continue on my way. Catch you later."

Mei-chou almost believed she'd get past him. He was shaking his head. It looked like he was trying to roll the pieces of his brain into their proper holes. She strolled toward him. *Mustn't show any fear! These primitive types can sense fear.* At that moment, an Azghun Demon streaked from somewhere; it hovered before Han Chung-li's snout. He snapped to attention. With his right talon, he threw a spray of gravel in Mei-chou's path. "Now, I remember! Prepare to die. You are mine, fur turd!"

"I would have thought you'd learned from Lei-kung that nothing you maniacs think is yours really is. Don't you know that there are beings and things you can't own?"

"You won't confuse me again!" The smoke came in great billows from his nostrils.

"These plans you have. Tell me about them. You know, cats don't yield to regimentation very well. We don't care for such things." Now another development was an added cause for Mei-chou's concern. Up behind Han Chung-li's head, she saw Chu-Chu. Sleep and senility were far gone. His eyes were wide; his concentration complete. He was playing out the ageless discipline of the stalk: ears back, body low, tail-fur fat with anger, its tip twitching. His fine, gossamer fur lifting in the faint breeze, he moved on the dragon with murderous intent.

She remained poised, if deeply concerned: *He'll have a heart attack. Where's Pita?* Confidently, successfully fighting fear, she looked up at the rearing dragon, his fire rising like bile. "Dragon, you cannot harm me. I am the First of the First. Friend to Ao Rue, last and greatest of the sorcerers. I summon the Bond of Talon and Claw, Fire and Fur."

Han Chung-li laughed grotesquely—shrieking. He almost choked on his own joy, drawing in more air than he let out. "Your words are nothing. You inferiors have no minds worthy of note. You are good only for orders and menial tasks. I will think for you! I am the first of the new dragons! We make our own bonds. There will be oaths of fealty and submission to us. All of nature will yield before our superior power and intelligence." His mouth opened; flames began to lick around his tendrils.

Mei-chou stood firm. *So this is how it ends. Cooked by a half-wit!* Then, from out of the corner of her eye, she saw Lord Chu spring. She knew the distance was too great—*too much age, too much weight.*

Lord Chu looked like a dolphin in the sea. His body was stretched out, a smooth blur in the air. Just before he got to Han Chung-li's head, he opened up. All four legs were fully extended. Every claw caught the red glow of the dragon's fire. He screamed his success, Han Chung-li's first sign of disaster. The dragon had no time to turn his head. Chu's front claws stabbed into the dragon's eyelid. Immediately, his hind legs began to snap up and down. He raked the naked eye with his claws. Han Chung-li wildly swung his head from side to side. His wings beat the ground, throwing great clouds of dust and stone. His pinions and claws ripped splinters and hunks from the granite. He flung fire everywhere, but all his struggles couldn't dislodge the squalling monster that was taking his sight.

"Run, Mei-chou, run! Hide, hide, until I finish him."

Mei-chou was paralyzed. All she could see was her Chu-Chu's beautiful fur charring as fire rushed from Han Chung-li's snout and ricocheted off the rock.

"Get, girl! Move! For once do as I tell you!"

Mei-chou responded automatically to that old tone. It was kitten and teacher again. Obediently, she turned and ran beneath a ledge into a crevice. Her ears were filled with the fury of the spitting, screaming tomcat. Han Chung-li's roars filled her with terror. She cowered in her hole, trembling in fear. She was horrified at the thought of life without Chu-Chu: *Who will tell me? It's not time! Too soon! Too soon! Who will care? My poor Chu-Chu.*

Suddenly, all noise vanished—the total silence of a world without ears. Despite her fear, concern dragged Mei-chou on her belly back to the canyon. She could see nothing amid the holocaust. It was as if the fire of the earth had punished the mountain. Great shards of rock were thrown and broken everywhere. The white granite was cursed with blackness. There were places it had melted and run, forming macabre sculptures of beings beyond madness. All had been scoured by evil, scourged by a dark pain. Mei-chou fell in upon herself in despair: *He is gone. I didn't help!* Then, something moved and moaned beneath the thrown slabs. As she ran to it, she almost didn't recognize him. So little of his rich colors remained. He was black with char, too brittle to touch. So little blood. All burned away. Yet a shadow of bright life remained. Lord Chu's voice was faint ashes: "Couldn't get to that other eye. Couldn't get across the snout. So far, seemed so far. Dragons must be wider between the eyes these days. Are you all right, kitten. You were my best student! My sweetest child!"

"Lie still; I am here." With all hope and love, Mei-chou cried out soundlessly and futilely: *Ao Rue, Ao Rue, where in the seven hells are you when I need you!*

"Wasn't much of a dragon. Would've liked to go out on a big one."

"Oh, Chu-Chu, it was the great father of all dragons. Nothing could have stood before him. Not now, not in the old days." *Ao Rue, Ao Rue! He's fading.*

"Was he really big?"

"He was a monstrous rogue. All the ancient blue-eyed sorcerers couldn't have stood before him, my brave Chu-Chu. I should have helped; I should have!" *Ao Rue! Here! Here!*

"No, this was no job for a kitten. And don't call me Chu-Chu. Best left to us adults. How I miss your mother." He had begun to babble in pain.

"I knew if I waited, if I was silent, I'd have you again, stupid cat." Han Chung-li had returned. His head was tilted so he could see them with his one good eye. Blood welled from scratches across the bridge of his snout. Chu-Chu had almost made it. "Gonna cook some kitties now, I am, I am." He was clearly in great pain, almost incoherent. Yellow ichor formed a shiny smear on his scales, clotted in the tendrils below the ripped eye. Its flaccid membrane was pink with diluted blood. "Cook you slow, I will. My agony will be nothing to yours." His head reared back; his jaws opened; Mei-chou curled herself around Chu-Chu. His gathering fire mocked her meager protection.

Nothing's happening. His head was coming forward

again. Mei-chou braced and cringed. Hugged Chu-Chu. *Again, nothing.* Han Chung-li's head wavered in confusion. Mei-chou looked up, gently cradling Chu-Chu's head as it slid from the curve of her throat. Han Chung-li's swinging head finally brought his good eye toward the summit of Bogdo-ola. He screamed in terror.

Ao Rue had come around the Mount of God and was plunging down upon the canyon. His silver body blew a valley in the peak's snow; white waves leapt away in great sheets from the stone as he roared down. Silver sparks trailed the edges of his wings. His speed burned and cut the air. He threw his anger before him. Ao Rue flew through his own fire. Again and again, he burst anew out of flame. He was the purity and might of lightning without storm, thunder without noise. His eyes blazed in great whirlpools of blue. Billows of energy streamed from his scales. Great swells of broken air cracked in his wake. He rode all his power to Mei-chou's call! His talons reached out for Han Chung-li.

"Now, the fear is yours, little general." Mei-chou's fear had turned to anger; she rose to stand astride Chu-Chu. "He is your death. The perfection of fur and fire. The last of the great sorcerers. He has stilled your hot breath. He has taken your fire. Now, for Lord Chu, he will take your life!" Han Chung-li, half-blind, turned in panic. He scrambled down the mountain. Too witless to fly, he banged against the stone. Ao Rue was almost upon him.

Mei-chou's rage suddenly vanished as she felt a faint stirring of Chu's body. "No, No, Ao Rue, here. Here, to me, to me!" Her cry stopped Ao Rue so quickly that he had to sink his talons into the granite to keep from flying by. As he cracked out of the stone and moved to her, concern marked every step. He offhandedly threw a blue orb in the direction of the fleeing Azghun Demon; it popped out of existence.

"What is it, Mei-chou; I came as fast as I . . . Oh, no!" He had seen the black body. "Who is this?" His voice dropped to a whisper.

"This is Lord Chu, the real First of the First. My teacher. I should not mourn; I should not. He wouldn't like it. This is as it should be. He has had a full life. He saved me. It was important to him. Important that he die for his student. Important he die this way." It was all Mei-chou could do to talk. "He dies a hero. Now, at least, I know. I never believed his stories. He was the dragon slayer. He was the legendary tom! Our greatest hero. Legend incarnate. To think I never knew. So much wisdom and courage in one body. Can anyone be this much again? Chu-Chu, my Chu-Chu, Chu-Chu!" She had begun to shake.

"Easy, my little friend." She was almost hysterical. Ao Rue found himself wishing he could hold her. "There's still some life. I think I can save him, heal him." The swirling blue magic rose in his eyes. "Yes, a small spark. Nothing's broken inside. The fur and flesh will come back. Climb up on my claw while I hold him, Mei-chou; I need to feel you with me."

Ao Rue carefully slid one claw under Chu-Chu's brittle body. Covered him in a light clasp with the other. Mei-chou climbed up on top. Blue light began to pulse within his folded claws as he concentrated. She could feel the magics that moved from him to Chu-Chu. They were summer breezes, budding flowers, small things stirring in warmth, awakenings, the warm loam, tender shoots. Despite the moment, she felt good, healthy. Ao Rue lifted his head. He let out his breath in relief. Mei-chou jumped down. Ao Rue opened his claws to let her look within. Chu-Chu was curled up, happily sleeping. His new, pink skin was already covered with a light fuzz, a promise of wonderful fur.

Just as Mei-chou was able to speak again and as Lord Chu began to stir, Pita arrived. She was tearing, sliding, skittering through the rocks and sand. One shoulder was marked with blood where she'd scraped a boulder. For once, a cat didn't seem to care about being awkward or dirty.

"Pita, you're a mess. You're not even smart enough to groom!" Lord Chu had climbed down out of Au Rue's claw and was standing. He was shaky but working to recover his dignity.

"You old fool, what's the matter with you. I go out for

one second, for one jerboa for myself, so as not to touch your precious larder. And what do you do. You wander off. Get lost. I've been all over this mountain looking for you."

"Watch your tone, silly kitten. How could I get lost? Why I knew every crack of this mountain before you were born. I have been protecting Mei-chou."

"You're too old even to protect yourself. Get back to the cave where I can take care of you. Leave this First of the First stuff to Mei-chou; you're too old."

"I hardly need your protection, madam." Nonetheless, he began to move. "I'm not that old. I've been doing some dragon slaying."

"Those stupid, old stories again. You've started to believe them yourself." She walked at his flank, herding him in the right direction. "Don't give me any of that nonsense. You get your tail to bed. You look terrible. What did you do to your fur? I can't trust you for a minute. You'll be the death of me."

"Just who do you think you're talking to, pink-nosed Pita! Why I remember when the best you could do was get a teat in your mouth. Don't use that tone on me, little Pita. It wasn't so long ago that your eyes weren't open. Funny thing, you were, stumbling into everything."

"How dare you, you senile lout."

As their yelling faded into the distance, Mei-chou smiled. Ao Rue was nonplussed: "Why is she so furious with him? Doesn't she think he did the right thing, was noble?"

"Ao Rue, how can you be so powerful yet so naive. She's not angry, just relieved. She loves him."

"He's twice her age."

"Age isn't the factor. Genuine affection is; loyalty is. Rare commodities in this age or any other for that matter. There are some that say that the young, like Pita, are to be avoided. Too mercuric, too fickle. I don't know. There are few rules in such things. Look at us. Interspecies friends. Good love? Luck, maybe? More likely the wisdom to pick well. Who knows?"

"Yes, you're right." Ao Rue was recovering his poise. "I'm so pleased I found my love, my Nü-kua, now when I'm smart enough to know what she is. She is so special.

She makes me more than I ever thought I could be. It's good to find the right one." Ao Rue was obviously proud that he could interpret the moment in his own terms.

"Well, try not to be too quick. It's early yet."

"Mei-chou, you're being cynical again. Isn't Nü-kua at least the equal of Pita? After all, Pita's only a cat."

"Only a cat?" Mei-chou quickly stifled her anger. "You might also entertain the idea that fidelity isn't species-specific."

"Enough. It's not up to you to question Nü-kua; she is mine. Anyway, Lord Chu can now rest without being disturbed again."

"I wouldn't be too sure. Chàos is loose in the world. We all may yet play roles none of us expected. But that's something no one can predict. For now, I must thank you. Bless all that's holy that you were nearby. If you hadn't seen us." Mei-chou let her voice trail off into a future she didn't want even to think about.

"I didn't. I was off listening to the whales sing. You called me!"

"I did?"

"Well, I heard you. Now that I think of it, how can that be? I know dragons and cats are bound, but telepathic contact?"

"Maybe great moments do summon great powers. We'll probably never know. Now I must go fix something. I never believed he was a hero. It just seemed he was born old, a creature of mind, not courage. I need to tell him he is a hero and, more importantly, that I know."

"I have to go, too. As much as I'd relish going after Han Chung-li, I have an important kaochang; I hate meetings. Do you think Lord Chu will listen to you?"

"Chu-Chu? He'll make fun of me, but it's something I have to say. And he'll listen. He'll pretend not to, but he'll listen."

CRITICAL CATS

by Susan Shwartz

So much they know, those two-legs. So many words they have for what they think they know. Like the way they take away our names, replacing them with noises of their own. They make a lot of noises.

I have learned to turn my head away when the two-legs push through the door here. The bells above the door ring, startling decent Folk into breaking off their leaps. All the other two-legs stare rudely as the newcomer, its face sat and sad, sets down a box holding yet another of the Free Folk, who is sick. Those who share my dish in this place of strange smells, cold ground, and unexpected aches sniff at the two-legs and purr for them: but not I.

There is little good in pleasing two-legs, as my kindred, trapped in small cages and waiting for the two-legs healers to hurt them, could tell you.

The two-legs who come here call me Puff. A foolish name, but I have learned that the words "Puff doesn't warm up to people" do keep the other two-legs away. I do not know my own true name. Two-legs took me away too early from my mother and dumped me in this place, where the air reeks of fear and pain and the bitter waters that the two-legs bathe us in or make us drink.

Any Soulhealer of the Free Folk knows better, not that I know so much about them. Lick the hurt. Keep the injured creature warm. But let the willing spirit go. Two-legs, I suspect, do not have Soulhealers. Instead, they have two-legs wrapped in loose white pelts, who rush from room to room to run clever hands over the Free Folk or prick them with thorns. Because they do not have quiet, hidden lairs, they make places like this one where two-legs come in with water pouring from their

283

eyes as they bring in the Free Folk they have captured. Some of these Folk are simply scared or spoiled—idle beasts who have forgotten their pride because life is easy and food is free.

Night, though, is the bad time. At night, the two-legs lug in what they call the "critical cats."

Truly, these kindred of mine are not "critical." They are simply ready to start on their Hunt, abandoning the bodies they have outlived like a gnawed bone. But foolish two-legs pull them back.

I said that I, Puff, do not go to the two-legs and let them stroke me. Nor do I watch them. Not where they can see me do it. Still, I learn much. They are a troubled lot, but they make their trouble for themselves.

This past night, they have come in again with the trapped Free Folk they claim to "own." Too many have brought with them kittens of their own breed. They watch with even more fear than they study what they call "their cats." What a breed they are, these two-legs. Outcasts of their kind turn on their kittens and they fear to fight back!

"Puff isn't comfortable with children," says the two-legs who sits behind a low wall and stops a bell from ringing by talking to it. Usually, then, a two-legs bats away its youngling, which saves me from a pounce by a staggering two-legs kit. It is dangerous to approach such kittens. Two-legs will let others of their kind hurt their young; but the bad manners that would earn our kittens a swift cuff must go uncorrected, lest I start to hunt the Dreamtrails before my body is outworn.

I run from where the two-legs and the sick Folk wait into the inmost lairs where the food bowls are. Enticing smells of meat and fish rise from the bowls. The other two Folk who live here, Fenster and Purvis, are not around. For the moment, all the bowls belong to me.

"There you are, Puff! We need your help, boy!"

Big hands sweep me up. The food was just a trap! I squall and kick out with my strong hind legs, but the two-legs female holds me fast. So clever they are, those two-legs, with their deft hands. So much they take from us.

The two-legs holds me. Her littermate brings up a stick that buzzes like hornets and chews away my fine full ruff. Bitter water splashes upon my now-bare hide. I see the glint of the thorns the two-legs healers use, and I kick wildly.

"Now, be good, Puff!" I hear, and a hard hand scruffs down upon my neck. Trapped like the Folk outdoors! The thorn in the eldest's hand pricks me and hurls me out into the sleep that has no Dreamtime.

When I wake, I know the two-legs have taken something else from me—strength. Now I lie in the inmost lair where the smells of bitter water and sick, frightened Free Folk make my nose twitch. Gum clogs my eyes, and I feel weak, like a female after her first litter. My breath pants in and out.

"Puff's awake now. Here, Puff. You were a good boy." A piece of chicken, too cold from how they keep it fresh, drops beside me. I wrinkle up my muzzle and turn my face away. Let them worry.

Bloodscent tinges the air: mine. This time, the two-legs have stolen my blood itself from my poor body while I slept. What won't they sink to? I trace the scent over to a cage. One of the Folk is lying in it on the special cushion that brings the warmth of sunlight to lairs where the only light comes from the walls.

The newcomer is of a fine size. He has a deep, sleek coat, except where his neck is bound with cloths. They smell of bitter waters and hold in place the clear, hollow thorn that feeds my blood into his throat.

He twitches and flexes his paws. They have *seven* toes, and that, as all Free Folk know, means strength and craft. I fight up onto my haunches, nip up my bribe of chicken to give me strength and walk unsteadily to stand before him.

He opens his eyes, and I am trapped. His eyes are huge and wise as the full moon, full of shadow from the Dreamtrails. And then I know.

"I greet my younger brother," purred a voice inside my head, "and thank him for his gift, which makes me strong." *For now*, the sense came, though the voice does not admit it.

I drop my head to my paws. I would bow further and
show my underbelly, but the stranger flicks up a corner
of his lip: no need. Respectfully I curl my tail around my
haunches and set myself to listen. It is not every day that
one meets a Soulsinger; cut off too early from my mother's teaching, I have never met one before.

My fur fluffs up and I start to squall with rage. It was
his time, yet two-legs had drawn him back, him, a
Soulsinger, and stuck him with their awful thorns. How
dare they?

"Be quiet, or you'll bring them here," he warns. Again,
he uses the inner voice. "Yes, we can talk thus. Your
blood is in me, as much as if the same female had borne
us."

He looks as if he has to fight to raise his head. He
closes his eyes, and I know he fights his body for more
strength.

Why would a Soulsinger fight the call? Surely the
Dreamtrails can hold no fear for him.

"Do you wish to take the Trails?" I ask. So clever
these two-legs are, yet it is not hard to puzzle out their
tricks. I could open that lock, dislodge the thorn, and
send the Singer forth.

The Singer twitches his head: no. When his eyes blink
open again, they are calm. The leafshadow has grown
dim.

"I would not profane your gift by wasting it. Stay and
talk with me."

"What is your name?" A Soulsinger, he has the right
to ask that, and I, the obligation to reply. Untaught in
the ways of the Free Folk I may be, but I know what is
owed to those who deal with souls.

Not knowing my true name, I put my nose down again
in shame. "I am called Puff," I say, wrinkling my muzzle
in contempt for the two-legs sound.

"Perhaps you are too big and strong for a Puff," he
agrees, then pauses. "I am Merlin."

"That is a two-legs' name," I sniff before I think.

"*My* name," he corrects me. "I am a named being,
named by my human after a Soulsinger and healer of the
human kind. Many songs come with this name, my hu-

man says. He who bore it hunted in a great wood and was accounted very wise in human dreams—which, you may be surprised to know, are as rich as our own. My human gave me the singer's name, but I have taken it for my own."

He holds his head proudly, despite the thorn. Then his eyes soften, fond as a tabby with one fine kit.

"Did you see my human when she brought me in?" he asks.

Was it for his *two-legs* he had stayed? I would not have thought a Soulsinger could be so great a fool. And yet, there it shone in his eyes. *Love* for a two-legs. *Worry* for a two-legs, though he was the one who was ill.

I start to tell him I do not look at two-legs, but those wise, troubled eyes force me to hunt back on my memory's trails. His human—there had been just one. Had she brought a kitten of her own? No, not that one . . . I shut my eyes . . . yes!

"The short two-legs with the long head-fur. The she who yowled all the while she brought you in—was that your two-legs?"

Merlin glares at me. "You should not call them two-legs."

"*We* are the People, the free kindred. *They* are just two-legs."

"You can still be polite!" A hiss tinges his mind-voice.

"The . . . person," I correct myself, unwillingly obedient. "I saw her."

"She is a fine human," Merlin tells me. "I do not wish to leave her. We have been together all my life. Kind hands, a soft voice, a generous heart. And pleasant to look at, once you know how to judge humans as they judge themselves."

Sickness had turned his brain. What a disappointment! Cut off so early from my kin, I had hoped to learn more of the ways of the Free Folk from this Soulsinger. And instead, what does he do? Maunders about a *pretty* two-legs. Some Soulsinger, indeed.

"She looks like the kind of two-legs who would feed a kitten till he cried with pain, but walk past a starveling stray," I snarl.

"*I* was a stray! You speak with less sense than a sick kitten!" This time, Merlin uses his voice as well as his mind. His yowl would have sent me flying against the wall if it had been a swipe of his paw. With it came an image of his human, crowned with light, bringing food to the Free Folk who rove the back streets. Wary they are, but they do come to her call.

Merlin's anger brings the youngest two-legs over fast. "Puff, are you bothering poor Merlin? Get down, Puff. Merlin's sick."

Her littermate calls over a shoulder. "Get him ready. Ms. Black is here to see him."

Both two-legs firm their lips and shake their heads.

"She's very upset, isn't she?"

"She's always upset. She's crazy about that cat. Look how she always gets one of us to come and sit for him when she goes away. And brings us gifts, too."

"He's a neat cat. Dr. Colt and Dr. Bell are worried about him. He's how old—thirteen? And he had this last year, too?"

"Dr. Bell says it's worse this time."

"It hasn't been a good week," sighs the elder two-legs. "That carriage-snatcher . . . there's lots of crazies. You haven't been here long enough to remember, but I do. Forest Hills used to be safe. You expected trouble in Manhattan, but not here. Now, we have people climbing in windows, and people grabbing babies right off Austin Street. Did you see how many people brought their kids in to office hours today? They're scared to leave them out of their sight."

"They drove Fenster and Purvis crazy. Puff ignored them."

"That's Puff for you. He was a good donor for Merlin today. *Come* on, Merlin. Good cat, pretty cat. Here we go. Want to see your mommy?"

The youngest two-legs lifts him from the cage. He protests and struggles a little. But "Merlin . . . Merlin. . . ." they practically sing his name, and he is calm again. He rests his head against the shoulder of the she who holds him, and lets her run gentle hands over his fur. It is still glossy, with its ordered markings of night and moonlight, but I think it will dry out fast. I also think that the Soulsinger is enjoying the attention.

"*Shame* on you, Puff, upsetting Merlin."

The door swings wide. Borne out to see his two-legs, oh, very well, his *human*, Merlin flicks a sly, triumphant glance at me.

I follow him out. Once again, Merlin's she is talking, with salt water running down her hairless face. She smells scared and sad. As he sees her, he tries to lunge from the arms of the one who holds him. As his two-legs sees him, her whole face shines. She does not smell as unhappy as she had.

"Merlin!" she calls. "*There's* my good cat."

The two-legs shut the door upon them. She, too, smelled unhappy. Fenster, who shares the foodbowls with me, trots up and paws at her knees. The two-legs swoops her up and holds her like a human kitten, seeking comfort. Fenster, the slut, purrs.

"Kitty!" squalls a two-legs kitten. I flee beneath a table and shut my eyes. Over and over the bells ring. There are a lot of critical cats coming in tonight, a lot of two-legs—well, enough—*people* speaking in soft, nervous voices.

"I didn't want to come out, but what could I do when Samantha was so sick?"

"We're picking up Dook. He was just fixed."

"They had cops patrolling Seventy-first. It's good to see cops on the beat again."

"I hope they catch that . . ."

The people growl in anger and in hope.

I lick the last traces of bitter water from my mangled ruff and wait.

The light beneath the door grows, waking me from my nap. One of the sisters carries Merlin, who protests separation from his human, back to the inner lairs. Merlin's two-legs stands before Dr. Bell: both females, but how different. Merlin's human is soft, long-furred, the wrappings that two-legs hide their bodies with carefully arranged and sparkly with the toys their females like. Dr. Bell is thinner, less carefully groomed: a lean barn dweller facing off against an indoor drowser upon cushions.

Their feelings hurt. Merlin's human fears and aches; Dr. Bell wants only to escape to the inner lairs and the Free Folk who watch and do not ask hard questions. Clearly, she forces herself to remain and meet the other female's eyes. Both females' mouths move in sounds that, ordinarily, I would ignore. But Merlin has stuck a thorn in my feelings as well as my curiosity. I can not turn away.

"I know you're on the cat's side," says Merlin's human. "So am I. I want him back, of course I do. But I want what's best for him. You're the doctor. What you say to do, I'll do." Her eyes fill, but her voice is quite steady.

Dr. Bell flicks an eyebrow up in surprised respect at this pampered-looking female. "We're trying our best. It's not leukemia or feline AIDS. It could be his spleen or his liver. We just don't *know* yet. But I have to say, it doesn't look too good."

The human looks down. "I know," she whispers. She makes the hand and voice gestures of respect that two-legs use. "Thank you, Doctor," she says and turns to go.

"You might wait a minute till you calm down," Dr. Bell suggests. "So you can watch out on the way home. God only knows what's out there."

Which is why I like it here, her undervoice tells me clearly. *I cure pain. And the cats I work with are decent; they don't turn on their own kind.*

Merlin's human nods thanks. She draws a deep breath and forces calm upon her face the way we lower our inmost eyelids when we gaze into the sun.

"Who's this?" she asks.

To my surprise, it is me she is talking about this time. I stroll out from beneath the table to let her admire me.

"That's Puff. He was Merlin's donor this morning."

The next instant, Merlin's human is down on her knees before me. She is quick in her movements, and her hand gestures are graceful, almost like paws. "Oh, the brave cat, good cat. But look, his ruff is shaved, and it was so pretty," she croons at me. She glances up at the one called Dr. Bell. "Puff's a hero-cat."

If she keeps that up, I think I may have a hairball, just

to teach her. I raise a forepaw to clean it and ignore her outstretched hands.

"Puff's a little standoffish tonight."

"Is he all right? Did you take a lot of blood from him?" Dr. Bell nods. "A good bit. He was scared."

"Poor Puff. Thank you, Puff. Tell me," again, she appeals to the other two-legs. "May I bring Puff treats when I come tomorrow? Whatever happens, I'm grateful to him."

Still talking, she wraps heavy clothes about her and vanishes into the night beyond the lights where the critical cats and the noisy kittens of both breeds wait.

If I had come to her, she might have felt better. What is that to me? She is just another noisy two-legs. Still, there had been that promise of treats. . . .

I head for the inmost lairs. Merlin lies upon the sunshine pad. He is breathing too fast, but purring as he breathes. I paw the cage lock open and come in beside him, nuzzling his side. His eyes blink open, lazy, satisfied. Seeing his human has eased him; he seems stronger and happier. I am angry at myself that I care.

"She groomed me; we don't like it when my fur is matted. She praised me and sang my name. Said I was a good cat and whatever I did was fine. I wish I were going home; I could run it to suit myself now. Such a good human." He shuts his eyes, musing on what would have appeared to be the most delightful of Dreamtrails, but what I know has to be that idiot human of his.

"Did you see Her?" he asks eagerly.

"I saw her," I admit. "She thanked me and would have stroked my back. But I was washing. Tell me, does she keep her word? She promised me food for helping you."

"That sounds like her," Merlin says, pleased. "She'll bring you treats. And she understands what we Free Folk like—tender beef in tiny cans; fat salmon and cream and things you can steal off plates."

If *he* keeps it up, I think again that I will have a hairball, and never mind the respect due to Soulsingers.

"You have made me strong for now, my brother," he praises me. "She will be afraid without me."

"Why is she afraid?" I hate to ask it, but my curiosity stretches and leaps. "She is sleek and well." *Not like you*, I think. "And she is old enough to be as wise as a female who has raised many litters."

Merlin shrugs, a ripple of massive shoulders on which the fur already has begun to wilt. "Humans fear more than we . . . pain, voices, fights. Even the pieces of paper that they carry scare them. My human more than most."

He looks up. For a moment, the pain he has suppressed this evening twists his face and drives the wisdom from his eyes. It is not just body pain. "If she conquers her fears, she will be a Soulsinger, too. That is a hard choice for humans, who do not respect the soul art as we do. She fears, but I know she wants to slay her fear. I do not want to leave her till she does. I do not think I could hunt in peace if I left her now."

The moment passes, and his eyes are deep and bright again as the autumn moon. "She will go to ground tonight, just like we do when we hurt. But she should not be left alone. Tonight, I shall watch her dreams. You shall help me, if you will. Have you never stalked a human's thoughts? I promise, my brother, you will find this an interesting game."

Once the two-legs turn down the lights and leave, we huddle together and hunt down the trail of Merlin's human's thoughts. She dodges in and out of the crowd of two-legs, watchful of the huge, foul-smelling things that honk and screech and have two-legs in them playing mating calls. She looks carefully away from the kittens trundled in their carriers by cautious two-legs.

Merlin was all the child I had, the thought lingers like rain in her thoughts. *Not was*, is. *But for how long?* Her eyes keep blurring. At that her fear nips her more shrewdly, like a rat. It is not safe to walk the streets with blurring eyes. *It has not been a good year*, she thinks. Faces shift and go . . . some clearly remembered; some blurred by years longer than the lifespan of Free Folk.

It is no kindness, the long memories of two-legs, I realize, and I wonder at the thought. Merlin shifts beside me and tries to chirp reassuringly. This far away, his two-legs does not hear him.

She does not look at the little suns that light up the sparkly toys behind clear walls. She does not sniff at the thousand intriguing food smells—or wince at the stenches of foul waters and foul air, or the wild two-legs whom not even a besotted Soulsinger would ever call "human" again.

At a gate scent-marked a long time ago by such two-legs, Merlin's human pauses. To my surprise, she calls, not in the speech of the Free Folk, but in what sounds like it.

"I *told* you she feeds the Folk who wander," Merlin's "voice" nudged me.

"Does she know what she is saying?" I ask. Merlin grimaces at me.

"She doesn't need to."

Two thin Folk drop from the undergrowth sloping up toward tracks on a bridge and trot toward her. "He's sick, fellows. Red Brother, wish me luck, will you?" The larger cat starts toward her; a smaller one bats him away. Both withdraw.

"I see your point," she whispers. "I didn't bring any food, and I smell sad. I guess I'm not very good company for you today. Sorry."

She turns and trots toward her lair, her eyes flicking in all directions as she crosses the street into a darkened square. Fears squeak in her thoughts: of the two-legs who leap from cars, the ones who pounce from hiding in the bushes, the ones who rush up in the street, or who linger in the halls. From her pouch, she pulls a jangling clutter of metal, an image of the Free Folk dangling from it, and uses it to get into her lair. I am surprised that any two-legs respects the Goddess of the Folk, much less bears Her image.

She sighs with relief when the door shuts behind her. Odd how doors mean prison to the Free Folk and safety to . . . all right, I won't call them two-legs.

Her lair is small, scent-marked as though Merlin were a full male, and full of toys. Stacks of paper lie on shelves, ready to be tumbled into cozy nests; warm wraps lie on chairs and cushions; a dark cave full of things that bear her scent yawns open.

Merlin's mind flickers into mischief. "'*Shoes,*' she says those are. For her hind paws. When I don't like my litter, I mark them to teach her better. She calls me 'rotten cat' and laughs. I don't do it much. It *is* a dirty trick."

He leads me on a thought tour of the tiny lair. "My dishes . . . and my box . . . and that's where I nap, on the fancy rug below the window. Someone sent it just for me from halfway round the world."

A bell rings, and the human stops it. "No, they haven't found the thief," she tells it. "None of the papers even have a picture of him. But they found the first kid. All right, thank God. I'd like to find that crazy myself." Her voice turns hard and angry. If she were one of us, her hackles would rise and her tail would lash like a mother in the kittening box with her litter when a stranger gets too close.

"Yes, I'll be careful. Yes, the door's locked. Stop *worrying* about me. I've got a sick cat to worry about. I have to visit him tomorrow. No, they don't know what's wrong with Merlin." Her voice quivers and breaks. "I'm scared he won't make it."

Beside me, Merlin's body tenses as if he wants to hurl himself through space and land beside her. Her hand goes out as if she seeks the comfort of his fur. Her face twists.

"Just thirteen. Yes, I know, it's old, but they live to be twenty, sometimes. . . . Thanks for thinking of us. He's a hell of a cat, and he's putting up a fine fight. Whatever's best for him. I'll take care. Bye."

She lays down the bell and walks over to the cold box.

"Sliced turkey in there," Merlin says. "She bought it for me."

Ignoring the delicacy, she pours herself some bitter water. I wrinkle my nose. Merlin shrugs. "It's like catnip, but they lap it up," he explains.

She sits in a chair before a table on which rests a box that holds a window screen. She touches it, and it lights and purrs. She rests her fingers on a pad and moves them, clacking, back and forth. Suddenly, she glances down, looking. "I always come and sit on her lap when she tries to makes songs. . . ." Merlin tells me. She tightens her muzzle and blinks her eyes. Salt water runs from them.

The Soulsinger beside me yearns forward, but he is beginning to tire. His body sags and cools.

"Come back," I coax. "You cannot hunt her dreams all night."

"I cannot leave her. Something is going to happen. I know it. Help me stay."

I am Puff. I walk alone. I cannot imagine caring that much about any of the Free Folk, let alone a two-legs. But the big soulsinger already has my blood; he might as well have the strength of my heart, too. I crouch by his side and let my spirit flow toward him. He sighs and the cold at his heart eases.

Again, we hunt forward. The human prepares to sleep. When her breathing slows, Merlin nudges his spirit-self forward beside her head and extends a seven-toed insubstantial paw to touch her face. It melts against her skin. Merlin looks unhappy again. But the human smiles as if she feels the touch. Satisfied by that, Merlin purrs and settles his dreamself by his human's side.

When I feel his breathing steady where his body crouches by mine, I reach out. Like a tabby tugging a stray kit back against her side, I ease his spirit back into his flesh. Then, as if an eyelid I didn't know I had opened, I find that I can see within my companion. None of his bones are broken; no organs are diseased; no blood flows. Yet matters are all awry; his body has turned on itself, devouring its own strength.

I am surprised that his heart is only the size it is. It seems as if it should be much bigger.

"Gently done," comes the familiar undervoice. I start.

Merlin turns his head slightly, wincing at the pain of the thorn in his neck. "As if you had known how to hunt a human's thoughts thus all your lives. Do you know, deny it as you may, you are in the right place, my brother Puff? Puff, as you're called, with your fur like smoke and your face with a smoke smudge across its muzzle, floating across minds to heal them. The humans are not the only healers here."

The Soulsinger looks up at me, his eyes glinting too brightly. "They were not total fools, the humans who named you. But let me give you your true name now; your inner name."

He jerks his head so our noses touch, and I feel his pain jolt through me. I know I do not want to hear this, but those eyes hold me. " 'Healer' I name you. Be the healer of souls you were born to be."

No! Careful not to yowl, I back away. I do not want to be a soul healer. I do not want to care so much—or care at all. I have already done too much. I am Puff who stands aloof, who takes my food and whatever else I can. I give as little as I can, and I go my own way.

"Who understands more than 'now'?" he asks me. "Who fears for humans, even when he most scorns them? Who watches the sick Kindred and fails to hold aloof— even from one as sick as I?"

No! I start to yowl as I back out of his cage, then mute my cry lest I wake the sick kindred. I do not want to be like Merlin whose body fails and who yearns for the Dreamtrails—but who forces himself to stay and watch . . . because he loves. I do not want to heal bodies or souls and run the risk of failure, or of fear. It is too hard, too much for me.

The whole lair is empty, except for the breathing of the Folk. Many are caged. I sense their fear as if it were my own.

Fenster and Purvis lie curled up together. They blink when I try to edge into their warm huddle. I do not think they are altogether pleased.

"You have always gone your own way, slept your own sleep, dreamed your own dreams. Why should we welcome you?" Fenster asks.

How happy they look, wrapped in warmth and the forever "now" of happy Folk. *Please let me share*, I ask. It comes out as a kitten's whimper.

"Because I am alone, and I'm frightened," I confess.

Kinder far than I, they lick my shoulder till I sleep. I

fear that Merlin stays awake, watching his two-legs dream.

I vow to myself I would stay away. But morning finds me again at Merlin's cage. He is cooler, weaker, and his eyes have dulled.

"Good morning, Healer," he mocks me. "Making your rounds like the human doctor?"

I show him my teeth. "Keep that up, and you can haunt your human's dreams alone today."

But I lie, and I know it.

"Rest," I tell him. "I will follow your trails for you until she returns."

I no longer doubt that she will do so.

Lazy Puff, the two-legs would call me. But I am not lazy. I hunt the strangest trail I have ever known as I track Merlin's two-legged she.

It is hard, the life they have, these people. They ride, all crammed, standing together, on fearsome wagons through runs worse than the maze of any mouse, deep beneath the ground: places of fearful sounds and smells. They do not look at each other because, if they do, they may fight.

We know the rules for who goes belly up, who slinks away, and when. These two-legs have no such rules that I can see.

And yet, I saw a male offer a female heavy with young a seat, saw people pull back to give kittens room to breathe. Merlin's human sits, too, blinking at a paper that she holds. "Child Snatcher At Large," huge letters shout at her above a darkened square. She shuts the paper and blinks. An old male leaning on a stick limp into the wagon, and she rises for him. I sense his surprise and his pleasure. She has courtesy, this she of Merlin's. He has trained her well.

Courtesy and neat hands; and yet she fears and remembered her fears. It must be hard for any two-legs, harder still for one with the rudiments of proper conduct.

Noise in the lair forces me back. I leap from Merlin's cage just as Dr. Colt comes in. He too is neat-footed—for a two-legs male. He lifts Merlin from the cage, and the Soulsinger yowls.

"Did that hurt, boy?" he asks. Why does he have to treat the Soulsinger, whose mind and spirit outshine him as catnip outshines sawdust, like a kitten? But Merlin lowers his head to rub against his hand. "Wish I knew what you had." He is suddenly grave.

I run out. All that day, I dream in a chair, not even noticing when people draw close and pet me. "Puff's gotten friendly. Think he's all right?" someone asks.

"He's not friendly. He's sleeping," replies the female who carried Merlin to his human. "Aren't you, Puff?"

I'm not. Instead, as often as I was drawn back to my lair, I send my spirit forth in dreams to hunt the strange trails of a two-leg's—a human's—mind. It is like setting weight on a leg too recently broken. It hurts, but I have to try it.

So much the humans have that they fear—not just dogs or claws or hunger; not even rogues like the mad two-legs who stole human kittens. But of being cold inside, as I was last night, without friends to curl up beside, of long, long years of being cold. They live far longer than we do. I used to hate them for it. Now, I know it is nothing I should envy.

Fears and sounds and scents boil about me, a frightening brew that causes even a human to freeze in her footsteps. Abruptly, I am a kitten again, jerked from my mother and littermates, dumped in a bag, then left on cold stone.

These two-legs feel that way every day, I realize, and yet they go about their lives not complaining, just as we do not complain when we are ill. Things get better, or they do not.

"How are you?" they greet each other.

"Fine," they reply, though they are not.

They are not cowards, though they are often fools.

Except the rare ones: the singers and healers of souls. I am not fit to be one of that breed. I will admit it—I fear the task. Yet I cannot look away.

When Merlin's human returns that evening, she arrives with red eyes and a sack that looks most gratifyingly heavy. I think I scent catnip. The cans in the sack are the tiny, delectable ones.

"These are for Puff," she declares. "I promised I would, and here they are. Besides, I may not need them. And if I do, I'll buy more. Lots more."

Everyone makes comforting sounds. No one is fooled. Whatever else they are, two-legs—I mean "people"—are not always stupid.

"Chicken," I tell Merlin, licking my lips. "Very good, too. Don't you want any?" I would have given all of mine if he had eaten.

He blinks his eyes shut. They are glazing. Any other cat would have turned his face to the wall, abandoned his traitor body, and set out on the Dreamtrails long before.

"Do you want more strength?" I ask. I do not want the bitter water and the thorn and the weakness again, but they might make him strong for a little while.

"It would be wasted." Even with the sunshine pulsing through the pad beneath him, he is cold. "She thanked me and said I was free to go. But I am *not!*"

"Don't you want to go?" I ask.

Merlin sighs. "I want the pain to stop. It would be good to be young again and leap into the air for the joy of it once more. I want to see those trails I've dreamed of and learn whether the water is as sweet, the birds as fat and slow as instinct tells me. But the Dreamtrails will be very lonely without humans."

He meets my eyes.

"Do you still deny your inner name is Healer?"

There is something he wants of me—hope, perhaps?

I put my head upon my front paws. "I looked, Singer. I did. I cannot help you any more than *they* can. But your spirit is too strong to slip away. You must choose, or they will send you."

"Not yet," Merlin tells me. "The thing I dreamt lies in wait, and I must track it to its lair. That is my gift, as sharing strength in yours. Help me hunt."

I hunker down by the big cat. He smells old now and sick. His fur is dull, and his mouth dry. But the spirit that leaps forth to hunt his human's thoughts is young and spry.

"You won't admit it, but I think you like her," he says, his whiskers set at a smug angle. "Most Free Folk do."

When we next track her thoughts, she is walking down
a street, her eyes following the movements when a movement catches them. From a narrow way between two
lairs darts a two-legs, lean and thin and fast. Though his
jaws do not foam, I know he is mad. A long thorn glints
in one hand. Quickly, he stalks his quarry: a female
pushing another's kitten in a wheeled box. No sooner
seen than pounced upon.

The female human screams and falls, blood steaming
in the cold air. The kitten sets up a thin wailing as the
mad two-legs snatches it up. The other people stand
trapped as one of us might alone at night on a road with
two suns racing toward you and a horn blaring.

"He's got a knife!" someone whispers.

"Call 911. . . ."

" 'Fraid to move. . . ."

The mad two-legs starts to back off, clutching the
two-leg infant he has stolen. He kicks the wheeled box
away.

"No," whispers Merlin's human. Again, she is afraid.
The smell of the other's blood turns her sick.

"No," she says again. She cannot take her eyes from
the mad one's thorn. She cannot shut out the smell of the
blood, the thin wail of the human kitten. She can not
run away. She is afraid to move, afraid to die. The fear
builds up and up past bearing. And then—

"No!" she screams, a yowl of battle fury that would
have done any of the Free Folk proud. "Oh, no, you
don't!"

She tugs her pouch from her shoulder, runs forward,
swings it, and lashes down with it upon the arm that
holds the thorn. The thorn drops. It rings upon the dirty
stone.

"Get the knife!" she screams. Carrying his prey, the
mad one starts to run off.

"No!" Merlin howls. "Let's stop him!" He flings his
spirit self clear of his body toward his human. I yowl and
follow him. In that instant, our strength burns through
the ties that hold him to his flesh and her to her fear. She
shrieks and hurls herself forward, stumbling on her fool-

ish "shoes," and toppling forward. At the last instant, she reaches out and grasps the madman's knees.

"Help!" she gasps. Blood pours down her muzzle. The mad one begins to thrash. As small as Merlin's human is, she cannot hold him long. Merlin and I pour our strength into her, and her grasp tightens. Her eyes blaze like the full moon in a fighting cat's eyes, sweeping round the people who stand, still too afraid to move, and kindling them.

"Great tackle, lady!" yells a burly male and leaps in to help. Two others join him.

"I'll call 911!"

And Merlin's human, creeping forward fast, snatches the baby from the mad two-legs, clutches it to her breast as if it were her own, and runs to the female who lies bleeding on the ground.

"The baby's fine," she tells the woman. "But you're not." She hands the baby over to a friend, then reaches about her neck and pulls free a wrapping much like Merlin has to wear. "So much for this scarf," she mutters and begins to wind it about the hurt one's arm.

She has the blood flow stopped when a pack of male humans arrives, as alike in what they wear as littermates can be in markings.

"Police," she says. "Thank God."

She wipes at the blood on her muzzle. When the men came up to her, she speaks calmly. We can see them shake their heads and purse their lips in admiration.

"Lady, you've got guts," one tells her as he writes down her name.

"She's not afraid, did you see that?" Merlin exults. "She's not afraid! Not any more! Not ever again!"

His spirit leaps in the air for joy . . .

. . . and comes down in nothingness. "Free!" he whispers. "At last I'm free to hunt!"

His eyes fill with awe and wonder. "How beautiful it is. And look—!"

I see him leave his body behind and race toward the deep, darkness of a stand of trees I have only seen in my dreams. I follow him in thought. Within the Dreamtrails would be patches of sun and shadow, clear, clean streams, and fat, stupid fowl and fish. He will hunt until he tires and sleep on soft grass, then rise to hunt again or roll in a meadow, letting the sun shine upon the fur of his underbelly. There will be mates for him, and kittens. He will be young again, forever.

Still, he had feared to be alone. Well, perhaps I could follow. And I do want to see. I hurl myself forward, but a door I cannot see slams before my nose, and I go sprawling. My thoughts reel, but I think I hear Merlin meow with joy at the sight of a tall, stocky human male, whose face I had seen in his human's dreams and whom she had mourned as gone ahead. He comes walking beside a creature that dwarfed us all in size and length of fangs: one of the Free Folk of the very longest time ago.

"Look at the furball, Steelsheen," booms the human. "I think I know this one."

So humans do hunt the Dreamtrails, companioned by the eldest Folk of all.

Merlin runs toward him and is swept onto his shoulder where he chirps and purrs like a kitten. They disappear into the lush shadows . . .

. . . and I awake beside the cage in which Merlin's husk lies cast aside.

I nose open the door and begin to groom him. He and his human had been vain of his fur; when she returns, as I know she will, it would hurt her to see him with a matted coat.

The vision at the last of Merlin entering the Dreamtrails dazes my senses, or I would hear my people come in.

"Puff? What are you doing in . . . ohhh, Merlin slipped away. Do you think Puff knew?"

"That one? He doesn't care. Not Puff." Pain quivers in the young human's voice as she moves me gently aside and reaches to straighten Merlin's body's limbs. "Not like this one. What a neat cat. Well, I'm not looking forward to seeing Ms. Black come in, are you? At least Dr. Colt will have to be the one to tell her, not me."

She shuts the door to the cage and moves away, walking slowly, her shoulders bent. I smell sadness on her. It hurts me, too.

I pad toward her, slip between her legs, and sit before her feet. I mew.

"Why, Puff! What is it, lad?"

I mew again, arch up, and paw at her knee.

"You want to be picked up? *You*, Puff? Feeling all right?"

Again I cry. She bends and lifts me. To my surprise, the teeth of pain that clench me loosen a little. I begin to purr. As if the sound eases some pain-rat gnawing her, she holds me tighter—though never too tight—and lays her face against my head. Her skin is warm. Under the masking scents of bitter waters, it smells sweet, like a faint dream of my mother and my littermates.

I put up a paw as I had seen Merlin do and pat her face. Salt water falls upon my fur, but for once, I do not care.

We both still feel the pain, but it is less—for both of us. Then, she sets me down.

"Thank you, Puff. I needed to hold someone."

Another of the things that humans say; this time, I know she means it. I need it, too. She was a healer, or she would be. Well, I am a healer, too. We are all in our rightful places—though she does not know yet just how right they are. Well, she is young for a human; she will learn. I will see to it.

I trot out where the humans and their sick friends wait. If they can take comfort from me, they are welcome to it. Perhaps it will ease the pain I feel: so little time to know a Soulsinger; but losing him aches like a clawed nose.

So much they know, these humans, and so little. So much they take from us—and so much they give.

* * *

For Merlin, who has gone hunting.

IN CARNATION

by Nancy Springer

She materialized, stood on her familiar padded paws and looked around at an utterly strange place. After every long sleep the world was more changed, and after every incarnation the next lifetime became more bizarre. The last time, a Norwegian peasant woman fleeing "holy" wars, she had come a long sea voyage to what was called the New World. Now she found it so new she scarcely recognized it as Earth at all. Under her paws lay a great slab of something like stone, but with a smell that was not stone's good ancient smell. Chariots of glass and metal whizzed by at untoward speeds, stinking of their own heat. Grotesque buildings towered everywhere, and in them she could sense the existence of people, more people than had ever burdened the world before, a new kind of people who jangled the air with their fears, their smallness, their suspicion of the gods and one another.

As always when she awoke from a long sleep she was very hungry, and not for food. But this was not a good place for her to go hunting. It terrified her. Running as only a cat can, like a golden streak, she fled from the chariots and their stench, from the buildings and the pettiness in their air until she found something that approximated countryside. Outside the town there was a place with trees and grass.

And on the grass were camped people whose thoughts and feelings did not hang on the air and make it heavy, but flitted and laughed like magpies. *We don't care what the world thinks,* the magpies sang. *Some of us are thieves and some of us are preachers, some are freaks and some are stars, some of us have three heads and some can't even get one together, and who cares? We all get along. We are*

*the carnival people. Whether you are a pimp or a whore
or a queer or a con artist, if you are one of us you belong,
and the world can go blow itself.*

A cat is one who walks by herself. Still, *A carnival!
Yes,* thought she, the golden one. *This is better. I may
find him here.* For she was very hungry, and the smells of
the carnival were good. She was, after all, a meat eater,
and a carnival is made of meat. The day was turning to
silver dusk, the carnival glare was starting to light the sky
and the carnival blare rose like magpie cries on the air.
The cat trotted in through the gate, to the midway,
where already the grass was trampled into dirt.

"Come see the petrified Pygmy," the barkers cried.
"Come see the gun that killed Jesse James. Come see the
Double-Jointed Woman, the Mule-Faced Girl, the Iron
Man of Taipan."

High striker, Ferris wheel, motordrome, House of
Mirrors—it was all new to her, yet the feel in the air was
that of something venerable and familiar: greed. Carnival
was carnival and had been since lust and feasting began.
French fries, sausage ends, bits of cinnamon cake had
fallen to the ground, but she did not gnaw at them.
Instead, she traversed the midway, past Dunk Bozo and
bumper cars, roulette wheel and ring toss, on the lookout
for a man, any man so long as he was young and virile
and not ugly. Once she had seduced him and satisfied
herself, she would discard him. This was her holy cus-
tom, and she would be sure she upheld it. A few times in
previous lives she had been false to herself, had married
and found herself at the mercy of a man who attempted
to command her; she had sworn this would not happen
again. Eight of her lifetimes were gone. Only one remained to her, and she was determined to live this one
with no regrets.

On the hunt, she found it difficult to sort out the
people she saw crowding through the carnival. Men and
women alike, they wore trousers, cotton shirts, and shapeless cloth shoes. And leather jackets, and hair that was
short and spiky or long and in curls. She became confused and annoyed. True, some of the people she saw
were identifiable as men, and some of the men she saw

were young, but they walked like apes and had a strange chemical smell about them and were not attractive to her.

"Hey there, kitten! Guess your age, your weight, your birthdate?"

The cat flinched into a crouch. Though the words of this New World language meant nothing to her, she could usually comprehend the thoughts that underlay words, and for a moment she had unreasonably felt as if the guess-man's pitch had been directed at her. Narrow-eyed and coiled to run, she stared up at him.

"Yes, Mother! Congratulations." He was facing a pudding-cheeked woman with a pregnant belly. "What would you like me to guess? Name? Age? Date of your wedding day? Yes? Okay. Fifty cents, please. If I don't get it right, one of my fine china dolls is yours."

He was not talking to the cat after all. *Why would he?* she scolded herself. He offered his invitation to the dozens of people walking by. And many of them stopped for him, perhaps because there was a wry poetry in his voice, or perhaps because he was young and not ugly. Slim, dressed in denims and boots, he stood tall though he was in fact not very tall. In front of the booth that marked his place on the midway he took a stance like a bard in a courtyard. Something about him made her want to see his eyes, but because he wore dark glasses she could not. His face was quiet, unexceptional, yet he seemed like one who had something more to him than muscle and manhead.

Not that she needed anything more. It was enough that he was young and not ugly. He would suffice.

She trotted on, looking for a private place to make the change. It would take only a minute.

Within a few strides the familiar musky scent of lust touched her whiskers. Her delicate lip drew back from her tiny pointed teeth, and she slipped under a tent flap. She had reached the location of "Hinkleman's G-String Goddess Revue."

This will do.

Inside, all was heat, mosquitoes, dim light, and the smell of sweating men. Forty of them were crowded in

there, watching a stripper at work on the small stage.
The golden visitor leapt to a chair back and watched also.
No one noticed her. She sat with her long tail curled
around her slender haunches, and its softly furred tip
twitched with scorn for what she was seeing.

*Stupid, simpleminded cow. She uses her body like a
club. She does not know how to walk, how to move, how
to tease. Her breasts are huge, like melons, and that is all
she knows.*

The thoughts of everyone in the tent swarmed in its air
thicker than the mosquitoes. Therefore the cat quickly
knew that the stripper, called a kootch girl, was expected
to more than mildly arouse the men, called marks. She
knew that the kootch girl's repertory was limited by her
meager talents, that the girl was planning to get out of
her G-string in order to achieve maximum effect. She
knew that several of the marks were thinking in terms of
audience participation. She knew that in back of the tent
was a trailer where those with fifty dollars might buy
some private action later.

The men roared. The stripper was flashing her pu-
denda. Jumping down from her perch, the cat darted
backstage, hot with scorn and anger.

*Is that what they call a woman these days? Can no one
show them how it should be done?*

Backstage were two more strippers, spraying one another's semi-naked bodies with mosquito repellent. Mr.
Hinkleman, the owner, was back there also, lounging in
a tilted chair, bored, drinking gin between hot hoarse
stints in the bally box. Off to one side was a booth with a
flimsy curtain, a changing facility, not much used by
women who were about to take off their clothes in front
of an audience anyway. The golden cat walked into it. A
moment later, a golden woman walked out.

"Carrumba!" Mr. Hinkleman, who had seen a lot over
a career spanning twenty-three years in the carnival, nevertheless let his chair legs slam to the floor, jolting himself bolt upright. "Hoo! Where did you come from,
honey?"

She answered only with a faint smile. There had been a
time when she was more fully human, when she could

talk. But that ability was a thousand years and four lifetimes gone. And she did not regret the loss. With each incarnation she found there were fewer to whom she wished to speak. Talking meant little but lies. Thoughts told her more truth.

"What's your name?"

The level look she gave him caused him to suddenly remember, without any resentment, the training his mother thought he had forgotten years before. He stood up to greet the naked visitor more properly.

"Hello, ma'am, welcome to—to wherever the heck this is. I'm Fred Hinkleman." His hand hovered in air, then went to his head as if to remove an invisible hat in her presence. "What can I do for you? Do you want to be in my show?"

"She don't got but little tits," one of the strippers put in scornfully. The girl from onstage had joined those backstage, and the three Hinkleman Goddesses stood huddled together like moose when the scent of panther is in the air.

"I know how she gets to look glowy like that all over," complained the dark kootch girl who was billed as the Wild Indian. "She just eats carrots, that's all. Any of us could do it. Eat carrots till they're coming out the kazoo."

Fred Hinkleman seemed not to hear them at all. His gaze was stuck on the newcomer. "Tell you what," he said to her. "You go onstage and show the yahoos what you can do. I'll go introduce you right now. What should I call you?"

Her mouth, smiling, opened into a soundless meow.

"Cat? Good. Suits you." He went out, and a moment later could be heard promising the marks "the hottest new talent in the adult entertainment business, the sleek, feline Miss Cat, uh, Miss Cat Pagan."

"Just another pussy," one of the strippers muttered.

She made her entrance onstage. Contrary to the logic of the word "stripper," it is not necessary for one actually to be wearing anything in order to perform. Cat was wearing nothing at all, but that was not what made the already-sated marks go wild and leap up and stand on their chairs in order to see her. It was the way she wore it.

She did not bump or grind or flash for them. All she did was walk, pose, hint at possibilities, and possess the stage as she had once possessed the known world. Dignity clothed her as if in robes of gold. No mark thought of touching her. Every mark knew that the price of going to her afterward would be more than he could afford.

Looking out over them, she knew she could have any one of them—and many of them were young and well built, far more showily muscled than the man in sunglasses on the midway. But no. It was him she wanted. There was something about the way he stood. He had dignity, too.

When she considered that the marks had seen enough, she went backstage and helped herself to clothing: a short strapless red dress with a flared skirt, a wisp of lace to throw around her shoulders, a picture hat. The other Hinkleman's G-String Goddess Revue girls watched her silently and did not try to stop her. Now that she had showed her stuff she was one of them. In the backstage air she could sense their stoical acceptance, and it surprised her. She had expected dislike, even enmity. But these women were carnies. They breakfasted with snake-eating geeks and sword swallowers, they bathed in buckets, camped in mud, and every day they were expected to perform magic, creating glamour out of dirt. So what was one more freak or freakish event to them? If the stranger wanted to show up out of nowhere, that was okay. They had weathered storms before.

"Honeycat, you're a walking advertisement," Hinkleman remarked when he saw her. "Go on, go do the midway. Have some fun."

The kootcher with the melon breasts went along with Cat—in order to be seen with her, Cat surmised, noticing the other woman's thoughts the way she noticed gnats in the air, with only a small portion of her attention. Melons wanted to make the best of a situation. Melons was not unwise.

"Been around the carousel a time or two, honey?" Melons chirped.

Married, she meant. Ignoring her, Cat headed straight toward the Guess Anything stand. Now that she was in her human form, she would make sure that the man there saw her. From her experience she knew this was all that would be necessary. She would smile just a little and look into his eyes, and when she walked away he would follow her as if she led him by an invisible chain of gold.

There was a crowd around the stand. The Guess Anything man was popular. Asked the standard questions concerning age and weight, he was often wrong, always on the side of flattery, and he gave away many prizes. But asked to guess far more difficult things—birthstones, marital status, number of children or grandchildren, home address, the place where a mark went to high school or nursing school or prison—he was often correct, uncannily so. And there was a quiet charisma about him. People stood listening to him in fascination, giving him their money again and again.

At the edge of the crowd Cat waited her turn with scant patience. She was not far away from him; he should see her. . . . Wishing to enjoy his reaction, she felt for his mind with hers and found it easily. In fact, it awaited her. And yes, there was an awareness of her presence in him, but it was unlike any awareness she had ever experienced in a man before. His cognition of her had no lust in it. Despite her lithe, barefoot, red-clad beauty, her appearance did not affect him in that way. Not at all.

"Who's next?" He took the mark's money and handed it to a boy in the stand, a good-looking youngster. His son, Cat knew from touching his mind at that moment. The mother was long dead but still very much missed. He was raising the boy himself.

As the boy made change, his father guessed the mark's age and weight, both incorrectly, then handed over the cheap ceramic prize with a smile. It was a warm, whimsical smile. Amusement in it: the "fine china dolls" were so worthless he made money even when he gave them away. But also something of heart: he liked to make people happy. Cat suddenly found that she liked his smile very much.

"Who's next?"

"Right here, Ollie," Melons said, nudging Cat forward. "Hey, Ollie, this here's Cat."

"I know. We met earlier." He faced her. His smile was wonderful, but he still wore the dark glasses, even though night had fallen. She could not see his eyes.

"Hello, Cat," he said. "Welcome."

Melons said, "She wants you to guess her age, I guess. I don't know. She don't seem to talk none. Cat got her tongue." Melons laughed at her own weak joke, chin angled skyward, breasts quaking. Ollie smiled but did not laugh.

"Some other time I'll guess for her if she wants," he said. "Not right now. I don't think that's what you really want right now anyway, is it, Cat?" His tone was mild, friendly. There was no flirtation in it.

Frustrated, she thought, *I want you to take off those barriers over your eyes. I want to see into them and make you follow me. I want to know you carnally, and I want to know what you are.*

No, his thought replied directly to her thought. *No, sorry, I can't do any of that. Not even for you, milady Cat.*

Back at the girl show tent, an hour later, she found herself still quivering in reaction. This man had made her feel naked, unshielded, exposed in a way that no lack of clothing could ever make her feel exposed. Whoever or whatever he was, he could touch her mind. Perhaps he could even tell what she was—or had been.

Partly, she felt outrage, humiliation, vexation. As much as she had ever wanted any man she wanted him, and he had not responded as he should have. It is no small matter when a fertility goddess is thwarted in lust.

And partly she felt great fear. The deities of the old religions are always the demons of the new. Once in her thrice-three lives Cat had been found out and put to death, while still in her feline form, by burning. She still remembered not so much the horrible pain as the helplessness of her clever cat body enslaved by rawhide bindings, the leaping, ravenous flames of the bonfire, the stench of her own consumed skin and fur. It was not a death she ever wanted to experience again.

Strutting and posing through her next kootch show,

she picked out a broad-shouldered, handsome young mark and summoned him with her eyes. As she had wordlessly commanded, he was waiting for her in back of the tent afterward, not quite able to believe what was happening, his mouth moving uncertainly, soft as a baby's. She led him away into the darkness beyond the edge of the carnival, and he did what she wanted, everything she wanted, and he was good, very good. Afterward, she drove him away with her clawed hands. More punishment was not necessary. She knew he would go mad with thinking of her before many days had passed.

She should have been satisfied. Always before she had been satisfied by the simple, sacred act of lust. Yet she found that she was not.

She should have gone away on four speedy unbound paws from that dangerous place where someone had apprehended her truly. Yet she found that she would not.

Confusion take this Ollie person. He has shamed me and he has made me afraid, but he has not yet bested me utterly. We shall see whether he scorns me in the end.

Scorn was perhaps too strong a word, for when she came back to the carnival, walking alone, she found him waiting for her outside Hinkleman's trailer. "I just want to say I'm sorry if I offended you, Cat," he told her aloud. "I didn't mean to."

The words meant nothing to her. But the thought underlying them was clear as tears. *I didn't mean to stir up anger, and I don't want enemies. I just want to be let alone with my son and my sorrow.*

Sentiment annoyed her. She bared her teeth at him, nearly hissing, then passed him and went inside to sleep in the bunk Hinkleman's girls had cleared for her. When Hinkleman came, a few minutes later, to see if he could share it with her as was the kootch show owner's tacit right, she struck at him, leaving four long red scratches across his face. Then she listened in disgust as he comforted himself with the Indian instead. He was aging, potbellied, foul of breath, altogether repulsive. How could he be so goatishly eager while this man who attracted her, this Ollie, was so indifferent?

*Men. Hell take them all. So Ollie wishes to be let alone?
That will be no heartbreak for me.*

Yet the next day when the carnival lights came on at
sunset, she went first to the flower stand, and took a
blossom—smiling, the old Italian woman gave it to her.
Carnies give other carnies what they can. This was a
flower like a woman's petticoat, frilled and fringed and
fluted, white once but dipped in a stain that had spread
from its petal tips along its veins and into its penetralia,
blood red. It was very beautiful. Cat placed it in her
golden hair. Then she walked the midway in her red
dress again, and came to a certain booth, his booth, and
stood there staring at him. It was her curiosity, she told
herself, that drew her back to him this way. And she
knew that partly this was true.

Hello, Cat, he greeted her without speaking and without looking at her.

Hello.

You are the only one I can talk to this way.

You are the only one I can talk to at all.

There was a pause. Then he thought to her very softly,
*Yes. Yes, I see. It had not occurred to me, but there is
such a thing as being too much alone.*

No, not really. I like being alone.

*Still . . . if you wish to talk sometimes, it is no trouble
for me to talk with you.*

It would be a way, perhaps, of finding out how much
he knew of her. As for the other thing she wanted of him
. . . she still desired it badly, and still felt no response in
him. And there was no way in cold frosty hell she was
going to ask it of him again. The flower in her hair
should have been invitation enough. That and the summons in her eyes.

She made mental conversation as casually as if she
were hostessing a court function, chatting with the lesser
vassals. *So you comprehend thoughts. When people come
to you and ask you questions, then you can find the
answers in their minds?*

*Yes. And also many things they would not want me to
know. Very beautiful things sometimes, and sometimes
very ugly.* She heard a poet's yearning in his tone of

mind. He wanted to take what was in people and make a song, a saga great enough to hold all of it, everything he had heard and learned. But she did not wish to be in his song.

She could not ask him how much he knew of her. Why would he tell her the truth, anyway? He lied constantly.

So whatever questions the marks ask you, you could answer correctly every time.

Yes.

They why do you so often give the wrong answer?

To please them. People like to win. So I let them win sometimes, and then they come back, you see, and try again.

She turned and walked away. Behind her she could hear him as he started ballying: "I can guess your age, your weight, your occupation! Challenge my skill, ladies and gentlemen! Ask me any question. See if I can answer."

Cat made sure she was well down the midway before she allowed herself to think it: *He keeps them coming back. He keeps me coming back.*

And then she thought, *If I win, will it be because he has let me?*

And she thought, *Who is he? What is he?*

But her sense of fear felt eased somewhat. If she did not know those things of him by touching his mind, there was little reason to think he knew more of her.

That night she lay with a mark again, and found that she despised him and what she did with him. "You should charge," Melons told her crossly after the man left. "It's stupid not to charge. You're making it bad for the rest of us." She glared at the kootcher, but she could not have loathed herself much more if she did indeed perform the holy act for pay. Even the thought of how insanity would punish the man for his daring did not comfort her.

The next morning she went to find Ollie in his trailer with his young son. For hours she sat in their kitchen, and conversed in her silent way with Ollie, and had fried trout, fresh caught, for breakfast with both of them. The boy tended to the breakfast, mostly, just as he tended the booth in the evenings, making change for his father, and for the same reason. The Guess Anything man could not do it for himself.

Ollie was blind.

Blind? But—I didn't know!

Hardly anybody does. Keep it to yourself, will you? His smile told her this was a small joke—he knew she could speak to no one. Yet it was no joke. A guess-man is supposed to see, to find clues with his eyes, to surmise, not to know. Anything else is too frightening. Ollie would be out of business if the marks knew the truth.

Of course.

Cat felt at the same time very foolish and strangely lighthearted. So he had never seen her in her red dress, he did not know how golden her hair glowed in the carnival lights, he had never seen the carnation softly bobbing at her temple, he could not see how beautiful she was at all. Yet he had been sorry to offend her. Yet he had greeted her the first time he felt her walk by.

Your eyes—how did it happen?

In the accident.

The fiery tragedy that had killed his wife. Afterward, he had sold his home, quit his job, and started traveling with the carnival. Built a life for himself the way he liked it. Letting people win. Giving them happiness.

Or—touching their minds, and learning all the truth about them, then telling them lies.

There was a pause. Then Cat asked gently, *May I see your eyes now?*

He hesitated only a moment, then reached up and removed the dark glasses. His eyes were not ugly. Really, she had known they could not be ugly. They were gray, misty, and seemed to stare far away, like the eyes of a seer. And his face, without its dark barrier in the way—how could she ever have thought his face was commonplace? It was exquisite, with arched aspiring cheekbones, brows that dreamed.

You are very beautiful.

You—they tell me you are also, Cat. I know—the feel of your mind—it is beautiful to me. It is proud, like a golden thing, a sunset thing.

You knew everything. Right from the start.

A silence. Then he admitted aloud, "Yes. I know."

I do not understand this strange barbaric language. I understand only what I feel in your mind. Which is now a great sadness. You know I want you. But you are still in love with your wife.

I think—I am now only in love with my memories of my wife.

You are afraid, then. You think I would punish you, as I did the others.

No, I am not afraid. Danger is part of the beauty of you. Everything that is beautiful is full of risk.

But when I came to summon you, you did not want me.

I do not know. . . . I am stubborn. Mostly I did not like the way you planned to take me.

You did not want me.

I want you now.

She had won. But perhaps he was letting her win?

The boy, who had finished scrubbing the dishes, smiled in the same winsome way as his father and went outside to wander the carnival grounds, to admire the motorcycle daredevil's new Harley, and watch the roughies play poker, and talk with the Bearded Lady, the Breasted Man, the Wild Woman of Borneo, the Amazing Alligator Girl.

Cat touched Ollie's fine-sculpted face. He leaned toward her, and let her touch guide him, and kissed her.

His body, she found within the next hour, was as beautiful as his face, and as ardent and clumsy as if he were a boy again. It truly had been years since he had given himself to a woman, a verity that made the gift all the more precious to her. She hugged him, she cradled his head in her arms and kissed him, she adored his awkwardness, she felt her heart burst open like a red, red flower into love of him.

Afterward, she was afraid. She was afraid. Love harrowed her with fear. She had sworn never to give her heart to a man again.

He said softly, "The carnival moves on tomorrow."

Yes.

"There is this about a carnival, it takes in all kinds of people. Criminals, whores, freaks, geeks, holy rollers, crap shooters, it doesn't matter, we're all carnies. We all belong. You, too."

Yes. She heard the wistfulness in herself. *I like that.*

"But there is also this, that we're like wild geese, we

carnies. We move with the seasons, everything is always changing. We get used to leaving places behind, people behind, losing bits of ourselves. My problem is I look back too much. I've got to learn not to do that."

She no longer cared that he was letting her win. It was his gift to her, this offering of a choice. He knew what she was. He knew that a cat must walk by herself.

And perhaps he hoped to keep her coming back.

But she did not leave him yet. She put on her dress, but lay down again on his bed. A dying blossom fell from her hair. Her fingers interlaced with his. She thought to him quietly, *Guess my name and age?*

Why, Cat?

You said you would guess for me someday.

Okay. Because you want me to. He took a deep breath. Or perhaps he sighed. *Your name is Freyja. Or that is one of them, anyway. You were the great goddess of fruitfulness, you had many names in different places.*

Yes.

Your age? A lot older than I can comprehend. About four millennia?

Yes. Though for most of the time I have slept.

Catnaps. She felt his gentle smile in his tone of mind and knew he would never betray her.

Yes.

She lay silent awhile before she asked him, *Now tell me. What are you?*

Cat. He was both rueful and amused. *I must give you a prize, a little china doll. That is the one question that baffles me.*

Of course. Otherwise she would have been able to find the answer in his mind. *You do not know?*

Milady—I feel that there is a dream I have forgotten. I keep trying to find the words for the song, but they are gone. I truly do not know.

She lay with his head on her shoulder. Stroked his cheek and temple and the side of his neck. At her mercy and in her arms, he succumbed to her touch, he fell asleep, as she wished him to. When that had happened, very softly she withdrew herself and made the change.

Her dress lay on the bed now. She, a golden cat, stood by her lover's pillow.

There is magic in the soft, twitching, fluffy end of the tail of a cat. Countryfolk know this and will sometimes cut off a cat's tail to use in their spells. This act is an abomination. The world that no longer remembers the holy ways of the golden goddess is full of danger for a cat.

Freyja curved the end of her tail so that it resembled the heavy head of a stalk of ripe wheat, her emblem. Softly she brushed it across the lidded eyes of the sleeping man.

Odin, my sweet faithless lover, when you awaken you will be able to see again. Give me no place in your song, do not remember me. And hang yourself no longer from the tree of sorrow, beautiful one. Be happy.

Not far away, the carousel calliope started to sound. The cat bounded to the floor, landing softly on padded paws.

There is still time to stay. Will I regret leaving him?

But perhaps there was no such thing as life without regrets. And a strange new world awaited her wanderings. She pushed her way through the loose screening of the kitchen window, thumped quietly to the ground, and trotted off.

The man would live long and bear her blessing. And it was an odd thing, now at last she felt satisfied.

She slipped away, a golden shadow quick as thought, into the silver dusk. But as she went, she felt the song of the carnival flitting on the air behind her, a fey and raucous magpie melody. *We don't care what the world thinks*, the minds of freaks and barkers and vendors sang. *We are old, we have been gypsying around this world for a long time. Come see a splinter of the true cross! Come see the pickled brains of the frost giant Ymir. Come see Napoleon's little finger. Come see a pressed flower from the Garden of Eden, from the Tree of Life.*

DAW

Great Masterpieces of Fantasy!

Tad Williams

☐ **TAILCHASER'S SONG** (UE2374—$4.95)

Meet Fritti Tailchaser, a ginger tomcat of rare courage and curiosity, a born survivor in a world of heroes and villains, of powerful gods and whiskery legends about those strange, furless, erect creatures called M'an. Join Tailchaser on his magical quest to rescue his catfriend Hushpad—a quest that takes him all the way to cat hell and beyond.

Memory, Sorrow and Thorn

THE DRAGONBONE CHAIR: Book 1
☐ **Hardcover Edition** (0-8099-003-3—$19.50)
☐ **Paperback Edition** (UE2384—$5.95)

A war fueled by the dark powers of sorcery is about to engulf the long-peaceful land of Osten Ard—as the Storm King, undead ruler of the elvishlike Sithi, seeks to regain his lost realm through a pact with one of human royal blood. And to Simon, a former castle scullion, will go the task of spearheading the quest that offers the only hope of salvation . . . a quest that will see him fleeing and facing enemies straight out of a legend-maker's worst nightmares!

STONE OF FAREWELL: Book 2
☐ **Hardcover Edition** (UE2435—$21.95)

As the dark magic and dread minions of the undead Sithi ruler spread their seemingly undefeatable evil across the land, the tattered remnants of a once-proud human army flee in search of a last sanctuary and rallying point, and the last survivors of the League of the Scroll seek to fulfill missions which will take them from the fallen citadels of humans to the secret heartland of the Sithi.

NEW AMERICAN LIBRARY
P.O. Box 999, Bergenfield, New Jersey 07621

Please send me the DAW BOOKS I have checked above. I am enclosing $_____ (please add $1.00 to this order to cover postage and handling). Send check or money order—no cash or C.O.D.'s. Prices and numbers are subject to change without notice. (Prices slightly higher in Canada.)

Name_____

Address_____

City _____ State _____ Zip _____

Allow 4-6 weeks for delivery.